W9-BHK-771

By W.E.B. Griffin
from Jove

BROTHERHOOD OF WAR

The
Colonels

BROTHERHOOD
OF
WAR
BOOK
IV

BY W.E.B. GRIFFIN

A JOVE BOOK

The Colonels was written on a Lanier "Super No Problem"
word processor maintained by Joe Steele.

THE COLONELS

A Jove Book / published by arrangement with
the author

PRINTING HISTORY
Jove edition / December 1983

ISBN: 0-515-07351-2

Jove books are published by The Berkley Publishing Group,
200 Madison Avenue, New York, N.Y. 10016. The words
"A JOVE BOOK" and the "J" with sunburst are trademarks
belonging to Jove Publications, Inc.

PRINTED IN THE UNITED STATES OF AMERICA

BROTHERHOOD OF WAR
THE COLONELS

When available, a caparisoned stallion, with boots reversed in stirrups, to be led in the procession, is authorized for military funerals of officers and noncommissioned officers assigned to Armor or Armored Cavalry, or for officers and noncommissioned officers formerly assigned to Cavalry.

A ground crew—two sergeants in fatigues and field jackets—was pulling camouflage netting off *Big Bad Bird II* when the three-quarter-ton truck rolled up to the small clearing in the pine forest and discharged its passenger.

The passenger was a tall, handsome, mustachioed major wearing pinks and greens, a uniform which, in three days, he would no longer be authorized to wear. The uniform was superbly tailored. It had, in fact, come from the London tailors which had outfitted General George Smith Patton, Jr. There had been a joke (paraphrasing J. P. Morgan's comment about his yacht) that if you had to ask what uniforms from Hartwell & Hay cost, you couldn't afford one.

The major's green tunic was heavy with ribbons and devices

1

testifying to his service, the ribbons ranging downward in importance from the Distinguished Service Cross, the nation's second highest award for valor, to the red-and-white ribbon of the Enlisted Man's Good Conduct Medal. There was an Expert Combat Infantry Badge with a star signifying a second award. There was a set of Senior Army Aviator's wings. There was a four-inch-wide ribbon around his neck, holding a three-inch gold medal awarded by the Greek government.

The major was carrying a small, folded, somewhat frayed guidon in his hands.

A chief warrant officer, a gray-haired, florid-faced, middle-aged man in an Ike jacket, jumped to the ground from the cabin of Big Bad Bird II. His eyes went up when he saw how the major was dressed. He walked to him. He did not salute.

"My," he said, *"don't you look splendid."*

"I thought I told you to stay out of this, Dutch," the major said.

"If this one went in, that would really be the end of it," the chief warrant officer replied.

"That wasn't your fault, Dutch," the major said.

"So you said."

The camouflage netting was now clear of Big Bad Bird II. One of the sergeants, a stocky master sergeant in his early thirties, dragged it to the side. The other, also a master sergeant, but younger and leaner, walked up to the major and the chief warrant officer. His eyes ran over the major's tunic, but he said nothing.

"I had an unpleasant thought on the way out here," the major said. *"Is there any gas in that thing?"*

"Shit," the sergeant said, as if that thought had occurred to him for the first time. He trotted to Big Bad Bird II, climbed up the fuselage, and leaned in the cockpit window.*

Big Bad Bird II was a Sikorsky H-19 helicopter, a twelve-passenger, single-rotor aircraft. The H-19 was the first really successful transport helicopter (it had been used in the waning days of the Korean War) and was now about obsolete. It had been replaced by the Sikorksy H-34, which was larger and more powerful, although with roughly the same lines. The H-19 was now used only for training.

Big Bad Bird II was an unusual H-19. For one thing, it had been painted black rather than olive drab. For another, on each landing strut there had been mounted a rocket-firing mechanism. It was the only armed helicopter in the U.S. Army. There had been another, but it had blown up a few days earlier: hence Big Bad Bird II. On the fuselage was a skillfully done cartoon of Woody Woodpecker, leering as he threw beer bottles.

The master sergeant standing on the fuselage steps withdrew his head from the cockpit.

"You've got about forty-five minutes fuel, Major," he called down.

"That'll be enough," the major replied.

He walked to the helicopter and looked up at the rotor head, moved to the rear, checked the blades on the tail rotor, and then walked to the front again. By then the sergeant had the engine compartment open, and the major examined the engine.

"What I need now is a set of cans," the major said. "And a roll of masking tape."

The master sergeant nodded and walked to his truck. The major climbed into the pilot's seat and disconnected the helmet he had found on the seat. He looked down at the ground, saw the sergeant, and tossed the helmet to him. The sergeant caught it, laid it on the ground, and then climbed halfway up the fuselage to hand him a set of headphones and a roll of gray masking tape.

"What are you going to do with the tape?" the sergeant asked.

"Stick this in the copilot's window," the major said. He shook the guidon open. It was a small yellow flag, yellow for Armor, onto which the numerals "73" had been stitched. Below them was a hand-lettered legend, in grease pencil: T/F LOWELL.

The major had commanded Task Force Lowell of the 73rd Heavy Tank Battalion (Reinforced) during the Korean War. Of all his military souvenirs, this meant most to him.

The sergeant nodded and ripped off strips of tape. The major leaned across the copilot's seat and taped the guidon over the window. Then he put the earphones on his head and flipped the Master switch and the radio buss. He listened to the traffic between the ground controller and the aircraft participating in the funeral ceremony. He listened for five minutes, and then he looked down from the cockpit again.

The two sergeants and the chief warrant were standing by a fire extinguisher mounted on what looked like oversize bicycle *wheels. None of them were looking at him. The major whistled to catch their attention. Then he made a "wind it up" gesture with his index finger.*

One of the master sergeants took the black fire extinguisher nozzle and pointed it at the engine compartment.

The major primed the engine, adjusted the throttle and the richness, and lifted up on the Engine Start toggle switch. The starter whined, and the machine shook as the 700 horsepower Curtiss-Wright radial engine labored. Then it caught, and the three blades overhead began to turn. The major watched the dials, making minor adjustments, until the engine smoothed out and the needles moved into the green.

Then he looked out the window by his side at the three men on the ground. He winked, put his hands on the controls, and advanced the throttle by twisting it. Simultaneously he raised the control itself. Big Bad Bird II shuddered and then went light on the wheels. First one wheel left the ground, then another, and then the machine was in ground effect hover. When he was two feet off the ground, he lowered the nose and moved across the small clearing, gaining speed. As he came to the trees at the end of the field, he pulled it up to fifty or sixty feet, and then made a 180 degree turn.

He was able to see the men on the ground. They were doing something very unusual for two master sergeants and a warrant officer. For their hands were raised in formal salutes. The major, touched, moved the joystick between his legs, and the helicopter swung from side to side.

He flew the treetops to Parade Ground No. 2, as low as he dared, popping up every once in a while for a quick look. The funeral cortege was still making its way from the chapel on the main post. The head of the snake, the tank with the casket on it, as well as the family, the other mourners, and the brass, were already in the bleachers at the parade ground; but the tail of the snake was still moving.

He would wait until everyone was in place.

He saw the T34s, Russian tanks, still wearing red stars, parked at the end of the parade ground. They were now American tanks, of course, used by a special unit at Fort Riley to provide realism for manuevers. But nevertheless, it was still surprising to see them lined up for a funeral ceremony.

There were five T34s. They had been ordered to Fort Rucker in a high-level public relations ploy against the air force. The air force, which according to the Key West Agreement of 1948, had a monopoly on all aerial weapons systems and armed aircraft, had been reluctant to develop an antitank helicopter. In fact, it had announced that such a device was impractical.

So in violation of the Key West Agreement the army had developed its own rocket-armed helicopter—the Big Bad Bird—and had planned to shoot up the Russian T34s before television cameras. Once that had happened, the air force would be forced to accept a fait accompli, and the army would be able to proceed with the development of the weapons system.

The plan hadn't quite worked: during a dry run before the demonstration, one of the rockets had misfired, setting off a chain of accidents that destroyed the Big Bad Bird and the young pilot flying it. What was left of the pilot was in the casket now on the back of the M48 Patton tank.

The army ploy had crashed with the Big Bad Bird. The crash had been filmed by the television networks, and now all the brass could do was to salvage what they could by staging a large funeral for the pilot. Once they had been caught doing something forbidden by the Key West Agreement, they could not repeat the violation by putting rockets on another helicopter—or at least so the brass understood.

The brass, the major thought, were wrong again.

"Unidentified helicopter operating in the vicinity of Parade Ground No. 2, you are ordered to immediately leave the area."

That was the traffic controller at the parade ground. He didn't want anything to interfere with the flight of the aircraft that would pass over the casket in final tribute.

The major lifted Big Bad Bird II high enough to get another look at the parade ground. The tail of the snake had arrived.

Instead of dropping back out of sight, he pulled up, rising vertically until he was almost out of power. When he felt the copter start to slip into a stall, he dropped its nose and made a full speed pass over the parade ground, so low that he had to pull up to get over the tank with the flag-draped casket.

The traffic controller's voice came again. He seemed annoyed that his orders were being ignored.

Big Bad Bird II flashed over the Russian T34s at the end of the parade ground. The major looked carefully at them as he turned. Then he flew back down the parade ground, turned again, and came to a hover directly over the tank with the casket.

He looked down and saw two of the official pallbearers jump onto the tank so that the rotor blast wouldn't blow the colors covering the casket away.

Then he looked at the T34s again. And squeezed the trigger on the joystick.

There was a dull rumbling noise and Big Bad Bird II shuddered as twenty-seven 3.5 inch rockets fired from the device on the left landing strut, and then twenty-seven 3.5s came off the right strut.

For fifteen seconds a train of rockets swept across the line of Russian T34s. When it was over, the five tanks were nothing but piles of warped and ruptured metal. Then the fuel from their tanks caught fire, and thick pillars of dense smoke rose into the sky.

The air force, the major thought, would no longer be able to claim that rocket-armed helicopters could not kill tanks.

And that, he thought, was really a much more fitting tribute to the late First Lieutenant Edward C. Greer, Armor, who had been flying the Big Bad Bird when it went in than a caparisoned stallion with reversed boots in the stirrups.

He flew through the dense diesel smoke, then turned the helicopter toward Laird Army Airfield. As he approached the Aviation Board parking ramp, he was not really surprised to see a military police sedan coming to meet him with its red warning lights flashing.

By the time he had shut the H-19 down, there were two military police cars parked by him. He reached across the copilot's seat and tore the Task Force Lowell guidon from the window. He tore the masking tape from the guidon and folded the guidon again. Then he put on his cap and climbed down from Big Bad Bird II's cockpit.

Two of the MPs were officers, both second lieutenants.

They were both obviously excited and not quite sure of themselves. One of them, the major thought, looked on the verge of drawing his pistol.

One of them finally saluted. The major returned it.

"Sir, are you Major C. W. Lowell?" he asked.

Major Lowell raised his hands in a gesture of surrender.

"The charge, I gather, is Grand Theft, Helicopter?" he asked.

I

(One)
Plantation No. 3
Société Générale de Produits Alimentation de l'Indochine
Phu Hot, South Vietnam
25 December 1958

Paul Hanrahan, a trim, pleasant-faced, balding Irish-American, was wearing what he thought of as his civilian class "A" whites: white shirt, white tie, white linen suit, and white shoes. These made him feel very much like a frog colonial—and also a bit overdressed for a 10,000 mile journey. By the time he got to Tokyo—much less to Hawaii or San Francisco—the suit, shirt, shoes, and tie would no longer be white, and he would look like an unsuccessful traveling salesman with a drinking problem.

On the other hand, he thought, as he sipped the too-bitter coffee, where he was going he wouldn't dare appear in public in these clothes, so he might as well wear them while he could.

Paul T. (Red) Hanrahan was a lieutenant colonel in the

regular army of the United States. Until 2359 hours the previous day, until the last minute of Christmas Eve, he had been Chief, Signal Branch, United States Army Military Advisory Group, Vietnam. As of the first minute of Christmas Day, he had been relieved of duty and ordered to proceed to Fort Bragg, N.C., for duty with the U.S. Army Special Warfare School.

Earlier, as soon as they had heard the faint tinkle of his alarm clock, two houseboys had come into the bedroom with orange juice, coffee, and croissants. Breakfast proper was served on the east patio of the rambling, white-frame building where Hanrahan and his family were staying as the guests of the Janniers. Here, among other offerings in silver serving dishes on a long table covered with crisp white linen, were laid *oeufs sur le plat avec jambon*.

His French hosts, Paul Hanrahan thought somewhat ungraciously, were determined to do their best. If the American barbarians couldn't face a new day without an enormous breakfast which included ham and eggs, then these would be provided to them.

If Paul Hanrahan had had his way, he and his family would not have been the guests of the Janniers at all. A final couple of weeks in Vietnam spent in a suite at the Caravelle Hotel was by no means like two weeks in the Black Hole of Calcutta. Christmas at the Caravelle would have been just fine.

But Patricia Hanrahan had met Christine Jannier at the Cathedral not long after she and the children had arrived in Saigon. Christine soon took Patricia under her wing; and became something like an older sister. Since the Janniers had been in Indochina for generations, they had dozens of contacts which Christine had been willing to use in Patricia's behalf. She'd gotten the Hanrahan kids—Paul, Jr., Kevin, and Rosemary—into the best of the "French" schools, without any of the trouble Hanrahan had been told to expect by his people in the American Embassy. Then Henri Jannier had arranged for the installation of a "local" telephone (as opposed to the Embassy line, which connected to the local system through the Embassy switchboard) overnight—after the Embassy people had told him he could expect it to take four months or longer.

Patricia was no fool, and it had not been necessary for Paul to tell her that there was more than one motive in the Janniers' friendship. He was a lousy light bird in the American army, and Jannier was the general manager of a French company which owned tens of thousands of hectares of rice paddies, vast plantations of rubber trees, and fleets of trucks and river boats. He didn't think his Irish charm was the reason they had been so nice.

At first he thought the Janniers wanted information from him. He gave them a little, after he was sure it had already been compromised. He'd also discussed them with Sandy Felter when Felter had passed through Saigon last January. Felter had been one of his junior officers on the Albanian border in Greece more than ten years earlier and had subsequently become a highly placed intelligence officer. Felter had heard out Paul's suspicions, and then, with that steel trap logic that had caused him to rise so far so fast, outlined the possible explanations.

First, possibly, the Janniers simply liked the Hanrahans. Second, it was equally possible that Jannier was a French intelligence officer. Or for that matter a Frenchman serving as eyes for the communist Vietminh. But what was most likely, according to Felter, was that Jannier was simply doing favors so that Hanrahan would be in his debt.

The next day, Felter had come up with still more. Overnight, somehow, Felter had checked the Janniers out. And it had turned out that Christine Jannier was General Jean-Philippe Dommer's daughter. Dommer had been one of the more ruthless fighters against the Vietminh, and was passionately hated by them.

"You say that Christine Jannier stays with you when she's in Saigon?" Felter had asked.

"Yes. All the time."

"If I were Henri Jannier, and I could arrange to have my wife stay in an 'American' house in Saigon and ride around in an American Pontiac, and all it cost me was a few favors, I'd think I'd made quite a bargain," Felter said.

"You think that Patricia's in danger?" Hanrahan had asked, alarmed.

"Not yet," Felter had replied, matter of factly. "The Vietminh seem to be leaning backward not to create an incident involving Americans."

And so there had been no way for Paul Hanrahan to say no when Patricia told him that the Janniers "insisted" they join them for Christmas on their plantation, ninety miles from Saigon.

Two things at the plantation had surprised Hanrahan. The

first was the Janniers' son. Hanrahan had understood he was supposed to have been in France; nevertheless he was waiting when the Hanrahans had climbed out of the two Citroen sedans the Janniers had sent to fetch them and their luggage.

The son was named Jean-Philippe, after his Grandfather Dommer, and like his grandfather, he was a soldier. Until recently he'd served as a parachutist in Algeria; and he had been wounded there.

Hanrahan liked Jannier from the moment he met him. He was that rare breed of parachutist, whose parachutist's credentials, like Hanrahan's, were impeccable, but who also understood that the parachute was an inefficient—and maybe absurd—means of getting a soldier into position.

Jannier, a tall and muscular, dark-haired and dark-eyed young man of twenty-six, was a graduate of L'Ecole Polytechnique in Paris. Now that he was recovered from his wounds, and apparently hadn't been tainted by the treason some other French parachutists had been involved in, he was being sent to America, to Fort Rucker, Alabama, where he would undergo training as a helicopter pilot. After becoming a pilot, he would then serve as one of the French Army liaison officers to the Aviation Center. It was, Hanrahan understood, the sort of assignment given to very bright young officers for whom a rank-heavy career is prophesied.

Before traveling on to the States, Jean Philippe had come to Vietnam to see his parents; and by a marvelous coincidence (which was about as coincidental, Hanrahan thought, as Christmas Day following Christmas Eve), he was on the very same flight to America as the Hanrahans.

The favors owed were being called in. Certainly a dear friend of the family, who happened to be a West Pointer, and who happened to meet the son under the family roof at Christmastime, would simply not abandon the son in America. He could arrange introductions, that sort of thing.

He was being used, Hanrahan understood, but he couldn't be angry. If he was smart enough, he told himself, and further removed than a generation from his own lace-curtain Irish neighborhood, he would do the same for his own kids. And Christ, he did owe the Janniers. There was no question about that.

The second thing Paul Hanrahan had been surprised to find at the plantation was a turkey. It was the entrée for Christmas

Eve supper. The only way Jannier could have gotten a turkey, Hanrahan realized, was to have it shipped frozen by air from Hawaii. It was an incredible gesture, and if he could pay it back in some small way by fixing up Captain Jean-Philippe Jannier at Fort Rucker, he'd certainly give it a hell of a try.

In fact, it all couldn't be easier, he thought. Colonel Bob Bellmon was at Fort Rucker, running Aviation Combat Developments. Bellmon was sort of a stuffy sonofabitch, but he was the man to take care of young Jannier. Like Jannier, his family had been officers for generations. More important, both Bellmon and his wife spoke French. Barbara Bellmon was not only a really nice woman but the daughter of Major General Peterson K. "Porky" Waterford, who had led the famed 40th "Hell's Circus" Armored Division in War II.

The Bellmons were Establishment, and they would be delighted to take care of the son of their French counterparts.

(Two)

As Paul was closing his attaché case, Patricia came out of the bathroom, looking crisp and desirable. She was red-haired and fair-skinned, but without the washed-out look Paul disliked in so many redheaded women. He had been enormously relieved when Patricia had kept her figure after the children. Even after three kids she was still very sexy and trim.

Patricia Hanrahan scowled at her husband.

"Do you really think you need that?" she asked, gesturing in the general direction of his pistol.

He picked up the Colt .45 from where he'd placed it next to the attaché case, and slipped it into a skeleton holster in the small of his back.

"We're not at Bragg yet," he said. "And you..."

"Never need a pistol until you need one badly," his wife finished his stock answer.

"That's right, honey," he said.

She shook her head in resignation—and disgust.

The houseboys wordlessly asked permission to take the luggage. Paul went to them and tried to give them money, which they politely but firmly refused. He gave up and gestured for them to take the luggage.

The Jannier family was gathered on the wide, red-tiled walkway that ran from the house to the curving drive. The Janniers were not going to go into Saigon with them. It was a ninety-mile drive each way over rough two-lane macadam roads.

The two Citroen sedans that had brought the Hanrahans from Saigon were in the drive. There were two Vietnamese drivers to a car, which was known as "sharing the rice bowl." Thus four men (in this case, four extraordinarily large men), doing the work of two, were "busy" tying luggage with great care to chrome racks on the roofs.

In addition, two houseboys were on the walkway, each with a tray of champagne glasses.

The departure turned out to be quite emotional when everyone realized that, excepting for the son, they were probably seeing one another for the last time. The chances of the Hanrahans returning to Vietnam, at least if Paul Hanrahan had anything to do with it, ranged from zero to highly unlikely.

Paul was not surprised when Christine Jannier kissed him, but he was surprised and touched when Henri wrapped his arms around him in an affectionate hug, and then actually kissed him. There was nothing whatever sexual in it, obviously, but it was a strange and disturbing feeling to feel a man's whiskers grating on his own.

They finished their champagne and got in the cars. Then, with waves and tootings of the horn and shouts of "Bon voyage!" and "Bon chance!" and "Au revoir!" the two cars, their tires grating on the macadam, drove away from the house.

Paul, Jr., and Kevin rode in the first car with Jean-Philippe Jannier, while the Hanrahan women went with Paul in the second. Their protracted departure for home now seemed just about over, Paul thought thankfully. All that remained was a "cocktail" at the Hotel Caravelle in Saigon. That would give them a chance to exchange a final word with a few friends as well as with the first secretary of the Embassy, the ambassador having sent his regrets, and make a quick visit to the facilities (the ones at the airfield left more than a little to be desired). Then they would be off to the VIP lounge and the Air France Constellation to Tokyo.

Hanrahan had been in Vietnam for more than three years, since the spring of 1955, when he had been one of the first American "advisors" sent there following the French defeat at Dien Bien Phu. He was glad to be getting out. It was his judgment that it had been a mistake to send Americans here in the first place. What he had seen of Vietnam since he had come had convinced him that what he had witnessed in Greece was not going to happen here, that this was a lost cause.

In Greece, the communists had been defeated. In part, this had been possible because Harry Truman had quietly ordered the army to send a group of officers and enlisted men to train and equip the Greek Army. This enabled them to protect their border with Albania and suppress Soviet-directed native communists.

Paul Hanrahan had first parachuted into Greece during World War II while on detached service to the OSS. Later, during the struggle with the communists, he had stayed on in Greece as an advisor. It had been touch and go for a while, especially at first, but then things had been turned around. American supplies had helped, of course, and so had the expertise of people like Hanrahan, whose extraordinary skill in counter-guerrilla activities was based on his own experience *as* a guerrilla. But what had kept the Soviet Union from taking over Greece had been a mind-set: the Greeks hated the communists not only for the ordinary reasons, but for religious reasons. They believed that the communists were the Antichrist, and they were willing to die for those convictions.

Hanrahan had rarely found such *pure* anticommunism in Vietnam. There was a little (among some of the hierarchy of the Roman Catholic Church, for example), but it was not widespread. Aware that he had become cynical, Hanrahan divided most of the South Vietnamese into two groups: those who really didn't give a damn who ran the country, and those who wanted to run it for their own benefit. Most of the anticommunists were in the second group. They were *not* anticommunist because they hated, as Hanrahan did, what communism really meant. And because of that, Hanrahan was convinced that the red flag, sooner or later, would fly over all of Vietnam.

But he was a soldier. He went where he was ordered to go and did the best job he could when he got there. That nobility of purpose, however, did not stop him from recognizing fault where he saw it. And it was his judgment that it was a mistake to send the army to Vietnam. In addition, the army itself was making the same mistake it had made in Greece. They were sending the same low caliber of officers to Vietnam that they had sent to Greece. When he was cynical (and he seemed to be cynical more and more of the time), he often thought that USAMAG (Greece) had been successful despite its officer corps, not because of it.

When a levy for personnel was issued, the best officers were given commands—of a platoon to a regiment—and the ones who weren't quite good enough for a command or for a staff position were the ones who could be "spared" to go to USA-MAG (Vietnam). And even the good officers who were sent over were the wrong kind. They could probably command an American battalion or regiment and fight a conventional war. But the war here was unconventional. Fighting it required skills that most of the people Hanrahan had met simply didn't have.

He forced those thoughts from his mind, and told himself to look on the bright side. He was going home. He was going to Bragg, where he had been stationed three times before; so that was sort of like going home, too. And he was pleased with his new assignment. He had crossed swords with the commanding officer of USAMAG (Vietnam) on a number of issues, and his efficiency reports, through a technique of "damning by faint praise," had reflected that officer's disapproval. But despite the lousy efficiency reports, he was being assigned to the newly organized Special Warfare School. He thought there was at least a chance that the school could set up some kind of valuable training program for officers and noncoms about to be sent to Vietnam—or wherever else the brass decided "advisors" were needed.

It would have been pleasant to think that he had been assigned to the Special Warfare School despite his efficiency reports rather than because of them. But Hanrahan was a realist. He had been a lieutenant colonel longer than just about anyone in the army. It was entirely likely that he had risen as high in rank as he was going to rise. It was expected of West Point graduates that, at appropriate points in their career, they be given commands. The only commands Paul Hanrahan had ever had were of small detachments of advisors.

Command, he sometimes thought bitterly, was judged by numbers of troops. Command of a 1,200-man battalion involved in maneuvers in Louisiana was considered far more important than command of a 50-man advisory detachment, even though the advisors might be in *de facto* command of a division and a half of indigenous troops in contact with a real enemy.

Of course, it was possible that he would get the eagle of a full colonel. It was even possible that five years later he could get to be brigadier general. He was, after all, a graduate of the United States Military Academy, and there was the West Point Protective Association, which was supposed to see that West Pointers got promoted no matter what.

It was also possible, Lt. Col. Paul "Red" Hanrahan thought, that a pig could be taught to say the rosary and then be taken bodily into heaven.

He looked out the window of the Citroen at the rice paddies and told himself that in seventy-two hours, when he looked out a car window, he would see either a billboard urging some kind of beer on him, or a farmer riding a tractor, not one standing up to his hips in muddy water.

Ten minutes later, roughly three-quarters of an hour from the plantation, as the two Citroens drove at what Hanrahan thought was an excessive speed down the winding road between flooded rice paddies, the skin at the back of his neck began to crawl.

The first thing he thought was that he was concerned with their speed.

Vietnamese, particularly those at the wheel of a Westerner's car, think that automobiles have two speeds, on and off.

And then he realized it was more than just the speed. There was a reason for the speed.

He turned over his shoulder and saw they were being followed by a General Motors Carryall.

The sonofabitch is right on our bumper!

And then he knew.

"Get on the floor!" he ordered sharply.

Patricia looked at him in disbelief.

Hanrahan reached over his wife and put his hands on Rosemary's shoulders, then jerked her violently out of the corner and threw her onto the floor of the car.

"My God!" Patricia shrieked. "Paul, what in the world . . ."

Hanrahan put his hands on his wife's hair and pulled her downward to the floorboard.

He felt the car brake, and then skid. Next he was flying forward, slamming into his wife, and then bouncing against the back of the front seat.

"Stay where you are!" he ordered.

Rosemary began to whimper.

He got his hand on the .45, tugged it free of the holster, and worked the action. Then he opened the door and crawled quickly out between the two Citroens. They had both skidded to a stop, crosswise on the road, facing in opposite directions.

He got to his knees and moved to the rear of the car he had just left.

Vietnamese in black pajamas were spilling from the GMC. The man in the lead was raising an American Thompson .45 caliber submachine gun to his shoulder, aiming it at the rear car.

Hanrahan put both hands together on the .45 to steady it and shot the man twice, first in the chest and then again in the face.

Then he ran the four steps to the edge of the road and dived into the ditch.

There came the sound of submachine guns, not the slower blam-blam-blam a Thompson makes, but a lighter, ripping sound. And then other weapons were firing. His pistol held in both hands in front of him, Hanrahan popped up from the ditch.

The firefight was over.

Not all the Vietnamese in black pajamas had made it out of the GMC. Those that had were sprawled in spreading pools of blood behind the man with the Thompson he had dropped. The others were hanging at obscene angles from the open doors of the truck. The windows on the GMC were stitched with holes, and steam was rising from the hood and radiator.

The Vietnamese in the Citroens had not been "sharing a rice bowl," he now realized; they'd been riding shotgun. Now they were advancing toward the GMC, holding French MAT-49 9 mm machine pistols in their hands. The man Hanrahan had shot was obviously dead; the .45 bullet had blown the back of his head away. There was some question about the others on the ground behind him, or hanging from the GMC.

One of the Vietnamese matter of factly ejected the clip from his MAT-49, inserted a fresh one, and then emptied it into the bodies.

"Formidable, mon Colonel," Jean-Philippe Jannier said, and then switched to English. "But I fear you have dirtied your suit."

He had a MAT-49 hanging loosely at his side. Hanrahan saw vestiges of smoke curling from the open action.

"Fuck my suit," Hanrahan said. He rushed to the Citroen,

and for a moment his heart stopped. Patricia and Rosemary were not moving.

"Oh, my God!" Hanrahan wailed.

And then Patricia looked up at him, wide-eyed, terrified, unbelieving.

"Honey?" she asked, and then she repeated herself.

"It's OK, Patty," he said. "It's all over."

"Honey?" she asked again.

When she saw the bodies on the road, Patricia became nauseous, and that caused a sympathetic reaction in Rosemary.

There was more carnage than anyone would have thought possible. He was able to reconstruct what had happened: it was an ambush, a carefully planned ambush, probably intended to get Jean-Philippe Jannier, and probably because of his grandfather. The ambushers had known the cars were coming. They had waited along the road to positively identify Jannier, and then chased him in the GMC. The GMC also served as a signal to men on the highway. When they saw it coming, they turned a bullock-drawn cart across the road to block it. The car had then been pinned between the GMC and the cart.

If there had been just one car, if Jannier had been traveling alone, the ambush would have succeeded. He would have been caught the moment he stopped.

But there had been a moment's hesitation when the two cars had skidded to a stop, sufficient time for the bodyguard in the rear car to direct his fire against the GMC. It was possible, Hanrahan decided, that he had been unnecessary, that the man in his car could have taken care of the man he had shot.

He was suddenly violently angry that the Janniers could put his wife and his children in such jeopardy.

But then he realized that was emotion speaking, not reason. They had done nothing of the kind.

The bullocks were unhurt. They hadn't even run. One of the Vietnamese went to them, urged them into motion, and got the cart off the road. The others picked up the weapons of the ambushers and loaded them into the trunks of the Citroens. Then they resumed their journey to Saigon.

Before they got to Saigon, Hanrahan had calmed down enough to realize that there would very likely be all kinds of Vietnamese officialdom interested in what had happened on the road. If that happened, their departure would be delayed. He told the driver to signal the other car to stop so he could discuss the problem with Jean-Philippe Jannier.

"I can look into the future, mon Colonel," Jannier said immediately. "Two hours from now, as they return from an uneventful trip to Saigon, my father's cars will be assaulted without warning. Unfortunately, lives will be lost."

"That sounds too simple to be workable," Hanrahan said.

"Put the matter from your mind, mon Colonel," Jannier said. "It might be wise to have a word with Madame Hanrahan. And perhaps leave the children somewhere while we are at *le cocktail*."

In the end, a generous bribe put the children in the billiard room while *le cocktail* was being held. And Paul's dirty suit was explained by a story of a flat tire.

Kevin Hanrahan, looking at the door of the billiard room, saw his father making his way to the men's room. He came running in after him, wrapped his arms around his father's leg, and hung on tightly.

"I don't ever want to come back," Kevin said.

(Three)
Honolulu, Hawaii
27 December 1958

The Hanrahans were less than twenty-fours out of Saigon, but they had crossed the international date line. December 26 had forever vanished from their lives.

They were not supposed to deplane at Honolulu, which was simply fueling stop. Kevin and Rosemary slept through the landing.

The stewardess came down the aisle.

"There is an urgent telephone call for you, Colonel," she said.

"I guess the Embassy heard about the attack," Paul, Jr., said evenly. "And now we'll have to go back for the investigation."

Hanrahan thought angrily that such a sophisticated analysis from a kid that age was less an indication of his intelligence than proof that he had taken his kids where they shouldn't have gone.

"'Never take counsel of your fears,'" Hanrahan quoted. "'General George S. Patton.'"

"What are you going to do if they have?"

"Tell the truth," Hanrahan said. "I didn't volunteer any information, but I didn't withhold any, either."

"That logic is invalid," Paul, Jr., said.

"You spent too much time with the Jesuits," his father said. "The truth is the truth."

"Truth is a perception," Hanrahan said to his son, as he pulled up his necktie, and gave what he hoped was an encouraging smile to Patricia.

"What does that mean?" Paul, Jr., asked.

"Ask the Jesuits," Hanrahan said, and then he walked down the aisle and down the ladder into the inhospitable atmosphere of a deserted airport.

There was a white telephone immediately inside the terminal building. He picked it up.

"This is Colonel Hanrahan," he said. "Have you a call for me?"

"I have a call for *Lieutenant* Colonel Paul. T. Hanrahan," the operator said.

"This is he," he said.

He felt like a fool, as if he'd been caught in a pretense. According to army regulations, the "lieutenant prefix is customarily not used in informal communication." He was right by the book, but he felt like an ass.

"One moment, please," the operator said. And after a pause: "I have Lieutenant Colonel Hanrahan for you."

A male voice demanded: "Is this Lieutenant Colonel Paul T. Hanrahan?"

"Yes, sir."

"This is Major Ford, sir. I'm the field-grade duty officer at Headquarters, USARPAC."

If Headquarters, U.S. Army, Pacific, had bothered to stop him en route home, his ass was obviously in a deeper crack than he had thought.

"What can I do for you, Major?"

"DA has advised by radio of a change in your orders, Lieutenant Colonel Hanrahan, and directed Headquarters, USARPAC, to relay them to you."

Hanrahan picked up on the "lieutenant colonel" business. Maybe USARPAC had a local rule that lieutenant colonels be fully identified.

"I was afraid of that," Hanrahan said, "when I was damned near home."

"May I read them to you, Lieutenant Colonel Hanrahan?"

That's what it was, a local rule. Maybe it made sense. He would have to think about it.

"Please," Hanrahan said.

"I'll just touch on the highlights, Lieutenant Colonel," the major said.

"Go ahead," Hanrahan said, impatiently. What he was going to hear was that he was to interrupt his travel, and report to Hq USARPAC to await further orders.

"So much of Paragraph 34, General Order 203, Headquarters, Department of the Army, Washington 25, D.C., dated 1 November 1958," the major read, "as pertains to Lieutenant Colonel Paul T. Hanrahan, Signal Corps, is amended to read, 'Colonel Paul T. Hanrahan, Signal Corps, detailed Infantry,' and so much of subject paragraph as pertains to subject officer reporting for duty with USASWS is amended to read 'to assume command of USASWS.'"

"I'll be goddamned," Hanrahan said. "I wasn't even on the list."

"You were on somebody's list, Colonel," the major said, with a chuckle. "Am I the first to be able to congratulate you?"

"Yes," Hanrahan said.

"My congratulations, sir."

"Thank you," Hanrahan said.

Actually stunned, Hanrahan hung the telephone up without even saying good-bye.

He stood with his head bent looking at the telephone.

"Bad, honey?" Patricia's voice said behind him.

He turned and saw the concern in her eyes. It took him a moment to find his voice.

"How would you like to kiss a bird fucking colonel?" he asked.

Her eyebrows went up.

"Failing that, how about the new commanding officer of the Special Warfare School?" he said.

She ran to his arms.

And then, after a moment, very softly, she whispered in his ear: "If I had my druthers, I'd rather fuck the full fucking colonel."

II

(One)
Hartwell Field
Atlanta, Georgia
1615 Hours, 28 December 1958

There had not been time in San Francisco to get on the telephone to Bob Bellmon, and there had not been time here in Atlanta to make any calls before Captain Jean-Philippe Jannier had to board the Southern Airlines DC-3 which would carry him to Dothan, Alabama, the nearest field to Fort Rucker. There was barely going to be enough time now, before they had to board Piedmont to fly to Fayetteville, N.C., the last leg of their journey to Fort Bragg; but Hanrahan thought he should at least try.

A surly attendant at the newsstand changed a ten dollar bill into quarters for him. After some difficulty in finding a telephone booth, rather than what looked like giant clam shells mounted to the walls, he began to make his call. With a little bit of

21

luck, he could catch Bellmon and have him send someone to meet Jannier's plane.

There was no answer at Bellmon's quarters. Next he called Combat Developments, but a none-too-bright sergeant who was charge of quarters informed him that "the general and his wife is at the funeral, probably."

"I'm asking for Colonel Bellmon, Sergeant."

"Yes, sir. They made him a general, as of this morning."

"You say he's at a funeral?"

"Yes, sir. Lieutenant Greer's."

"Do you have any idea when he'll be back?"

"No telling, sir. It's a great big funeral, with the band and everything. The place is crawling with brass."

Hanrahan was curious about that 'great big funeral, with the band and everything' for a simple lieutenant, but he didn't have the time to pursue his curiosity.

"Sergeant, have you got a pencil?" he asked.

"Yes, sir."

"My name is Hanrahan," he said. "I'll spell it for you." He did. "Will you please give General Bellmon a note saying that I telephoned, that I extend my congratulations on his promotion, and that I will call again."

"Yes, sir. Be happy to."

"Thank you very much," Hanrahan said, and hung up.

It wasn't the end of the world. He could call again, as soon as he got to Fayetteville, and still have someone call Jannier and welcome him to Rucker once he was actually there. Certainly someone official would meet him, and Captain Jean-Philippe Jannier was not an innocent second lieutenant. He could make it from the airport to the post by himself.

Then Hanrahan thought of Sandy Felter.

Now that he was out of Vietnam, he knew he simply could not forget the ambush on the road. He had realized on the plane that he had erred in not reporting it. He should have stayed and dealt with it, no matter what a pain in the ass that would have been.

The attack itself was worthy of official note. The Vietminh, if that's what they were, had made a daylight assassination attempt on a Frenchman. Even more important, it followed that if they knew as much about Captain Jean-Philippe Jannier's movements as they obviously did, then they knew that the guests of the Janniers were an American MAG officer and his family: That had not stopped them. That was something new. Felter had told him the communists were going out of their way not to attack Americans.

The very least he could do was tell Felter. Perhaps that would, in some small way, permit him to squirm out of his failure to do in Saigon what he knew damned well was the correct thing to do.

He took out his address book again and found a Washington number that Felter had told him was sort of an answering service. The operator took what seemed like an endless amount of quarters, and then put the call through.

"Liberty 7–1221," a pleasant female voice said.

"Major Felter, please," Hanrahan said.

"May I ask who is calling, please?"

"This is Colonel Paul Hanrahan."

"One moment, please, Colonel," the woman said.

The woman wore the five stripes of a sergeant first class on her khaki shirt, and she was sitting with three other soldiers before a switchboard in a small room with eight-foot-thick walls fifty feet under the White House.

She raised her hand over her head and snapped her fingers to attract the attention of a young Signal Corps captain who was in charge. He walked quickly over to her.

"Colonel Paul Hanrahan for Felter," she said. "There's a Lieutenant Colonel Hanrahan, Paul T., on the list." She pointed out a name in a loose-leaf notebook in front of her. These were the names and telephone numbers of those that the fifty-odd people on what was known as "the A List" (those with unlimited access to the White House communications system) might wish to talk to. "But the number here is in Saigon."

"Probably the same guy," the captain decided. "Put him through."

"Yes, sir," she said.

"One moment, please, Colonel Hanrahan," she said, pleasantly. "We're trying to locate Major Felter for you."

She pushed a button on her control console.

"Go," a male voice said. He was speaking from a heavily guarded underground room in the Defense Communications Agency, a large, featureless building across Washington.

"Scramble One for Mouse," she said.

"Hold," he said.

There was another voice on the line a moment later, another female, this one in a temporary communications link in the Signal Telephone building at Fort Rucker, Alabama.

"Canary verifies scrambler."

"Mouse, please," the White House operator said.

"Mouse is 60 to 120 seconds from scrambler," the operator at Fort Rucker replied.

"Advise Mouse call is from Colonel Hanrahan."

There was the sound of a telephone ringing.

"Captain Parker."

"Major Sanford Felter, please," the Fort Rucker operator said.

"Just a second," the man who answered the phone said, and then, more faintly, as if the telephone was away from his mouth, "Mouse, it's for you."

The White House operator restrained a giggle. Obviously the people who had given Major Sanford T. Felter his code name weren't the only ones who thought him mouselike.

"Major Felter."

"Major, this is not scrambled," the Fort Rucker operator said. "You have a call from a Colonel Paul Hanrahan."

"Put it through," Felter said.

"Colonel Hanrahan," the White House operator said, "we have Major Felter for you."

"Yes, sir?" Major Felter said, happily. "How are you, sir?"

"Exhausted, Felter. I just got off a plane from Saigon."

"Welcome home, sir. I'll look forward to seeing you very soon."

"Mouse, there's something I've got to tell you."

"This is not a secure line, Colonel. Is it classified?"

"You tell me. Is an attack by the Vietminh on Americans classified?"

"Why should it be?" Felter said in a moment. "I guess the Vietminh already know about it. Anybody we know?"

"Pat, the kids, and me," Hanrahan said. "I think they were after a Frenchman named Jannier . . ."

"Father or son?"

"Son. We were on our way from the plantation to the airport."

"Any damage?"

"Not to us. I think he expected it."

"Forgive me, Colonel. I didn't think to ask about Pat and the kids."

"They're all right. Scared, but all right."

"Thank God," Felter said. "I'm glad you told me, Colonel. It may have some significance."

"That's the point, Mouse. I didn't say anything over there. I wanted to get out of the country, and I knew..."

"If there was no damage to you, that was the smart thing to do. I'd have done the same."

"I hate to admit how relieved I am to hear you say that, Mouse," Hanrahan said.

"Forget the whole incident, Colonel," Felter said.

"I didn't ask about Sharon and the kids, either."

"Fine, just fine," Felter said. "And trying to take the phone away from me this very moment is another familiar face."

"Who?"

"The Duke," Felter said.

"And what outrage has he been up to lately?" Hanrahan asked. Major Craig W. Lowell had earned his nickname, "the Duke," as a second lieutenant under Hanrahan in Greece.

"At two this afternoon, Colonel, there were ten T34s in the inventory. At two fifteen, Duke blew half of them up."

Hanrahan chuckled. He didn't know what was going on, but nothing Major Craig W. Lowell did would surprise him.

"Put him on, Mouse," Hanrahan said. "I want to hear about that."

"Colonel, sir," Lowell's happy voice came on the line.

Hanrahan saw Patricia gesturing frantically at him, pointing to her watch.

"Hello, Duke. Call me at Bragg. Good-bye, Duke," Hanrahan said, and hung up.

"Oh, hell," Lowell said.

"Major Felter, please," the White House operator said.

"They want to talk to you again, Mouse."

"Felter."

"Major, your party disconnected. He was calling from a pay booth at the airfield in Atlanta."

"Thanks very much."

"Yes, sir."

There was a click when Felter hung up.

"Breakdown Scrambler One for Mouse."

"Clear."

"Clear."
"Clear."
"Standing by."

(Two)

Dr. Antoinette Parker had never been quite able to control her feelings that military courtesy was an amusing absurdity. One man calling another "sir" went back to the medieval "sire," with its implication that the senior was the father of the junior. Her husband had pointed out to her that military courtesy wasn't very much different from the protocol of academe or medicine. Her father, he pointed out with infuriating logic, was more than a little sensitive about his prerogatives as a professor. None of *his* subordinates dared fail to call him either "doctor" (or, preferably, "professor"). He added somewhat smugly that she herself was outraged if a nurse called her anything besides "doctor."

Intellectually, she had to agree with him. Emotionally, she still thought it was absurd.

But when Major General Jiggs appeared at the screened-in porch at the end of the World War II hospital ward that had been converted to quarters, what she said, without thinking about it, was, "Good evening, sir."

"I'm sorry to intrude, Doctor," General Jiggs said. "But I had an idea Major Lowell might be here. I suppose I should have called first . . ."

"They're celebrating his reprieve," she said, stepping away from the door, gesturing with an inclination of her head and a smile for him to come in.

"I suspected they might be," he said. Then he looked at her. *"They're?"* he asked.

"At the moment, General," she said, "it's the brotherhood. I felt out of place."

"Oh," he said, and smiled at her.

"That will change," she said. "Barbara Bellmon's on her way over here with Roxy MacMillan and Sharon Felter."

"I thought," General Jiggs said, "that it was bad news that was supposed to travel fast."

There was the sound of tires on gravel, and they both looked toward the street. A Buick convertible, Barbara Bellmon's car, had pulled in beside General Jiggs's staff car. There were three women in the front seat, Barbara Bellmon, tall, lithe, attractive (who looked, Toni Parker often thought, as if she had just stepped from an advertisement in *Town & Country*); Roxy MacMillan, buxom, redheaded, with prominent teeth ("jolly," Toni thought); and Sharon Felter, a small, dark-haired woman (whom Toni thought was probably the most gentle, understanding person she had ever known).

"The sisterhood seems to have arrived," Jiggs said dryly.

The women spilled out of the car and walked onto the porch.

"Where is Jane?" Barbara Bellmon said to General Jiggs, accusingly. Jane was Jiggs's wife.

"The last I heard, Barbara," Jiggs said, "she was at the Duttons with you and Melody Greer."

"I dropped her at your quarters," Barbara Bellmon said. "She was going to the club to get you and bring you here. I don't know where Bob is."

"He and Mac MacMillan are on their way to Washington," Jiggs said. "How did you find out there is cause for celebration?"

"Sandy Felter called Sharon at the Duttons," Barbara said. "What's Bob doing in Washington?"

"E. Z. Black sent for him," Jiggs said. "He didn't say why. But my guess is that Bob's due for a new job."

"When are they coming back?" Roxy MacMillan asked.

"Bob will be back in time for New Year's Eve, Black said. Mac, probably tonight or in the morning."

"I'll call Jane at the club," Barbara said.

"Thank you," Jiggs said.

He made a gesture halfway between a nod and a bow and went into the apartment. When he got to the living room, there were four officers sprawled on the Danish modern chairs and couches, and two others leaning on a bar. Each clutched a glass dark with whiskey.

Major Sanford T. Felter was the first to see Jiggs when he entered the room. Felter had been leaning on the bar, and when he saw Jiggs he straightened up, almost coming to attention. The officer he was talking to, "Dutch" Cramer, the old-time, middle-aged, Ordnance Corps chief warrant officer whose rockets had blown up the five Russian T-34s, glanced over at Jiggs; and he too straightened up.

Their movement caught the eyes of the others, and the four men on the chairs and couches started to stand up.

"Keep your seats," General Jiggs said.

Captain Philip Sheridan Parker IV walked over to General Jiggs.

"What can I get you, sir?" he asked.

"First a drink of that scotch," Jiggs said. "And then I want a moment of Major Felter's time."

"Yes, sir," Parker said, walking to the bar.

"And after that, probably more of the scotch," Jiggs said.

Parker made him a drink and handed it to him.

"Thank you," Jiggs said, with a smile, and then looked at Felter. "Major, if you please?"

Felter followed Jiggs out of the room and down the corridor of the building and then outside, so they were standing under the covered walkway that had been built to roll body carts from one part of the hospital to another.

"This is far enough," Jiggs said.

"Yes, sir," Major Felter said.

Jiggs thought that Felter looked as if he was wearing his big brother's, or at least somebody else's uniform. Felter was in greens, and the tunic was loaded with an impressive array of medals, insignia, and devices. To the shoulders were sewn the patches of the 40th Armored Division, in which Felter had served as a young lieutenant in the waning days of World War II; that of the Military District of Washington; and a curved strip with the word RANGER embroidered on it.

There were four rows of ribbons above the breast pocket, representing the Distinguished Service Cross, Silver Star, and Purple Heart, and others representing medals awarded by the Greek, French, and Korean governments. There was an Expert Combat Infantry Badge with a star signifying the second award. There were U.S. and French parachutist's wings. On the lapels was the starred insignia of the General Staff Corps, and on a tunic pocket the medallion signifying three years' service on the General Staff. Hanging from the right epaulet was a heavy, woven golden rope, the insignia of an aide-de-camp to the President of the United States. On his finger was the ring worn by graduates of the United States Military Academy at West Point.

There was an automatic reflex on Jiggs's part: *The GSC insignia on the lapels was wrong. He should be wearing the insignia of an aide-de-camp to the President.*

But Jiggs immediately remembered that there was no one

who was about to correct Major Felter. Felter was in fact
assigned to the General Staff Corps, and he was in fact an aide
to the President of the United States. Not the sort of aide,
however, who stood tall behind the President in his dress blues
or the even more ornate blue mess uniform, whispering the
names of distinguished visitors. Nor was he expected to dance
with the ugly daughter of the Swedish ambassador to the strains
of the Marine Corps Band in the Blue Room.

Major Felter was a very special kind of aide. In each of the
personal safes of the directors of the CIA, the FBI, and the
Defense Intelligence Agency, and of the chiefs of Army, Navy,
Air Force, and State Department Intelligence, there was a typewritten note on the President's personal stationery:

> Major Sanford T. Felter, GSC, USA, is an-
> nounced as my personal liaison officer to the in-
> telligence community with rank of Counselor to
> the President. No public announcement of this ap-
> pointment will be made.
>
> DDE

Major Felter did not wear his medals, or his uniform, on
duty.

When Paul Jiggs had heard that Felter was coming to Rucker,
he had been curious to know why. Jane Jiggs had found out
for him from Barbara Bellmon.

By coincidence, many of Felter's old friends were for various reasons at Rucker, and Roxy MacMillan had impulsively
called Sharon and asked her to come down for the New Year's
Eve party. At first the idea had seemed absurd on its face, but
then Sharon Felter had realized how very much she wanted to
be what she was, an officer's lady, rather than what her neighbors thought she was, the wife of a middle-ranking economic
analyst at the CIA. Sharon very much wanted to walk into an
officer's mess for the traditional New Year's party on the arm
of her dress-uniformed, highly decorated husband.

Sharon had confessed to Barbara Bellmon that she had had
to get a little drunk to find the courage to demand of her husband
that he bring her to Rucker. But it had worked. Felter had
reluctantly agreed. They had arrived at Rucker just before Ed
Greer crashed to his death. And their arrival had been preceded

by a directive from the Defense Communications Agency calling for the installation of a secure radiotelephone, radioteletype link to Washington for Felter's exclusive use. The nature of his duties were such that Felter was never supposed to be more than 30 seconds away from a commo link to the White House, never more than 120 seconds from a secure, scrambler connection to the commander in chief.

He didn't look like a Counselor to the President, Jiggs thought, or a highly regarded, very influential intelligence officer. He would never be asked to pose for a recruiting poster. Ranger-qualified majors with the Combat Infantry Badge and the DSC are supposed to look like John Wayne, and Major Sanford T. Felter was a stoop-shouldered, balding, bespectacled little Jew.

"Yes, sir?" Felter asked politely.

"If you are in a position to do so, Major," General Jiggs said, "I would like you to tell me what happened between Lowell and General Black."

Jiggs was aware that Felter was considering whether he should answer the question. It took him a long moment.

"Craig's story is that the army couldn't afford, in a public relations sense, to court-martial him," Felter said, finally. "That, in effect, Colonel Tim F. Brandon saved his skin."

Colonel Tim F. Brandon was the Pentagon public relations officer handling the rocket-armed helicopter "problem."

"Is that what he told you?" Jiggs asked.

"No, sir, he told me what really happened."

"And you are not in a position to tell me?"

"I've been considering if I should," Felter said, frankly. "Apparently what happened, General, is a combination of things. The root of General Black's anger with him was based on Lowell's direct disobedience to an order of General Black's."

"What order was that?"

"General Black thought it best that Lowell keep his distance from me. He ordered him to do so."

"I hadn't heard about that," Jiggs said. "Why? Because of where you work?"

"Primarily that, of course," Felter said. "But also, I think, because of Craig's involvement with the rocket-armed chopper. From the general's point of view, of course, it was logical."

"And, of course, Lowell didn't keep his distance?"

"He came to see me, and my wife and children often used

the swimming pool at his house in Georgetown."

"You didn't know about Black's order?"

"No, sir."

Black, Jiggs thought, was not about to tell a man who saw the President of the United States at least once a day who he was not supposed to see, even if that man was only a major.

"And that's the real reason they were throwing him out of the service?" Hanrahan said.

"The specific reason was Craig's affair with the senator's wife," Felter said. "The straw that broke the camel's back."

"I tried to talk to General Black," Jiggs said. "Lowell is just too valuable an officer to lose just because he satisfied some unsatisfied woman who happened to be a senator's wife. He wouldn't even hear me out."

"He reminded me that I am a major," Felter said, "when I tried to speak to him about Lowell."

"Then what changed his mind?" Jiggs asked. This was the question he hoped he would be able to ask Major Sanford T. Felter.

"Craig told me that General Black told him that he had come to understand that he had violated a basic principle of command, sir," Felter said. "That one should never issue an order that one knows cannot be obeyed. Lowell is closer to my wife and children, and to me, than to anyone else in the world. With the best intentions, he could not cut us out of his life. General Black apparently finally understood this. That, in any event, is what he told Lowell. I believe it to be the case."

"And how do you see his putting Lowell in charge of the rocket-armed helicopter program?"

"I believe the general was rather pleased with Major Lowell's demonstration of the capability of the rocket-armed helicopter," Felter said, dryly. "I don't see, now, how the air force can take it away from us."

"No," Jiggs said, "neither do I." And then he added, "One more question, Major?"

"Yes, sir?"

"Why did you decide to tell me this?"

"I don't know of anyone Lowell respects more than he does you, General," Felter said. "I hoped that you might be able to speak to him, to convince him that this is, in fact, his last chance."

"I'll tell you what I'm going to do, Major," General Jiggs

said. "I'm going to go back in there and get drunk with him, and swap war stories, and then tomorrow morning, when we're both hung over, I'm going to call Duke Lowell into my office and read him the riot act like he's never heard it before. When I get through with that sonofabitch, he'll rush right over to the chaplain's office and sign up for the men's choir."

"I believe, sir, the general has a splendid idea," Major Felter said.

(Three)
Fayetteville, North Carolina
1945 Hours, 28 December 1958

The five Hanrahans—father, mother, two sons, and the baby, a daughter aged ten—came down the ladder from Piedmont Flight 223, a turboprop Convair, into the surprisingly bitter cold. They were mussed, tired, and groggy.

They shuffled into the terminal.

There were two signs just inside the terminal. One pointed to the baggage pickup area, and the other had an arrow pointing at a shallow angle toward a telephone booth. The legend on the sign said: TELEPHONE FOR INCOMING MILITARY PERSONNEL FOR FORT BRAGG.

"Paul, go with your mother and help with the bags," Colonel Paul T. Hanrahan said. "I'll call and get us some wheels."

Patricia Hanrahan, holding the hands of her youngest children, marched off to the baggage pickup area while her oldest child walked tiredly behind her. In seventy-some hours, they had traveled 10,000 miles, and they were still some distance from bed. They hadn't eaten since lunch, and both Kevin and Rosemary were getting whiny.

Hanrahan went to the telephone booth, closed the door, and sat down. He expected a pay telephone, but the booth offered instead a dialless desk telephone firmly bolted to a tiny shelf. There was a sign on the wall. He studied it:

MILITARY PERSONNEL REPORTING TO FORT BRAGG ON TRAVEL ORDERS:

Between 0730–1630 Hours, Weekdays:

Officers: Call Ext. 3546.

EM: Call Ext. 3606.

Between 1630–0730 Hours, Weekdays:

Officers: Call Ext. 3202.

EM: Call Ext. 3290.

Saturdays, Sundays, and Holidays:

All Personnel Call Ext. 4333.

He said, aloud: "I'll have to figure that out."

He found a battered package of cigarettes in his mussed suit jacket, and searched for a match. Then he read the sign again.

"Is this a holiday or isn't it?" he asked aloud. And then he said, "Fuck it," and stood up and opened the door and left the telephone booth.

He looked around for more signs, and found the one he was looking for: "RENTAL CARS THROUGH THE CORRIDOR."

He went through the corridor and looked at the rental car booths, passing over Hertz and Avis for Econo-Car. They probably charged just as much as Hertz or Avis, he thought, but maybe not.

There were three people in line ahead of him.

As Hanrahan waited, he kept looking toward the baggage pickup area. It was entirely possible, he thought, that Fayetteville would have baggage handlers of extraordinary zeal who would get the bags to Patricia before he expected they would. If so, she wouldn't know where the hell he was.

Finally, it was his turn.

"I'd like a car, please," he said.

The girl took out a sheath of forms.

"Do you have an Econo-Car card, sir?"

"Do I have a what?"

"One of our credit cards," she explained impatiently.

"No."

"American Express, Visa, Air Travel?"

"No."

"Then there will be a one hundred dollar deposit, sir."

"OK," he said.

That wasn't all there was to it. She wanted his driver's license, too, and when he presented his New York State operator's permit, it was two years out of date. He gave her his Adjutant General's Office identification card (AGO card), which identified him as a lieutenant colonel of the regular army, and explained to her that according to the laws of the State of New York, military personnel returning from service outside the country have thirty days in which to renew expired driver's licenses.

She had to check on that. While she was calling her superiors at Econo-Car in Raleigh, Paul, Jr., found him, and delivered the latest bulletin. They now had their luggage, except for one piece which had apparently not been loaded on the plane in Atlanta. It would be delivered the next day. And Rosemary had shit in her pants.

"Don't say that word," Paul Hanrahan said.

"Mother wants to know how long it's going to take them to send a car."

"I'm renting one," he said. "Tell your mother that."

There was one other problem. He didn't know where he was going.

When the Econo-Car girl came back, visibly surprised to have been informed that his driver's license was indeed valid, he asked her about a motel.

"The biggest is the Fayetteville Inn," she said. "On Bragg Boulevard."

"Could we call them, and ask if there's room?"

"You'll find a pay telephone in the main lobby, sir," the girl said. "Thank you for renting from Econo-Car."

He didn't call first. When he found his family, Rosemary was weeping from her humiliation.

"It was that whatever-it-was they gave us on the plane from San Francisco," Paul Hanrahan said. "It almost got me, too."

"She stinks," Kevin said.

"Shut up, Kevin," Paul Hanrahan said. "We're on our way to a motel." To Patricia, he explained: "I'm too beat to go out to the post."

She nodded her understanding.

They loaded everybody in a Chevrolet. Kevin was right. Rosemary, sitting beside her father, stank.

It was fifteen minutes from the airport to Bragg Boulevard and another five before he found the Fayetteville Inn, a large motel with a complex of two-story buildings.

He went in. They could give him a room with two double beds and put a cot in it for only six times what it would have cost him to go to Fort Bragg and put up in the officer's guest house, a barracks converted into apartments to provide temporary accommodation for newly arriving officers and their families.

The cot was delivered while Patricia was cleaning up Rosemary in the bathroom. When she came out, he saw that her chest was beginning to swell under her little girl's undershirt.

You're getting old, Hanrahan. The last of your children is really growing up. And you were just too old and tired to comply with your orders.

"Well, let's go someplace and get some dinner, and then hit the sack."

"You *promised*," Kevin, hurt and angry, challenged.

"What did I promise?"

"You said that when we got here, I could have a hamburger."

"If nothing else, I am a man of my word. A hamburger joint it is."

"Her stomach..." Patricia said.

"She can have something else," Hanrahan said.

"I want a hamburger, too," Rosemary said.

They went out and got in the rented Chevrolet. A mile from the Fayetteville Inn, he found a large hamburger joint, a white concrete building with an enormous tin hamburger outlined with neon lights on its roof.

It was called the ParaBurger. Fort Bragg, N.C., was the home of the paratroops.

When they walked inside and he smelled the burning ground beef and the onions, his mouth watered and he was amused at himself. They crowded into one of the booths, and a waitress promptly arrived to take their order. Kevin ordered a Super ParaBurger with french fries and a chocolate ice cream soda. That meant that Kevin was probably going to run to form, gulp too much food down, and then throw it up. All the same Paul didn't even warn the kid to take it easy.

The hamburger joint in a sense was really coming home, and he didn't want to be a spoilsport.

A great bull of a man came to the booth. He was florid faced and crew cut, and the skin of his neck hung in folds. He wore a plaid sports coat with a blue shirt collar spread on it, and he was towing a tall, skinny woman with a nervous smile.

"Colonel Hanrahan?" the man asked.

"Yes," Hanrahan said, forcing a smile, getting to his feet, and offering his hand.

"Sergeant Wojinski, sir," the bull of a man said. "I thought it was you, Colonel."

"It's good to see you again, Sergeant," Hanrahan said.

But it would have been better at some other time.

"I'm sure the colonel doesn't remember me . . ."

You're familiar; I've seen that bullneck before. But where? Greece!

"You were with the 119th Regiment, 27th Royal Hellenic," Colonel Hanrahan said.

"Well, goddamn, Colonel, I'm flattered," Sergeant Wojinski said. "That was a couple of wars ago."

"I remember you," Hanrahan said, "very well."

"Colonel, could I let you meet my wife?" Wojinski blurted.

"How do you do, Mrs. Wojinski?" Hanrahan said.

"We didn't want to bother you, or nothing," Mrs. Wojinski said, "but Ski says, 'that's the colonel, I know goddamn well it is,' and I couldn't stop him."

"I'm very glad you didn't," Hanrahan said. "And this is my wife, Patricia, and Paul, Jr., Kevin, and Rosemary."

"I'm pleased to meet you, I'm sure," Mrs. Wojinski said. "You have a real nice family, Miz Hanrahan."

"Thank you," Patricia Hanrahan said, with a smile. "Won't you sit down?"

"Thanks just the same, but we was just leavin'," Mrs. Wojinski said.

"Another time, then," Hanrahan said. "I'll probably see you out at the post, Ski. We're just reporting in. Where are you?"

"Special Warfare School, sir," Wojinski said.

"Well, then, I will see you. That's where I'm going."

Wojinski gave him a funny look.

"You got any idea what you'll be doing there, Colonel?" he asked.

"I'll be running it, Ski," Hanrahan said.

"Commanding officer?"

"They call it 'commandant,'" Hanrahan said.

"Colonel, I'm glad to hear that," Wojinski said. "Real glad."

"I was, too, Ski," Hanrahan said. "I only found out a couple of days ago. On our way here, as a matter of fact."

"Well, then, sir, I will see you out at the post," Wojinski said. "It was nice to see you and to meet Mrs. Hanrahan, and I hope we didn't butt in or anything."

"Don't be silly," Hanrahan said.

(Four)

Master Sergeant Stefan Wojinski, whose intention it had been to grab a burger or something and then go bowling (just to get off the fucking post), instead drove immediately back to Fort Bragg, onto the main post, and into a small area of brick cottages behind the barracks.

He got out of his Buick, bounded up the stairs, and hammered with a massive fist on a door.

A tall, crew-cut man in his middle thirties, his civilian shirt stretched tight across his chest, opened the door. He was Master Sergeant Edward B. Taylor, Sergeant Major of the U.S. Army Special Warfare School.

"I thought you said you were going bowling," he said.

"You dumb sonofabitch," Wojinski said. "You and your 'candy-ass political colonel with connections in the White House.'"

"What the hell are you talking about, Ski?" Sergeant Major Taylor asked, patiently.

"Your 'absolutely straight poop' is full of shit, is what I'm talking about. I just met our new commanding officer."

"And?"

"It's Paul Hanrahan, Shit-between-the-ears."

"You know him, then?"

"I was with him in Greece," Wojinski said. "They don't come no better."

"And how do you know he's taking over?"

"He told me, that's how," Wojinski said.

"And he's a good man?"

"You bet your fucking ass, he is. I seen him work."

"Come on in, Ski, I'll give you a beer," the sergeant major said.

The Wojinskis followed Taylor into the kitchen of his quarters, where he opened the refrigerator and passed out bottles of Miller's High Life and the church key to pop the top.

Mrs. Taylor, a small, firmly bodied redhead, came into the kitchen.

"I thought you were going bowling," she said, yawning. "Give me one of those, honey, will you?"

Her husband got another bottle of beer and handed it to her. But he looked at Wojinski as he did.

"My poop is straight, Ski. I saw the orders. He was assigned, DP, as commandant. You know what that means?"

"No, I don't. All I'm telling you is that Colonel Paul Hanrahan's as good as they come."

"DP means 'Direction of the President,' Ski. He was personally assigned by the President. More likely, since the President has other things on his mind, by somebody who can put a piece of paper in front of the President and have him put his signature on it without asking too many questions. This guy has friends in very high places, Ski."

(Five)
The Fayetteville Inn
Fayetteville, North Carolina
0930 Hours, 29 December 1958

Patricia Hanrahan sat on the bed and ran her fingers down her husband's face, finally tickling him under the chin. She noted that the stubble on his chin was no longer pure red; it was turning gray.

He grimaced, making her chuckle, and then his eyes popped open.

"Good morning," she said.

He looked at his watch.

"I let you sleep," she said. "You were beat. How do you feel?"

He looked around the room. The children were nowhere in sight.

"Like taking you up on that offer you made in Honolulu," he said.

She gestured frantically toward the bathroom. One of the children was obviously in there.

"Sorry about that," she said.

"I've got to get up and get a uniform pressed," he said.

She pointed to a clothes rack, where a uniform covered with dry cleaner's plastic wrap was hanging.

"Done," she said. "And I made Paul shine your boots."

"I bet he loved that," Hanrahan said.

"He must be sick," she said. "He didn't even complain."

"You've been busy," he said.

"Busy, busy. I even have half-bought a Volkswagen."

"Where'd you find that?"

"There was a stack of *ParaGlides* in the restaurant," she said. "With classifieds. A captain going to Germany's got one."

"The *ParaGlide,*" he said, referring to the semiofficial newspaper published for Fort Bragg personnel. "God, it's been a long time since we've seen one of those."

"Who would have ever thunk," Patricia said, smiling, "that Second Lieutenant Hanrahan would one day come back here wrapped in the glory of a full colonel."

"Glory," he mocked, gesturing around the room.

"The wife, the one with the Volkswagen, is coming to show it to me," Patricia said. "If it's not falling apart, I think we should buy it. You want to look at it before I give her a check?"

"You'll be driving it," he said. "If you want it, buy it."

She nodded.

"Who's in there?" he said, nodding toward the bathroom.

"Rosemary," she said. "The boys found pinball machines in the lobby."

"Rosemary," he called, raising his voice, "you have thirty seconds to get out of there."

Patricia waited until he'd come out of the bathroom, his face ruddy from his shave. She watched as he sat down on the bed and put on the glossy pair of Corcoran jump boots, laced them up, and pulled his trousers on over them. She waited until she saw a look of concern on his face, and then tossed him a small, square cellophane-wrapped package.

"Don't ask where I got them," Patricia said. "I'll see if I can't get you some rubber bands today."

"I do believe you're blushing," he said, as—concealing what he was doing from Rosemary, who was watching television—he broke open the package of rubber prophylactics, unrolled them, twisted them, and tied them around the top of his jump boots. Then he tucked the hem of his trousers under the rubbers, "blousing" them.

After that he put on his shirt, tied his tie, and took the tunic from its hanger.

"Even the eagles," he said. "You done good, Patty."

"And the crossed rifles," she said. "Don't miss the rifles."

"Where the hell did you get them?"

"I went down to Blood Alley and banged on the door of one of those junk stores until they opened it for me. I'd hate to tell you how much they cost."

"Thank you," he said.

She waited until he had put on the tunic and his hat before she went and kissed him.

"Congratulations, Colonel," she said. "You look very nice with those eagles."

He squeezed her buttocks and she yelped, and Rosemary turned from the TV and said, "Daddy!"

(Six)
Fort Bragg, North Carolina
1015 Hours, 29 December 1958

The office of the commanding general of Fort Bragg, N.C., was on the ground floor of the two-story brick building (originally built as a barracks) directly across from the main post theater.

Paul Hanrahan walked in, and the sergeant major stood up.

"Good morning, sir," he said.

"My name is Hanrahan, Sergeant," he said. "I'm reporting in."

"We've been expecting you, sir," the sergeant said. "Can I offer you a cup of coffee, Colonel?"

"Thanks, no," Hanrahan said.

The sergeant pushed a lever on his intercom, and lowered his head toward it.

"Colonel Hanrahan is here, sir."

There was no reply, but in a moment a stocky lieutenant colonel wearing parachutist's wings and the insignia of the General Staff Corps came out of an inner office, his hand extended.

"Welcome to Fort Bragg and the Airborne Center, Colonel Hanrahan," he said. "My name is Field, and I'm SGS." (Secretary of the General Staff)

"Thank you, Colonel," Hanrahan said. "It's good to be home."

"Sergeant Major, would you see if the general is free?"

The sergeant major left the room, and returned immediately.

"The general will see you, Colonel Hanrahan," he said.

He held open a door, and then trotted ahead of Hanrahan to open a second one.

"Come on in, Colonel," a voice called.

Hanrahan marched in, stopped three feet from the general's desk, and raised his hand in a crisp salute.

"Colonel Hanrahan reporting to the commanding general, sir," he said.

The general, a tall, lithe man with somewhat sunken features was wearing the three stars of a lieutenant general. His name was H.H. "Triple H" Howard. Although Hanrahan knew who he was, he had never met him before.

General Howard returned the salute and smiled, then gestured Hanrahan into a chair.

"You'll have some coffee, Colonel?" General Howard asked.

"Thank you, sir."

"How do you take it, Colonel?" the sergeant major asked.

"Black, please."

"How was your trip?" General Howard asked.

"Tiring, sir."

"They take care of you all right at the guest house?" General Howard asked, and then went on without waiting for an answer. "We had no word on when you were coming. Just that you were."

"We took a motel in town, sir," Hanrahan said.

The coffee, served in fine china cups, was immediately delivered, and the sergeant major left, closing the door after him.

"I don't recall, Colonel," General Howard said, "having met you before."

"No, sir, I don't believe we have met."

"And your assignment as commandant of the Special Warfare School was, what shall I say, unexpected."

"I was surprised myself, sir," Hanrahan said.

"And I was at a further disadvantage," General Howard went on. "I couldn't even check on your records."

"I believe they're maintained by DCSOPS when you're on a MAG assignment," Hanrahan said. (Deputy Chief of Staff, Operations; Military Advisory Group)

"Yours are being maintained by DCSINTEL," General Howard said. (Deputy Chief of Staff, Intelligence)

"I didn't know that, sir," Hanrahan said, genuinely surprised.

"You seem surprised," General Howard said.

"Yes, sir, I am," Hanrahan said.

"Obviously, there are some things some people have elected not to tell either of us," General Howard said. And then he smiled. "From outward appearances, Colonel, let me say that you seem to be fully qualified to run the school."

"Thank you, sir."

"When did you graduate?"

"Class of '40, sir."

"Who were you with? 82nd, 11th, 101st?"

"I was with the 82nd when it was the 82nd Infantry, General. In the Parachute Test Battalion."

"Oh," General Howard said, obviously pleased. "You go back that far, do you? And you stayed with the division through the war?"

"No, sir. I didn't serve with a division during the war."

"You've got combat jump stars on your wings," General Howard said, making it more of a question than a statement.

"I jumped into Greece, twice, with the OSS," Hanrahan said.

"And that's considered a combat jump?" General Howard said. "I didn't realize that."

The implication was that jumping behind enemy lines wasn't really a combat jump. Combat jumps were made en masse— by *soldiers*—not by spies who sneaked in someplace. Hanrahan was not surprised. He had heard it all before.

"Yes, sir, it is."

"And you got the CIB the same place?"

"No, sir. I got that after the war."

"In Korea?"

"No, sir, in Greece."

General Howard debated a moment about asking for an explanation, but then changed his mind.

"Well," General Howard said, "sometimes you have to go on first impressions, Colonel, and let me tell you that somebody who has been airborne since before it was airborne, and has subsequently earned a DSC and a Silver Star and a CIB, makes a very fine first impression."

"Thank you, sir."

"Frankly, Colonel, when we heard where you were coming from, we thought they had all gone mad and were turning the Special Warfare School over to one of those unconventional warfare nuts."

That's just what they've done, General. Guilty as charged.

"I see," Hanrahan said.

"Don't misunderstand me, Colonel," General Howard said. "There is a place for that sort of thing. I have the highest respect for what the OSS did in War II. But that was then, and this is, after all, Fort Bragg, the Airborne Center."

"Yes, sir," Hanrahan said.

"I'm very happy to have the Special Warfare School here at Bragg," General Howard said, "as part, so to speak, of the airborne family. I think of it as sort of a continuation of the Rangers, and I'm convinced that, in proper hands, it can make a contribution of great value to airborne."

"I understand, sir," Hanrahan said.

All too fucking well.

"I was a Ranger myself," General Howard said. "I don't think there was ever a finer body of troops anywhere."

"I haven't had that privilege, sir," Hanrahan said.

"Well, maybe we can get you Ranger qualified while you're here," General Howard said. "Most of my senior officers have found time to go through the course."

"Perhaps I will be able to find the time, sir."

It was Paul Hanrahan's studied judgment that the World War II deployment of the Rangers had been a stupid expenditure of assets. To begin with, parachutists were generally more highly qualified than any other troops. And then rangers were selected from the ranks of parachutists, intensively trained, and sent into situations where extremely high casualties were expected. In his opinion, it was World War II's version of Balaclava, ordering men into the valley of death, into the mouth of cannon. In this, at least, Paul Hanrahan was a disciple of George S. Patton, Jr., who believed the function of soldiers was to kill the enemy, not to die themselves—no matter how gloriously.

General Howard smiled at him and nodded, and Hanrahan knew he was about to be dismissed.

"I know you've got a lot to do, Colonel," General Howard said. "To settle your family, and that you're anxious to see your new headquarters."

"Yes, sir."

"You know where it is? Smokebomb Hill?"

"I think I can find Smokebomb Hill, sir," Hanrahan said.

"Yes, of course. You've been here before."

"Yes, sir."

"There is one thing more, however," General Howard said. He pushed his intercom levers. "Will you bring in the flowers, Sergeant Major?"

Flowers?

The sergeant major entered the office a moment later, literally hidden behind an enormous floral display. He set it on the floor and adjusted the legs of its metal easel so that it would stand alone.

There was a floral representation of a horseshoe, large enough to hold inside it a floral representation of the national colors. A purple ribbon, six inches wide, was stretched across the whole thing. Onto it had been glued in gilt letters the words, "To Our Leader. Welcome Home."

It was garish and ugly, and Hanrahan tried and failed to guess what it had cost. At least a hundred bucks, he thought. Maybe twice that much. There was no question whatever in his mind who had sent it.

"They arrived this morning, Colonel," General Howard said, disapprovingly. "Addressed to you, in care of the commanding general."

"I see," Hanrahan said.

"There is a card," the general said, and the sergeant major handed him a small envelope. Hanrahan opened it. The card read, "The Duke and the Mouse."

The Duke and the Mouse my ass. The Duke sent this god-damned thing, and signed Felter's name to it. Felter has more sense than to do something like this.

"One of my former officers has more money, General, than common sense," Hanrahan said.

"And a very strange sense of humor," General Howard said. "Shall I ask the sergeant major to dispose of it?"

"No, sir, thank you. I'll take it with me."

"As you please," General Howard said, stiffly. Then he went on: "Feel free, Hanrahan, to call upon me at any time for anything I can do to help you get settled."

"Thank you, sir."

"If there is nothing further, Colonel, you are dismissed," General Howard said.

Hanrahan saluted, the general returned his salute, and then Hanrahan picked up the floral display and carried it out of the post commander's office.

(Seven)

He knocked a good many of the flowers off the floral display getting it onto the back seat of the rented Chevrolet. Then he got behind the wheel and started out for Smokebomb Hill, the portion of the post on which the Special Warfare School was located.

Impulsively, he went the long way through the 82nd Airborne Division area, and drove slowly, looking at the routine army activity. The army, he thought as he often did, had more to do with hauling garbage and passing out groceries and standing in line for mail and laundry than it did with close order drill or practicing "The Platoon in the Attack."

And he wondered again, as he often had, if he had made a mistake nearly seventeen years before when he had taken the offer to go to the Office of Strategic Services and leave the 82nd Airborne.

If he'd lived through the 82nd's campaigns, and a surprising number of his peers had, he would have had an entirely different career than he had had. He would have spent a lot of time here at Bragg, and his kids would have grown up American, and not international gypsies.

But he concluded again, as he always did, that he had made the right decision, that he had made a greater contribution doing what he had done than he would have had he gone up the ladder of command in airborne to platoon, company, and battalion. Besides, he thought wryly, you can break your ass jumping out of airplanes. If God had wanted men to do that, he would have given them a parachute growing out of their backs.

Ten minutes later, he found the sign:

HEADQUARTERS

U.S. ARMY SPECIAL WARFARE SCHOOL

FORT BRAGG, NORTH CAROLINA

It was a typical "temporary" two-story building, built for World War II. He remembered that the last time he'd been on Smokebomb Hill, the area had been occupied by an engineer regiment.

He turned off the road and drove to the rear of the building. There were reserved parking spaces for the Commandant, Deputy Commandant, Chief of Staff, Adjutant, Sergeant Major, and two for Official Visitors. The commandant's space was empty, but Hanrahan nosed the rented Chevrolet into one of the visitor's spots; the man he was replacing might still be here, and he didn't want to tread on his toes.

As he got out of the car, a very natty and very young-looking lieutenant colonel came trotting up. He threw a crisp salute.

"Sir," he barked. "The acting commandant reports to the commandant, sir."

How the hell did he know I was coming?

Hanrahan returned to the salute, wondering what he should say next. The young lieutenant colonel didn't give him a chance to say anything.

"Sir," he barked, "if the commandant will be good enough to come with me, sir?"

And then he started walking around the end of the building. Hanrahan followed him. When they got to the front, there was something there he hadn't seen before. Two groups of soldiers, twenty-five officers and close to forty noncoms were lined up at attention.

"Sir," the lieutenant colonel barked. "The staff is formed, sir. Will the commandant troop the line, sir?"

"Yes," Hanrahan said.

"Sir," the lieutenant colonel barked. He saluted, then marched stiffly to a position in front of the formation, did an about-face, and stood there at attention.

"Stand at ease," Hanrahan called out. And when they had come to "at ease," he went on: "Where the hell did you come from? You weren't here sixty seconds ago."

There was pleased laughter, and then Hanrahan walked to the lieutenant colonel and offered his hand.

"Paul Hanrahan, Colonel," he said. "I'm impressed and grateful."

"We wanted to make you feel welcome, Colonel," the lieutenant colonel said, with a smile.

"I'm going to troop the line informally," Hanrahan said, raising his voice. "Please give me your name, so I can say hello."

He was impressed with what he saw. The officers and non-coms were neatly turned out, with one notable exception, in stiffly starched fatigues. Their boots were shined, their faces shaved, their hair cut, and they looked bright and proud.

The one exception, the last man in the rear rank of the enlisted platoon, was Master Sergeant Stefan Wojinski. He wasn't wearing glossy jump boots. He was wearing battered boots with hobnail heels and soles. He was wearing a soiled, patched British Army battle jacket and baggy British trousers, which had pockets sewn to their knees. There was little, un-authorized, handmade (from a brass cannon casing) pin in the shape of technical sergeant's stripes pinned to one collar point, and the insignia of the 27th Royal Hellenic Mountain Division to the other.

"My name is Wojinski, sir," he said, trying to look innocent.

"I know your name, you ugly bastard," Hanrahan said, close to tears. "You hung on to that crap, did you?"

"What the hell, Colonel, in some ways they was good days."

"Yes, Ski, they were," Hanrahan said.

"Colonel, we had the mess hall make a cake, and there's coffee, inside," the lieutenant colonel said.

"Thank you," Hanrahan said. "Ski, there's something in the back of my car, from another couple of Gone Greeks. Would you get it and bring it inside, please?"

"Yes, sir," Wojinski said, and trotted around the far corner of the building.

"I wasn't sure the colonel would be amused," the lieutenant colonel said.

"They're all crazy, the old Greek hands, Colonel," Hanrahan said. "Wait till you see what I've got in the back of my car."

He walked in front of the formation again, and made a gesture with his hand over his head.

"Break ranks and follow me," he called.

The lieutenant colonel held open the door for him. And immediately on stepping inside the door, a tall, crisply uni-formed master sergeant thrust a clipboard and a pen at him.

"May I have the colonel's signature on this please?" he said.

Hanrahan looked at it.

HEADQUARTERS

U.S. ARMY SPECIAL WARFARE SCHOOL

FORT BRAGG, N.C.

GENERAL ORDER   29 December 1958

NUMBER 41

The undersigned assumes command effective this date.

> Paul T. Hanrahan
> Colonel, Infantry
> Commandant

Hanrahan scrawled his signature on the document. "You're very efficient, Sergeant."

"I try to be, sir," Sergeant Major Taylor said. "Your office is this way, sir."

There was a sign, with his name on it, on the commandant's door.

He sat down behind the commandant's desk. A sergeant brought him a cup of coffee and a piece of cake. Wojinski carried in the flowers.

"Jesus," Wojinski said, "you'd know the Duke would do something like this. The Duke and the Mouse. Christ. I remember the day the Duke nearly got blown away . . . it brings back memories."

"He's a major now, Ski," Hanrahan said. "Both of them are. I talked, for a couple of minutes, to the Mouse yesterday."

He remembered the circumstances, and that reminded him that he had not called Bellmon about Captain Jean-Philippe Jannier. He would have to call, and right now. But to hell with it, he'd call the Duke first. He'd cut him off yesterday.

"Until I get a post phone, I don't know how they're going to bill me," he said to Sergeant Major Taylor, "but I want to put in a personal call to Major Craig W. Lowell right now. I don't have the number, but he should be in the Washington book, and if he's not, get his number through MDW." (Military District of Washington)

"No problem, sir."

The floral display had made a hit with the troops, he saw. He finished off his cake and was sipping his coffee when Sergeant Major Taylor was at his ear.

"I got Major Lowell's number, sir, and called it. Someone who said he was the butler told me that Major Lowell is at Fort Rucker, but that he has no number where he can be reached."

He must have just gone to Rucker, then. Because the Mouse said he was with him.

"Get me Major Felter on this number, then, please," he said, writing it down. "Also in Washington."

Major Sanford T. Felter was on the phone in ninety seconds.

"Mouse, I just got your flowers," Hanrahan said.

"Sir?"

I knew goddamned well the Mouse knew nothing about them.

"Well, ask your pal the Duke about them when you see him again."

"He's right here, sir."

"I heard he was at Fort Rucker."

"We are, sir," Felter said.

"Oh," Hanrahan said. "They switch your calls, do they, Mouse?"

"Yes, sir," Felter said, evenly, "they do. Here's Craig, sir."

"Good morning, sir," Lowell said, cheerfully.

"Your flowers dazzled the post commander, Craig."

"I was hoping to dazzle you," Lowell said.

Hanrahan felt emotion surging up inside him.

"The Mouse leads me to believe you had your ass in a crack again," Hanrahan said, to change the subject.

"There was, frankly, an awkward moment or two," Lowell said. "But all has been forgiven, and I now have a new job."

"I was about to offer you a job," Hanrahan said.

"That would be at Fort Bragg, sir," Lowell asked, "where perfectly sober people leap from functioning airplanes?"

"I'm commandant of the Special Warfare School," Hanrahan said. "I could use you."

"If it would involve jumping out of airplanes, running obstacle courses, sleeping on the ground, and things of that nature—and I'm sure it would—thank you, no, sir."

Hanrahan let it drop.

"I need a favor, Craig," Hanrahan said, and told him about Captain Jean-Philippe Jannier. Then he put Master Sergeant Wojinski on the horn, and let him talk to both of them.

He sipped thoughtfully on his coffee. He would offer Lowell a job again. The very reasons Lowell didn't want a job, were the reasons he would be valuable. Hanrahan didn't want super-troopers. He wanted people like Lowell, who had led foreign troops, and thought jumping out of airplanes was idiocy.

It was very interesting, now that he thought of it, that his records had been maintained by DCSINTEL. Felter was in intelligence, high enough up so they transferred his calls around the country as if he was a member of the White House staff.

III

(One)
Fort Rucker, Alabama
1430 Hours, 31 December 1958

Mrs. Jane O'Rourke Cassidy, Administrative Assistant, GS-7, of the U.S. Army Aviation Board, stood at the door to Major Craig W. Lowell's office, leaning against the jamb, so that her sweater was drawn tightly against her breasts. It was the first thing Lowell noticed when, sensing her presence, he looked up from the papers on his desk.

Jane Cassidy, who had just turned thirty, was a tall lithe woman. She wore her natural, pale blond hair parted in the middle and drawn tightly into a bun at the base of her neck. She looked more Danish than Irish, and the family joke had been that long ago a visiting Viking had paid more than casual attention to one of the lasses on the auld sod.

Her job at the Aviation Board was new, her assignment to Major Craig Lowell even newer; and it was the second real job she had ever had. She had married Tom Cassidy the week

50

she had graduated from Spring Hill College in Mobile. She became pregnant that fall, and there were now two children. The youngest, Tom III, was now eight; Patricia a year and two days older.

She had lived in Enterprise all of her married life. Six months before their marriage Tom had come out of Auburn University with a master's degree in chemical engineering, to a job at Enterprise's major (some said only) industry, the Wiregrass Peanut Oil Company. Tom joked that he had been offered the job because he graduated cum laude, and the Wiregrass Peanut Oil Company was determined to stay on top of Leguminosae technology—and also because his uncle, John Patrick Cassidy, not only had not been blessed with a son, but was president and major stockholder of the company as well.

Raising the kids, Jane had not had the time to learn to really hate Enterprise until Tom III had started school. She had been and was still a good mother. Caring for the children and making a home had kept her busy. But with the kids off at school, there was a lot of free time, and the interesting things to do in Enterprise were few and far between. She was, because of Tom and John Patrick Cassidy, part of the Enterprise Establishment, but her peers in this social class bored her out of her mind.

Jane had been born and raised in Mobile, where her family had been in the ship chandlery business since before the Civil War. Mobile was a somewhat unpleasant three-hour drive from Enterprise. When she made the trip, every month or six weeks, there was a chance to be with her peers, the girls she had grown up with. There was the country club, which her grandfather had helped found, and the Althesan Club, and half a dozen restaurants. Her peers scorned most of this, and went another three hours down the road to New Orleans for their escape from the boredom of children and home.

There was nobody to blame but herself. She had made her bed . . . her father had tactfully pointed out to her that Enterprise was not going to be Mobile . . . and now she would lie in it. Tom was happy. He was now out of the lab and into the plant manager's office, and clearly the heir apparent. He had to travel a lot which was fun—for him. But even at home, the life for men in Enterprise was more varied than it was for women. The men had their golf, and they hunted in season, and there was an illegal bar in two rooms of the Hotel Enterprise where they met after work.

The idea of going to work at Fort Rucker had come to Jane as soon as the post had reopened and begun the transition from World War II infantry training base to the Army Aviation Center. When she had brought the subject up to Tom, he just didn't understand why she should want a job. They didn't need the money, and wives of members of the Enterprise Establishment generally, and the wife of the plant manager of the Wiregrass Peanut Oil Company specifically, did not take jobs.

"What would you do, anyway? Punch a typewriter?"

She had driven out to the civilian personnel office at the post one afternoon, where she was given a large packet of material describing careers in government service, plus a list of the available jobs. Tom had been right about one thing: she was unqualified to do anything but punch a typewriter, and truthfully, not even that. When she took the typist's examination, she just barely passed, qualifying only for a job as a Typist (Trainee) GS-1.

And then Tom had thrown another monkey wrench in the gears: "Honey, if you took a job like that, you'd be taking it away from some woman who really needs the money."

That had put the idea of working at the post to rest, and for good, she had thought . . . until there was an advertisement in the *Enterprise Star*, announcing an examination for "Federal Service Interns." College graduates would be taken into the federal service as GS-5s, to be trained for a year in some specialty, afterward, they'd enter into a "career field" as a GS-7.

It took only the price of a stamp to apply. So Jane applied, more than a little embarrassed that she could fill only one line in the large blank for "educational and work experience": B.A. (French) Spring Hill College, Mobile, Ala., 1949."

In spite of that, two months later she received a letter announcing that she had been selected for the intern program. She was to report to the U.S. Army Hospital the following Tuesday "not later than 1330 hours" for her physical examination.

Tom, it turned out, wasn't nearly as upset as she thought he would be. He just laughed: "Working for the government will drive you out of your mind," he told her. "You really want to waste your time, go ahead and try it."

Her interview with her first boss was more than a little disappointing. He was a colonel, Robert F. Bellmon, and he was in charge of something called "Aviation Combat Developments." He had been politely blunt: "The fact is, Mrs. Cassidy, that I did my level best to avoid getting an intern. I consider what we're doing here very important, and I tried to make the point that I don't have time to run a training program. I lost. I will have an intern working here. Frankly, if you come to work here, you'll probably be more trouble than you're worth. On the other hand, you're head and shoulders above the other people they've sent over for me to interview. If you're willing to lend a hand here, wherever you're needed, and clearly understand that any training you get will be on the job, I'm willing to give it a try."

She had taken the job, convinced that what she was going to do would be what Tom has prophesied, punch a typewriter, and badly. But punching a typewriter was better than sitting around the house watching the maid polish the silver.

And there was already sort of an office manager, a dentist's wife from Dothan, who was equally jealous of her prerogatives. Instead, Jane O'Rourke Cassidy spent her year's internship maintaining the flight records of the aviators assigned to Combat Developments, and doing what was called "Updating the Jep."

Every pilot's entire flying time had to be accounted in his record: what kind of airplane; how long the flight had been; and whether or not the flight had been under instrument flight conditions. In addition, a certificate had to be sent each month to the Finance Office stating that the pilot had flown the four hours required to qualify for flight pay.

Because they flew all over the country, all the pilots at Combat Developments were issued a set of manuals in a salesman's case. The manuals contained loose-leaf binders containing information about every airport in the United States, maps of the airfields, radio frequencies, and NOTAMs—"Notices to Airmen" about hazards or closed runways.

These were published by the Jeppsen Company, who each week mailed each pilot an update, reflecting changed information. The old sheets had to be removed from the binders and the new sheets inserted.

"Updating the Jep" struck Jane as an idiot's job, but none of the clerks who had been doing it had been able to do it correctly or on time. But there were several things in the job's favor: it allowed her to get out of the house every day and to meet interesting people. The pilots seemed to be very nice guys, very grateful to have an updated Jep and their flight pay certificates filed on time. Before long they began to take her to lunch at the officer's club with them.

To her great relief, none of them made passes at her. Most of the pilots were married, and the ones that weren't were so young they treated her with a respect that was almost embarrassing. Gradually, Jane began to do other services for them, typing up forms of one kind or another that the typists were either unwilling or unable to do.

She had made a good deal, Jane thought, in taking the job. It wasn't quite what she had expected, but it was better than nothing. She also thought it was making a contribution to her marriage: she was more alive than she had been before she'd come to work. Though the magic—a nice word for lust—had long been gone from her marriage, at least now she could talk to Tom over dinner about something interesting that had happened to her during the day.

Socially, Tom was in an awkward position regarding the post. The brass made overtures of friendship to the mayors and other officials of Enterprise and Ozark. These had been given associate memberships in the officer's open mess. And the doctors and lawyers met regularly with their counterparts in uniform. But there was no counterpart to a peanut oil mill manager at Rucker; so Tom was left out.

But if Jane lasted the first year and was promoted to GS-7, she could join the officer's club herself, since a GS-7 rating carried with it the "assimilated" grade of lieutenant. She wasn't sure how Tom would respond—if he would feel embarrassed about being his wife's guest. So she decided that if he objected, she wouldn't join the club. But when she told him, all he wanted to know was whether he could use the golf course at the post.

"Find out about that, honey, will you?" Tom had asked.

The internship year passed quickly, and one day Colonel Bellmon had called her into his office.

"I had sort of a dilemma about you, Jane," Bellmon said. "On the one hand, I'm more than a little grateful for the way you've been running flight records and the Jeps, and God knows what will happen when you're gone. But on the other hand, it wouldn't be fair to you or the taxpayers to keep you on as a clerk and pay you a GS-7's wages. So I talked to Colonel

Roberts at the Aviation Board about you, and next Monday
you report out there to him."

"I don't quite understand," she said. It was the first time
she had thought about leaving Combat Developments.

"Well, I've signed the papers making you an Administrative
Assistant, GS-7," Bellmon told her. "And if there was someplace I could put you here, I would. But there isn't. And
Colonel Roberts says he's sure he can find a place for you out
at the Board where your talents can be properly utilized."

They had a little party for her that Firday, coffee and cake,
and gave her a plaque: aviator's wings and the Combat Developments insignia mounted on a piece of mahogany. And on
Monday she had gone out to the Army Aviation Board's new
building at Laird Army Airfield.

For two weeks, she had trailed the Board adjutant around,
to get a feel of the place, and it had looked during the second
week that she would be assigned to the Technical Publications
Section. TBS functioned both as the technical publications library, and "publisher" for the reports the Aviation Board issued
on aircraft and other equipment it tested. TBS was under a
woman, an "imported" DAC (a Department of the Army civilian transferred to Fort Rucker from someplace else), and
Jane had met and liked her.

But then she had been called into the office of Board president Colonel William R. Roberts. The adjutant was there when
she walked in.

"Mrs. Cassidy," Colonel Roberts said, "the Board has
been directed to immediately set up a new section within the
Flight Test Division. It will need an administrative assistant,
and we think you could hold the job down. Would you be
interested?"

She wondered if she was going to be clerk-typist under a
fancier name, but she smiled and said she would.

"If it doesn't work out, we'll think of something else,"
Colonel Roberts said to her. "Major Groppe will walk you over
there—it's in Hangar 101—and introduce you to Warrant Officer Cramer."

Jane had been around the army long enough to know where
a warrant officer fitted into the hierarchy, so she knew that she
was going to be a clerk to someone with no authority or responsibility. She was disappointed until she reminded herself

that being a clerk was better than sharing tuna fish sandwiches with the maid.

When they walked into an office in a concrete block structure built onto the street side of the hangar, CWO Cramer was standing on a chair, nailing a sign to an interior door. The sign read:

MAJOR C. W. LOWELL

CHIEF

ROCKET ARMED HELICOPTER SECTION

Jane O'Rourke Cassidy knew a good deal about Major C. W. Lowell. She had met him several times when he had visited Combat Developments. He was a friend of Colonel Bellmon. He was rich, and even owned his own airplane. And she knew that he was in deep trouble with the army.

Being assigned to work for him was proof that, rather than building on a career, she was being pushed aside. She would be working for a man who would shortly be out of the army.

Without meaning to, she had overheard a conversation between Major Lowell and Colonel Bellmon. Lowell had been caught in an affair with a U.S. senator's wife in Washington, and they had sent him to Rucker, where Colonel Bellmon had told him he could either resign from the army immediately or be assigned as garbage disposal officer in the Panama Canal Zone until the board of officers was convened that would throw him out.

Lowell had agreed to resign as of January 1, 1959, but he told Bellmon that he intended to spend the holidays with his friends on the post. When Jane had told Tom about Lowell one night at dinner, he'd laughed.

But then the next day, Ed Greer had been killed when the Big Bad Bird crashed and exploded. Jane had known Greer, of course; Greer had been assigned to Combat Developments, but he was also married to Melody Dutton, the daughter of Howard Dutton, the mayor of Ozark. Howard and Tom were good friends.

Jane and Tom Cassidy had been sitting in their reserved seats in the bleachers on the parade ground for Ed Greer's funeral services when the black-painted helicopter had appeared out of nowhere, buzzed the field, and then blown up a line of Russian tanks.

Before they left the parade ground, one of the Combat Development guys had told her what had happened. Major Lowell had stolen an H-19 from the Aviation School. He'd taken it somewhere out on the post—in the pine thickets—and hidden it there. Then he'd made all sorts of unauthorized modifications to it: he had another door cut in the fuselage; had mounted rocket launchers on the skids; and then he had used it to shoot up the Russian tanks lined up at the funeral ceremony.

Jane thought she understood why he had done it. The rocket-armed helicopter was important to the army, and it was liable to go down the tube because of Ed Greer's accident. Lowell had decided in effect, to commit suicide in order to prove beyond question that a helicopter could kill a tank. It was generally agreed that Lowell would be court-martialed for what he had done, and would probably spend some time in the federal prison at Leavenworth.

Thus, when she walked in on Cramer hanging up the sign with Lowell's name on it, she believed she had been assigned to an office where nothing would happen until they court-martialed Major Craig Lowell.

As it turned out, Jane was wrong. She soon learned that Major Lowell was not going to be court-martialed, nor was he going to resign. The Rocket Armed Helicopter Section of the Flight Test Division was indeed what Colonel Roberts had said it was, a brand new division of the Board, and she was its administrative assistant.

And Major Lowell himself was not what she expected him to be. She had thought he was a swinging bachelor—and had learned that he was instead a widower; a widower with a son, whose photograph in a silver frame was the only decoration in Lowell's office. About the first thing he ordered Jane Cassidy to do was to put in a telephone call to his son in Germany.

Neither did he look at her as a man on the make looks at a woman. He spoke to her briefly when Mr. Cramer introduced them, telling her that if she had worked for Bellmon for a year, that was all the reference she needed. He was polite, but not charming.

Other small things about him surprised her, too. For instance, he immediately proved that he was the best and most accurate typist in the office. She would not have expected a somewhat dashing pilot to be a skilled typist . . . Tom couldn't type at all.

And she saw something else that interested her. The officers and men who worked for him, with whom he dealt casually and jokingly, regarded him with great respect and admiration. Colonel Bellmon had been known behind his back as "Old Iron Britches." But Lowell was either "the Duke," a flattering reference to his finely tailored uniforms and to the mustache, or he was simply "the Major."

By the end of her first day working for Major Craig W. Lowell, Jane O'Rourke Cassidy had learned something else: she was as attracted to Major Lowell as she had been to Tom Cassidy, Auburn halfback, the first time she had seen him up close.

At 2:30 P.M., there was a phone call for the Major, and she had to wait before he looked up at her. He had an ability to concentrate on what he was doing—to shut everything else out—that was almost frightening. Despite his casual manner, she knew right away that he was probably the most intense individual she had ever met.

"Colonel Bellmon's wife," Jane said, then immediately corrected herself, "I mean *General* Bellmon's, is on the phone if you're not busy, Major."

Lowell picked up the telephone, idly thinking that tension had done it again, had made him aware of Jane Cassidy's breasts and her sexuality. Whenever he was tense, he got horny. Of course, after the ass-chewing session he had had with Paul Jiggs, he would not have jumped her if she had come into the office starkers.

And besides, this was not your typical Rebel broad, ready to jump into the bed of her dashing lover. This one was a lady; married, Cramer had told him, to a former football hero now running the peanut mill. She would not be interested in fun and games with Craig Lowell.

"Hello, Barbara, what can I do for you?" he said to the telephone.

"Southern's having 'equipment problems' again," Barbara Bellmon said. "The next flight to Dothan is at 11:15 tonight."

That translated to mean that General Bellmon was stranded in Atlanta, Southern Airways having decided again that safety required that they delay their flight to Columbus, Georgia, Dothan, Alabama, and Panama City, Florida, until they were reasonably sure the wings of their DC-3 wouldn't fall off.

"How can I help?"

"Bob tried to call MacMillan," she said, "so Mac could fly over and pick him up."

"Mac is on the golf course," he interrupted.

"Where else?" she laughed. "So when he couldn't get him, he called me and asked me to find Mac and see if Mac could arrange to have somebody else come pick him up. Get a plane from the school fleet I mean. But he can't."

"Let me call you back in a couple of minutes," he said. "I think I can fix this."

"I hate to bother you, Craig," she said.

"No problem," he said. "I'll call you right back."

He told Jane Cassidy that if there were any calls, he would be in Colonel Roberts's office.

Roberts's office, which occupied the left rear corner of the two-story concrete block building, was guarded by Florence Ward. Florence was a heavyset, southern Alabama farmer's wife who, like Jane Cassidy, had "gone out to the post to see if she could find some kind of work." She had surprised everybody, including herself, by turning into a crisply efficient administrative assistant.

"Is the colonel in, Mrs. Ward?"

She didn't reply, but instead went to Roberts's open door and asked if he could see Major Lowell.

"Come in, Lowell," Roberts called.

Lowell walked in the office and saluted.

"What can I do for you?" Roberts asked.

"I know I just got here, Colonel, but could I take a couple of hours off?"

"Still getting settled are you?" Roberts asked. "I don't think the place will collapse if you take off. It *is* New Year's Eve."

"I want to go to Atlanta," Lowell said.

"How're you going to do that?" Roberts asked, puzzled, and then answered his own question. "In your airplane, of course."

"Barbara Bellmon just called," Lowell explained. "Southern cancelled, and Bob's . . . the general . . . is stranded."

"Isn't that a shame?" Roberts said, dryly.

"Barbara asked me, Colonel," Lowell said.

"Well, we can't turn her down, can we?" Roberts said. "Go ahead."

"You're going to go up and come right back?" Florence Ward asked.

"Yes," Lowell said. "I'll be at the party." Then he realized that wasn't what she had been asking. "Colonel, could I take your secretary with me?"

"Sure," Roberts said.

"Thank you," Florence said to Colonel Roberts.

"I'll see you tonight, Lowell," Roberts said pointedly. Earlier that day Roberts had "suggested" to Lowell that he make sure he came to the New Year's Eve party. Lowell had no more wanted to go to the officer's club party than he was thrilled with the notion of taking the fat farmer's wife for a ride.

"Thank you, sir," Lowell said. "Mrs. Ward, when you're ready, will you come to my office?"

"I'll be right there," Florence said.

Lowell returned to his office in the hangar and told Jane Cassidy to call Mrs. Bellmon.

"Problem's solved," he said, when she came on the line. "Where's Bob now?"

"In a phone booth at the airport, waiting for me to call back."

"Tell him to catch a cab to Fulton County Airport," Lowell said. "I'll be there in about an hour, maybe a little longer."

"I am now forced to become a dishonest wife," she said.

"I don't think that's a proposition," Lowell said.

"He said I was not to ask you," she said. "You know how he feels about your airplane."

"Then screw him," Lowell said. "Let him wait for the 11:15."

"Then he would miss the party," she said, plaintively.

"OK. So I'll go get him," Lowell said. "I'll think of some imaginative excuse which requires his riding in my airplane."

"Oh, Craig, would you?" Barbara asked, happily. "I'd really be grateful. I'll pay you for the gas, or whatever, of course."

"You want to fly up with me, Barbara?" Lowell asked. "That way *you* could face the wrath of your righteous husband."

"Oh, I can't, Craig," she said, laughing. "I've got to have my hair done. And a hundred other things."

"Coward," he said. "But all right. You call him back, and

tell him somebody's on the way to pick him up at Fulton County. You don't know who."

"Craig, you're a darling," she said. "I owe you one."

"One what?"

"You bastard," she laughed, and hung up.

Lowell hung the phone up and looked at Jane Cassidy. She had listened to—and understood—what the call was about.

"Call Sergeant Kowalski and ask him to bring my airplane to Base Operations, will you, please, Mrs. Cassidy?"

She nodded.

And then Florence Ward appeared.

"Ready any time you are, Major," she said.

Lowell saw the surprise on Jane Cassidy's face, when she realized that Florence Ward was going with him.

"Would you like to come along, too, Mrs. Cassidy?" Lowell asked.

"Would there be time?" Jane Cassidy heard herself replying. "Before quitting time I mean?"

"God willing," Lowell said, mockingly pious. He immediately regretted it, thinking that either or both of the women were likely to take offense.

"I don't know if I should," Jane Cassidy said. She had joined the officer's club as soon as she had been promoted and she and Tom would be going to the party at the officer's open mess tonight (in black tie and formal dress), instead of the one at the Enterprise country club.

"Come along," Florence Ward said.

"I've got to get ready for tonight," Jane said. "We're going to the club."

She knew she was lying. All she had to do to get ready was take a quick shower and put on her dress.

"Another time," Lowell said. He wasn't sure if he was disappointed or relieved.

"I'll go," Jane said, suddenly.

"Fine," Lowell said.

Florence Ward had commandeered Colonel Roberts's staff car for the thousand-yard ride from the Board building to the hangar, and then for the second thousand-yard leg from the hangar to Base Operations. Although Lowell moved as far as he could to the left, there was not room enough in the back of the Chevrolet for the three of them. His hip and upper leg were pressed against Jane Cassidy.

At Base Ops, Sergeant Kowalski, the noncom in charge of the Aviation Board's flight line, was standing, beneath a bad oil portrait of Major General "Scotty" Laird, Jr., which was next to the double glass doors to the transient aircraft parking area.

Shortly after they had given Scotty Laird his second star, the week before the $97 million main airfield complex had been completed, Laird had picked up an H-13 in front of post headquarters. Climbing quickly, his mind apparently on other things, he had forgotten to turn on the carburetor heat. His H-13 went down in the woods just the other side of the golf course, within sight of his brand-new two-starred flag flapping from the Rucker flagpole.

The airfield had been named for him: Laird Army Airfield. But the Morse code from the Omni identifying the field had remained what it had been, OZR. Everytime Lowell heard OZR on his earphones, he thought of Scotty Laird, a passenger in Lowell's H-13 on the way to Bad Godesburg, Germany, immediately after Laird had turned down an assignment as deputy commander of the 2nd Armored Division to become, at forty, an aviator.

"She's all ready to go, Major," Kowalski said.

"You want to load the ladies aboard while I check the weather and file the flight plan?" Lowell replied.

"I want to watch that, too," Florence Ward said firmly, and marched after him into the plotting room. Jane Cassidy, after hesitating, walked after them. Both women bent over the map as Lowell showed them how he plotted the flight. Over the years Lowell had flown back and forth between Atlanta and Fort Rucker so often he could do the flight planning from memory; but, rather enjoying his role of high priest explaining the mysteries to the novices, he went through it step by step for them to watch.

Once, in bending over to see what Lowell was writing, Jane Cassidy's breast brushed his arm. He looked at her, more in annoyance than anything else, and saw her face flushing.

It's all right, Madame. I not only understand that that was quite accidental, but I have personally given my word of honor as an officer and a gentleman to the post commander that I will not go within ten feet, sexually speaking, of a married woman.

"I'm not going in there," Florence Ward laughed, when Lowell invited her to sit in the cockpit. "As fat as I am, I'd bump into something important."

After she settled herself in one of the chairs in the cabin, Lowell thought that Jane Cassidy would sit in the one opposite her. She did not. *She* elected to ride in the copilot's seat—and *that* pleased him, somewhat to his dismay.

There were airline-type lap belts in the seats in the back; and Lowell saw that Florence had figured out how they worked. But the pilot's and copilot's seats had over-the-shoulder harnesses, which Jane Cassidy had to be shown how to fasten. In the process, his arm brushed against her breast; and his hand, more or less, had to be placed in her crotch when he snapped it all together. Close enough to be aware of the softness of her thighs.

Down, boy! Don't you dare forget that you are now Sir Pure of heart, who took the vow, if not quite of chastity, of nonadultery.

He adjusted his own harness, saw that Kowalski was standing by with a fire extinguisher, yelled "contact" at him and hit the switches. The left of the Aero Commander's engines coughed into life, smoothed out; and in a moment, the right engine too belched blue smoke and caught.

Lowell put on his earphones and pressed the mike switch.

"Laird, Commander One Five in the transient area for taxi and takeoff, VFR, direct Atlanta Fulton County."

Jane Cassidy looked around the cockpit and located a set of headphones on a hook over her head. She had ridden in private planes before—though none as plush as this—but Tom had always managed to sit beside the pilot. It was now her turn, she thought. She put the earphones on in time for her to hear the tower giving Lowell taxi instructions to the active runway.

This is exciting, she thought. Going to Atlanta after lunch and still getting back before supper. And the airplane itself was impressive. Her previous experience had been in single-engined airplanes upholstered in plastic. This was something like a miniature airliner; it had a separate cockpit, airline-type seats upholstered in leather, and even a row of stainless steel thermos bottles, one of which Sergeant Kowalski said he had filled with coffee.

Jane was surprised at the roughness of the ride as they moved along the taxiways. At the end of the runway itself, Major Lowell stopped the airplane and raced the engines, one at a time. To make sure they were working, she supposed.

"Laird," the earphones said, "Commander One Five on the threshold of the active for takeoff."

It took her a moment to understand the voice in her earphones was Major Lowell's. It had been clipped, metallic sounding, and hadn't sounded like him.

"Laird," the earphones said, in another voice, "clears Commander One Five as number one to go on three eight. The time is one five past the hour, the barometer is two niner niner niner. The winds are negligible from the north. There is traffic at one mile to your left."

Lowell's hand reached for the stalks in front of him and pushed on them. Jane understood, as the engines began to roar, that these were the gas pedals.

Lowell's voice came over her earphones: "One Five rolling."

The airplane began to pick up speed at an alarming rate, accompanied by even more alarming rumbling sounds and the roaring of engines. And then, all of a sudden, the rumbling noises stopped. And the ground, which had been rushing past them, dropped away. Jane glanced at Lowell and saw him flip a lever. There was a whining sound, and then a little sign on the dashboard lit up WHEELS UP AND LOCKED.

They were flying.

She glanced at Major Lowell. His face bore the same look of concentration it had when she had gone into his office. She wondered what he was doing when he threw switches and adjusted levers, or soon after when he was making little notes on a clipboard that was attached to his leg with what looked like a bicycle clip.

During the fifty-five minutes before they landed at Fulton County Airport, Jane Cassidy several times caught herself glancing over at the face of Major Craig W. Lowell.

(Two)
Fulton County Airport
Atlanta, Georgia
1550 Hours, 31 December 1958

Brigadier General Robert F. Bellmon and another officer Lowell didn't recognize at first were waiting to be picked up at Martin Aviation, the private aviation operator at Fulton County Airport.

Bellmon, a medium-size, athletic looking man, was standing just outside the door, drinking coffee from a plastic cup. He was wearing a grayish pink trenchcoat over his greens. There was an overseas cap on his head, with the solid gold piping of a general officer. There was a star on the cap, and also on each of the trenchcoat epaulets. The second officer, Lowell saw, as he turned the Aero Commander into line with the other transient aircraft, was wearing one of the new brimmed caps, which provided for gold embellishment ("scrambled eggs") on the brim to identify field-grade (major through colonel) officers.

He got another look at the other officer, and recognized him. He was a portly man of fifty with a pencil-line mustache and eagles on his epaulets.

It's that horse's ass of a Pentagon press agent, Colonel Tim F. Brandon. What's that sonofabitch doing here?

He cut the engines and took off his headset.

"If you'd like to go to the rest room, Mrs. Cassidy," he said, "or you, Mrs. Ward, this is your chance." And then he added, to Mrs. Cassidy, "I think the general will rank you out of your seat on the way home, Mrs. Cassidy."

"You'll have to help me out of this," Jane Cassidy said, angry rather than embarrassed that she couldn't unfasten the harness itself.

He unfastened her harness, carefully avoiding her breasts as he worked, and then waited for her to walk down the aisle to the door. She didn't know how to open that, either, of course, and their bodies made contact again as he squeezed by her to do so.

He let the women off the airplane first. Then he followed. He saluted Bob Bellmon.

"Good afternoon, sir," he said. Bellmon and Brandon returned his salute.

"I didn't expect to see you here, Craig," General Bellmon said, evenly.

"I was taking the girls for a little ride," Lowell replied smoothly, "and they got on the horn and told me you were stranded in Atlanta, and asked if I would come and get you."

"I see," Bellmon said.

"I didn't expect to see Colonel Brandon here," Lowell said, with a smile. "Not on New Year's Eve."

"When you're in public communications, Major," Colonel Brandon said, "you learn to go where you're sent on a moment's notice."

While the rest of the army sits home by hearth and fireside, right? You fatuous sonofabitch!

"The Chief of Information thought it would be a good idea," General Bellmon said dryly, "if Colonel Brandon personally kept an eye on the public relations picture as the armed helicopter story develops."

"I see," Lowell said.

"What kind of a plane is that?" Brandon asked.

"An Aero Commander, Colonel," Bellmon said.

"I don't quite understand," Brandon said. "It doesn't have any markings."

"Army markings, you mean?" Bellmon asked.

"Yes, sir," Brandon said.

"That's because it's not an army aircraft," Bellmon said. "We are about to be hauled to Fort Rucker through the courtesy of Major Lowell."

"Oh, you mean you talked the manufacturer out of the airplane, Lowell?" Brandon said, approvingly.

"Sir?" Lowell asked, not understanding.

"I checked you out, Major. And you *are* an operator."

"All it took to promote that airplane, Colonel," Lowell said, smiling, "was my usual charm, and a check."

Brandon was astounded.

"You mean you personally own that airplane?" he blurted.

"Yes, sir, I personally own it," Lowell said.

"You surprise me, Colonel," Bellmon said. "I thought everybody knew Major Lowell owns Manhattan Island."

"You're kidding, of course, General."

"Just the part from Washington Square to the Battery," Lowell said.

Bellmon laughed, and Colonel Brandon took the opportunity to get out of deep water by joining in. He knew that his leg was being pulled, but he didn't know how. Bellmon had laughed because a few years ago he had seen the Counterintelligence Corps/FBI Complete Background Investigation report on then Second Lieutenant Craig W. Lowell:

"Without access to Internal Revenue Service records, it is impossible to develop an accurate estimate of SUBJECT's *total financial worth. Information obtained, however, from the Securities Exchange Commission and the Village of Glen Cove, L.I., reveals that* SUBJECT *owns 43.6% of the outstanding stock of Craig, Powell, Kenyon and Dawes, Investment Bankers, Inc. (13 Wall Street, New York City, N.Y.) and property in Glen Cove ("Broadlawns," which* SUBJECT *has designated as his Home of Record) which has been appraised for tax purposes at a value of $3,935,000."*

At the time Bellmon had read the report, Second Lieutenant Lowell and his German wife (who at the time hadn't known her husband had a dime) were living in quarters on Fort Knox that Craig had furnished with battered junk from the quartermaster warehouse. The way Lowell handled his wealth in the army was one of the few things about him that Robert Bellmon admired without qualification. There were exceptions (the Aero Commander, for one; his town house in Georgetown for another), but generally Lowell appeared to live as if all the money he had was from his monthly check.

Bellmon really couldn't put his finger on any but petty reasons that made him dislike Lowell, but he simply did not like him. It was a bone of contention between Bellmon and his wife. Barbara Bellmon loved the handsome young major like a mischievous younger brother.

Jane Cassidy and Florence Ward came back from the ladies' room, interrupting Bellmon's chain of thought. And Jane's expression when she looked at Lowell started another: was it possible that Lowell was already ignoring the "talk" General Paul Jiggs had had with him only two days before, and was off in pursuit of the blond, long-legged Jane Cassidy? Was he that much of a fool?

He decided that *he* was being the fool. Jane Cassidy was a level-headed woman, happily married to a very nice fellow. She doubtless already knew Duke Lowell's unsavory reputation with women. There was nothing going on, Bellmon concluded. Lowell had simply taken the women for a ride. Period.

Never, Bellmon thought, as he made his way down the aisle of the Aero Commander to slip into the copilot's seat, *look a gift horse in the mouth*.

As soon as they were in the air, and the drone of the engines would keep Colonel Brandon from hearing his voice, Lowell picked up the microphone, threw the switch for the intercom, and raised the question: "Am I permitted to ask, Bob, what you've been doing in Washington? Rumors are going around that you have a new job."

"The rumors are true," Bellmon said.

"Then would it be presumptuous for the major to ask the general what that job is?"

"No, Craig, it wouldn't; but keep it under your hat until official word is out."

"I never break confidences, General . . . well, hardly ever," he chuckled.

"Make this time one of your nevers"—he paused—"Major." He let that sink in, then added, "I'll be Director of Army Aviation in DCSOPS."

"Excellent, Bob! I'm really pleased."

"Thank you, Craig, so am I."

"May I also ask the general," Lowell said, moving to something else he was curious about, "what's Fatso doing with you?"

"You heard what I said before we took off," Bellmon replied a little stiffly. "The Chief of Information has ordered Colonel Brandon to run the PIO thing about the rocket-armed choppers for a while."

"He had to come on New Year's Eve?"

"Colonel Brandon will be the guest of Combat Developments at the party, and my houseguest; and I am sure everyone will make him feel welcome," Bellmon said.

"I'm sure everyone will be polite," Lowell said. "Welcome's something else. It was his PIO bullshit that got Ed Greer killed."

"Lieutenant Greer," Bellmon said, icily, "was killed by a malfunctioning rocket."

There was a long silence.

"You're right," Lowell said, two minutes later. "You're right, Bob, and I was wrong, and I'm sorry."

"If any of the others are in similar error, Lowell," General Bellmon said coldly, "it would behoove you to correct them."

At the last moment he had fought down the temptation

(recognizing that it would have been chickenshit) to remind Lowell that majors do not customarily refer to general officers by their first names, no matter how long they have known them.

"Yes, sir," Lowell said. "But I would suggest the general have a word with Major MacMillan. The major is prone to ignore me."

"I'll talk to Mac," Bellmon said. "And forgive me, Lowell."

"Sir?"

"I haven't thanked you for coming to get us. It was nice of you. And important to Barbara. When we get on the ground, I'll give you a check for gas and maintenance."

"My pleasure, sir," Lowell said, smiling. And then, as if he had been reading Bellmon's mind, he added: "I always try to get on the right side of general officers, General."

"I'll give you a check when we're on the ground," Bellmon repeated.

(Three)
Ozark, Alabama
1600 Hours, 31 December 1958

The three cars, an Oldsmobile 98, a Buick convertible, and an olive-drab Ford staff car formed a little convoy—the Oldsmobile leading. As they approached the Ozark gate of Fort Rucker, one of the two military policemen on duty spotted the Oldsmobile.

"Charley," he said, "heads up."

Both of them stepped out of their little guard shack and assumed the position of "parade rest," and then together popped to attention and threw a crisp salute as the Oldsmobile passed them.

On the Oldsmobile's bumper was a plastic sticker. It bore a representation of aviator's wings, the legend "Ft. Rucker, Ala" and, on a blue field, the numeral "1." The Oldsmobile was the personal automobile of Major General Paul T. Jiggs, the post commander. General Jiggs, who was in the front passenger seat (Mrs. Jiggs was at the wheel), returned the salute casually and smiled at the MPs. The MPs completed their salute and immediately saluted again, just about as crisply, as the Buick convertible, which carried the numeral "7" on its bumper, passed them. Brigadier General Robert F. Bellmon was at the wheel of his wife's car.

The staff car was driven by one of the civilian drivers, and its passenger was Master Sergeant P. J. Wallace, whom they recognized. Master Sergeant Wallace was the senior photographer of the Post Signal Detachment, and he took pride at being present whenever something interesting (by which he meant an aircraft crash or a spectacular auto accident) happened. The MPs and Master Sergeant Wallace waved at each other.

"I wonder where they're going?" one of the MPs said.

"Who gives a fuck?"

"I meant, all together, with a photographer?"

"And I said, 'Who gives a fuck?'"

The little convoy drove five miles down the two-lane macadam highway (now in the process of being widened to four lanes) and then turned right between two curved brick walls, standing alone. On the walls a sign had been mounted: WOODY DELLS.

They shortly began to pass houses on both sides of the road—new houses. Some of these were occupied, and the others had four-by-eight-foot wooden signs erected on their new, sparse, lawns. The brightly painted signs displayed the model name of each house such as ("The Colonial," "The Ranchero," "The Presidential,"), the model's price, and the information that VA, FHA, and conventional mortgages were available. The bottom line of each sign was identical: "Dutton Realty Corporation. Howard Dutton, Pres."

The little convoy wove its way through the gently curving streets until it came to Melody Lane. Howard Dutton had named the streets of his subdivision after his friends and the members of his family. The most prestigious street of all looked down onto the lake and the Woody Dells Community Center offering tennis courts and a putting green, as well as a kitchen and a party room available at a nominal cost to Woody Dells residents. That street he had named after his daughter Melody.

When, over his silent but deep objections, Melody had become engaged to Lieutenant Ed Greer, Howard Dutton had a Presidential built for the kids as a wedding present. But after Greer had broken the engagement and jilted Melody, he had quickly sold it—only to have to buy it back at a premium after Melody ran away to Algeria (where Greer was serving as an advisor to the French) and succeeded in getting him to the altar of the English church in Algiers.

The Oldsmobile and the Buick pulled into the driveway of 227 Melody Lane, which had a Cadillac Coupe de Ville and a Volkswagen parked in its double garage. 227 Melody Lane was also a Presidential, the most luxurious of Woody Dell's offerings. The Presidential provided four bedrooms, three and a half baths, a separate dining room, a living room (which Dutton Realty called "the Great Room"), and a den with a wet bar. The staff car stopped on the street, and Master Sergeant Wallace got out, carrying a press camera. He also had a canvas ditty bag loaded with film packs and flashbulbs hanging from his shoulder. Wallace trotted up the driveway, reaching to the house just as the kitchen door was opened by Mrs. Roxy MacMillan.

"Does he know?" Barbara Bellmon asked.

"No," Roxy giggled. "He hasn't the foggiest."

"Who is it?" Mac MacMillan called from inside the house.

"Bob and Barbara," Roxy called, and giggling again, added, "And some other people."

"Come on in the den," MacMillan said, raising his voice. "The Mouse and me are having a beer."

The five people trailed through the kitchen and into the den. Mac MacMillan, wearing brilliant yellow golf slacks and a striped, knit golf shirt was standing by the wet bar with a can of beer in his hand. Major Sanford T. Felter, in more subdued golf clothing, held a scotch and soda. When he saw Bellmon, he put the drink down on the bar.

When General Jiggs came through, a look of puzzlement came on Mac's square, ruddy face.

"What the hell?"

"Get yourself in uniform, Major," General Jiggs said.

"What the hell is all this?" MacMillan said.

"The way it works, Mac, is that I'm the general and you're the major, and you do what I say."

"Sir?" MacMillan asked.

"Greens will do nicely, Mac," General Bellmon said. "Just shake it up."

After MacMillan left, Felter smiled at General Bellmon.

"It came through, did it?" Felter asked.

"I brought the orders back with me," Bellmon said. "You think he knows?"

"By now, I think he does," Felter said.

"Well, we kept it quiet until now," General Jiggs said. "With Mac, that's an accomplishment. He has spies at every camp, post, and station in the army."

They laughed.

MacMillan returned in a surprisingly short time wearing a green uniform.

"Where do you think, Wallace?" General Jiggs asked.

"Against the wall would be nice, sir," Master Sergeant Wallace said, nodding at a wall on which more than a dozen framed photographs of army aircraft were hung.

"Come over here, Mac," Jiggs said. "And you, too, Roxy."

Roxy MacMillan, flushed with excitement, stood on one side of her husband, and General Jiggs stood on the other.

Bellmon took a folded sheath of papers from his tunic pocket.

"Attention to orders," he said formally, but smiling. And then he began to read: "Extract from General Orders Number Two Thirty-one, Headquarters, Department of the Army, Washington 25, D.C., dated 31 January 1958. Paragraph 32. The following promotion in the Army of the United States is announced: Major Rudolph G. MacMillan, 0-678562, Infantry, to be Lieutenant Colonel, with date of rank from 1 October 1958. Official. James B. Pullman, Major General, U.S.A., Acting, The Adjutant General."

"Jesus," Lieutenant Colonel MacMillan said smiling, embarrassed.

"Who's got the leaves?" General Jiggs asked. Barbara Bellmon handed him a small piece of cardboard onto which were pinned two silver oak leaves. He tore one off and handed it to Roxy. Next he tore the other off. Then, at Master Sergeant Wallace's direction, they mimed pinning on the symbols of MacMillan's new grade and moved a little closer, so there would be a good photograph for the press release.

IV

(One)
Quarters No. 33
Fort Bragg, North Carolina
1616 Hours, 31 December 1958

The commandant of the U.S. Army Special Warfare School, the sergeant major of the school, and three other of the school's senior noncommissioned officers were sitting in fatigue uniform on the floor of the living room drinking beer. A galvanized iron washtub rested on newspapers spread on the floor. It held a case and a half of Miller's High Life on a bed of ice. On a kitchen chair by the door from the foyer to the living room were a pile of green felt berets.

The commanding officer and his senior noncommissioned staff looked exhausted.

M/Sgt Wojinski, after a couple of beers, asked Colonel Hanrahan a very odd question.

"If you don't mind me asking, Colonel, who's your pal in the White House?"

"My pal in the White House? You mean as in Washington, D.C., that White House?"

Wojinski nodded his massive head solemnly.

"I don't know a soul in the White House," Hanrahan replied, truthfully. "Except General of the Army Eisenhower, of course. He's an old buddy."

"No shit?" Wojinski asked, impressed.

"Oh, sure, Ski," Hanrahan said. "He called upon me for tactical advice all through the war."

"Bullshit," Wojinski said.

"You want to know where I met Eisenhower?" Hanrahan asked, and then went on without waiting for a reply. "In 1944, in London. I was back from Greece, and somebody got the brilliant idea that I should brief the Supreme Commander on what was going on in Greece. So I spent three days writing a speech, got all dressed up in a brand-new uniform, and went over to SHAEF prepared to dazzle him with my all-around brilliance. So I waited patiently in the theater while a dozen other officers—none less than a bull colonel—made their pitch. When it was my turn, Eisenhower glanced at his watch, stood up, looked at me, and said, 'Sorry, Son, we've run out of time.' That's how Ike and I came to be buddies. I don't know anybody in the White House, Ski."

"Got it," M/Sgt Wojinski said, and winked at Colonel Hanrahan. "You don't know a soul in the White House."

"Good Christ, Ski!" Sergeant Major Taylor said.

"What the hell is he talking about, Taylor?" Hanrahan demanded of his sergeant major. "Do you know? Or has a little honest sweat and a couple of cold beers blown his mind?"

Taylor shrugged. Hanrahan didn't like the look on his face.

"I asked you a question, Taylor," Hanrahan said. There was a very subtle change of tone in his voice. It wasn't the joking tone it had been a moment before.

"Sir," Taylor said, "I happened to get a look at the directive. You were given command of the school DP."

"DP? What the hell is that?"

"It means 'Direction of the President,' sir," Taylor said.

"Are you sure?" Hanrahan asked.

DP did mean Direction of the President, the highest authority possible to cite in the military—an order from the Commander in Chief. Eisenhower got a DP during War II: Invade France. A DP had ordered the dropping of the atom bombs. But a DP was unlikely to be wasted on the assignment of a lowly colonel to a small school.

"Yes, sir, I am."

"I have no idea what it means," Hanrahan said. "But, I repeat, I don't know a soul in the White House."

"Yes, sir," Taylor said.

Quarters No. 33 was a two-story, brick house built in 1937 on what was now known as the main post. In 1937, there had been nothing but the main post. But in World War II, Fort Bragg, an artillery base, had been designated as the training center for airborne (parachute) divisions, and vast tracts of sandy scrub land and pine had been converted within a matter of months to a "temporary" base capable of housing nearly 40,000 men and all the service facilities necessary to train and care for them.

When it was built, it was intended that Quarters No. 33 serve as family housing for officers in the grade of captain. One captain, who had memorialized his time at Bragg by carving his name, rank, and the dates of his occupancy on the inside of an upstairs bedroom closet door, had occupied the quarters for not quite two and a half years. By the time he was transferred and Quarters No. 33 became vacant for reassignment, the army had already grown much larger. The second officer to be assigned Quarters No. 33 had been a full colonel, and so had every officer since. The sixteen identical houses built to house captains and their families had long been known as "Colonel's Row."

Each occupant of Quarters No. 33 had perpetuated the custom of carving his name, rank, and dates of occupancy on the closet door, until there was no more room left. Then a sergeant skilled with his hands had taken the door down, sliced the part with the carvings thin enough so it could be framed, and mounted it in the foyer. A substantial majority of the colonels who had once lived in Quarters No. 33 had gone on to achieve high rank. The first occupant, for instance, had reached lieutenant general before being retired.

Assisted by Sergeant Major Taylor, M/Sgt Wojinski (the Operations Sergeant), M/Sgt Richard Stevens (the Armorer/Artificer), and M/Sgt Dewey F. Carter (the Communications Sergeant)—in other words, Ski and his cronies—the present occupant of Quarters No. 33 had spent all day searching through the quartermaster Family Furniture warehouse for sufficient furniture so that his family could survive until their own furniture, now en route from Saigon, arrived.

There was not much furniture in the warehouse, and Hanrahan had concluded that the family furniture he had drawn from the exalted position of full colonel was even more beat up than the furniture he had drawn as a newly commissioned second lieutenant. But it would be enough to keep them afloat until their own furniture arrived. More important, it would get the family out of the Fayetteville Inn.

When Ski had asked him if he could "use a little help with the furniture," he had accepted. If Ski went to the motor pool and drew a truck, that would mean that the PFC or the SP4 assigned to the truck would not have to drive it on a day that everybody else had off. And with Ski's broad shoulders, between the two of them they could move anything.

Ski had shown up with the sergeant major and two other master sergeants in tow. Later when Patricia and the kids dropped by to see how things were going, he sent her to the PX for beer. There was no other way to compensate his noncoms. They would have been insulted if he had offered them money for their services: the only time that a master sergeant dirties his hands or works up a sweat is when it pleases him to do so.

The doorbell rang. It was, Hanrahan thought, an anemic buzz.

He pushed himself off the floor and walked to the door.

It was a full bull colonel from the 82nd Airborne Division, in greens, a great big guy festooned with all the regalia: colored woven cords hung from the epaulets, the gold-framed blue oblong of the Distinguished Unit Citation and the regimental colors flashed beneath the parachute wings, and there was an impressive array of individual decorations.

"Good afternoon," Paul Hanrahan said.

"Well, Paul," the bull colonel said, "I really didn't expect a warm embrace, but I did think you would at least remember who I was."

"Jesus," Hanrahan said, finally realizing who he was, "Foster!"

"Try to remember that you're an officer and a gentleman, Paul," Colonel J. Thomas Foster said to his roommate and classmate at the United States Military Academy at West Point. "Say something like, 'Foster, Old Man, I'm glad to see you.'"

"I am," Hanrahan said. "Jesus, Jerry, it's good to see you!"

They shook hands.

"Come on in and have a beer," Hanrahan said.

"What I really had in mind was an icy martini at the club," Foster said.

"Look at me," Hanrahan said, gesturing at his mussed and soiled uniform. "I can't go in public like this."

"And you probably don't have any gin, either, do you?" Foster said.

"Come on in, anyway, and have a beer," Hanrahan said, and led Foster into the living room.

The noncoms were on their feet when the two colonels entered the room. Two of them were in the act of adjusting their green berets.

Hanrahan introduced them.

"They've been helping me get stuff from the quartermaster," Hanrahan said.

"I never would have guessed," Foster said.

"Colonel, with your permission," Sergeant Major Taylor said, "we'll be going."

"Take the beer," Hanrahan said. "And thank you, fellas."

"We'll leave you the beer."

"Take the damned beer," Hanrahan said. "I am not being generous. It's starting to leak through the newspapers."

"Well, if you put it that way, Colonel," Wojinski said, and gestured for Stevens to pick up the other end of the galvanized tub.

"Happy New Year, fellas," Hanrahan said, "and thanks a lot."

There was a chorus of "Happy New Year, Colonel."

"I guess I should have taken a couple of beers before they left," Hanrahan said when he and Foster were alone.

"You have always been unable, Hanrahan," Foster said drolly, "to think ahead. You now leave us no alternative but to make the perilous trek to my house."

"Which is how far?" Hanrahan asked.

"Two houses down," Foster said.

"I'll have to leave a note for Patricia," Hanrahan said. "She took the kids to the movies."

"It apparently never entered your mind to read the name signs in front of the quarters. Or perhaps you did read them and decided that Joan really wouldn't want to be bothered with one of her bridesmaids and her brats."

"Hey, I just got here, for Christ's sake," Hanrahan said. "I'm not firing on all cylinders."

"Obviously," Foster said. "Obviously."

Hanrahan wrote a note for Patricia, and wedged it in the door jamb. Then he put on his beret.

"You really look absurd in that, you know," Foster said, "ignoring other considerations. You look like a girl scout."

Hanrahan thumbed his nose at him.

They walked down the tree-shaded street to Quarters No. 31. It was identical to No. 33, but the furniture was personal and there were carpets on the floors. The difference in the atmosphere was like day and night.

"Joan's not here," Foster said. "I sent her away."

"I'm sure she jumped at your command," Hanrahan said.

"I wanted to spare her the embarrassment of listening to me give you my routine Dutch Uncle speech," Colonel J. Thomas Foster said.

"God, I can hardly wait," Hanrahan said. "You have no idea how lonely and afraid I am when I don't have your wise counsel to steer me down the straight and narrow."

"Would you like a martini, or are you still a barbarian?"

"If I drink martinis, I make an ass of myself, you know that."

"And sometimes you don't even need the martini," Foster said. "Scotch all right?"

"Fine."

"And take off that silly hat," Foster said. "Someone's liable to see you and think I know you."

"This hat really bugs you, doesn't it, Jerry?" Hanrahan said, chuckling.

"Not only me," Foster said, handing him a glass of scotch. He interrupted himself. "It's good to see you, Paul," he said. "Really good."

"Yeah, me too, Jerry," Hanrahan said. They touched glasses.

"Absent companions," Foster said.

"Absent companions," Hanrahan repeated, lifting his glass with Foster.

"Incidentally, the next time you need some strong backs give me a call. I'm running a daily average of 121 in the stockade, and they're supposed to do manual labor not six-stripers."

"One of them is an old friend of mine, Jerry," Hanrahan

said. "The others are his friends. I didn't order them to help me move."

"Appearances are what count," Foster said. "Which brings us back to the girl scout hat."

"OK, tell me about the berets," Hanrahan said. "You are obviously obsessed with the subject."

"The general doesn't like them," Foster said. "Make that plural. The generals: mine, Howard, and all the others."

"Piss on 'em," Hanrahan said. "I do."

"I know for a fact, Paul, that Howard sent a 'the commanding general desires' letter to every commander on the post, specifically dealing with headgear."

"I saw it," Hanrahan said.

"To which your predecessor responded by ordering his men into the authorized headgear."

"So I understand," Hanrahan said.

"What did they do, Paul, have them on when you arrived? So you would think that's the way things were?"

"No," Hanrahan said, "they were wearing regular headgear, and I asked about the berets. I'd heard about them. So my sergeant major showed me Howard's letter."

"And?"

"I directed their wear," Hanrahan said.

"So it *is* true," Foster said.

"Yeah," Hanrahan said.

"Oh, I knew you'd authorized them," Foster said. "I meant about your having friends highly placed enough so you can thumb your nose at Howard."

"So far as I know, I don't have any highly placed friends," Hanrahan said. "Although everybody seems to think I do."

"Paul, I'm probably the oldest friend you have in the army. Don't tell me that."

"OK. Between friends, I've been trying to figure it out. I have no idea why the DP was on my orders. For that matter, I was genuinely surprised at the promotion. I wasn't even on the bird colonel's list."

"And you don't have any idea who's been laying hands on you?"

"No, but I guess someone has. My last efficiency report had the phrase, 'for someone of his limited experience, this officer has performed adequately.' That didn't get me an eagle, nor the command of the school."

"No," Foster said, shocked at the language, "it didn't."

"You want a straight answer about the berets?" Hanrahan asked. Foster nodded. "I got a welcome speech from Howard when I reported in. He made it clear he thinks the Special Warfare School belongs to airborne. He used the phrase 'the airborne family.'"

"And you don't think it does?"

"No, I don't. It's just what it says, 'special.' Airborne is conventional."

"You could find an argument about that, Paul," Foster said. "From me, among others."

"You establish a position by superior firepower, invest the terrain with troops, and hold it. That's conventional," Hanrahan said. "It doesn't make any difference if you invest the position with a skirmish line, or by parachute, or by landing barge."

"And 'special'?"

"Guerrillas," Hanrahan said. "Irregulars. Hit and run."

"That doesn't work," Foster said.

"I know better," Hanrahan said. "It worked in Greece during the second war. You do know how many divisions the Germans had there, don't you? If those divisions hadn't been tied up fighting guerrillas, they could have made the difference, possibly, in Russia. Or Italy. Or France."

"That was World War II," Foster said.

"Vietminh guerrillas defeated French paratroops at Dien Bien Phu," Hanrahan said.

"A couple of American divisions, probably the 82nd Airborne alone, with an artillery regiment and a combat command of tanks, would have been able to send those people back to their rice paddies."

"Oh, God," Hanrahan said, laughing sadly. "You're dreaming, buddy. *Dreaming.*"

"I'm not going to fight with you the first time I've seen you in fifteen years," Foster said. "We'll put that aside for the moment."

"Good," Hanrahan said, and then: "Can I have another one of these?"

Foster made him the drink.

"Get back to the berets," he said.

"Do you know the status of the school?" Hanrahan asked.

"I don't quite understand the question," Foster said.

"It's a class-two activity of DCSOPS," Hanrahan said. "It's not under Bragg."

"It's on Bragg. You're a colonel. The general has three stars. It's under Bragg."

"Fort Bragg has been directed to support me logistically . . ."

"'Me'?" Foster interrupted. "My, aren't *we* drunk with power?"

"Which means Howard has to feed us, and pay us, and let us use his physical assets, but does not mean he commands us."

"Who does?"

"DCSOPS," Hanrahan said.

"And how long do you think it will take them to find a new commandant after Howard calls the DCSOPS and tells him 'your colonel here is annoying me'?"

"I don't know. I'm going to find out, I suppose, pretty quickly. To tell you the truth, Jerry, I feel a little silly in the green beret. That 'girl scout hat' line occurred to me, too. But I either jump when Howard says 'jump,' or I run the school. He's ordered my troops to do something that I don't think he has the authority to do, wear what kind of hats he thinks they should wear. If I give into him on this, I give in all the way."

"In other words, you don't want to be a general," Foster said. "Or for that matter, commandant of the Special Warfare School. You ever read any Mao Tse-tung?"

"Yes, indeed," Hanrahan said.

"'The reed bends with the wind, and then snaps up again,'" Foster quoted.

"'When the enemy is strong, withdraw,'" Hanrahan quoted back. "'When he is weak, attack.'"

"You don't think he's strong?"

"I don't think he picked Paul Hanrahan to command the Special Warfare School," Hanrahan said. "On the contrary. I'll bet he spent a lot of effort trying to pick a commandant who thinks Special Forces are 'part of the airborne family.'"

"And besides, you have friends in high places, right?"

"I told you, Jerry—do you want my word of honor?—I don't know any more about the DP business than you do. Probably less."

"But you're willing to use it, right?"

"Within reason," Hanrahan said. "Why not?"

"I think we had better change the subject, before we start saying things we'll regret later."

"In other words, you think I'm being devious?"

Foster did not reply to the question.

"I heard about the flowers," he said, chuckling, and obviously to change the subject. "They really sent Howard up the wall, from what I hear."

"Jesus," Hanrahan said, also chuckling. "If I'd have had that bastard here, I'd have killed him."

"An old friend?"

"Right after War II, in 1947, I was in Greece. I had two young lieutenants, a guy named Lowell, and a guy named Felter."

Foster's eyebrows went up.

"This is a pretty good story, Jerry," Hanrahan said. "Lowell's got more money than God. He was an eighteen-year-old draftee who knew how to play polo. So Porky Waterford arranged to have him commissioned so he could play polo against the French. And then Waterford dropped dead, so they got rid of Second Lieutenant Lowell by sending him to Greece, and they got rid of him in Athens by sending him to me."

"He's the guy who sent the flowers?"

"Yeah. Truth being stranger than fiction, he's still in the army..."

"Tell me about the other one," Foster said. "What was his name, 'Felter'?"

"Yeah," Hanrahan said. "He's a West Pointer, smarter than a whip, and was in Greece because he wanted to learn about counterguerrilla operations..."

"And he sent you the flowers, too?"

"No, Lowell sent the flowers, and signed Felter's name to the card."

"But they're both friends of yours, right?"

"Yeah, they are. Both of them turned out to be pretty damned good warriors. Lowell made a battlefield promotion to major in Korea, and..."

"And you don't have a friend in the White House, right? Your word of honor. With the single small exception of Major Sanford T. Felter, GSC, who just happens to be...this is supposed to be classified, but it's certainly not a well-kept secret...standing at the right hand of God. With rank as Counselor to the President."

"Jesus H. Christ!" Hanrahan said, genuinely surprised.

It all fell in place now. And he felt like a fool. He'd heard about the Special Warfare School from Felter in the first place. He and Felter had agreed that it was high time the army stopped planning to fight the next war with the tactics of the last, and started training guerrilla and counterguerrilla forces. The mysterious, instantaneous switching of his telephone call to Felter, from Washington to Fort Rucker, now made sense. Felter had access to the White House switchboard, the world's most sophisticated telephone communications system.

"You didn't know, Paul, did you?" Foster said, after a moment.

"No," Hanrahan said.

"This puts me on a bit of a spot," Foster said.

Hanrahan looked confused for a moment, and then he understood.

"You were sent to see me, right?" he asked.

"If I had known, I wouldn't have had to be sent," Foster said. "But, yes, Paul, I was sent. My general had a call from Howard, who thought that you might listen to a few words of advice, about the berets and other things, from your roommate."

"And you will go back reporting that not only am I intransigent, but that I have in fact a patron in the White House?"

"I'll have to report that you're going to prove difficult," Foster said. "But if you don't want me to say anything about your knowing Felter, I won't."

"Don't," Hanrahan said.

"Who?" Foster asked.

"Thank you, Jerry," Hanrahan said.

"You want another drink, Paul?"

"No. I'd better be getting back," Hanrahan said. "Patricia'll be getting back from the movies about now."

"We'll see you at the New Year's Eve party, then?"

"'Not I, said Cock Robin.' Red Hanrahan will be sound asleep long before midnight."

"For your general information," Foster said, "General Howard feels very strongly about his New Year's Day reception. He expects all unit commanders, battalion and up, to be there."

"I'll be there," Hanrahan said. "With my bells on. And my beret."

(Two)
Hangar 104
Laird Army Airfield
Fort Rucker, Alabama
1745 Hours, 31 December 1958

Major Craig W. Lowell had just settled himself back in his office, after rescuing General Bellmon from the Fulton County Airport in Atlanta. His desk was littered with technical manuals, field manuals, Department of the Army pamphlets, tables of organization and equipment, and a foot-high stack of army regulations, plus—neatly stacked—the ten pages he had written so far on the IBM electric typewriter of ***SECRET*** (Draft) TO&E 1-XXX Helicopter Company (Rocket Armed) (Tank Destroyer). The document provided in precise detail for the personnel and all the equipment of a tank-killing chopper company.

He was sorry he hadn't drafted this months before when he was in Washington. He had not written it then because he hadn't realized that he would find himself in a position where he would officially have to "write" it, that is, get it into the system. He had thought then that his only contributions would be made after the first draft had been written by someone else and was being circulated among the concerned agencies for comment. At some point, he would have been asked for his comments. He would have made a few, officially, because that would have been a waste of effort. He was a major, and majors—at the Department of the Army level—were expected to be seen but not heard, like small children.

Instead (for he had very positive ideas how the company should be organized and with what it should be equipped) he would have made extensive unofficial comments which he'd have sent to Major General Paul T. Jiggs. Jiggs would then have made some minor changes of his own, and submitted the comments over his signature. The comments of major generals—especially those of the major general commanding the Army Aviation Center—would be very carefully weighed by the major generals in DCSOPS and the three-star who was the DCSOPS. These comments would probably be accepted and incorporated into the final draft sent to the Chief of Staff for his approval.

That was all changed now. As Chief, Rocket Armed Helicopter Section, Aircraft Division, the U.S. Army Aviation

Board, Lowell had become the minor underling expected to prepare the first rough draft. As the draft TO&E made its way upward through the layers of bureaucracy, this would be improved upon by his superiors.

Now he would not have the services of professional Washington secretaries to type and refine the basic document. They were not nearly as attractive to look at as Jane Cassidy, but they had an expertise in bureaucratic finesse that the Cassidy woman could never be expected to have. He was going to have to somehow or other provide that expertise himself, as well as create the raw material.

If he didn't do the thing *just right,* then as the draft TO&E moved slowly upward, every other dumb sonofabitch and his brother was going to make changes to show their grasp of the big picture—or for some other half-ass reason. In the process they'd really fuck it up.

It was proving a very difficult TO&E to write. The tank-killing chopper company(s) he envisioned would be separate—not part of a battalion or larger organization. To be effective, they would have to have the capability of being sent anyplace at anytime to counter an armored advance. That meant they would not be able to draw their logistical support from a larger organization. That meant they had to be able to support themselves. And that meant the company would have to have its own mess sergeant and field ranges, its own ordnance ammunition detachment, its own ordnance artificer section, its own signal corps avionics maintenance section, and its own quartermaster aircraft fueling trucks. Everything a regiment had, in other words—except perhaps a chaplain and a public relations officer.

The task of writing such a TO&E normally would be handed a major such as himself with the expectation that he'd make a progress report in maybe ninety days, with the first rough draft following ninety days after that. Major Craig W. Lowell intended to deliver within thirty days a final draft of the TO&E that would be left ninety percent intact after it had gone through all the reviews.

The rocket-armed helicopter was important. Without it, the next war might very well be lost. Although Lowell saw no war on the immediate horizon, the lead time—the time between the official acceptance of a rocket-armed helicopter company in the army, and the time the first company would join the field army—was at least a year. Equipment would have to be procured, personnel trained, and a thousand bumps ironed out.

When the knock came at his door, Major Lowell was dealing with a personnel problem. Since there was absolutely no question in his mind that if the army was going to arm its helicopters with tank-killing rockets, then choppers armed with machine guns would soon follow. The .30 caliber Browning machine gun had been invented in 1917. Its big brother, the .50 caliber, had come along in time for War II. Among the documents on Lowell's desk were Air Corps documents from War II reflecting their experience in maintaining .50 caliber machine guns in P-51 and P-47 fighter squadrons. It had taken a good many machine guns to insure that each time a P-51 or a P-47 took off, there were eight functioning machine guns on it. Lowell thought that there would no more than four—and possibly as few as two—.50 caliber machine guns mounted on army helicopters. But even halving the Air Corps' spares and maintenance personnel, he was going to have to have a large detachment of ordnance weapons men in the armed chopper company. The people he needed were senior enlisted men. And this was going to cause problems, because with the exception of truck drivers and cooks, the enlisted men required for other logistic support (avionics, aircraft maintenance, and so on) also needed to be highly trained and thus with stripe-heavy sleeves.

In other words, he was going to have far more sergeants and sergeants first class than privates and PFCs. And that was going to cause trouble when the draft TO&E was sent for review to armor, infantry, and artillery. They were not going to go along happily with high-ranking enlisted men in some oddball candy-ass helicopter company when there were PFCs in tanks, at the cannon, and carrying rifles.

There was another knock at his door. Major Lowell got up from his desk, went to the door, and pulled it open. He was very annoyed at the interruption.

A civilian was standing there, a tall, good-looking guy with a silk kerchief knotted around his neck. He was wearing an open overcoat with a fur collar. Beneath it he wore a suede jacket. He looked, Major Lowell thought, European.

"What can I do for you?" Lowell asked somewhat coldly.

"Have I the honor of addressing Major C. W. Lowell?"

European, all right. A frog, more than likely.

"I'm Lowell," he said.

"You are a difficult man to find, mon Major," the man said. He raised his hand, palm facing forward, in the French military salute.

"Captain Jean-Philippe Jannier at your service, M'sieu le Major," the frog said.

"What can I do for you, Captain?" Lowell asked. He made a vague gesture with his right hand in the direction of his temple which could have been a return salute.

"I have been asked to deliver this to you, mon Major." He handed Lowell a small, Northwest Orient Airlines envelope. It bore the address of the town house in Washington and the telephone number there.

Lowell, still annoyed at the interruption, was now curious. He tore the envelope open and read the short handwritten note:

NORTHWEST ORIENT AIRLINES

Inflight Letter

Duke:

    Captain Jannier is a friend of mine. All courtesies to him gratefully received by your friend and mentor,

                    Paul T. Hanrahan
                    Colonel, Infantry
                    Commanding, USASWS*

*I got the word as we were refueling in Hawaii.

Lowell raised his eyes to meet Jannier's.

"You come very well recommended, Captain," he said, in French. "Paul Hanrahan is one of our finest officers. I will now repeat my question, meaning it this time, 'What can I do for you?'"

Jannier did not seem at all surprised that Lowell spoke in French.

"I don't quite understand," he said.

Lowell handed him the note. Jannier read it.

"That was very kind of Colonel Hanrahan," he said. "But I need nothing, thank you just the same."

"You've been assigned here?"

"I am to learn to fly, and then I will be a liaison officer," Jannier said.

"When did you get in?" Lowell asked.

"Two days ago. On the twenty-eighth."

"You tried to call me in Washington at this number?"

"Yes."

"Are you settled? Do you have a BOQ?"

"In the same building as the major's," Jannier said. "I saw the major's name on his door."

"Please call me 'Craig,'" Lowell said. "If you're a friend of Paul Hanrahan's . . ."

"I have that privilege, I believe," Jannier said.

"May I ask your plans for tonight, Captain?"

"If I am to call you 'Craig,' you must call me Jean-Philippe," Jannier said. Lowell nodded. "Madame le General Bellmon has been most kind to ask me to join them for the evening," Jannier said.

"I cannot, regrettably," Lowell said, smiling, "offer you a cinq-à-sept, but I am about to take on some liquid courage to face that party, and I would like it very much if you were free to join me."

"A little Scots whiskey is, I suppose, the next best thing," Jannier said.

Lowell realized he liked this man. And if Hanrahan liked him, he must have something going for him.

"Let me put some papers in the safe," Lowell said. "And then we will have a little drink to toast le Colonel Hanrahan's promotion."

(Three)
227 Melody Lane
Ozark, Alabama
1945 Hours, 31 December 1958

Lieutenant Colonel Rudolph G. MacMillan, in the master bedroom of 227 Melody Lane, examined his reflection in the full-length mirror on the closet door. He was wearing, for the first time, his new blue mess uniform.

"Jesus!" he said.

"You look real nice, Mac," Roxy said, approvingly.

The blue mess uniform had been Roxy MacMillan's Christmas present to her husband. They had known back in October that Mac had made the promotion list, but had had no idea when the promotion would actually come through. That had been enough for Roxy to decide to buy the uniform, even if he wouldn't be allowed to wear it until the promotion orders were cut.

Blue mess was the army's most ornate uniform: a short jacket, which MacMillan thought made him look like a bartender, was worn over a white shirt with a formal collar and a white piqué vest. The sleeves were decorated with golden cord in ornate loops, reaching almost to the elbow. The number of golden loops indicated rank. A second lieutenant got one loop. There were four loops on MacMillan's sleeves. The lapels of the vest were the color of the officer's branch of service, in MacMillan's case the powder blue of infantry. Miniatures of the medals to which the officer was entitled were pinned to the lapel. The jacket was worn with a cape, lined with satin in the branch color and fastened at the collar with a thick gold rope.

There weren't very many blue mess uniforms around the army. They were mostly worn by officers assigned to the White House and by senior military attachés at important embassies (London, Moscow, Paris, Tokyo, and Rio de Janeiro, for example), but they were frighteningly expensive and there were few opportunities to wear them. Consequently, few officers had them, even though their acquisition was officially "encouraged."

Roxy had wanted Mac to have one from the very first time she had seen one. Years ago, before the Korean War, there had been an official reception at the Fort Knox officer's open mess for a visiting British Royal Tank Corps general officer. The invitations (actually commands to appear) issued to the officers of the Armor School had paid lip service to the notion that blue mess uniforms actually hung in most officer's closets. The bottom line had said: "Dress: army blue or blue mess."

The post commander had shown up in army blue. Second Lieutenant Craig W. Lowell, then fresh back from Greece, had shown up in blue mess, wearing a Greek medal the size of a coffee saucer hanging from a three-inch-wide purple ribbon stretched across his chest. Bob Bellmon had thought he'd done it to be a smart-ass, and was furious. But Lowell had actually been trying to be a good guy. When he'd seen the invitation, he'd gotten on the telephone and called Brooks Brothers in New York and told them he didn't give a damn what it cost, he wanted a blue mess uniform cut and sewn that day, and en route to Kentucky, via air freight, the next.

Despite the furor it had caused, Roxy thought Craig had looked wonderful; and she'd promised herself that one day she would get a uniform like that for Mac. Thus when his name had come out on the light bird promotion list, she knew it was time.

Though blue mess *was* expensive (some would even say extravagant), they were doing all right money-wise, and there would be a bigger pay check when the promotion came through. And besides, it wasn't as if they had to put money away to send the boys to college. As sons of a Medal of Honor winner, they were entitled by law to go to West Point. And there was other money, too, if something went wrong with that.

Right after World War II, Mac got a whole bunch of money. It was his back pay for the time he'd been in the POW camp. Instead of blowing it on a car or something, they'd set Roxy's brother Jack up in a bar in Mauch Chunk, Pennsylvania. They put in the money, and Jack put in his time. Jack had worked hard, and done well, and was a good manager, and the Hardesty House became the best restaurant and cocktail lounge for miles around. Now they split the profits right down the middle.

And then there were the houses. Soon after they'd loaned Jack the money to buy the bar, they'd been assigned to Bragg, and they'd bought a house on the GI Bill in Fayetteville, outside Fort Bragg. Mac's housing allowance had more than covered the mortgage payments. Later they'd sent him to flight school at Fort Riley, and Roxy had figured out there was no sense in selling the house when they could keep it and rent it to some other officer for more than the mortgage payment. Before long Roxanne and Rudolph MacMillan, husband and wife, in joint tenancy, owned houses in Fayetteville, N.C., outside Bragg; Manhattan, Kansas, outside Fort Riley; Columbus, Ga., outside Fort Benning; and here in Ozark, in the Woody Dells subdivision. The Cadillac in the carport was paid for—and Roxy often wished there was some way she could tell that to the people who wondered out loud how a major could afford the payments on a Cadillac.

"You know what I was wondering?" Mac MacMillan asked his wife, and then went on without waiting for a reply. "I wonder is there any chance they might give me Combat Developments?"

"The TO&E calls for a bird colonel, Mac," she said. She had thought about that before he had, and she had been afraid that notion would pop into his head. She knew it would never happen. They wouldn't give him Combat Developments even if he was a full colonel. It wasn't, she thought, that she was putting her husband down. Mac was as smart as anybody—but, she reasoned, in a different way. There was probably no better warrior, no better fighter, in the army, period. And he was a good leader, the kind that made the people who worked for him like him, and who did what he said as best they could. He knew how to make people feel like part of the team.

But Mac just wasn't made up like Bellmon, or for that matter, like Lowell or Phil Parker or Sandy Felter. If the brass told Mac to take a company or a battalion and go take that hill, he could do it as well as anybody she had ever met. But that wasn't enough for doing what he was hoping for now. She didn't know the exact word for it, maybe "intellectual," but the others were "intellectual." They could talk about the army and plan for it in their heads. They knew history and could talk about people like Clausewitz, and things like Lee's campaigns, and "politico-military considerations." But when they did that, they might as well be talking Greek, for all Mac understood.

Mac was a nuts-and-bolts soldier, and Roxy was proud of him for being that. But she knew that he had no chance whatever of being given command of Combat Developments to replace Bob Bellmon.

MacMillan tugged one final time at the lower edge of his blue mess jacket, and then turned to face his wife.

"Jesus!" he said, as if something had just occurred to him.

"Jesus, what?" Roxy asked.

"With everything going on around here, you know what I forgot to do, Roxy?"

"No," she said. "What did you forget, Mac?"

"Roxy, you know how much I've had on my mind."

"What did you forget, Mac?"

"I forgot to go to the safety deposit box to get the Medal."

"Bullshit," Roxy said.

"Believe it or not, Roxy," Mac said, "that's what happened."

"You forgot on purpose, you bastard, the way I knew you would. You did that last year, too."

"I forgot, so like it or lump it," he said, righteously.

"Yeah, well, I figured that you were going to forget it, wise-ass," she said. "So I'm two full jumps ahead of you."

She went to her dressing table, opened a drawer, and took out a blue leather-covered case. She smiled smugly at her husband as she exhibited it to him, and then she opened it. She wiggled her finger at him to come to her. And when he did, somewhat sheepishly, she took from the box the Medal of Honor, the nation's highest award for valor, which Harry Truman had personally hung around his neck. Then she put the blue-starred ribbon around her husband's neck and arranged the medal on his shirt front. It really stood out, she thought, against the white shirt.

(Four)
BOQ No. 1 (Bldg. T-1703)
Fort Rucker, Alabama
2015 Hours, 31 December 1958

Major Craig W. Lowell had decided somewhat reluctantly that he had to wear his blue mess uniform to attend the New Year's Eve party at the Fort Rucker officer's mess. He would have preferred not to go to the party at all, but in keeping with his new straighten-up-and-fly-right code of conduct, he knew he had to go. Blue mess was a bit much for Fort Rucker. But because the Mouse would be there and wearing blue mess, Lowell thought he better wear his own. Otherwise he would have worn blues with a black bow tie.

He'd worn blue mess a good deal in Washington. Under the right circumstances, he rather liked to wear it. But not here, where it would earn him gapes of curiosity and resentment. Still, he consoled himself with the thought that he would not be the only one going to a converted service club to sit on folding chairs in a uniform that would have been more at home at a reception given by the President of France in the Hall of Mirrors at Versailles.

Barbara Bellmon had told him Bob would be wearing his, out of kindness to Sharon Felter. Sharon, whom Lowell admired and loved above most women, had bought Sandy blue mess. In her touching naiveté, she had thought his assignment to the White House would mean that they would become part of the social whirl there. And so she'd thought that he would

need it. As it had turned out, while he was frequently on White
House guest lists, the invitations were directed to Mr. and Mrs.
Felter, not Major and Mrs. Felter. Only a few people at the
White House even knew he was in the army. It was generally
believed that he was some sort of financial advisor, out of
Harvard or MIT, to the President.

Sharon had carried Sandy's blue mess uniform to Rucker
with her, and Sandy was going to wear it, aide-to-the-President
gold rope and all, to please her. And to insure that Sharon's
husband wouldn't stick out like a sore thumb, Bob Bellmon
would wear his. Even Mac would be in one, Barbara Bellmon
had told Lowell.

"Mac?" he had asked in disbelief.

"There's a reason," Barbara Bellmon had laughed. "You'll
see."

"They cut his promotion orders," Lowell said.

"Spoilsport," Barbara had laughed and hung up on him.

Craig Lowell, aware that there was probably an element of
sour grapes in it, thought that the only reason MacMillan had
been given the silver leaf of a lieutenant colonel was because
he was a Hero, First Class. He had a chestful: the Medal, the
Distinguished Service Cross, a flock of others. There was no
question that Mac had balls, and with the possible exception
of Phil Parker, there was no one he'd rather have with him if
he had to pick up a rifle and go shoot bad guys. Mac had been
the platoon sergeant of the 508th Parachute Infantry Regiment's
intelligence and reconnaissance platoon through five combat
jumps in War II—and lived. *Ergo sum,* he was an extraordinary
warrior.

But he simply wasn't bright enough to be a lieutenant colonel. He would have to be carried by his subordinates. Officers
at Combat Developments weren't going to be crawling around
in the boonies on their hands and knees matching wits with
riflemen; they were going to be sitting around conference tables
matching wits with some very bright people, guys who could
cut their throats as neatly with a well-turned phrase as some
guerrilla could with a sharpened carbine bayonet. Mac simply
wasn't up to handling that kind of combat.

And those conference room battles were not small unit fire
fights. If you lost one, you couldn't pull back and call for the
artillery to bail you out. If you lost these battles, the losses
would be irreversible. The army would not get its own air

mobility—or its own armed helicopters—as quickly as it had to have them. It might not get them at all.

There were two places where Major Craig Lowell thought the next war would be fought, and these weren't where most everybody else did: on the plains of Hesse in Germany. He thought the Russians were probably going to make their next move in the Near East. Or, alternatively (and perhaps simultaneously), in the Far East. In either of these areas mobility was going to be the key to success.

Trying to get information out of Sandy Felter was like trying to squeeze water from a rock, but he had known him long enough to get a few drops, and after a conversation with Felter about Vietnam, Lowell had concluded that Felter was convinced that American forces would find themselves engaged there. He hadn't yet had a chance to pump Hanrahan's friend, Captain Jean-Philippe Jannier, at length. But he had already learned from the Frenchman—over two beers at the officer's club—that he agreed with Felter . . . with the typically French certitude that Americans wouldn't do as well there as the French had. And the French had lost. Lowell had already decided that as soon as he could get a day off, he would go to see Hanrahan at Bragg. Hanrahan would have some answers.

But wherever the next war was going to be, the army was going to need its own aviation, and getting it at all, much less in the quantity and quality required, was going to be considerably more difficult than ordering the bugler to sound "boots and saddles."

Major Lowell examined himself in the full-length mirror on the wall. It was wavy and the reflecting material was beginning to flake off. They had bought the mirror, he decided, at a distress sale of shopworn merchandise at Woolworth's.

The cheap mirror, in the Spartan BOQ, triggered another line of thought.

Straighten-up-and-fly-right be damned. I am not going to live in this goddman BOQ like some sophomore working his way through Slippery Rock State Teacher's College.

He had not been *ordered* to live in it, he remembered. Paul Jiggs had *implied* that he should, the time when he had eaten Craig's ass out. The way Jiggs had put it, he was "to forego his flamboyant ways." Jiggs thought it was "flamboyant" for an officer to rent one of the two suites in the Daleville Inn, the newly built motel outside the gate. And so in a burst of righteous determination to do the right thing, Lowell had asked that he be assigned a BOQ. Even at the time, he had known in the back of his mind that he was acting the fool. There was no way he would be able to put up with either the Spartan accommodations of a BOQ or the forced camaraderie. He decided now he would move into the Daleville Inn tomorrow. There was no reason he couldn't straighten-up-and-fly-right in something approaching reasonable comfort.

He debated for a moment wearing what he thought of as "the Golden Saucer," and concluded he might as well go the whole hog. He took off his jacket and laid it on the bed. Then he went to an attaché case, which he thought of as "the things case." Inside the battered pigskin case, which had been his father's, were a number of things that experience had taught him should be kept together in a portable form in case of unexpected need.

It held a spare razor, comb, and brush. There was a change of underwear, still in plastic wrapping. There was paper and a package of six ballpoint pens. In an interior compartment which hooked to the top of the case were his passport and an envelope containing $2,000 in fifty dollar bills. There was a small leather-bound address book. A plastic bag held a 9 mm Pistol-08 Parabellum—more popularly known as a "German Luger"—and two loaded spare clips. There was a box, sealed with Scotch tape, of fifty Winchester-Western 9 mm cartridges. And there were several boxes holding insignia and his medals in their various forms: the medals themselves (in individual boxes), and a box which held the miniatures of the medals, assembled together on a single mounting for wear with either the blue mess or on the lapel of a civilian tailcoat. He had already pinned the miniatures to his blue mess lapel, but now that he had decided to go the whole hog, he took from a thin blue leather case the medal of the Order of Saint George and Saint Andrew. It was a spectacular sonofabitch, a four-inch hunk of sculptured gold hung on a three-inch-wide purple band. As he tugged the ribbon into place diagonally across the stiff front of the dress shirt, he almost changed his mind about wearing it. But in the end, he decided that wearing it was the right thing to do. If the Mouse showed up wearing all that aide-to-the-President crap, and Mac wore his Medal, and he showed up without his spectacular decoration, they would be liable to think he disapproved of them wearing theirs.

He was pleased with his decision, taking it as proof that he was now flying upright, behaving as behooved a field-grade officer of the Regular Army of the United States.

There was a knock at the door.

"Come!" he called.

It was Captain Jean-Philippe Jannier, now in dress uniform, complete to a round-crown cap adorned with gold braid. The uniform, Lowell thought, was absurd. The jacket was too short and looked too tight, but that was the custom, not bad tailoring. The French custom was that medals, not miniatures, were worn. And Captain Jean-Philippe Jannier had more than his share.

"Is there something wrong?" Jannier asked, aware that Lowell had been staring at him.

"I've been admiring your medals," Lowell confessed.

"And I yours, M'sieu le Chevalier," Jannier said. That was in reference to Lowell's French Legion of Honor, in the grade of Chevalier.

"A slight bow will suffice," Lowell said. "It will not be necessary for you to kneel."

Jannier bowed, mockingly.

"I think we are going to find mutual friends in the French Army," Jannier said. "You and I have been to the same places at different times."

Lowell smiled at him. Jannier returned it. They liked each other, because they understood each other.

"You're going to meet two honorary members of your regiment tonight," Lowell said.

"Of the *3ième Parachutiste?*" Jannier asked, surprised.

"Lieutenant Colonel MacMillan and Major Felter," Lowell said.

"Ah ha!" Jannier said, recognizing the names. "I have heard the story."

"What I will do," Lowell said, "is give you a good deal to drink and encourage you to jump off the balcony."

Jannier laughed.

"We might as well go," Lowell said. "I can't think of any way to get out of it."

When he got in his Hertz Chevrolet, he was reminded again that he was going to have to figure out how he was going to get his car down from Washington. Or would Paul Jiggs consider the car itself, a Cadillac Eldorado, unbecomingly spectacular? Maybe, instead, he should ask his father-in-law to use his influence on the Mercedes people in Germany to arrange for them to ship him one of the new Mercedes-Benz convertibles. The salesman at the Mercedes place in Washington had told him that there would be at least a nine-month's delay in delivery from the time he placed a firm order, and he hadn't wanted to wait that long.

He had always liked the Mercedes. His father had had several of them. The last of these, a 1939 convertible coupe, Craig Lowell at fifteen had wrecked after he had been chased all over Long Island, the papers reported, "by eight police cars in a fifty mile pursuit at speeds in excess of 110 miles an hour." He didn't think the new Mercedes was quite the car the prewar one had been, but there was something about the Eldorado that made people look at him, as if he had bought it with the wages of fallen women. It was time to get rid of it.

He would have to make a decision about that, and soon, and about the house and the staff in Georgetown.

He put those concerns from his mind as he concentrated on finding a place to park the rented Chevrolet near the mess.

V

(One)
The Officer's Open Mess
Fort Rucker, Alabama
2015 Hours, 31 December 1958

The officer's open mess was jammed by the time Lowell and Jannier arrived. Dale and Houston counties, which surrounded the Rucker reservation, were Bone Baptist Dry. So in addition to the officers, the Very Important Civilians from Ozark and Enterprise who couldn't drink anywhere else, were also in attendance.

Lowell started toward the stairway which led to the balcony but didn't make it. A lieutenant stopped Jannier.

He had been posted by Bellmon to look for an officer in French uniform, and to bring him to the Combat Developments tables.

Lowell spoke to Jannier in French: "My compliments to General et Madame Bellmon," he said. "Please tell them I will present my respects later."

98

"Certainly," Jannier replied.

The lieutenant was awed, as Lowell had smugly expected him to be, by someone who actually spoke a foreign language.

Then he went up the stairway to the opposite second-floor balcony, where the Army Aviation Board's tables could be found.

There were fifty-four commissioned and warrant officers assigned to the Army Aviation Board and twenty-five "senior civilians": Department of the Army employees whose classification was GS-7 or higher, thus entitling them to become members of the officer's club. Looking at the packed tables, Lowell decided that they were all in attendance. Including Jane Cassidy and a large, football player type in a dinner jacket who must be Mr. Cassidy. Mrs. Cassidy was wearing an evening dress, he noticed, the major attraction of which was her cleavage. Not vulgar, not even very low cut, but drawing the eye to the curves like a magnet. He saw her smile at him across the room and wondered if she had sensed his fascination with her chest.

More than a little uneasy, he walked quickly to the bar which had been set up to care for the balcony customers before going to the Board's tables. He had arrived, he saw, after the Board president, which was a faux pas. He wondered if Bill Roberts would take offense.

He looked down at the dance floor, and then across the room to the balcony opposite. There he saw faces he recognized—MacMillan's and Bellmon's—and somewhat cynically he concluded that the club officer, in his infinite wisdom, had physically separated the Board and Combat Developments as far as possible. There was friction between the two organizations, the Board thinking of CDO as a collection of upstarts without meaningful experience, and CDO thinking of the Board as a collection of gone-to-seed army aviators with no understanding of the role aviation was going to play in the army of the future.

Carrying his drink, Lowell went to the nearest of the Board tables. He worked his way down it and greeted the officers and civilians he knew. He came eventually to the table where Jane Cassidy and her husband were sitting.

"Good evening, Mrs. Cassidy," he said. "May I tell you how very lovely you look tonight?"

He realized that he had gone a bit overboard, but she didn't seem to be unnerved by it.

"Major, I'd like you to meet my husband," she said. "Tom, this is my new boss, the man I spent the afternoon in Atlanta with."

Tom Cassidy rose, smiling, and offered Lowell his hand. He was a good-looking, pleasant fellow, whose dinner jacket hadn't come from the racks at Sears, Roebuck.

"I'm pleased to meet you, Major," he said, with a smile. "Jane had a lot of fun with that."

"Pardon me?"

"I didn't believe her at first when she said you'd been back and forth to Atlanta this afternoon."

"All I could show her was the Fulton County Airport," Lowell said.

"Well, you thrilled her, and I thank you for it, although it made me a little jealous."

Oh, Jesus!

"I've got to catch a plane tonight," Tom Cassidy said. "Which means that I have to leave here early, drive thirty miles to Dothan, and then pray Southern is flying when I get there. It must be very nice to have your own airplane."

Lowell smiled at him, wondering why he was so relieved that Cassidy was talking about airplanes and not his wife.

"Tom's going geese shooting near Huntsville," Jane Cassidy explained.

"Now that sounds like fun," Lowell said.

"Do you hunt, Major?"

"Yes, I do. When I can find someplace to hunt."

"We've got a club, about nine hundred acres of marshland, on the flyway; and I'd be honored to have you join me sometime."

"I accept," Lowell said. "Thank you."

"Come hunting with me," Jane Cassidy said. "Bring your airplane."

"Jesus!" Tom Cassidy said, embarrassed.

"You let me shoot on nine hundred acres on the flyway, and I'll be happy to bring my airplane," Lowell replied.

"I had nothing in my mind at all about your airplane," Tom Cassidy said. "I hope you can believe that."

"Your wife was pulling your leg," Lowell said. "And now

I'd better pay my respects to Colonel Roberts and find my seat."

"You've found it," Jane Cassidy said. "I hope it's all right, but when the secretary called and asked where you wanted to sit, I put you here. I wanted you to meet Tom."

"Well, that was thinking ahead," Lowell said. "Thank you. I'll be right back."

He made his way to the head table.

"Good evening, sir," he said to Colonel Roberts, adding "ma'am," to his wife.

"You're . . . *splendiferous* . . . Craig," Jeanne Roberts said.

"Thank you, ma'am," he said.

"Yes, you are," Roberts said, dryly.

"When things settle down a little, will you come to supper?" Jeanne Roberts asked.

"I'd be delighted," Lowell said. He saw from the look on Roberts's face that the invitation had not been planned.

"There was a Frenchman looking for you today," Roberts said. "What was that all about?"

"He's come here for chopper school," Lowell said. "And then he'll stay on as a liaison officer."

"He found you, then?"

"He had a note from Colonel Hanrahan," Lowell said, "asking me to look after him."

"Hadn't you better introduce him to us, then?" Roberts asked.

"I will, sir," Lowell said. "He's across the room, as General Bellmon's guest."

"I see," Roberts said. He obviously didn't like that at all. "He's a friend of Bellmon's, is that it?"

"I believe General Jiggs arranged it, sir," Lowell said.

"You could have gone with Combat Developments tonight," Roberts said, "if you'd preferred."

"I'm assigned to the Board, sir," Lowell said. "And I would have been out of place over there."

Roberts, he thought, was making no secret that he questioned Lowell's loyalty to the Board.

Their antagonism went back to the day Roberts had recruited Lowell for army aviation. Fully aware that Lowell's career was then in very bad shape, Roberts had wanted him in aviation for two reasons. He had political influence, and Paul Jiggs had told him Lowell was the best young staff officer he had ever met. Roberts and Lowell had disliked each other at sight— almost a chemical reaction—and things had not gotten any better between them over the years.

Roberts, a West Pointer, had presumed that Lowell, a non-West Pointer whom he had rescued from military oblivion, would align himself out of gratitude, with his faction. Lowell, however, was not only an unrepentant sinner but had made it clear almost immediately after graduating from flight school that he did not share Roberts's vision of army aviation's future. So far as Roberts was concerned, Lowell was both an incredibly lucky wise-ass to still be in the army at all and entirely too close to Bob Bellmon, the head of Combat Developments.

They had already had a clash, on Lowell's first day of duty with the Board.

"I'm not simply putting the best face on a *fait accompli,* Lowell," Roberts said then, making reference to General E. Z. Black's unexpected, nearly incredible order assigning Lowell to the Board as project officer for rocket-armed helicopters, "I really think you're the man to run the rocket-armed helicopter program."

That was true. Obnoxious as he was, he was the best man for the job.

"Thank you, sir."

"Having said that, I will add that under the circumstances, you can have any assets at my disposal to carry out your job."

"Thank you again."

"And having said that, I feel constrained to add that there is no room in the Board for your flamboyance. There will be no clever little deals, no clever little shortcuts, no deviation from standard Board operating procedure. I hope you understand that."

"Yes, sir."

"For your general information," Roberts said, "Big Bad Bird personnel and equipment have been transferred to the Board."

"I didn't know that," Lowell said.

"Neither do they."

"I see."

"Is there anything in addition to the men, and their equipment, that you think you need?"

Lowell was ready for the question. "There is one officer I would like to have transferred to work with me, Colonel."

"Who?"

"Captain Parker."

"Out of the question."

"May I ask why, sir?"

"For one thing, he knows nothing whatever about this project," Roberts said. "And for another, I dislike cronyism."

"Captain Parker, in addition to being one of my best friends, is a highly skilled, highly intelligent officer who is at the moment being underutilized."

"He's an instructor pilot," Roberts said. "You don't think that's important?"

In fact, Major Craig W. Lowell did not. He had a number of heretical ideas, but perhaps the most heretical—in the sense that it was the one most likely to see him burned at the stake—was his feeling about flying generally, and army aviators in particular.

So far as Lowell was concerned, flying was too romanticized. From the beginning of flight there'd been too much glamor about the guys that roamed the skies. You could see it in the early movies like *Dawn Patrol*, where handsome young men flew off to their deaths with silk scarfs flapping in the slipstream and smiles on their faces. The words of the Army Air Corps song in War II was another instance of the myth, "We live in fame or go down in flame."

Lowell was qualified as both a fixed and rotary-wing aviator. He had flown multiengine planes, seaplanes, and planes with skis, and had a Special Instrument Certificate. That experience had taught him that flying was a skill that could be acquired by anyone with average intelligence and reasonable depth perception and coordination.

As far as he was concerned, there was no justification whatever for the rule that pilots had to be either commissioned or warrant officers. The Luftwaffe and the Royal Air Force and even the U.S. Marine Corps had done very well with enlisted pilots. The army entrusted a multimillion dollar tank with a crew of four to a sergeant, while it insisted that a $75,000 two-seater observation plane required the ministrations of an officer and a gentleman.

Certainly, instructor pilots were important. Stripped of the heroic bullshit, they were probably nearly as important as a second lieutenant at Fort Benning teaching a sergeant how to take a squad of eight men and blow up a squad of the enemy in a pillbox. There was no question in Lowell's mind that it was infinitely more difficult to teach someone of limited intelligence and education how to lead men into a situation where they are liable to lose their lives than it was to teach someone of above-average intelligence when to lower the flaps and chop the throttle on an approach.

But he could not say this to Colonel William Roberts, who had been an army aviator since the very first Piper Cubs had been leased to the army.

"I think, sir," Lowell said, "that because of his experience commanding tanks in combat, Captain Parker would be of more value to the army in developing an aerial antitank weapon than he is sitting in the right seat of an H-13 teaching some kid how to fly."

Even that had been too much. Roberts's face had turned white, his lips had thinned, and for a moment Lowell had been sure Roberts was about to lose his temper. But he kept control of himself.

"You can't have him," Roberts said, finally, flatly, icily. "Unless, of course, you go over my head. Is that your intention?"

"You will permit me, Colonel, to respectfully take offense?" Lowell replied angrily. "You have no reason to believe that I would go over your head."

"I'm pleased to hear that, Major," Roberts said. "Have you anything else?"

"You recruited Parker when you recruited me," Lowell said. "What have you got against him? Or, for that matter, me?"

"I have nothing against either of you," Roberts had said. "But there is no place in the army for cronyism."

That had happened only three days before. Tonight Roberts was apparently still nursing the rage he had worked himself into when he had had time to consider that he had been assigned an officer he really hadn't wanted, and whom he would not be able to control completely.

Roberts did not ask him to sit down, so Lowell returned to his table. He found himself sitting beside Jane Cassidy.

"I hope," Tom Cassidy said, "that this isn't a breach of military manners, but I've been wondering about that medal." He pointed to the medal suspended from the purple ribbon. "Is it all right to ask what it is?"

"It's beautiful!" Jane Cassidy said. He could feel her breath on him; she smelled like spearmint. "I'm glad he asked, faux pas or not."

"It's Greek," Lowell said, smiling, pleased that he had not responded as he normally did, by saying that it was "second prize in the All-Army bowling contest" or some other wise-ass remark.

"Oh? And what do they call it?" Tom Cassidy asked.

"The Big Round Medal," he said, smiling, unable to stop himself, then he forced a laugh. "It's the Order of St. George and St. Andrew," he explained.

"Is that gold?" Tom Cassidy asked.

"I believe it is," Lowell said. He took the ribbon from around his neck and handed it to Jane Cassidy. Their fingers touched. There was absolutely no reason that he should be excited by the innocent touch, he told himself, but he was.

You have just jumped on the soda wagon, Romeo.

He was saved from further discussion of the medal when lines of white-jacketed GIs, moonlighting as waiters, began to serve dinner. Dinner (roast beef, baked potatoes, French green beans, a salad, and a dessert) was included in the price of the party ticket. When Lowell saw it, his mind groaned at the thought of the perfectly pink standing ribs, the smoked turkey, and the salmon flown in from Scotland that Hester, the bone-thin black woman who was his cook in the house in George-town, would have put on his table in Washington an hour or so ago at the party at which he, the cohost, would be missing.

The party had been Constance's idea. Constance was his next-door neighbor in Georgetown, the thirty-two-year-old wife of a sixty-eight-year-old United States senator. Rather than do something common, such as going to Burning Tree, or the Club on F Street, where they would have to mingle with the riffraff, Constance had decided that, provided Craig was willing, there was enough room to have a "nice" party for the nicer people in both of their town houses. All they would have to do would be hire someone to build a stairway over the brick wall that divided their adjoining gardens.

If Craig would provide the food, she would provide the booze, which would cause the guests to move toward her town house in the shank of the evening. With the bar in her house, his house would be empty.

"With a little bit of luck," Constance had said, "I can have you tucked in bed by the time they're finished singing 'Auld Lang Syne.'"

One of the last things he had seen before he had been sent in disgrace to Rucker was the bill for the temporary stairway. It had cost him $2,970.60.

Constance, he thought, admiringly, was a survivor. When news of their affair had reached the Chief of Staff, she had accepted it philosophically.

"We were getting a bit obvious, I suppose," she said. "Does this mean I can't go ahead with the party?"

At this moment, he thought, Constance was already looking at the younger males at the party, picking out the one she would entice into bed. *His* bed. Constance had planned the evening carefully. The only thing that was going to be changed was the stud.

For reasons he couldn't imagine, he rarely had complaints about food he got from an army mess, even if it had been prepared by an unshaven sergeant on a gasoline-fueled field range. But he almost always found food from officer's open messes to be nearly inedible. He did so again. The only thing he could eat was the baked potato.

After dinner, he was expected to dance with the wives of the officers and civilians at his table. There were six of them, and only one said, "perhaps later." He danced with Jane Cassidy last, and it wasn't until they were on the dance floor that he realized she had been drinking. She was tight. *Tiddly.* Proper, but *tiddly.*

He was uncomfortable dancing with her. There was no place for his hand but on her bare back, and her back was warm and soft. And then he got an erection. He wasn't sure she knew, since they were dancing with inches separating them—but it enraged and shamed him.

And then, when they were walking up the stairs back to the table, she turned to him and said: "I understand that's an involuntary reaction. But wipe that guilty scowl off your face or my husband will be suspicious."

He did not sit down again. He asked to be excused. He had people to see, he said.

(Two)

Lowell went down the stairs to the main dining room to look for Phil and Antoinette Parker. A seating map had been posted on the wall, showing the location of various units within the club. After he'd looked at it, he headed for the cafeteria. Tonight, the cafeteria was "Drawing Room C" and had been set aside for the officers of the hospital and their ladies.

He looked in vain for the Parkers for several minutes until he realized the Parkers would be with the school. Tonight, Toni would be the wife of Captain Phil Parker, rather than Dr. Parker, U.S. Army contract surgeon.

It took him another couple of minutes in the main ballroom to spot them. He made his way along the edge of the dance floor, and then bent over Toni and whispered in her ear: "Doctor, I have this little pimple sort of thing on the tip of my . . ."

"God!" she said, looking up at him, laughing. Then she got up and he led her to the dance floor.

While they were dancing, she snorted in his ear.

"Most ladies tell me I'm a very good dancer," he said.

"I just realized why people are looking at us."

"Oh, I don't think they are," he said.

"We are," she said softly, amused, in her luxurious Bostonian accent, "what they call the cynosure of all eyes. And until just now I thought it was because the dinge lady doctor was dancing with the white guy in the Imperial Hussar's uniform," she said.

"Screw 'em," he said.

"You *are* spectacular, Craig," she said. "But that isn't it."

"What is it? What is 'it'?"

"You're sort of a hero," she said, and then corrected herself. "Not sort of. A hero, period."

"I beg your pardon?"

"To the officers Phil works with. Because of what you did at the funeral. You did something they can only dream of. More important, you got away with it."

"Come on, Toni," Lowell said, embarrassed.

"When we go back to the table, can I show you off? I know Phil would like it."

"No, you can't."

She chuckled. "I will anyway."

"You send them to medical school, let them wear shoes,

and the first thing you know they're running your life," he said.

"Nature abhors a vacuum," she said.

"Just dance," he said. "Just dance."

"I'm more than a little surprised that you actually showed up."

"Command performance," he said.

"Phil, too," she said. "He hates these things."

"I understand social gatherings of this sort are very important to the ladies, and the military axiom is that a well-laid husband is an efficient officer."

"Then you and Phil should be generals," she said.

"Give us time," he said.

"You really believe it, don't you?" Toni said, suddenly serious, and a little sad. "The both of you. That you'll be generals."

"I believe there's a chance," he said.

"And that's so important to you?"

"Yeah. I guess it is," he said. "I didn't realize how much the army meant to me until I was about to be thrown out."

"I don't understand that," she said. "For some of these people, sure. It's social security, and you get to wear a pretty uniform that tells the world how important you are. Do what you're told and the system takes care of you. That's very important to a lot of people. But it shouldn't be to people like you and Phil."

"How about people like Phil and me and Jiggs?"

"Jiggs too. I don't understand any of you bright ones. Does that make me a disloyal wife, do you think, Craig?"

"It makes you a smart wife, and there aren't a hell of a lot of them around."

The music stopped. Toni put her arm in his, and led him back to the table.

(Three)

Major Craig Lowell was uncomfortable at the Parker table. Toni had been right. He was sort of hero to Phil's fellow officers. He was the guy who had the balls to tell the system to go fuck itself and had, as a result, saved the armed helicopter from being squashed by the goddamned air force. So there was a steady stream of drinks, more than he wanted. When it became apparent to him that the liquor was getting to him, he excused himself by saying that he had to get back to the Board's tables.

On the way to the stairway to the second floor, he changed his mind. He was not anxious to return to sit beside Jane Cassidy, especially now that he had had more to drink. She was really getting to him, actually making his heart beat faster, and under those circumstances being half in the bag was very dangerous indeed.

What he needed, he decided, was something to counter the effects of the liquor. He went to the bar, a long, curving affair with windows behind it that looked out on the officer's swimming pool, and beyond that, to the scraped-away land where the contractors were about to build more dependent housing.

At the crowded bar there was one empty stool between two groups of drinkers, but there wasn't enough room to climb onto it without pushing his way in.

A red-jacketed bartender, a black man in his thirties, one of the regular bartenders, came down the bar.

"If you gentlemen would be good enough to move down just a foot or so," he said to one of the groups of drinkers, "the major could sit down."

They moved, but not without giving both the bartender and Lowell dirty looks.

"What can I get you, Major Lowell?" the bartender asked with a smile. Lowell was surprised that the bartender knew his name.

"A large glass of straight soda water with a couple of large squirts of bitters in it, please," Lowell said. "Evil companions have been plying me with spirits."

The bartender chuckled and filled the order.

Without knowing it, Lowell enjoyed a very good reputation among the black troops on the post. He had come to their attention the first time he had flown to Rucker to see Phil and had immediately become "the white dude with his own *personal* Aero Commander." He had brought further attention to himself when they learned that he visited the post for the sole reason of visiting Captain Philip S. Parker IV and his wife, the lady doctor.

There was, especially among the senior black noncoms, a good deal of resentment toward do-gooders—a do-gooder being defined as someone who publicly professed admiration for his black brothers-in-arms and devotion to their welfare. The blacks knew that stuff was patronizing and humiliating.

But the white dude's friendship with the Parkers, they had come to understand, was not that sort of thing. Captain Philip Sheridan Parker IV and his wife were held in high esteem by the black military community. The old-timers knew that Captain Philip Sheridan Parker was the fifth generation of soldiers holding that name. His great-great-grandfather, after he'd ridden with General Philip Tecumseh Sheridan, had named his firstborn after the great cavalry officer. First Sergeant Philip Sheridan Parker had gone up Kettle and San Juan hills with the regular 10th U.S. Cavalry (Colored) and Teddy Roosevelt. First Sergeant Parker was buried in the cemetery at Fort Riley, Kansas, between his father, Sergeant Moses Parker, and his son, Colonel Philip S. Parker, Jr., who had commanded the 179th Infantry in France in World War I.

Colonel Philip Sheridan Parker III had commanded the 393rd Tank Destroyer Regiment in General Porky Waterford's famed "Hell's Circus" 40th Armored Division in World War II. Captain Philip Sheridan Parker IV had earned his promotion to captain at twenty-four in command of a tank company on the battlefield in Korea. In other words, he did not need the benevolent interest of a white major.

The feeling among the black troops and officers was that "if Phil Parker calls the guy a friend, he's got to be all right."

Lowell extended a bill to the bartender.

"Soda water's free," the bartender said, waving the money away.

"In that case, Sergeant," Lowell said, "I'll give you all my business."

Lowell sipped at his bitter soda and stared out the windows behind the bar—fascinated by the flickering lights—until he sensed that someone was standing behind him. He glanced over his shoulder, and then got off his stool.

"Major Lowell, I believe," the young woman said. She was, Lowell thought, a younger version of Jane Cassidy. Long-legged, lithe, blond, and exquisitely feminine. A genuine Alabama magnolia blossom, he thought. She was wearing a simple white evening dress with a string of pearls plunging into the valley of her breasts. The pearls were real, he saw, and so was the diamond on their clasp.

"May I be of some service?" Lowell said, his voice at once formal and gentle.

"Do you know who I am?" she asked.

"Yes," Lowell said, "I do."

"You could offer me a drink," Melody Dutton Greer said. "I don't belong here anymore."

Without taking his eyes from her, Lowell raised his hand over his head and loudly snapped his fingers. The bartender who had served him the soda looked down the bar in annoyance, even anger, and then when he saw who it was, hurried down the bar.

"The lady would like a drink," Lowell said.

"What can I get you, Mrs. Greer?" the sergeant asked.

"What is Major Lowell drinking?" she asked.

"Soda water and bitters," Lowell replied.

"In that case, I think I'll have a scotch and soda," Melody Greer said.

"Yes, ma'am," the bartender sergeant said. He quickly made the drink, and after he returned and handed it to her, he said: "Ma'am, if you'll let me, I'd like to buy you that. I knew the lieutenant. He was a fine officer, a fine gentleman."

She looked at the sergeant and then at Lowell, and then she said: "My mother has the baby. He's asleep, of course, and I didn't want to be with them. And I just couldn't stand being alone in the house. Can you understand that?"

"Yes, ma'am," the bartender said.

"Certainly," Lowell said.

"And I thought maybe I would see you," she said to Lowell, "so I could say 'thank you.'"

"You owe me no thanks," Lowell said.

"Coming here seemed like a pretty good idea an hour ago," Melody Dutton Greer said, uncomfortably. "I'm not so sure, now."

Lowell said nothing.

"We had reservations," Melody Greer went on. "I wrote the check for them."

"You've missed dinner, I'm afraid," Lowell said.

"I don't need dinner," she said.

"I can get you something, ma'am," the sergeant said. "Be happy to."

"Thank you, no," she said. "And thank you for the drink."

"My pleasure, ma'am," he said and excused himself.

"I went out to the cemetery this afternoon," she said.

There was a pause before Lowell replied.

"You had to go, of course," he said. "But don't make a habit of it."

She looked at him with anger in her eyes.

"You have to let go," he said, simply.

"That's easier said than done," she said.

"Yes," he said.

"How soon did you let go?"

"My wife is buried in her family crypt," Lowell said softly. "There's a marble bench down there. For two nights I slept on it, with a bottle of scotch."

"And then?"

"And then I let go," he said.

"Just like that?"

"Just like that," he said. "I faced the fact that she was not going to come out of her crypt, that things weren't ever going to be the way they had been."

"What did you do?"

"I beg your pardon?"

"I mean, what did you do?"

"Oh," he said. "I went back to Korea."

"To the war, you mean?"

"Yes."

"I don't have a war to go to," she said, simply.

He did not reply.

"Do you think it was a mistake for me to come here?" she asked.

"I think Ed would understand," Lowell said, after a moment.

"But the others won't? Is that what you're saying?"

"I don't know," he said. "I think you can count on somebody being shocked."

"I told my father today that I would have to go out to Texas and close the house, and he said he'd already taken care of that. So I can't even go out there."

"I thought you said you were alone in your house here?" Lowell asked, immediately wishing he had thought before he spoke.

"I was," Melody explained. "We ... *I* ... have a house here, too. In Woody Dells. It was our wedding present from my father."

"Oh," he said. Now that she'd told him, he remembered hearing about the wedding present.

"Do you think I should just walk back out of here?" she asked.

"Do you care what anybody thinks?"

"I don't know," she said.

"You're here," he said. "You can't take that back."

"But I am going to shock some people?"

"Yes, I think so."

"Then I might as well get it over with," she said, and drained her glass. She put it on the bar, and looked up at him. She touched his arm. "Thank you, Major Lowell," she said.

He averted his eyes from hers and found himself looking down her dress, shamed the moment he realized that her breasts were unrestrained beneath it, and that a mental picture of her without the dress popped into his mind.

"I'll go with you," he said, offering his arm.

She took it, and together they walked out of the bar and toward the stairs to the balcony. They were almost there when Lowell heard his name being called, and then recognized the voice. He put his hand on Melody's hand, which was holding his arm, and stopped.

It was Jean-Philippe Jannier, in what Lowell thought again was his rather comic-looking French dress uniform.

"I'll be with you in minute, Jannier," Lowell said. Melody looked at the Frenchman curiously, which Lowell attributed to the uniform.

"May I present," Lowell said, in French, "Madame Greer."

"I have the honor of knowing Madame," Jannier said, reaching for Melody's hand and bowing over it. "May I have the privilege, my dear Madame Greer," he went on, "of offering my most sincere condolences on the loss of your husband?"

There's no two ways about it, Lowell thought. *The frogs have it over us, language wise. That would have sounded ridiculous in English.*

"Thank you very much," Melody said, in English. Lowell was surprised at first that she understood what Jannier had said, until he remembered that Melody had been in Algeria with Greer.

"It was my privilege, Lowell, to have served with the late Lieutenant Greer in Algeria. He was a valiant officer and a distinguished gentleman, and I am proud to say that I claimed him as a friend."

Is that the straight poop, I wonder, Jannier, or have you homed in on the boobs?

"*Vous-êtes très gentil, M. le Capitaine,*" Melody said, in not bad French.

"I wasn't aware you spoke French," Lowell said, in French.

"Enough," she said, easily, in French, "to get by saying things like that."

"I stand at your command, my dear Madame Greer," Jannier said. "To render what service you may ask of me in your grief."

"Now that you mention it, Jannier," Lowell said in English, "you've solved a bad problem." Both of them looked at him in surprise. Lowell switched back to French. "What I am going to say, when we go upstairs and face General Bellmon and the others, is that *you* convinced Melody it was her duty to go through with the plans she and Greer had made to entertain you, their old friend, on New Year's Eve."

"I am at your service, of course," Jannier said. "But I don't quite understand."

"Mrs. Greer did not want to spend the night alone. So she came here. I am afraid that some people might not understand."

"*D'accord,*" Jannier said. "If that is your pleasure, Madame."

"Major Lowell has been too polite to tell me I made an ass of myself," Melody said.

"You are incapable, Madame, of doing anything in bad taste," Jannier said.

"You'd better call me, 'Melody,'" she said. "Since we are such good pals."

"I am honored, Melody," Jannier said. "May I ask a question, Lowell?"

"Certainly," Lowell said.

"Is that what you intended doing, telling General Bellmon that you were responsible for Melody being here."

"He couldn't do that," Melody answered for him. "Everyone would think he was trying to get in my pants."

Lowell realized for the first time that Melody Greer had gotten the courage to come to the party from a bottle.

"Well," Jannier said, drolly, "no one will think that of me. I am French, and everyone knows that Frenchmen have no interest in beautiful women."

"I love the both of you," Melody said, and took both their arms as they started up the stairs to the balcony.

(Four)

Major General Paul Jiggs sought out and danced with Antoinette Parker, for several reasons. For one, the commanding general should have at least one dance with the wife of a company-grade officer. Somewhat cynically, he also thought dancing with Phil Parker's wife killed two birds with one sedate fox trot, for a commanding general should also be seen dancing with the wife of any officer who happened to be black, Hispanic, American Indian, or a member of some other minority group. There was a Chinese-American major, he recalled, in the Department of Flight Instruction, and a Korean-American in the Flight Safety Section.

There were very few people, he thought, who would really believe that he was dancing with Toni for the very simple reason that he was an old friend of her father-in-law. Jiggs wondered if he really qualified as a friend of Colonel Philip Sheridan Parker III. He had been a young shavetail when he had met then Major Parker at the Ground General School at Riley the summer he'd graduated from the Point. Among his other distinctions, General Jiggs was a graduate of the last course in advanced equestrianism ever offered by the U.S. Army, and Major Parker had been the officer-in-charge.

Was that position a distinction, Jiggs had often wondered. Had Parker been given that privilege because he was the son, and grandson, and great-grandson of cavalrymen, or because, with horses and cavalry on their way out of the army, it had been a suitable assignment for a darky who had somehow wound up with a major's gold leaves on his epaulets?

He'd learned a hell of a lot more than how to ride a horse from Major Parker, although he'd learned that well enough to qualify for the Olympic equestrian team. While Parker was probably not a dark-skinned Von Clausewitz, he came damned close. He had given Jiggs an understanding of the role of cavalry in warfare that few other people in the army had.

The tall, stiff-backed, curt-mannered Parker had been the first to see in Second Lieutenant Jiggs the seed of whatever it was that separated those who were destined to run the army, to control its direction, from those who would spend their careers doing what they were told to do to the best of their ability.

Jiggs could still quote from memory from his first efficiency report as an officer. He had been friendly with Parker, but he knew that would have nothing to do with what Parker would have to say about him as an officer. He had been stunned by what Parker had written:

> Second Lieutenant Jiggs is a trim officer of average height. He demonstrates the personal characteristics required of an officer. He is possessed of an unusual intelligence which permits him to evaluate circumstances and form from them a well-thought-out plan of action far more quickly than can be reasonably expected from someone of his age and experience. Coupled with his natural ability as a leader, this combines to suggest that he is an officer of unusual potential. The undersigned considers him without qualification capable of assuming the responsibilities of a captain in combat. The undersigned recommends that future assignments and professional education of this officer be made taking into consideration his value to the military service when he is a senior officer rather more than the immediate needs of the service.
>
> > P. S. Parker III
> > Major, Cavalry
> > Commandant

"What do they call these, General?" Toni Parker said in his ear. "Duty dances?"

It was not the sort of thing a captain's wife is supposed to say to the General. But then, Toni was not a typical captain's wife, and it also occurred to Jiggs that Toni had probably had a drink too many.

"New Year's Eve," Paul Jiggs replied, "gives me the bad mouth, too, Toni."

"Sorry," she said.

"Is it anything in particular?" he asked.

"Between us?"

"Between us," he said.

"I wish I was at the staff party at Mass General tonight,

rather than dancing with an army general here. No offense," she said.

It took Jiggs a moment to translate that. When Toni had married Phil, she had been an associate professor of pathology at the Harvard Medical School and on the staff of Massachusetts General Hospital.

Jiggs chuckled, and then asked: "The hospital giving you trouble?"

"No. They're glad to have me. I am a very big fish in a little pond. I meant that I'd rather have it the other way."

"Whither thou goest, I will go," he said. "I guess that's tougher on someone like you than on somebody else."

"I've got the sorries for Phil," she said.

"Anything in particular?"

"Craig wanted him to go out to the Board and work with him," Toni said. "Roberts said no."

"He say why?"

"He said something about cronyism, according to Craig, but Craig thinks he was simply putting him in his place. He and Roberts have never gotten along."

"How do you know that?"

"I was there," Toni said, "the first time they met. At Riley." She laughed deep in her throat. "That was the night I accepted Phil's proposal of marriage."

"And Bill Roberts was there?" Jiggs asked, surprised.

"Phil and Craig were on, forgive the expression, the shit-list," Toni said. "In nothing assignments at Riley. They were living in a house Craig had bought in one of those picture window developments. I was commuting out there every other weekend, and I'd almost had Phil convinced to resign."

Jiggs knew the story, but he let her go on.

"Craig had hooked up," Toni went on, "with a redheaded banker. We were having Sunday afternoon dinner. Large steaks and lots of martinis, and then the phone rang, and it was Roberts, and he invited himself and his wife over."

"Why did he do that?" Jiggs asked, feeling dishonest.

"Because not everybody in the Armor Establishment, and I think that included you, General, thought they should be drawn and quartered."

"Meaning what?"

"Meaning that somebody had told Roberts to recruit them for aviation, somebody he didn't dare tell 'no.'"

"Would you believe, Toni," Jiggs said, "that the decision to recruit Lowell and Phil for aviation was for the good of the army?"

"Is that an admission you were responsible?"

"I was one of those responsible," Jiggs said. "I think they both know that."

"Roberts didn't like having to do it," she said.

"Colonel Roberts sometimes thinks he owns army aviation," Jiggs said. "I don't think he resents Lowell or Phil, any more than he resents me or Bob Bellmon. We're all Johnny-come-latelies."

"He can't get at you or Bellmon," she said. "But he *can* tell Lowell he can't have Phil transferred."

"What Phil needs at this point in his career is a routine assignment like that," Jiggs said, telling her what he had concluded before sending Parker to the school to teach the final phase in the Cargo Helicopter Course. "He'll show up against the mediocrities."

"So he tells me," she said. "But do you know what it's doing to him?"

"No," he said.

"He got drunk after Lowell told him that Roberts had refused to have him transferred. Very drunk. The picturesque phrase he used to describe his opinion of his usefulness made reference to teats on a boar hog."

"Somebody has to be an instructor pilot," Jiggs said.

"I notice Craig isn't doing it," she said. "What does Phil have to do, steal a helicopter?"

He decided to be brutal.

"What Phil doesn't need is anyone thinking he's somebody's pet nigger."

"Now you sound like the Colonel," she said. There was no question that she meant Colonel Philip Sheridan Parker III.

"I hope so," Jiggs said. "He's one of the brighter men I know."

"I shouldn't drink," she said. "It causes my mouth to runneth over."

"It's New Year's Eve," he said. "Originally a pagan rite where everybody got drunk and danced naked to take their minds off the threat posed by the saber-toothed tiger."

She laughed. "I'm sorry, General," she said.

"Unless you want me to start calling you 'doctor,' you'd

better start calling me 'Paul,'" he said. "At least while we're dancing and exchanging confidences."

"I've got a confidence for you," she said. "You've always reminded me of someone, and I never could figure out who. Now I know."

"I can hardly wait," he said.

"My father," she said. "He has the same extraordinary ability to make people bawl themselves out when they're making asses of themselves."

"You don't think I think you're making an ass of yourself, do you?"

"You see, you see?" Toni said.

VI

(One)
Balcony "B"
The Officer's Open Mess
Fort Rucker, Alabama
2250 Hours, 31 December 1958

The head table of the Aviation Combat Developments group was presided over by Brigadier General and Mrs. Bellmon. At the head of the table, beside Barbara Bellmon, was Colonel Tim F. Brandon. Roxy MacMillan, in a tight, pinkish gown with waves of lace framing her ample, freckled bosom, sat beside Bellmon. Major Sanford T. Felter, wearing all the decorations to which he was entitled, plus the heavy gold rope of an aide-de-camp to the President of the United States, sat beside her. Sharon sat beside Brandon, and on her other side, MacMillan.

General Bellmon, Lieutenant Colonel MacMillan, and Major Felter wore the blue mess uniform. Colonel Tim F. Brandon was in blues, with a white shirt and bow tie. He wore his ribbons. The highest of these, Lowell saw as he approached the table, was the Legion of Merit, which he regarded as a decoration customarily awarded to senior officers who had spent six months on foreign shores without once contracting a social disease.

Barbara Bellmon, as Lowell had known she would, responded with exquisite grace, tact, and understanding to the appearance of Melody Greer at the New Year's Eve party.

"Oh, Melody," she said, "I'm so glad you decided to come. I was afraid you wouldn't."

And, as he had also expected, Brigadier General Robert F. Bellmon obviously wished the widow hadn't come.

Lowell kissed Barbara. Neither he nor Barbara were kissing types, but they had learned long before that it annoyed Bob when they exchanged noisy smacks, and they did so now with relish.

That set off a line of kisses. Having kissed Barbara, he had to kiss Sharon and Roxy as well. It occurred to him that it was an extraordinary coincidence that the only three women in the world he didn't mind kissing were at the same table. He then congratulated MacMillan on his promotion, sincerely, for in many ways he liked and admired the simple Scot and was happy for him and Roxy.

Lowell realized that there were more medals for valor on display here than at any other table in the club. The army didn't pass out that many Distinguished Service Crosses, and the one on his own lapel was duplicated on the lapels of Felter and MacMillan. And that didn't count Mac's Medal of Honor, the only one on the post. Nor the Medaille Militaire and Legion d'Honneur on Jean-Philippe Jannier's blouse. Nor the Silver Stars and Bronze Stars and Purple Hearts on just about every other Combat Developments officer. There was an exception, of course. To judge by the ribbons adorning the breast of Colonel Tim F. Brandon, the Pentagon Press agent, the man had somehow managed to rise to colonel without ever having heard a shot fired in anger.

He made the effort and smiled at Colonel Brandon. Except for Brandon, he liked everybody here, and he decided to stay.

If Bill Roberts didn't like it, fuck him. War between them had already been declared.

Peace in our time, he thought, *is just not possible*.

"Madame le General," Lowell said, "would you do me the honor of dancing with me?"

"Only if you promise to do something that will make people gasp," Barbara Bellmon said, giving her husband a broad smile as she got to her feet.

Major Craig Lowell and Madame le General danced very close with Barbara's lips next to his ear—like teenagers in love—because they knew that annoyed Bob Bellmon.

Barbara told him she didn't know what to think about Melody showing up, and hoped that it would simply be passed over.

"But don't believe for a minute that I swallow that tale about her being here because of Jannier," she said. "And it wasn't at all nice of you to set him up like that."

"If I had said I had asked her, you know what people would have thought."

"I wouldn't have," Barbara said.

"You would have stood alone," Lowell said.

"Probably," she agreed, and chuckled.

Once he had danced with Barbara, he had to dance with Sharon Felter and Roxy MacMillan. Sharon Felter told him that she was happy "the way things have turned out for you" and that she wanted to thank Craig for making Sandy come to Rucker.

Roxy MacMillan had had enough to drink to put her in a jovial mood.

She told him, as they danced, that the first time she'd seen a blue mess uniform was the one he had worn at Knox.

"Mac looks good in his," he said. "He even looks dignified."

"We're a long way from Mauch Chunk," Roxy said.

"We're all a long way from where we were," he said. "You even learned to play a passable round of golf."

PFC Craig Lowell had met Captain MacMillan's wife on the Constabulary Golf Course in Bad Nauheim, Germany, where he had then been an assistant pro.

"It's going to be good having you around, Romeo," Roxy said, laughing.

"Thank you, ma'am," he said.

"Who's going to replace Bob Bellmon?" she asked, suddenly serious. "You must have heard."

"I don't know, Roxy," he said, truthfully. "Hainey, I would guess. If Bellmon knows, he hasn't confided in me."

"Mac had the nutty idea they'd give it to him."

After a moment, Lowell said, "It calls for a bird colonel."

"Mac's sometimes not too bright about things like that," Roxy said.

"Mac wouldn't like the job if he had it," he said.

"Tell that to him," she said, a little bitterly, and then lightened her voice. "We do go back a long way, Romeo, don't we?" Roxy asked.

"Yes, we do."

"You better go back where you belong, Craig," she said.

"I like it where I am," he said.

"The story I get is that you've promised to behave," Roxy said. "Behaving means being with the Board. You're just going to make things worse with Roberts by hanging around with us."

"I'm very afraid you are very perceptive," Lowell said.

"Take me back to the table, and then go back where you belong," she said.

"Your wish is my command," he said.

Holding hands, they started back to the stairs to the balcony. Then, all of a sudden, Lowell pulled Roxy toward the bar.

"Where the hell are we going?" she asked.

"I just solved a problem," he said. "You just agree with me, understand?"

"I'd like to know what the hell's going on," she grumbled, but followed him into the bar.

Melody Dutton Greer was sitting on a bar stool. With her were Captain Jean-Philippe Jannier, Warrant Officer Junior Grade William B. Franklin, and several junior officers he didn't know, but whom he presumed were friends of the late Lieutenant Edward C. Greer. Melody Greer was visibly tight.

Roxy saw this and said so: "Christ, she's bombed!"

"Good evening, children," Lowell said. "I am about to issue orders, so everybody pay close attention."

The young officers he didn't know looked at him resentfully.

"Yes, sir," Melody Greer giggled and saluted.

"Melody," Lowell said, "when you're ready to go, which means when you finish that drink, Jean-Philippe will drive you home in your car. Bill will follow you in his car, so he can bring Jean-Philippe home. Is that clear, or does someone have a question?"

"I can drive myself home," Melody said, sharply.

"Listen to him, honey," Roxy said.

"Yes, sir," Melody said, saluting Roxy and giggling again.

"My car is at Hanchey, Major," Franklin said. "I'll need a ride out to get it."

Lowell put his hand in pocket, came up with the keys to the rented Chevrolet, and handed them to Franklin.

"Take mine," he said. "It's in the parking lot, way at the end by the chapel."

"Bring it back here?" Franklin asked.

"Pick me up in the morning for breakfast," Lowell said. "Then we'll go to Hanchey and get yours."

"Yes, sir."

"Well, that's settled then," Roxy said.

Melody Dutton Greer took Lowell's arm and pulled his face to hers. She kissed him on the cheek.

"When you're right, you're right," she said. She turned to Roxy. "Will you tell the Bellmons good night for me?"

"Sure thing, honey," Roxy said.

Melody slid off the stool and looked as if she was going to stumble. Jannier and Franklin caught her arms. Then they all walked out of the bar together and to the door.

"Now you go back to the Board," Roxy said.

"Yes, ma'am," Lowell said.

"You handled that pretty well, Romeo," Roxy said. "Sometimes you can be a very nice guy."

He climbed the stairs back to the Board area. When he got to his table, there were three men, two officers, and a civilian there.

Introductions were made. The officers were a major and a captain from the Department of Tactics, and the civilian was "with the Enterprise Banking Company." They were the other members of Tom Cassidy's hunting party.

"I was hoping to see you again before we left," Tom Cassidy said.

"I'm glad I got back," Lowell said.

"I'm trying to make up my mind whether I want to go home, or stay," Jane Cassidy said.

"There's no reason for you to go home," Tom Cassidy said.

"And if you go home," the banker argued, "Phyllis will think she has to go home." He turned to Lowell. "My wife is with the others . . ."

"The hunting widows' social club," Jane Cassidy said, a little bitterly.

"Oh, do whatever you want, Jane," Tom Cassidy said, impatiently.

"Go catch your plane," Jane Cassidy said.

The men shook hands with Lowell. Cassidy kissed his wife.

"Happy New Year," she said.

The men left.

Jane Cassidy looked up at Lowell.

"Logic tells me that I should get my coat and go home," she said. "But he was right, if I did that, Phyllis would take it as disapproval. Would you mind if I stayed?"

"Of course not," he said.

"In that case," she said, "you'll have to face the hunting widows with me. So that Phyllis will understand that I approve."

"All right," he said.

She took his arm as they went down the stairs. Then as they walked past the dance floor on their way to the Department of Tactics tables, she suddenly turned into his arms.

"They're playing a waltz," she said. "And I'll bet you can waltz."

"Can't everybody?"

She laughed a little bitterly.

They waltzed. Craig Lowell waltzed well. He had spent three hours every Saturday afternoon in his thirteenth year at a dancing school. It was his studied judgment that most women who liked to waltz did so badly. Jane Cassidy was the exception. They began sedately, but as they sensed the good dancer in each other they began to swoop gracefully around the room. By the time the dance was over, there were only four couples on the floor. The others had stopped to watch, and when the dance was over, there was applause.

Holding hands, Jane curtsied, and Lowell bowed elaborately. There was more applause and laughter, and then she hugged him. He was acutely aware of the pressure of her breasts against his abdomen, the soft warmth of her back under his fingers.

And then she took his hand and led him to the table where the other hunting widows were sitting.

It was a large table, and introductions took some time. It

would have been rude to refuse the drink he was offered, so he drank it. And he made small talk until he thought he could leave Jane with her friends without giving the impression he didn't care for their company.

He had just said his good-byes when the band began playing "Goodnight, Sweetheart." He looked at his watch and saw that it was almost midnight.

"If you were to ask, Major Lowell," Jane Cassidy said, "I would grant you the favor of the New Year's midnight dance."

She was already on her feet.

They danced again with six inches between them, but the smell of her hair and the warmth of her back had the same effect on him as dancing with her before had had. She was dancing with her head back, so that she could look up into his eyes.

And then the lights flicked on and off, on and off. The band stopped playing, and people began to count downward from fifteen. It was almost the New Year.

He looked down at Jane Cassidy and smiled. She hadn't let go of his left hand, and was standing so close to him that he could feel the pressure of her breasts on his arm.

The countdown finished. Everybody was kissing their partners. He bent to kiss Jane, chastely, because she obviously expected him to—and because he wanted to. He expected to get her cheek, and instead got her lips. Somebody lurched into them, first banging their teeth together, and then apparently pushing Jane's elbow, for he felt her lower wrist and the back of her hand against his erection. She would know, he knew, what it was.

"Whoops!" he said.

"Crowded," she said.

The band played "Auld Lang Syne," and everybody sang. Jane sang enthusiastically, swaying with the music, swinging the hand she held, looking up at him and smiling. When "Auld Lang Syne" had finished, the lights dimmed, and the band began to play again. He started to dance with her once more.

"We were cheated out of our socially permissible New Year's kiss," she said, pulling back to look at his face. He bent to kiss her again, telling himself *this time on the cheek*. But he got her lips again, and he just had time to marvel at the softness of them when her tongue came between them. Her middle came into to meet his, and he felt his erection pressing against the softness of her belly.

There came a scream, and then a crashing noise, and then silence, and then a male voice said, *"Ooooooooooh, shit!"*

(Two)

Lieutenant Colonel Rudolph G. MacMillan had a load on. First he'd had a couple of beers on the golf course with Sandy Felter, and then a couple more in the house before the general and Bob Bellmon and everybody had showed up with the photographer. They'd all killed three bottles of champagne after that, and he had been drinking bourbon since they had come to the club. A lot of bourbon. There had been a lot of people who had heard about his promotion and had insisted on buying him drinks. He could hardly turn them down or they'd think the promotion had gone to his head.

It wasn't an entirely happy occasion, his promotion notwithstanding. For one thing, it was so soon after they'd buried Ed Greer that a party didn't seem quite right. It made him feel a little guilty that he was here, all in one piece, and what was left of Ed was in the cemetery in Ozark. He could just as easily have been flying the Big Bad Bird. He wondered if it would have gone in, if he'd been flying it.

For another, he'd brought up to Bob Bellmon his chances of taking over Combat Developments now that he was a light bird. Bellmon had quickly shot him out of the saddle on that one. No chance. Bellmon gave him the same excuse Roxy had, that the TO&E called for a full bull colonel, but Mac had known that was so much bullshit. If they'd wanted to give it to a light bird, they would have. They just didn't want to give it to him, and probably because he hadn't finished high school. He thought that he should have been able to prove by now that he was just as smart as any of the others, high school diploma or no high school diploma, but that wasn't the way it worked. They gave command only to a certain kind of officer, one who had all the punches on his ticket.

Bellmon had told him that if he wanted him to, he thought he could arrange for MacMillan to be ordered to the Pentagon, to work for him in DCSOPS.

That was the *last* goddamn thing he wanted. A newly promoted light bird in the Pentagon ranked about as high as a corporal did here. Light birds in the Pentagon were errand boys most of the time, sent out to the snack bars to bring the full colonels and the generals their morning coffee and rolls. He wanted nothing to do with that kind of crap. He was a soldier, not a paper-pusher.

He wasn't even going to get the rocket helicopter project. General E. Z. Black had ordered the whole project transferred to the Aviation Board. He couldn't go with it, because Black had given it to Lowell. Besides, Mac didn't want to work for Bill Roberts, anyway.

Sending the project to the Board was so much bullshit, too. The Board was supposed to test equipment, not tactics, and the only equipment they had was the H-19 Lowell had stolen. The project should have stayed with Combat Developments until they really got it started. Mac thought there was politics involved. It must have been a real kick in the balls to Roberts when they gave Bellmon a star and made him Director of Army Aviation. Roberts had certainly expected that promotion—and that job—himself.

What really had happened, Mac thought, was that Colonel Tim F. Brandon, the Pentagon PIO—without whose bullshit Ed Greer would probably still be alive—had suggested that the Big Bad Bird go to the Board. Proud as hell, the sonofabitch had told everybody that he had recommended Lowell for the job for the public relations value. If he'd wanted to, Bellmon could have choked off that dumb idea right from the start. Maybe he hadn't been all that enthusiastic about the Board getting the Big Bad Bird, but he had gone along with it to try to make Bill Roberts feel better. They may not like each other, but they had to work together. It was for damned sure that Bellmon hadn't been very pissed about Mac *not* getting it.

And then Melody Greer had shown up. That had really got to him. Ed not yet cold in the ground, and here she was at a party in an evening dress with her boobs damned near falling out of it. He hadn't thought Melody was like that. But he was out of step with the rest of the fucking world about that, too. He thought the Bellmons would have a fit when they saw her walking down the balcony hanging onto Lowell's and that frog officer's arms, but they hadn't. They had acted like it was the most natural thing in the world for a widow with her husband hardly cold to go to a party.

"Oh, Melody!" Barbara Bellmon said, sweet as hell, as if it was the most natural thing in the world for a widow to do, "I'm so glad you decided to come. I was afraid you wouldn't."

And they'd found a seat for her and Lowell, too, right next to the Bellmons, which had meant moving the adjutant and his wife to the next table. And then Bellmon had even danced with her, and Mac had watched them from the balcony and had seen that even if Lowell and Bob and Barbara Bellmon didn't think there was anything strange in a widow going to a party so soon after her husband had gotten himself killed, a lot of other people in the club did. As many people stared at Bellmon and Melody as had stared at Lowell when he was dancing with Phil Parker's wife.

Mac thought that what Barbara Bellmon should have done was take Melody aside someplace and politely let her know that she didn't look much like an officer's lady doing what she was doing. Or Lowell should have told her. Except you couldn't expect Lowell to do something like that. Lowell didn't give a shit what anybody thought, which was proved by the way he danced with Parker's wife.

It wasn't Melody's fault. She was just a kid, not more than twenty-two or something like that, and she really hadn't been around the army all that long, so somebody should have told her. Nicely, but they should have told her, and they didn't. Melody was a nice girl, and he felt sorry for her. Ed was a good guy, and they'd obviously been happy, and it was a dirty goddamn shame, him getting blown away that way.

Roxy, who would have jumped off the goddamn balcony if Barbara Bellmon jumped first, had gone along and pretended that she didn't think there was anything wrong with Melody being here. She had even told Mac to dance with her. There was no way he was going to do that, and he said that to her, and then she told him not to raise his voice at her. And that pissed him off the way it always did.

And Colonel Tim F. Brandon had also pissed him off most of the night. He was a general all-around horse's ass anyway, and getting a little plastered made him even worse than when he was sober.

Mac had heard Brandon tell Melody, holding her hand, that he "admired her courage" for coming to the party. Then he asked her to dance. It had made Mac's skin curl to watch that fat old sonofabitch with his arms around that nice young girl.

He was old enough to be her father, for Christ's sake, and he was hanging on to her like some second lieutenant on his honeymoon.

Giving credit where it was due, Mac thought that Lowell had danced *proper* with Melody—that is, with enough room between them to drive a truck through, not trying to cop a cheap feel the way Brandon did. He had thought at first that Lowell, who did some strange fucking things, had been responsible for Melody showing up at the club; but when Melody was dancing with Bob Bellmon, Barbara asked Lowell where he'd found her. Lowell told her she'd come up and introduced herself to him at the bar. Then Jannier (who had known Ed and Melody in Algeria) had showed up. So he decided that it would look better if people thought Melody had come in order to be nice to Jannier than if she'd just decided to come, period. Mac concluded that Lowell was probably telling the truth. If Lowell wanted to get laid, he didn't have to run after some young widow. All he had to do was get on the phone. Sonofabitch had more pussy on the string than any man Mac had ever known.

Mac also concluded that so far as frogs went, this Jannier was a good one. He'd learned that Jannier had been a young officer at Dien Bien Phu. Mac had been there, too, and knew what a mess that had been. Later Jannier had gone to Algeria, which is where he had known Greer. More important, he was a paratrooper. That, of course, said a lot about him. There was no way that a guy like Jannier was going to make a pass at Melody. Which was a good thing, because any female who went around showing off her boobs in a low-cut dress like Melody was wearing had to expect somebody to make a grab for them—widow or no widow.

Melody wasn't the only one with her teats on display. There were acres of boobs around tonight. Christ, even Jane Cassidy, who was a real lady, had hers on display. That was the last thing he had expected of her.

Mac looked down from the balcony at the dance floor again. Lowell was dancing there with Jane Cassidy; and Mac wondered what her husband thought about that. But at least Lowell was on his good behavior. He was dancing with Mrs. Cassidy like he was a bishop and she was a nun.

The lights began to flicker, and Mac wondered what the

fuck that was all about, and then he heard people starting to count backward from fifteen. He looked at his watch.

Goddamn, it's midnight already.

Roxy was on the other side of the table, next to Colonel Tim F. Brandon. She stood up when Mac stood up and reached out for his hand.

"Happy New Year's, *Colonel*," she said. When they finished counting backward and the lights went off, she leaned across the table and kissed him.

"Yeah, you too, Roxy," Mac said.

Then they started to sing "Auld Lang Syne," and Roxy straightened up.

"Don't I get a New Year's kiss?" Colonel Tim F. Brandon asked.

Roxy MacMillan gave him her cheek, but the fat sonofabitch weaved his head and kissed her on the lips and wouldn't let go until she pushed him away.

Mac glowered at the sonofabitch while they sang "Auld Lang Syne." The fat chairborne fucker kept putting his arm around Roxy, trying to hug her.

When they'd finished singing, Colonel Tim F. Brandon offered his hand to MacMillan across the table.

"Keep your fucking hands off my wife, Brandon!"

Colonel Brandon looked shocked and angry, for Mac had spoken so loud that others were watching them.

"Now see here, MacMillan!" he said.

"See here, shit!" MacMillan replied.

A wave of rage swept through him.

Lieutenant Colonel Rudolph G. MacMillan hit Colonel Tim F. Brandon with his right fist. He hit him squarely, with the skill he had demonstrated when as a sergeant he had been All-Pacific boxing champion.

Colonel Brandon, his lip cut, his nose already beginning to bleed, fell backward against the balcony railing. There was a ripping sound as the railing tore loose. Then Colonel Brandon, realizing he was falling, screamed.

"Oh, Mac," Roxy said. "You *dumb* sonofabitch, you!"

(Three)

Out of habit someone called out "Medic," but the medical staff tables were in the cafeteria, and the first physician to respond to the call was Antoinette Parker, M.D., who had been on the dance floor with her husband.

Phil Parker ran interference for his wife. When Lowell saw him shoving his way through the crowd, and then glanced up at the balcony and realized that whoever had fallen from the balcony was from CDO, Lowell left Jane Cassidy on the dance floor and headed for the crowd of people under the balcony.

As soon as he saw that it was Colonel Tim F. Brandon, he suspected that Brandon had not fallen accidentally from the balcony. He looked up and met Bob Bellmon's angry, resigned eyes.

Bellmon cupped his hands: "Do what you can, Lowell!"

Lowell nodded.

He squeezed through the last line of spectators and dropped to his knees beside Toni. From somewhere, she had an ammonia ampule. She broke it and put it under Brandon's nose. He woke with a start.

"Don't move, Colonel," Toni said, reassuringly, "until we see if you've broken anything."

Brandon saw Lowell.

"Major Lowell," Colonel Brandon ordered, "have that son-ofabitch MacMillan arrested. Have him put behind bars, right now. I'll bring the charges."

"Take it easy, Colonel," Lowell said. "You'll be all right."

"I gave you an *order*, goddamnit, Major!"

"Yes, sir," Lowell said. "I heard it."

There were other doctors on the scene now, one of whom rudely pulled Lowell out of the way.

The physicians held a hasty conference, the consensus of which was not to move Brandon until they could get an ambulance team to the club. The team could put him into something Lowell didn't understand and immobilize him.

It took the ambulance about five minutes to arrive, five minutes during which Brandon was alternately in a rage against MacMillan and terrified that he had broken his back. Lowell, at first contemptuous, told himself that he would behave no differently in the circumstances.

Someone called his name and he turned and someone thrust a drink in his hand.

"You look like you can use one, Major Lowell," a complete stranger said.

After the ambulance crew had strapped Colonel Brandon to a plywood board that immobilized him completely (and further terrified him), they lifted the board onto a stretcher. The doctors looked on disinterestedly. Carrying stretchers, Lowell thought, was obviously beneath their dignity.

"You," Lowell said, pointing to a young lieutenant, "lend a hand with the stretcher." He and the lieutenant helped the enlisted men carry the stretcher out of the ballroom, through the foyer, and down the stairs to an ambulance backed up to the club. Its doors were open and its emergency lights were flashing.

"My wife will have to be notified," Colonel Brandon said. "God knows what that will do to her!"

"As soon as we get to the hospital, sir," Lowell said, "I'll get on the phone and explain the situation. I'll stay with you, sir."

When he started to get in the back of the ambulance with him, the medical officer, a young captain who was probably annoyed at being on duty on New Year's Eve, put his hand on his arm and stopped him.

"Medical personnel only, Major," he said, officiously.

"I'm going," Lowell said. "Get this show on the road, doctor."

"You are *not* going, Major," the medical officer said.

"Get in the ambulance, chancre mechanic, and shut your mouth," Lowell said.

"It's all right, Doctor," Toni Parker said. "I asked Major Lowell to accompany the patient."

The doctor's face tightened, but he went around and got in the front beside the driver.

"I'll see you at the hospital," Toni said to Lowell. "I can't let Phil drive."

She slammed the door, and the ambulance, siren howling, headed for the hospital.

(Four)
Married Officer's Quarters
U.S. Army Hospital
Fort Rucker, Alabama
0215 Hours, 1 January 1959

When Lowell called Bellmon's quarters, the phone was answered before the second ring.

"General Bellmon," the voice said.

"Lowell, sir," he said. "I've just spoken with Dr. Parker. Colonel Brandon has a cracked shoulder blade, which will require a cast. He has also suffered some torn muscles and ligaments and various bruises and contusions. But there is no damage to the spine, and he should be up and walking in a couple of days."

"I'm sure Mrs. Brandon will be greatly relieved when I call her back," Bellmon said.

"So, I'm sure, will Mrs. MacMillan," Lowell said.

Bellmon ignored that.

"Thank you, Lowell, for staying on top of this," he said.

"General, I have been ordered by Colonel Brandon to have Mac placed under arrest. It is the colonel's intention to bring charges."

"You have brought the matter to my attention, Lowell," Bellmon said.

"What do I tell the wounded elephant?" Lowell asked.

"You tell *Colonel Brandon,* Major Lowell," Bellmon said icily, "that you have brought his wishes to my attention."

"I tried to talk to him, Bob," Lowell said. "He is still greatly pissed."

"I'll see you tomorrow, Major," Bellmon said, coldly. "Thank you again for what you have done."

The telephone went dead in Lowell's ear.

"One suspects," Lowell said, picking up his glass and smiling at Phil Parker, "that one should not have referred to the victim of this brutal assault as 'the wounded elephant.' One gathers from his famous icy tones that General Bellmon considers this an affront to good military order and discipline."

"Screw 'em," Phil Parker said, drunkenly amiable.

"My sentiments, exactly," Lowell said. "I guess I better call Roxy and get her off the hook."

"I'll call her, Craig," Toni Parker said. "You go home."

"'Tis but the shank of the evening," Lowell said. "Phil and

I have just about solved all of the army's problems."

"Go home, Craig," Toni said. "Before you fall down."

"Well, if I didn't know better," Lowell said, mincingly, "I'd think I wasn't wanted."

Parker laughed.

"Oh, God, I'll have to drive you home," Toni said. "Your car isn't here." She chuckled. "Not that you'd be capable of driving it if it was."

"Where is it?" Lowell said, as if that information came as a great surprise.

"You loaned it to Bill Franklin."

"So I did," Lowell said, remembering.

"Where's your cape and your hat?" Toni asked.

"At the club," Lowell replied, after he'd thought that over. He was just sober enough to decide that if he couldn't remember where he'd left his car, his cape, and his hat, he had had more to drink than he should have.

There were two telephones on the table in the living room. One was an outside (post) line, and the other an internal hospital line. He picked up the hospital line.

"Duty officer," he said.

A sleepy sergeant came on the line.

"Sergeant, this is Major Lowell. Is there some reason your staff car can't run me to my quarters?" He listened briefly, and then added: "I'll be right there. Thank you, Sergeant."

"Now you can proceed immediately with your lecherous plans for my friend," he said to Toni.

"Good *night,* Craig," she said. "Can you find the front desk by yourself, or will I have to show you?"

"Good night, doctor," he said, and kissed her cheek. "And thank you." He leered at Phil Parker. *"Et bonne chasse, mon ami!"*

It was a surprisingly long walk from the Parkers' quarters to the front entrance to the hospital. And when he got there, Jane Cassidy was waiting for him, sitting in one of the plastic and chrome armchairs with her fur jacket over her shoulders. He felt his heart beat.

"I knew you would need a ride," she said, getting to her feet when she saw him. "You told me you gave your car keys to Mr. Franklin."

"I see I won't be needing you, Sergeant," Lowell said to the driver of the staff car. "Sorry to get you up."

"No problem, sir."

He had a very clear memory of Jane Cassidy's tongue against his, his erection stiff against her belly, the moment before MacMillan had sent Colonel Brandon flying through the balcony rail.

I am very drunk, he told himself, *but not too drunk to recognize this as a very dangerous situation.*

"How is Colonel Brandon?" Jane asked, as soon as she led him to her car, a Buick coupe.

"He's got a cracked shoulder blade," Lowell said. "We were afraid he'd hurt his spine, but the X-rays say not."

"That's good," Jane said.

She got behind the wheel and started the engine; but she did not put the car in gear or turn on the lights.

"You weren't really surprised to see me, were you?" she asked. "Here, I mean?"

"I was," he said, truthfully. "But now that you're here, no."

"I don't have in mind what you think I do," she said. "I don't cheat on my husband. I never have, and I don't want to."

"OK," he said.

He realized that he was deeply disappointed.

"After what happened at the club," she said, "I got in my car and started home."

"Why didn't you keep going?"

"Because I knew this had to be settled now," she said. "Right away."

"What had to be settled? A semi-innocent kiss?"

"You want me," she said.

He didn't reply.

"And I . . . respond . . . to you," Jane Cassidy said.

"We are adults," Lowell said, "who can behave ourselves."

"I don't think so," she said. "That's why I came back."

"I thought you just said you don't cheat on your husband."

"There's always to be a first time," she said. "If I'm around you, there would be a first time."

"Jane, I'm a little drunk, and I don't know what you're talking about."

"I don't want to work for you anymore," she said.

"Oh," he said.

"Oh, what?"

"Oh, if you ask for a transfer, everyone will believe—with

cause—that it is because I have made a pass at you."

"I hadn't thought about that," she said.

"And I have just had a speech from General Jiggs about my relationships with married women," he said.

She laughed.

"What's funny?"

"You don't fit the image of innocent victim," she said.

"I'll go see Roberts and tell him I think you're very nice, and very intelligent, but you just aren't working out," Lowell said.

"OK," she said, without enthusiasm.

"I'll make it clear that I think highly of you, but that I need someone with more experience. You can't be blamed for not having experience."

"If I had experience," Jane said, "I would be handling this better than I am, wouldn't I?"

"I think you're doing very well," he said.

"Damn you!" she said furiously.

"For what?" he asked, after a moment.

"For not trying to overcome my objections," she said. "For understanding. For not making a pass."

"Do you want me to make a pass?"

"If you gave me a chance to slap you, that would make things a lot easier," she said.

She looked at him. Even in the darkness he could see her eyes. He moved across the seat to her, slowly but surely, so that she understood his intention, and would have time to put the headlights on and put the car in gear.

He put his hand on her cheek and then kissed her. She didn't respond at first, but then her mouth opened and her tongue touched his. He let his hand move to her neck, and then inside the fur coat. The moment his fingers touched the first swell of her breast, she pushed him away furiously.

She pulled the lights on, jammed the Buick in gear, and backed out of the parking lot.

Lowell leaned back against the seat, furious. Simply talking with her had brought the erection back. Kissing her, and the first touch of her breasts, had aroused him.

With difficulty, he restrained himself from telling her that what she had done was known as cockteasing.

They approached his BOQ.

"There it is," he said. "You can just drop me in front."

She passed the BOQ without slowing.

"You passed my BOQ," he repeated.

"Just shut up," she said.

As they drove off the post, he asked, "Is it permitted to ask where we're going?"

She didn't reply for a moment.

"When you sent me to settle your bill at the Daleville Inn," she said, "do you remember what I told you?"

"No," he said, honestly.

"I told you they told me you had taken the suite for two weeks, and a bargain was a bargain, no refunds."

He took her meaning.

"By now, certainly," he said, "they have rented it out to someone else."

"No," Jane Cassidy said, as they approached the motel. "No, they haven't. I kept the key. At the time, I didn't want to think why I kept it."

She drove into the motel, past the office, to a parking spot by the door to the suite. She stopped the car with a squeal of brakes and got out without saying anything.

She went to the door and took the key from her purse. He saw that her hands were shaking. She finally got the door open, and he followed her inside.

She slammed the door and shrugged out of her fur jacket and turned to him.

"For God's sake, hurry!" she said.

VII

(One)
The Daleville Inn
0320 Hours, 1 January 1959

The phone rang so long that Lowell was just about to hang up before there was a click and a sleepy voice:

"Warrant Officer Franklin."

"I need a ride, Bill," Lowell said.

"Where are you, at the hospital?"

"At the Daleville Inn," Lowell said.

"I thought you moved out of there."

"I'm sorry to have to get you out of bed," Lowell said, avoiding the question.

"Five minutes," Franklin said, and hung up.

Lowell hung up the telephone and exhaled audibly. Then he stood up and started to pick up his clothing. He caught a glance of himself in the mirror over a chest of drawers.

"Christ!" he said at the reflection of a naked man stooping over picking up clothing like a Neanderthal man grubbing for roots. Then he saw the tooth marks and nail scratches on his body.

"Jesus!" he said.

He went to the door, which he had carefully locked after the departure of Jane Cassidy, and unlocked it. At least he had had enough sense to send her home, rather than have her take him back to the post. He went into the bathroom and ran the water. It was like ice, and it ran a long time before it got hot. He took a towel with him into the tub, and he did not pull the curtain shut while he scrubbed at elusive remnants of Jane's lipstick.

Lowell had come to a conclusion about Jane Cassidy: in bed she had been wild, demanding, because she had never in her life had a good screw. He believed her when she said that she had never strayed before. She had married the first love of her life, and he hadn't known any more about screwing than she had.

Lowell had been no better. He had married the first love of his life, too, and he and Ilse hadn't known much more than which part fitted where. He believed now that he was a good lover because any number of women had told him so. He believed that he was good because he was experienced. But that experience had come after Ilse. If she hadn't been killed, would Ilse have become unsatisfied because he would have remained no more experienced than she? What he knew now he had learned in several hundred beds. When he had been with Ilse their sex life, while satisfying, was almost touchingly innocent. He had learned the clever little tricks afterward.

He felt sorry for Jane Cassidy. He believed she was what she said she was, and therefore it followed she was now wallowing in regret, self-disgust, and shame. He was a little ashamed himself that he had participated in her first infidelity.

And God only knew what trouble it was going to cause when they went back to work.

He came up with two clichés: "A Stiff Prick Has No Conscience" and "If It Wasn't Me, It Would Have Been Somebody Else."

Neither provided any solace at all.

When he came out of the shower, Bill Franklin was sitting in one of the armchairs in the bedroom.

"I trust the Major had a pleasant evening," he said, dryly.

"Very nice, thank you."

"Anyone I would know?" Franklin asked.

"I don't think so, Mr. Franklin," Lowell said.

"I like the perfume," Franklin said, sniffing. "'*Essence de Rut*'?"

Lowell laughed.

"And how did you do, Bill?"

"I had to remain chaste, unfortunately," Franklin said. "There are two kinds of local quail, the white kind, who want nothing to do with a darky, and the dark kind, who ain't exactly my cup of tea."

"I've seen some good-looking black girls," Lowell said.

"I tried a couple," Franklin said. "They too come in two kinds: those who want me to get washed in the blood of the lamb—whatever the hell that means—and those who want me to blow up the post in the interests of racial equality."

Lowell dressed quickly, and they left the suite and went to Lowell's car.

Franklin got behind the wheel.

"Since we're already up, so to speak," he asked, dryly, "would you mind if we went out to Hanchey to get my car now?"

"Sure," Lowell said.

There was no conversation as they drove through the post from the Daleville gate to Hanchey Field. But when they pulled in beside Franklin's car, a red MG, Franklin said, "There's something I have to tell you, Major."

"*Major?*" Lowell said. "That sounds serious."

"How about delicate?"

"What's on your mind, Bill?"

"When I got to Melody's house," Franklin said, uncomfortably, "she and that frog captain were already inside. Half an hour later, he came out and told me that it was all right, he didn't need a ride back to the post, he would catch a cab."

"That sonofabitch!" Lowell exploded. "I'll have his ass for that."

"That presumes Melody would let him do something he shouldn't have."

"She was drunk, Bill."

"Well," Franklin said, "I figured I'd better tell you." Then he quickly opened the door, got out, and slammed it shut.

Lowell rolled the window down.

"Thanks, Bill," he said.

If Franklin, already inside the MG, heard him, there was no reply.

(Two)
BOQ No.1 (Bldg. T-1703)
Fort Rucker, Alabama
0845 Hours, 1 January 1959

Major Craig W. Lowell woke. The skin on the back of his neck was crawling, and his heart was thumping alarmingly. He was instantly wide awake, but forced himself to lie immobile, his eyes shut. He collected his thoughts. He was in his room in the BOQ, he told himself. There was somebody in the room.

The fucking pistol is in the things box, and the things box is on the desk, far out of reach. Do sneak thieves carry guns, or razors?

He groaned and feigned tossing in his sleep, then rolled over. The way he was lying, he faced the closet door. He forced himself to breathe slowly and naturally, and he counted to one hundred slowly. That would, he hoped, convince the sneak thief that he was really asleep.

Then he opened his eyes.

Captain Jean-Philippe Jannier, still in his comic French dress uniform, was sitting in the one upholstered chair in the room, his feet stretched out, examining the centerfold in *Playboy* magazine.

He looked over the magazine at Lowell and saw that Lowell's eyes were open.

"Good morning," he said, in French. "I hope that I didn't waken you?"

"You just came in to read the magazine, right?" Lowell said, in French. He was furious, and wondered how much of the fury was because of this bastard's fucking around with Greer's widow, and how much because he felt like a fool that the sneak thief had turned out to be a frog reading *Playboy*.

"It was necessary that I speak with you, Major Lowell," Jannier said.

"Was it?"

"I did something last night that I wanted to tell you about, before you heard it from your black warrant officer."

"Bill Franklin, *mon Capitaine*," Lowell said icily, "is a close friend, not 'my black warrant officer.' He was also, it seems germane to note, a close friend of Ed Greer."

"I know," Jannier said, sadly, shrugging his shoulders.

Lowell sat up in bed, then swung his feet onto the floor.

He couldn't find his slippers, so he strode naked and barefoot across the sticky linoleum to his closet, from which he took a silk dressing robe. The robe was old-fashioned, the striped silk sewn in squares. The belt had tasseled ends. The dressing robe had been bought at Sulka's in Paris in April of 1940 by Lowell's father.

"You have talked to Franklin since last night?" Jannier said.

"Yes, I have," Lowell said.

"I'm sorry," Jannier said. "I wanted to tell you first, before you saw him."

"Tell me what?" Lowell asked.

"What happened last night."

"I know what happened last night," Lowell said.

"You know what Franklin...that is his name, Franklin?...*thinks* happened last night."

"You tell me, then, what happened," Lowell said.

"That is why I am here, my friend," Jannier said, with a Gallic shrug of his shoulders. It was with the greatest difficulty that Lowell kept his mouth shut. There was a terrible urge to tell this frog sonofabitch that, whatever other failings of character he had, he had not stooped to being this man's friend.

"I'm waiting," Lowell said.

"In the car," Jannier said, "as we started to Ozark...that is right, 'Ozark'?"

"That's right, Ozark," Lowell snapped.

"Melody started to cry. She broke down."

So you "comforted" her, did you, you charming frog sonofabitch?

"I saw it as my duty to comfort her," Jannier said.

"How kind of you," Lowell said, sarcastically.

Jannier flashed him an angry glance, which immediately softened. He shrugged.

"I understand what Franklin thought," Jannier said. "What others would think. But I thought that you would understand."

"That I would understand what?"

"That nothing that should not have happened between Melody and I happened," Jannier said. "That I stayed with her until I could stop her from crying, that I spoke with her, of many things, and that I held her in my arms, as a father, as a brother, until she went to sleep."

"And why do you think I would believe that?" Lowell asked.

I'll be damned if I don't think he's telling the truth.

"Because you and I are much alike," Jannier said. "And not *only* because we are, in that delightful American phrase, 'formidable swordsmen,' but because—*primarily*—it is not necessary for men like *us* to take advantage of a woman when she is weak. *We* prefer the chase."

What the hell is that supposed to be, flattery?

"You seem to have learned a good deal about me in the few days since we met," Lowell said.

"I learned about you before I came here, when I was still in Paris. My uncle, the Baron de Pildet, was most insistent that while I was here I make an effort to know you. That you and Hanrahan are friends was a pleasant coincidence, permitting me to meet you first as a soldier."

"What the hell does all that mean?"

"You don't recognize the name, Baron St. Etienne de Pildet?"

"No," Lowell said.

"He would be crushed," Jannier laughed. "He is the general manager of the Banque de Commerce de l'Afrique du Nord."

"I'm awed," Lowell said.

In European banking, "general manager" was essentially the same thing as "president" in America.

"He said that when you and I were finished with 'playing at soldiers,' we would probably be doing business together."

"Why would he think that?"

"Because, among other positions, he sits on the board of Haymann Freres, in which I understand you own the controlling interest."

"My firm does," Lowell corrected him idly. "Is that why you think it important that I don't think you've sneaked into Melody Greer's pants?"

"It is important to me as a man," Jannier said. "If you like, as an officer and a gentleman."

"Shit," Lowell said. Jannier looked at him angrily. Lowell held up his hand. "Oh, I believe you, Jannier," he said. "Relax."

Jannier's relief was evident.

"Thank you," he said.

"As one 'formidable swordsman' to another," Lowell chuckled.

"It is the truth," Jannier said. "Why should one deny it? It happens. Some men are born to be great pianists. Others are like us."

"The money may have something to do with it," Lowell said.

"Of course it does," Jannier said. "A handsome poor man is a handsome poor man. But an ugly rich man is a rich man."

Lowell chuckled. He liked this guy.

"I am about to have a small hair of the dog," Lowell said. "Will you join me?"

"Hair of the dog?"

"I had too much to drink last night," Lowell said.

"A drink? Yes, please."

Lowell went to the window and, with a grunt, jerked it open. He had a six-pack of small cans of Bloody Mary mix on the outside windowsill, chilling in the cold outside air.

"Primitive, but effective," Jannier said, admiringly. "Let me ask that question."

"What question?"

"Is it necessary for people like us to live like this?"

He means more than "in the Spartan accommodations of the BOQ." He is really asking how far an officer is expected to go to conceal the shameful fact that he doesn't need to earn a living.

"No," Lowell said. "I decided that question yesterday. I have a suite in the Daleville Inn. I'm going to move back there today."

"Is there another vacant?" Jannier asked.

"I don't know," Lowell said. And then, impulsively, he went on: "The suite I have has two bedrooms, a sitting room, one other little room, sort of an office, I guess, or a big closet, two bathrooms and a kitchen. If two people lived in it, it would be less ostentatious."

The reply at first was raised eyebrows, a Gallic shrug of the shoulders, and finally an ingratiating smile.

"You do believe me, then," Jannier said. "I am very grateful. I accept, of course, your kindness."

Lowell opened two cans of Bloody Mary mix, poured them into glasses, and added a stiff shot of Beefeater gin. He handed one to Jannier, who raised his glass.

"To our new home," the Frenchman said, drolly.

Lowell noticed that Jannier had not asked what his share of the suite was going to cost. He told him. Jannier shrugged acceptance.

"Can we eat there?" he asked.

"We can, but the food is no better than at the club," Lowell said.

"Then I shall be obliged to cook," Jannier said.

"Splendid," Lowell said, chuckling. He was liking Jannier more and more, and the prospect of sharing the suite with him was pleasant. Among other things, having Jannier in the suite would reduce the temptation to have Jane Cassidy come to call.

"Now that I'm up," Lowell said, "bursting with energy to face the New Year and its many challenges, I'm tempted to throw this stuff in the car and go out there now, before the general's reception. How does that sound?"

"Marvelous," Jannier said.

"I wouldn't worry about last night anymore, Jean-Philippe," Lowell said. "As I said, Franklin is a friend of mine. I'll explain the situation to him."

"Thank you," Jannier said. "I would hate to have Melody embarrassed in any way."

"Just stay away from her," Lowell said.

"That may not be possible," Jannier said, draining his Bloody Mary.

"I beg your pardon?" Lowell said, his voice cold.

"She's an extraordinary woman, Melody," Jannier said. "Truly unusual. I was taken with her in Algiers, and even more taken with her last night. I have never felt this way about a woman before."

"What the hell is that supposed to mean?" Lowell asked sharply.

"I was thinking about that while I waited for you to wake up," Jannier said, innocently, obviously sincere. "Wondering if I am finally in love. I have never been in love, so I have no criteria to make a judgment."

"You had better hope it was the liquor," Lowell said.

"I thought about that," Jannier said, and met his eyes. "I don't think it was. There have been many women, and much alcohol, but never before for me a feeling for a woman like this."

(Three)
Quarters No. 1
Fort Rucker, Alabama
1330 Hours, 1 January 1959

The white-frame, ranch-style house sat on a small hill over-looking the senior officer's housing area. It was the largest quarters on the post, but the house was neither large nor elegant. Getting the dependent quarters appropriation through the Congress had not been easy, not even in a year when the Congress had voted to provide for its one hundred senators a second restaurant and a second gymnasium—at a cost of some $17 million.

There were four bedrooms; two full and two half bathrooms; a dining room; and a living room. There was a two-car carport. Off the kitchen was a screened patio where the general could take the afternoon sun, or charcoal a steak, out of view of his neighbors. The most visible differences between Quarters No. 1 and the quarters on Colonel's Row at the foot of the small hill, was that Quarters No. 1 sat alone on about an acre of land. The other houses, which looked not unlike a lower-middle-class housing development, had much smaller lots and one-car carports.

The street in front of Quarters No. 1 was crowded with cars, and two MPs did their best to make order out of the chaos. It was caused by the general's decision to revive the tradition that on New Year's Day the commanding general and his lady received the officers of the garrison and their ladies.

It was understood that the general expected to see only field-grade officers, that is to say majors and above. It would have been physically impossible to have all the officers on the post wind their way up the general's driveway, shake his hand in the foyer, take a cup of punch from a bowl in the dining room, sip it in the living room, and then leave. On another day, the general would receive the captains at his quarters. And on two other days, he would receive the lieutenants and the warrant officers. Not in Quarters No. 1, because it wasn't large enough for all of them at once, but in the officer's open mess.

In fact, there wasn't enough room in Quarters No. 1 for all the colonels (21), lieutenant colonels (130), and majors (208)—plus their ladies—no matter how brief their call. Fortunately, Major General Paul T. Jiggs thought wryly, a goodly number of the lieutenant colonels and majors had decided to duck the

New Year's Day reception. The *smart* ones, he thought, the ones who knew they probably wouldn't be missed and thought it improbable that their names would be checked off on a roster.

General Jiggs, in army blue uniform, stood with his wife and his aide-de-camp at the entrance foyer to his quarters. He shook hands and exchanged a brief word with each officer (and each wife) in a long line of army blue uniformed officers and hatted and gloved wives.

Then he saw something interesting in the shuffling line, a very familiar face indeed. Behind the familiar face was a young French officer, in a well-fitting tan gabardine uniform; more than likely the captain Barbara Bellmon had called his wife Jane about.

"Why, I'm so glad you could make it, Major Lowell," General Jiggs said, his voice dryly sarcastic. "Aren't you pleased to see Major Lowell, Jane?"

"I'm always pleased to see Major Lowell," Jane Jiggs said, her voice suggesting that she knew he was joking. "Happy New Year, Major Lowell."

"Happy New Year, Mrs. Jiggs," Lowell said. Then Lowell switched to French: "Mon General," he began, and then introduced Captain Jean-Philippe Jannier to them in French.

Jane Jiggs saw a colonel from the Department of Tactics actually put his hand on his wife's arm to hold her back. He didn't want to give the general the mistaken impression that he was with Major Lowell, whose pardoned status was not yet fully known, and who was saying God only knows what in a foreign language to the general.

Paul Jiggs was cordial to Jannier, asking him if Lowell was helping him to feel at home at Fort Rucker.

"We have established bachelor quarters together, mon General," Jannier said with an ease that told both Jane and her husband that he was accustomed to deal with senior officers.

"How interesting," Jiggs said, giving Lowell a significant look.

"We're splitting the cost," Lowell said, innocently.

Jiggs nodded. Still in French, he said: "It always warms my heart, Captain Jannier, when one of my bachelor officers, such as Major Lowell, is willing to tear himself away from the football game on television to pay his respects to his post commander."

"It is my great pleasure to be received by you and Mrs.

Jiggs, General," Lowell said, drolly. "It will be the high point of my day."

"How *kind* of you, Major Lowell," Jane Jiggs said, fighting to keep from smiling.

"Have you met my aide, Major Lowell?" the general asked, and gestured toward the neat young lieutenant at his side.

"Lieutenant Davis, sir," the aide said.

"How do you do?" Lowell said.

The aide shook hands with Lowell and Jannier.

Switching to English, Jiggs spoke to the aide: "Davis, if Captain Jannier can find the punch by himself, will you take Major Lowell into my study? If he can spare me a moment, I would be grateful for his wise counsel."

That man, Jane Jiggs thought, looking at the frozen smile on the colonel from Tactics, *is actually afraid.*

"Yes, sir," the aide said. "This way, please, gentlemen?"

General Jiggs turned to the wife of the colonel from Tactics and took her hand.

"How nice of you to come," he said.

Ten minutes later, Jiggs walked into the fourth bedroom of Quarters No. 1, which, at his own expense, he had turned into a working den. There was a desk and chair, and two walls were covered with bookcases. The third wall was nearly covered with photographs and other memorabilia.

Lowell had been looking at a photograph. Jiggs saw which one. It was a photograph of Jiggs himself, looking over the shoulder of his fur-trimmed parka. He was standing on the fender of an M46 tank, and he appeared to have been caught in the act of relieving his bladder.

The photograph had been taken by Major Craig W. Lowell as then Colonel Jiggs emulated General George S. Patton. If Patton could piss in the Rhine, Jiggs had told his wife, there was no reason he could not mount on his private study wall a photo of himself pissing in the Yalu. It was as far north as his battalion had gotten in the Korean War. The photo had been taken twenty-four hours before the chinks came in.

"You want a drink, Craig?" General Jiggs asked.

"I'd love one," Lowell said.

Jiggs poured scotch into glasses, and added soda. He handed one to Lowell and then raised his in a toast.

"Absent companions," he said, barely nodding his head toward the photo.

"Eight years ago today," Lowell said, obviously affected by the memory, "the 73rd Heavy Tank landed at Pusan from Hamhung. At right about this time of day, you and I were standing on Pier One in Pusan freezing our asses, watching them unload our tanks."

"And our dead," Jiggs said. He had a clear memory of a pallet stacked with wrapped corpses being swung over the side of the ship.

"Absent companions," Lowell repeated and they both raised their glasses again.

"What's with you and Jannier?" Jiggs asked.

"We have two things in common," Lowell said. "Neither of us like the BOQ."

"How do you know he can afford his half of your motel suite?"

"That's the other thing we have in common," Lowell said.

"I don't want to hear tales of wild parties with naked women and bawdy songs, Craig. Nor do I wish to receive a native with a shotgun and a daughter of childbearing age, demanding to know where he can find either of you."

"Following our last little chat, I am determined to be as pure as the driven snow," Lowell said.

Jiggs snorted and chuckled. "That'll be the day," he said. Then he asked: "What the hell happened last night?"

"The general refers, one gathers," Lowell said, his voice now lightly mocking, "to Colonel Brandon's devastating *vertical envelopment* of the post signal officer's table?"

"It's not funny," Jiggs said, chuckling.

Lowell mimicked Colonel Tim F. Brandon's scream of terror.

Jiggs laughed out loud. But then he pulled himself together.

"He could have been killed, for God's sake," Jiggs said. "It's really not funny; and besides, in thirty minutes I'm going to have to explain to Black what happened."

Lowell sobered. "Black? How did he get involved?"

"When he woke up this morning, Brandon called the Chief of Information."

"Oh, hell," Lowell said.

"He wants MacMillan court-martialed," Jiggs said.

"Last night, he ordered me to have Mac put behind bars," Lowell said. "Have you talked to him? Brandon, I mean?"

"I sent my chief of staff over to the hospital this morning. He was at C&GS with Brandon. They weren't close friends or anything, but I thought he might be able to calm him down."

"No luck?"

"None."

"Well, I guess now we test the folklore," Lowell said.

"What does that mean?"

"That you don't court-martial winners of the Medal," Lowell said. "No matter what they do."

"Why did he do it?" Jiggs asked.

"He was drunk," Lowell said. "Specifically, because he didn't like the way Brandon kissed Roxy."

"I haven't talked to Bellmon," Jiggs said. "What's he done to Mac?"

"Told him to go home and stay there until he sends for him."

"Did he make it official?"

"He can say he did, if it comes to that," Lowell said.

"Damn him," Jiggs said.

"Bellmon or Mac?" Lowell asked, innocently.

"Mac," Jiggs said. "Bellmon didn't knock Brandon off the balcony."

"Has anybody suggested to Brandon that his skirts aren't clean?" Lowell said. "Forcing your attentions on an officer's wife is conduct unbecoming an officer and a gentleman."

"He didn't do that, for Christ's sake," Jiggs said.

"If I were Mac, and they were going to court-martial me, I'd damned sure charge him with it," Lowell said.

Jiggs looked at Lowell, and then visibly decided not to say what came to his mind.

"Are you going to see Bob Bellmon today?"

"I'm taking Jannier there from here," Lowell said, dryly. "I am toeing the line, General, behaving in a manner reflecting my status as a regular army field-grade officer. I am going to *all* the general officers' receptions. And, of course, to Bill Roberts's."

"Don't be a pain in the ass, Craig," Jiggs said.

"You want me to talk to Bellmon?"

"See if he's got any ideas what we can do with Mac," Jiggs said. "We just can't let it pass. We've got to let Brandon save a little face."

"Yes, sir," Lowell said.

"I mean, find out what's on *Bellmon's* mind, Craig," General Jiggs said. "Keep your guardhouse lawyer opinions to yourself. Call me after you've talked to him. But let *us* handle this."

"Yes, sir."

Jiggs locked eyes with Lowell for a moment, and then he said, obviously making reference to returning to the reception line, "I would rather face a thousand deaths."

It was what General Lee had said before riding out to surrender to General Grant at Appomattox Courthouse.

"Yours not to reason why, General," Lowell said. "Yours but to go out there and shake hands."

(Four)
Quarters No. 3
Fort Meyer, Virginia
1345 Hours, 1 January 1959

The great majority of the officers who walked up onto the screened porch of the Victorian house that served as quarters for the Vice Chief of Staff of the U.S. Army wore the stars of general officers.

The screen door was pulled open for them by a white-jacketed orderly who smiled and directed them to the double doors of the house itself. There another orderly pulled open the door, while a third and fourth stood inside to take the coats and hats.

The Vice Chief of Staff and Mrs. Black greeted their guests, and then the guests went into the dining room, where there was a very large silver punch bowl with matching cups, also attended by an orderly, and a bar with bottles of whiskey for those who wanted something harder.

New Year's Day was one of the few times when the Vice Chief of Staff was jealous of the prerogatives of his immediate superior, the Chief of Staff. It might well be more blessed to give than receive, General Black thought, but it was obviously nicer to be on the receiving end of receptions on New Year's Day.

The Chief of Staff and his wife would spend the day going to other people's receptions, from the President's at the White House, down through those given by the Deputy Chief of Naval Operations, the Vice Chief of Staff of the Air Force, the Deputy

Commandant of the Marine Corps, and then those of various high-ranking bureaucrats.

The Vice Chief of Staff would spend the day holding a reception.

The Vice Chief of Staff spotted a face that he had been looking for coming through the door. He covered his mouth with his hand and spoke to his wife. "Hold the fort, here comes Chester."

She nodded.

General Black smiled at the people at the head of his line. "I'll see you in a moment," he said and walked into the house, trailed by one of his junior aides, a natty, crew-cut young major.

He went to his study and thought about having a drink, decided against it, and then changed his mind.

"Would you ask General Chester, alone, to join me?" he said to the aide de camp.

"Yes, sir," the aide said.

While he waited, he made himself a drink and was holding it in his hand when the aide tapped at the door, opened it, and announced: "General Chester, General Black."

"Come on in, Tom," Black said. "Have a little something."

"Thank you, sir," Major General Frederick Chester said. He was the Chief of Information for the Department of the Army. He had not asked for his job, did not like it, and was very much aware that General E. Z. Black held his future career in his hands. It would be up to Black to "recommend" to the Chief of Staff whether General Chester, after completing three years as P.R. Chief, would be retained in that job . . . or given a command . . . or retired.

General Chester *very* much wanted a final command, almost any kind of a command, before he retired.

He saw that General Black was drinking bourbon and asked for the same thing.

"I don't want to spend a lot of time on this," General Black said, as he handed Chester his drink. He was prepared to go along with practically anything Chester recommended in the matter of the assault upon Colonel Tim F. Brandon. MacMillan was no child. In this, he was going to have to take his lumps.

"No, sir," Chester said. "I presume the general is referring to that unfortunate business at Rucker?"

"What do you think should be done?" Black asked.

"It's not an easy one, sir," General Chester said, seriously.

"On the one hand, it's black and white—officers do not assault other officers—but on the other hand, there are very important public relations considerations."

"And have you a recommendation?" Black asked.

"There really hasn't been time to give the situation the consideration it deserves, General. I have, of course, several options to offer."

That does it, you paper-shuffling sonofabitch. This isn't a decision about where to invade the Asian landmass. It's what to do about two unimportant officers. If you can't make a decision like this in ten seconds flat, you shouldn't be an officer, much less a major general.

"I'll tell you what we're going to do, General," General Black said. "You're going to get on an airplane and go to Rucker and tell your colonel to count his blessings. He's lucky MacMillan didn't kill him, and he's lucky that I don't order his court-martial on charges of conduct unbecoming. If he wants to stay lucky, he is not even to think about pressing charges against MacMillan. You understand me?"

"Sir, I understand Colonel Brandon is the aggrieved party," General Chester said.

Black was surprised that Chester dared argue with him. His opinion of Chester rose a little.

"I know he is, Tom," Black said. "But, of all people, Brandon should know what an embarrassment this could be for the army."

"That's true, sir."

"He's just going to have to swallow his injured pride. If you think it will make him any happier, you may tell him that I have already ordered MacMillan's transfer."

"We couldn't really leave him at Rucker, could we?"

"No more than we could court-martial him, and give everybody a good laugh at our expense," Black said.

"When would you like me to go to Fort Rucker, General?"

"I was hoping that your schedule would permit you to go today," General Black said. "Will it?"

General Chester looked thoughtful.

"With a little shuffling, yes, sir," he said, finally.

"Good boy, Tom," General Black said. "I knew I could count on you."

After General Chester had left his office, General Black sat down at his desk. He took a battered telephone book from a drawer, found a number, and picked up the telephone.

"Bill this to me personally," he said, when the operator came on the line. And then he gave her the number.

The phone was answered on the second ring.

"Let me talk to him, Roxy," he said.

Roxy knew his voice. Mac was on the line in ten seconds.

"Yes, sir?"

"Pack your bags, you dumb sonofabitch," General Black said. "And write this on the palm of your hand so you won't forget it: This is the last time I am going to save your ass."

"Where'm I going, General?" MacMillan asked.

"This is the last time, Mac, the *last* time. Get that through your thick head."

Then he hung up.

That left only one thing to resolve. He had no idea where he was going to send MacMillan.

He sipped at his drink, and then smiled broadly. He had the answer to that one. It was so simple he wondered why he hadn't thought of it sooner.

He dialed the operator again.

"Get me Colonel Paul Hanrahan at the Special Warfare School at Fort Bragg," he said.

Paul Hanrahan had just gotten an eagle earlier than he would have gotten one without the personal intervention of the President—*and* he'd gotten command of the Special Warfare School. Mac was a paratrooper. Let Hanrahan sit on the stupid sonofabitch. Let him work off MacMillan's excess energy by running him around and around in the boonies at Bragg.

(Five)
Quarters No. 3004
Fort Rucker, Alabama
1500 Hours, 1 January 1959

Only officers and senior civilians (and their wives) assigned to the U.S. Army Aviation Combat Developments Office were invited to the commanding officer's New Year's Day reception. It wasn't much different from the regular unit get-togethers that Bellmon held frequently during the year, differing only in that this one would be the last one Bellmon would give before moving to Washington—and in that Mac MacMillan, who was in charge of Bellmon's official social calendar, was absent.

Bellmon's quarters were not nearly as crowded as General Jiggs's had been, and though there was a punch bowl, there was also a bar with a wide assortment of whiskey, which meant that much of the punch would eventually be thrown out.

There was a sense of relief when Lowell came in with Jean-Philippe Jannier. Everybody would much rather gather around to meet Jannier than to discuss Lieutenant Colonel Rudolph G. MacMillan, whose punching out of Colonel Brandon had made him invisible, Lowell thought, if not yet officially a nonperson.

When Bellmon waved him toward the small cubicle he had made into a den for himself, Lowell was sure, however, that the fate of MacMillan would be Item No. 1 on Bellmon's agenda.

It was not, however.

"Colonel Edmund G. Hainey will assume command of CDO officially on Monday," Bellmon said.

"I was afraid of that," Lowell said.

"But he will not be physically present for duty for approximately two weeks after that. That means that since Colonel MacMillan is leaving . . ."

"Is Mac going somewhere?" Lowell asked innocently.

"MacMillan has been reassigned to the U.S. Army Special Warfare School at Fort Bragg," Bellmon said.

"I wonder how he'll look in a green beret?" Lowell asked. "Like a Scottish leprechaun?"

"Just for the record," Bellmon said, "I heard that the berets are gone."

"Pity," Lowell said. "I would have cheerfully given two dollars to see Mac in a beret."

"I don't quite understand your attitude," Bellmon said. "I thought Mac was a friend of yours."

"I didn't say he isn't," Lowell said.

"You seem remarkably cavalier about his problems," Bellmon said.

"Who sent him to Bragg? General Black?"

"Yes."

"Where do you think they would have sent a light bird who damned near killed somebody, punching him off an officer's club balcony, who was neither a holder of the Medal or an old pal of the Vice Chief of Staff?" Lowell asked. Bellmon did not reply.

"Going someplace where they have your bust in the post

Hall of Fame is not exactly being sent somewhere unpleasant," Lowell said. "Such as, for example, the Southern Command in Panama, where they were going to send me. I don't feel sorry for Mac, Bob. Sorry."

"It was an entirely different matter," Bellmon said.

"Forgive me, General, for not realizing that pleasuring a willing lady in what I thought was the privacy of my home was not, by a quantum jump, a more serious violation of good order and discipline than almost killing another officer."

"You can wisecrack to me as a friend, Craig," Bellmon said, obviously making an effort to control himself. "But I would be grateful if you would avoid using my rank when you do."

"I certainly meant no offense," Lowell said.

"None was taken," Bellmon said, curtly.

"Well," Lowell said, mocking him, "maybe just a little." He held up his hands, the thumb and index finger spread just a little apart.

"Before we landed in the rough, as we so often seem to, Craig, I was about to thank you for what you did last night."

"I didn't do much," Lowell said. "The first thing Brandon did when he woke up this morning was call the Chief of Information and tell him about the brutal, unprovoked assault."

"Where did you hear that?"

"I was at Jiggs's reception."

"Oh," Bellmon said.

"He also told me that he had a call scheduled with Black. I didn't think they'd court-martial Mac, particularly since there is no permanent damage to Brandon. But I didn't think they would leave him here, either."

"It's a hell of a note," Bellmon said, sadly. "The day after you get promoted, you get sent somewhere in disgrace."

"Let me say something to you as a friend, Bob," Lowell said.

"I don't suppose I could say no?"

"Whatever you owed Mac—if indeed you owed him a damned thing—for leaving him behind in the POW camp in Poland in War II, you have paid back a hundred times. Unless he goes up there and immediately starts throwing people off balconies, Mac is home free. He's got his twenty years in, and he's got his silver leaf, and the worst that can happen to him now is that they'll force him to retire. You've done your duty to him, it's over."

"I wish that I possessed your ruthlessness, Lowell," Bellmon said. "When I telephoned him and told him to depart for Bragg no later than Monday, I felt like I was kicking my family dog."

"Well, just consider where the family dog will be on Tuesday night," Lowell said. "In the 82nd Division O club, with a litter of eager little puppies at his feet, listening to the old dog tell them how it was at Sicily or Normandy, or wherever. He won't be allowed to buy a drink, which will of course delight him; and no one will say, 'Mac, for Christ's sake, we've heard that story fifty times.'"

Bellmon looked at Lowell without expression for a moment. Then he smiled, and patted his arm.

"You're right, of course, Craig. Thank you."

"I told Jiggs I'd call him after I'd spoken to you," Lowell said.

"There's the phone," Bellmon said. "Help yourself."

Barbara Bellmon came into the office as Jiggs was telling Lowell that he had just heard from General Black about Mac's transfer to Fort Bragg.

When he hung up the phone, Barbara handed him a drink.

"Danke schoen, gnadige Frau," Lowell said.

"Did he ask you?"

"Did who ask me what?"

"Then he didn't," she said. "Damn him!"

"Ask me what?"

"About your house," she said.

"What about it?"

"About renting it to us," she said. "Just until spring, when my brother leaves the Farm."

"I presumed that's where *you* would be," Lowell said. The Bellmon family for four generations had owned a farm twenty miles from Washington. Any of the Bellmons who happened to be stationed in Washington lived there during his assignment.

"Not until May," she said. "Then Tommy's going to England."

"Well, as they say in Poland, my house is your house, of course."

"He won't ask you for it," Barbara said.

"Send him in," Lowell ordered. When she hesitated, he said, "Go on, Barbara."

Bellmon came in the office a minute later.

"I have this friend with a problem," Lowell began.

"I thought you had something from General Jiggs," Bellmon said.

"My friend's problem is that he suddenly had to move," Lowell said. "Which means that his house is empty. It's not a trailer, and he couldn't bring it with him."

"Barbara came to you," Bellmon accused.

"That's what friends are for. When you have a problem, you go to a friend. You will recall, Bob, that I've gone to you on occasion."

"The last time you came to me, I wanted to see you thrown out of the army," Bellmon said.

"So I forgive you, OK?"

"What are you going to do with the house?"

"Well, for the next three months, because I feel obliged to give them that much notice, I'll have to keep it staffed," Lowell said. "And I would much rather have them waiting hand and foot on Barbara than on each other."

"How many are there?"

"Three."

"And after that?"

"I'll think about renting it," Lowell said.

"Not selling?"

"My family got rich by following a simple principle," Lowell said. "Buy real estate, do not sell it. The house is owned by one of my companies."

"Tommy, Barbara's brother," Bellmon said, "is going to England in May or June. We need a place till then."

"You've got one, Bob," Lowell said. "Call it house-sitting for me."

"I'm grateful," Bellmon said. "It would solve a lot of problems."

"There is only one problem," Lowell said.

"What?"

"Keep your hand on your zipper. Otherwise the senator's wife will be trying you on, or in, for size."

"Some of us are not possessed by an uncontrollable desire to rut," Bellmon said.

"You tell me that as a friend, right?" Lowell said, and laughed.

VIII

(One)
Fort Rucker, Alabama
0945 Hours, 3 January 1959

When Brigadier General Robert F. Bellmon told Lieutenant Colonel Rudolph G. MacMillan that he had been reassigned to the U.S. Army Special Warfare School at Fort Rucker, N.C., and was to proceed there immediately, Mac asked only one question.

"Can I go TPA?"

TPA was "travel by personal automobile."

"I don't see why not," Bellmon replied, after a moment's thought. "You're going up there TDY until your orders can be cut. I don't even know if I'm supposed to cut your orders, or whether DA will."

TDY was temporary duty. MacMillan knew what it meant.

"'Get his ass off the post right now!' huh?" he asked.

Bellmon didn't reply.

"I'll leave in the morning," Mac said.

"All right," Bellmon said.

"How am I going to clear the post without orders?" Mac asked.

Bellmon thought that over a moment, too, before replying.

"Have Roxy pay your club bill, and the golf course bill, that sort of thing. Whatever she can't handle later, I will."

Mac nodded again.

"I'm sorry about this, Mac," Bellmon said.

"I did it," Mac said. "I'll take my lumps. How lousy an efficiency report is it going to cost me?"

"Officially, it never happened," Bellmon said. "If it never happened, then obviously I can't write that your well-known splendid attributes as a warrior are unfortunately overshadowed by your lamentable tendency to do goddamn dumb things when you're drinking."

It doesn't really matter what the efficiency report says, Mac thought. *People are going to hear that I belted Brandon off the balcony. And even those that don't are going to wonder why a new light bird aviator suddenly gets himself assigned back to airborne.*

"Just to keep the record straight," MacMillan said, "I was mad, not drunk."

"You ever hear the story about the New York advertising agency, Mac, where the boss put a notice on the bulletin board saying that executives were requested to drink anything they wanted to drink at lunch—except vodka?"

"No," MacMillan replied seriously, confused.

"He said that their customers couldn't smell vodka on the breath, and he would rather have them think his executives were drunk, not stupid."

"OK, it was a dumb thing to do."

"Yes, it was."

"You know what I was just thinking?" Mac said, and went on without waiting for a response. "The last time I was stationed at Bragg, they wanted to send me to flight school, and I didn't want to go. Now they're sending me back, and I don't want to go."

"Lowell pointed out to me that sending you to Bragg can hardly be termed cruel and unusual punishment."

"I wanted to stick around and finish the Big Bad Bird," Mac said.

"Drive up, Mac," Bellmon told him, ending the conversation by putting out his hand. "By the time you get there, your orders will probably be there. You know the number if you need anything from me."

MacMillan shook Bellmon's hand briefly, and then met his eyes for a moment. Then he saluted.

"Fuck 'em, General," he said. "Have the bugler sound the charge."

He had said almost exactly the same words fourteen years before when he had parted from Bellmon at a German POW camp in Poland.

"Take care of yourself, Mac," Bellmon said, returning the salute. "Keep in touch."

MacMillan left Bellmon's office and got in his Cadillac and drove home.

Roxy came out into the carport before he got out of the car.

"Sandy and Sharon get off all right?" he asked.

Major and Mrs. Felter had come to Fort Rucker for the holidays in Major Craig Lowell's Aero Commander. Colonel William Roberts, who was now Lowell's commanding officer, had denied Lowell time off to fly them back.

"I took them to Dothan to the airport," Roxy said. "We were waiting for the Southern flight when an air force jet, a little one, landed. They sent it for him."

"Why didn't he have it land at Laird?" Mac asked.

"He probably didn't want people to know," Roxy said, and then she blurted: "So what are they going to do to you?"

What they're going to do to me, Roxy, is give me some asshole assignment, deputy assistant garbage disposal officer, maybe, or officer in charge of service clubs, so that I will take the hint and put in for retirement. I'm getting thrown out of the army, is what they're doing to me.

He couldn't tell her that, not with that look on her face.

"Bragg," he said. "The Special Warfare School."

"What's that?"

"You run around in the woods and eat snakes," he said.

"Those guys who wear the funny hats?"

"You got it," he said.

"You off flight status?"

"Bellmon didn't say. Probably. I was thinking about that on the way home. I can probably get back on jump status. Pay'd be the same if I can."

"This is real bad for you, huh?"

"I won't know until I get there," he said. "Red Hanrahan's there. He'll give me the straight poop. The worst that can happen is that I'll have to retire."

"When are you going?"

"In the morning. You want to pack me enough for a couple of weeks?"

She nodded.

"What do we do with this house?" Roxy asked.

"Rent it out," he said. "What else?"

He walked to a utility room at the end of the carport. He took a can of beer from an extra refrigerator, opened it, and drank deeply. Roxy watched him, shaking her head "no" when he offered her a beer. Then he took off his tunic and laid it on the washing machine and started to put on a set of coveralls.

"What are you going to do?" Roxy asked.

"Change the oil, check it out," he said. "Take the god-damned Fort Rucker stickers off the bumpers."

"What do you want for supper?"

"I don't care," he said.

She nodded and went back into the kitchen.

(Two)
Aboard Special Missions Flight No. 59–34
1105 Hours, 3 January 1959

The pilot, a handsome air force major, pushed aside the curtain that separated the cockpit from the cabin. Stooping under the low cabin ceiling, he made his way to where Felter was sitting.

"There's a chopper waiting for you at Andrews, Mr. Felter," he said.

Felter, without thinking about it, closed the portfolio on the folding desk in front of him. The portfolio was printed with red diagonal stripes and the words "Top Secret." It had been put aboard the aircraft, in the custody of a courier, so that it could be given to Felter as soon as he got aboard. It contained the latest intelligence from Cuba.

On New Year's Day, a bearded doctor of philosophy named Fidel Castro had driven into Havana in a jeep and taken control of the country.

Felter looked at the pilot as if he were thinking of something else, and it was a moment before he spoke.

"Get on the radio, please," he said, "and kill the chopper. Put us into Washington National."

"Sir, I mean a presidential helicopter," the major said.

"I don't want to arrive on the East Lawn in a chopper to save five minutes," Felter said. "Put us into Washington National."

"Yes, sir," the pilot said, and, stooping, made his way back to the cockpit.

Felter reopened the Top Secret folder and returned his attention to the messages. There was an almost wistful tinge of hope in the reports that some of the people close to Castro were bona fide democratic revolutionaries, but Felter believed it was only a matter of time before Castro allied himself with Moscow and acknowledged that he was a "Marxist."

There were no Marxists, of course, in the Kremlin, or anywhere else in the Soviet bloc. Marx had not even envisioned communism for Russia. There was a totalitarian state in Russia, which called itself "communist," but which was, in fact, continuing the expansionist, colonialist foreign policy of the Russian Tsarist Empire. At the moment, Sanford T. Felter was one of perhaps a dozen men in the American intelligence community who knew how much aid the romantic, bearded hero of the revolt against the old Cuban government had received from Russia. And who understood the threat that a Soviet colony ninety miles off Florida would pose to the United States.

He read the file again, once or twice shaking his head in either disbelief or resignation, and then closed the red-striped cover. After he'd finished, he leaned into the aisle and motioned with his finger.

A tall, thin, clean-cut young man came to him. He was wearing a dark blue vested suit. His necktie was pulled down, and the vest unbuttoned. There was a Smith & Wesson .38 Special revolver in a holster on his belt. There was a briefcase attached to his wrist with a stainless steel wire and a handcuff.

Felter handed him the folder.

"Burn these," he said. "Send me confirmation."

"Yes, sir," the young man said, stuffing the folder into the briefcase and then locking it.

"We're going into National," Felter said. "Is that going to pose transportation problems for you?"

"No, sir. We have people there. I'll be all right."

"Thank you," Felter said.

The young man went back to his seat. Felter got out of his seat, made his way forward to the cabin, and knelt in the aisle beside Sharon, who had a copy of *Reader's Digest* and the remnants of a sandwich on the fold-down table in front of her.

"We're going into National," he said. "If the car won't start, take a cab, and leave word for me at the White House."

"All right," Sharon said.

"I don't know when I'll be home," he said.

"I know," she said, and placed her hand on his and smiled at him. "Is it bad, honey?"

"No," he said. "Nothing to worry about."

(Three)
The White House
Washington, D.C.
1155 Hours, 3 January 1959

The taxi turned off Pennsylvania Avenue and stopped before the gate. Felter got out of the cab as a guard came out of the guard shack. The guard recognized Felter and signaled to the guard shack. Felter paid the cab, and then held up his White House pass for the guard.

"Good afternoon, sir," the guard said.

As Felter walked to the gate, the gate slid open just wide enough to admit him. When he was inside, it closed after him. He walked up the curving drive and entered the side entrance. A guard and a marine sergeant in dress blues were waiting for him.

"You're to go to the Situation Room, Mr. Felter," the marine sergeant said, and led the way to the elevator. Once the door had closed after them, Felter reached under his coat and came out with a .45 ACP pistol. He handed it to the marine.

"Thank you, sir," the marine said.

There was a bank of television sets mounted on the wall in the Situation Room. One of them was carrying NBC, the others were blank. NBC was showing what looked like a New Year's Day celebration in Havana.

The President turned when he sensed the light from the corridor shining into the darkened room. He saw Felter, nodded, and then returned his attention to the television. Felter saw that most of the places at the conference table were already filled. As he took an empty place at the end of the table, a marine set a legal pad, three pencils, and an ashtray in front of him. A moment later, he added a china mug of coffee.

Felter nodded his thanks, and picked up the coffee.

The NBC news program ended. A commercial for Sanka coffee came on. The screen went blank, and the lights in the room came up.

A discussion followed, lasting forty-five minutes. Felter neither made notes nor opened his mouth.

"Well, then," the President said, finally, "to sum up, we're in a holding position. Until this . . . this victory party, I suppose . . . winds down, and we can either talk to Castro personally, or at least get an idea of what he's thinking from Valaquez, there's nothing we can, or should do."

Juan Valaquez, the son of a Havana hotel owner, had been educated, like his father, at Georgia Tech. He had joined Fidel Castro early on, in a naive belief that Castro was a patriot whose sole ambition was to liberate Cuba from an oppressive military dictatorship. When it had become obvious to him that Castro's plans for Cuba had nothing to do with providing a free and democratic government, he had contacted a Georgia Tech classmate who had entered the Foreign Service.

Who told Valaquez he had two choices: to drop out of the Castro rebellion (he was offered political sanctuary in the United States) or to stay where he was and report on Castro's activities. He had elected to stay with Castro.

Felter raised his hand from the table, its index finger extended. The President saw it.

"Felter?"

The faces at the table turned to Felter.

"Mr. President," Felter said, "Juan Valaquez was executed by a firing squad at 5:05 this morning, Havana time."

"Jesus!" somebody said.

"How the hell can you know that?" an army lieutenant general snapped.

Felter didn't reply.

"Can you expand, Felter?" the President said.

"He was arrested at two this morning," Felter said. "Shortly after he left Castro in the presidential palace. He was taken to a house on the outskirts of Havana, interrogated for several hours, and then taken to the garden and shot. I don't know how much he told them, but we have to presume they got what they wanted from him."

"Dick?" the President looked at the Director of the CIA.

"The last I have on Valaquez is that he was with Castro for dinner," the Director said. "I don't know where Felter gets his information."

If it was an invitation to Felter to expand on his sources, Felter ignored it.

"How do you assess this, Felter?" the President asked.

"Are you asking for my recommendation, Mr. President?"

"Yes," the President said, somewhat coldly.

"I think we should eliminate Che Guevara," Felter said, levelly.

"Absolutely not!" the Secretary of State said.

"Are you prepared to do that, Felter?" the President asked. "It's something you can do, I mean, rather than something you suggest should be done?"

"Yes, sir. At the moment, we have the assets."

"What would be the advantages to us, Felter?" the President asked.

"Assets?" the President's Chief of Staff said. "What he means is assassins in place."

"I believe the decision to eliminate Valaquez was made before they knew for sure he was working for us," Felter said. "I believe it was made by Che Guevara, not Castro, although of course with Castro's blessing, for one or more reasons. For one thing, he posed a threat to Guevara's position in the new regime, as number two to Castro. Guevara took the chance, in other words, that he could reinforce his own position by eliminating Valaquez—providing he could prove to Castro that his suspicions were justified. We have to assume he made his point. Castro is now convinced that the people around him, with the exception of Guevara, are not trustworthy."

"That's conjecture, nothing more," the lieutenant general said.

Felter ignored the comment. He went on.

"If we take Guevara out, it will accomplish several things. For one thing, it will make Castro uneasy, and thus easier to deal with; and it will eliminate Guevara, who is probably the most dangerous member of the inner circle."

"And when do you think, Major," the head of the Defense Intelligence Agency asked, icily sarcastic, "that, failing the assassination of Guevara, we may expect a Cuban invasion of Key West?"

"No one expects that, General," the President said, gently. But it was a reproof.

"It may well be, Mr. President," Felter went on, "that nothing we can do, including the elimination of Guevara, will keep Russia, or Russian missiles, out of Cuba. I suggest, however, that anything we do to delay that movement is in the national interest."

"Including murder?" the Secretary of State said.

"How would you characterize the execution of Valaquez?" the President asked, dryly, "if not murder?"

"As the execution of a traitor," the Secretary of State said. "Which is permitted under international law."

The President nodded, as if he accepted that interpretation. He looked at Felter.

"I don't want this man killed, Felter," he said.

"Yes, sir," Felter said.

"I would say this," the President said. "If this matter were brought to a vote, I think there would only be one vote, Colonel Felter's, to go ahead. He stands alone, in other words."

Felter glanced at the President. He had just been given a misspoken promotion to colonel.

"He stood alone six months ago, too," the President said, "when he said there was no doubt in his mind that this Castro was going to overthrow General Batista."

Then without another word, the President got up and walked out of the Situation Room.

(Four)
127 Rosemary Lane
Ozark, Alabama
1000 Hours,
3 January 1959

For MacMillan, the drive to Bragg was going to be by way of Benning, Gordon, and Jackson. That is to say, he would drive up U.S. 431 to Columbus, Georgia, where Fort Benning, the Infantry Center, sits on the Alabama–Georgia border. From Benning, he would take U.S. 80 across Georgia to Fort Gordon, at Augusta, and then U.S. 1 to Fort Jackson, at Columbia, S.C., and then take U.S. 15 into Bragg, which was outside Fayetteville, N.C.

He slept late, until almost ten, then got up, showered, and

got dressed. He put on civilian sports clothes, a dark blue golf shirt, light blue slacks, and an expensive yellow nylon jacket with an embroidered representation of a burning tree on its breast. Three months before, after he'd gone eighteen holes with Craig Lowell at Burning Tree in Washington, he'd seen the jacket in the pro shop. It was stuffed with some kind of miracle material that was supposed to be lighter and more efficient insulation than goose down. He liked the jacket for two reasons; first, because it was a really good jacket, light and warm as hell, and second, because he'd paid for it with the hundred and sixty bucks he'd taken from Lowell, who had needed eleven strokes to get through the last two greens. Mac didn't often get to take money from Lowell, and it was sweet when he did. The jacket made a pleasant reminder.

After he'd eaten the ham and eggs Roxy made for him, he kissed her perfunctorily, as if he were going no further than Fort Rucker for the day, and went out to the carport. He took a quick look to see that the stainless steel thermos bottle and the road atlas were on the front seat; that the briefcase was on the floor on the passenger side; and that the golf bag was on the floor in the back.

He didn't check the briefcase, confident that Roxy had taken care of it. He knew that when he opened it, it would contain a toilet kit, a checkbook, five $100 American Express Company traveler's checks, a .32 ACP Colt pistol, two clips and a shoulder holster for the pistol, a couple of handkerchiefs, a bottle of aspirin, and a small box of Kleenex. He did not even open the trunk. He had asked Roxy to pack enough for him for two weeks, and there was absolutely no question in his mind that when he opened the trunk at Bragg, there would be suitcases and zipper bags containing enough uniforms and clothing for at least two weeks. He saw that Roxy had even equipped him with a jar of Lowell's cigars and a box of large wooden kitchen matches to light them with.

Then he got in the Cadillac and backed out of the driveway. When Roxy waved at him, he tapped the horn, and then turned the corner.

There was absolutely no trauma of separation. The kids hadn't even said much when he told them at supper that they were going to Bragg. They were army brats, and used to his frequent absences and their own frequent moves.

He left Ozark at a quarter to eleven. At almost exactly noon, having driven the ninety-odd miles well above the speed limit, he crossed the bridge between Phenix City, Alabama, and Columbus, Georgia. A large sign gave the route to Fort Benning.

He had been at Benning years before, as a buck sergeant, when the concept of vertical envelopment, that is of landing military forces by parachute from aircraft, had been judged worthy of a test by a provisional company of the 82nd Infantry Division. He had made his first parachute jump at Benning. He and Roxy had lived in a tiny apartment in Phenix City, Alabama.

There was a Hall of Fame at Fort Benning. On its wall hung a photograph of First Lieutenant Rudolph G. MacMillan. In the photograph, President Harry S. Truman was hanging the starred ribbon of the Medal of Honor around his neck. Framed beside it was a copy of the citation that had accompanied the award.

He did not turn toward Fort Benning. Instead, he drove through town toward the intersection of U.S. 80. Then he nosed the Cadillac into the parking lot of a White Castle hamburger stand. He had been looking especially for the small white-tiled building. There they made very thin hamburger patties sort of steamed on the grill with chopped onions, which a waitress would bring to the car. There was no hamburger stand like it near Fort Rucker.

It was those burgers, he told himself, that made him look for the White Castle, rather than going out to the club at Benning for lunch. It had nothing to do with the fact that the way he had things figured, he was about to have his ass thrown out of the army and the less chance of seeing somebody he knew the better.

He looked around impatiently when no waitress appeared, and then saw a sign saying that curb service began at 4:00 P.M. He swore, and started the engine, and then shut it off again. The aroma of the frying onions and beef had penetrated the Cadillac. His mouth was watering.

"Fuck it," he said, and got out of the car and went inside the building, carrying the stainless steel thermos bottle.

There was a stool in the corner by the door. He sat down and ordered eight White Castles and coffee, black. Then he went to the john and threw out what was left of Roxy's coffee and rinsed the thermos.

The stack of White Castles was waiting for him when he

came out. He methodically made four double-patty burgers out of the eight White Castles, by throwing away the top half of the rolls and putting the bottoms together.

A quartet of instructors—two corporals, a staff sergeant, and a sergeant first class—from the Parachute School at Benning came into the White Castle. They paid absolutely no attention to him.

He thought that what he really would like to do was be sergeant major of the jump school. Shit, he'd been around airborne even before it *was* airborne. Then he realized that was a dumb thing to be thinking. He might be on the shit list, but the worst thing they could do to him was make him retire. That wouldn't be the end of the goddamned world. He had twenty-one years in, which meant that he would go out with a nice pension. When he left Mauch Chunk, Pennsylvania, at sixteen to join the army, he didn't have the price of a pot to piss in. So if he went home now, he would go home in a Cadillac, with a lieutenant colonel's pension, and half ownership of the nicest restaurant in miles. Things could be a lot worse.

Another soldier came in. A young one. He was in civilian clothes, but he was dragging a stuffed duffel bag along after him, his hair was clipped short, and he was tanned red. There was no mistaking that he was a soldier, and Mac guessed that he had probably just finished jump school.

The soldier took a stool down the counter and ordered two White Castles. That's all, just two of the tiny hamburgers. He was obviously broke. MacMillan debated striking up a conversation with the kid, and then buying him a meal, but decided against it. Dressed the way he was, in civvies, it might be misunderstood.

The kid wolfed down the two White Castles and drank the water that came with them, then visited the john. When he came out, he hoisted the duffel bag onto his shoulder and went out.

Mac ate his four double White Castles, ordered the thermos bottle filled with coffee, black, and paid his bill, got back in the Cadillac, and headed toward U.S. 80.

A hundred yards down the road, he saw the kid, sitting on the duffel bag with his thumb out.

Mac slowed, stopped, backed up, and lowered the passenger side window.

"I'm taking 80 North," he said, when the kid ran up.

"That's great!" the kid said.

"Put the bag in the back seat," Mac said.

The kid got in beside him.

"Watch your feet," Mac said, pointing to the jar of cigars and the briefcase. "Push that crap to one side."

"I appreciate the ride," the kid said.

"You're welcome," Mac said. "Where you headed?"

"Fort Bragg," the kid said.

"You're lucky, then," Mac said. "I'm going right through there."

"God," the kid said, "takes care of fools and drunks, and I am qualified on both counts."

Mac chuckled.

"Just finish jump school?" Mac asked.

"Does it show?" the kid said.

"Yeah," Mac said, "I guess it does."

"You were in the army?"

"I was in the 82nd during the war," Mac said. "War II."

"That's where I'm headed," the kid said. "The 82nd Airborne."

They were on U.S. 80 by then, and out of town.

"There's coffee in the thermos," Mac said. "The top makes a cup. You want some?"

"I would really like some coffee," the kid said.

"Here," Mac said, handing the thermos to him. "Broke, huh?"

"Does it show?"

"I saw you in the White Castle," Mac said.

"Stony," the kid said.

"You should have talked to your first sergeant," Mac said. "Not all of them are bastards. Maybe yours could have arranged a partial pay."

"Is that what you were, a first sergeant?" the kid asked.

"I used to be a technical sergeant," Mac said. "Platoon sergeant of the Pathfinder Platoon of the 508th P.I.R."

"No kidding?" the kid said, impressed. Mac was pleased.

"You jump into Normandy on D day?"

"I jumped every place the regiment jumped," Mac said with quiet pride.

"They showed us the movies of Normandy," the kid said. "Twice."

"How come twice?"

"Once in OCS and once in jump school."

"You were in OCS?"

"Second Lieutenant Ellis, Thomas J., at your service," the kid said.

"Why the hell are you broke and hitchhiking, Lieutenant?" Mac asked. He wasn't entirely sure that the kid was telling the truth. He didn't look old enough to be an officer.

"Because three kings doesn't beat three nines and a pair of sevens," Ellis said, simply.

"Jesus!" Mac said, sympathetically. "And you lost your whole month's pay."

"The pay didn't bother me," the kid said. "Losing the car really hurt."

"You lost your car, too?"

"Nice little red MG. And my watch. And a very nice ring with a diamond."

"You were in the wrong game," Mac said.

"Now you tell me," Ellis said, and chuckled.

"Were you taken?" Mac asked.

"No," Ellis said. "I thought the sonofabitch was bluffing. He couldn't play poker. He just drew the right cards. You know how it is."

Nice kid. No bitching about losing his shirt.

"What are you going to do until next month?"

"I'm praying that I'll be able to convince a banker at Bragg that as an officer and a gentleman on jump pay I'm a worthy risk," Ellis said. "You've solved my major problem, getting from Benning to Bragg. And I'm grateful."

"Are you old enough to smoke cigars, Lieutenant?" Mac asked.

"I'm nineteen," Ellis said. "Is that old enough?"

"Reach down to that jar and get a couple out," Mac said.

Ellis opened the wide-mouthed glass jar and took two long, thick, black cigars from it.

They were H. Uppmann "Churchills." Roxy had told Mac, years ago, that they cost two bucks apiece. Every year since 1947, the postman had delivered a carton from Alfred Dunhill in New York City. The cartons contained four wide-mouthed jars, each jar containing twenty H. Uppmann "Churchill" cigars. There was always a card, always the same message: "Merry Christmas, Craig W. Lowell." It wasn't his signature; somebody in the cigar store signed it. And every year, too, there was a package for Roxy, always containing the same thing, a bottle of Chanel No. 5, not the size bottle you saw in stores, a little one containing an ounce, but a big one, about a pint, and the same card, signed by somebody in the perfume store.

The cigar jars were too good to throw away. Roxy kept them and used them for sugar and coffee, and to put things in the refrigerator. The cigars were good, but Mac couldn't see where they were worth two bucks apiece.

He thought of Lowell now, watching the kid light the cigar. Lowell had always smoked cigars, even when he'd been an eighteen-year-old goddamned PFC and the golf pro at Bad Nauheim. Lowell had been eighteen when he'd put on the gold bars of a second lieutenant. And this kid at least had gone to OCS to earn his. They'd handed Lowell his on a tray, because General Waterford wanted him to play polo.

"How long you been in the army?" Mac asked.

"Almost a year," the kid said.

"You enlist for OCS?"

"No. I enlisted, believe it or not, for cook's and baker's school. I thought what I'd like to do is own a restaurant."

"That's what I do," Mac said, and wondered why. "I own a restaurant."

"Must be a successful one," the kid said, indicating the car.

"My brother-in-law runs it," Mac said. "In Mauch Chunk, Pennsylvania."

"That where you're headed?" the kid asked.

Mac nodded. He didn't want the kid to be scared off by his silver leaf.

"I saw the clubs in the back seat. I thought maybe you were going to Augusta."

"I've been South," Mac said. "So tell me, how did you get from cook's and baker's school to OCS?"

"By way of KP," the kid said, and laughed. "By the time I'd done my first day of KP, I decided that I did not want to spend the next four years of my life in a kitchen. And the only way I could get out of going to cook's and baker's school was to go to OCS. So I did."

"Being a second john is better than being a sergeant," Mac said.

"I think I'll like it," the kid said. "Anyway, I figured that since I was going to do it, I might as well go whole hog. So

I applied for airborne, and when I finished OCS they sent me to jump school."

"I never went to jump school," Mac said. "They didn't even have a jump school back then. What happened was they sent a guy from the Switlick Parachute Company down to Benning, and he taught us."

The kid was fascinated, and made a good listener, and Mac liked to talk about the old days. The time and the miles passed quickly.

Mac pulled into a restaurant on the outskirts of Augusta, Georgia.

"I'll stake you to chow," he said. "I've lost my ass at poker, too."

"Thank you," Ellis said simply. "Thank you."

Over a tough hot roast beef sandwich in a pasty gravy, the kid asked him his name, and a couple of minutes later, how to spell Mauch Chunk.

"Why the hell do you want to know how to spell Mauch Chunk?" Mac asked.

"So I can send you a check for my dinner," the kid said.

"Forget that," Mac said. "My pleasure."

"I really want to," the kid said.

He means it. He's just not saying that. A nice kid.

"I'll put it on my expense account," Mac said. "Forget about it."

When they came out of the restaurant, Ellis offered to drive.

Mac was surprised at himself when he walked to the passenger side of the Cadillac. He didn't usually let anybody else drive the Caddy. But he told himself the kid was trying to pay his way, and it was a long haul to Bragg yet.

"I'll crap out in the back seat," he said. "Wake me when you get tired."

(Five)

The kid shook him awake.

Mac sat up. They were in a truck stop. The kid was in uniform.

"Where are we?" Mac asked. He looked at his watch. It was seven thirty.

"A couple of miles outside of Fayetteville. I thought I'd better change into my uniform."

Mac got out of the back seat.

It was so much bullshit about eating where truck drivers ate—because the food was good. Truck drivers ate where they could find room to park their rigs. Still, he was hungry.

"Let's get something to eat," he said.

"I've mooched enough," Ellis said.

"When you've mooched enough," Mac said, "I'll tell you."

He opened the glove compartment, and pushed the trunk opener button.

He handed the kid a twenty dollar bill.

"Fill it up," he said. "Check the oil. I'm going to change, too. Then we'll get something to eat, and then I'll take you out to the post."

"That's out of your way. They must have a bus or something, and I've got enough money for that."

"I'll see you inside," Mac said, and picked up one of the zipper clothing bags and carried it into the truck stop.

Mac had never been in a truck stop this big before. The goddamned place was enormous, and it had something Mac had never seen before. For three dollars, you could rent a room for eight hours. That made sense, when he thought about it. It didn't cost them three bucks to wash a couple of sheets and towels, and for three bucks a driver got a place for a little shut-eye and a shower. And besides, he filled up his truck and ate probably two meals. Plenty of money changed hands.

Roxy's brother was talking about them building a truck stop. He would have to remember to tell Roxy to tell him about this.

And right now, three bucks seemed like a cheap enough price to pay for a quick shower, a private crap, and a clean place to change into his uniform. He handed over three bucks and a girl gave him a key.

As he tucked his shirt in his pants, Mac looked at the breast of his tunic. Roxy had pinned every goddamned thing he owned on it. There were decorations and insignia above both breast pockets. Above the right pocket were what the army called "metallic devices": there was a gold-rimmed blue oblong, the Presidential Distinguished Unit Citation, awarded to the 508th Parachute Infantry Regiment. It was both a personal and a unit award. If you were in the 508th when it was awarded, you could always wear the citation. You could also wear it if you were assigned to the 508th even if you had never heard a shot fired in anger. Beside it was the Korean Presidential Distinguished Unit Citation. Above those devices were French Army paratrooper's wings.

The upper left breast of the tunic was buried under ribbons and devices. There were five rows, each of three ribbons, each signifying an award. Above them, by itself, was the ribbon representing the Medal of Honor. Above that was an Expert Combat Infantry Badge, second award, above that the army aviator's wings with the wreathed star of a Master Aviator, and above the pilot's wings, parachutist's wings, onto which were fixed five stars, one for each jump into combat.

What the hell. What was it the kid had said about going "whole hog"? I might be coming to Bragg on the shit list, but there is no harm in wearing the crap that says you haven't always been on it.

He put the tunic on and examined himself in the mirror. Then he zipped up the clothing bag and carried it across his shoulder out to the dining room.

Second Lieutenant Ellis was sitting in a booth over a cup of coffee. He glanced at Mac, then did a double take and stood up.

"Keep your seat, Lieutenant," Mac said, and slid onto the seat across from him. "You order for us?"

"No, sir, Colonel," the kid said.

"Life is full of little surprises, ain't it?" Mac said.

Ellis was studying the ribbons.

"Is that one on top what I think it is?" he asked.

The waitress appeared, so Mac didn't have to answer.

"Bring us a couple of 'Long Haul Specials,' medium," Mac said. He had noticed an advertisement for it. It was steak, eggs, and hash browns.

"Coffee for you, too?" she asked.

"Yeah," Mac said, and then said, "Hold it a minute, honey." He took out his wallet and two one-hundred-dollar traveller's checks and his AGO card. He scrawled his name on the checks and handed them and his AGO card to her.

"Cash those for me, will you?"

She walked away.

"You must think I'm a real horse's ass," the kid said.

"No," Mac said, and smiled at him. "Anybody who can lose all his dough, and his car and his watch and his ring, betting on three kings can't be all bad."

"You're stationed at Bragg, Colonel?" Ellis asked.

"I'm reporting in, like you," Mac said.

The waitress returned with a mug of coffee and a wad of battered twenty dollar bills. When she had gone, Mac pushed the money across the table to Ellis.

"I expect two monthly payments of a hundred bucks," he said. "I'm going to be at the Special Warfare School. You know my name."

"I can't take that, Colonel," Ellis said.

"Yeah, you can, and you will," Mac said. "Don't argue with me."

Ellis was looking at his ribbons again.

"That is the Medal of Honor, isn't it?" he asked.

"Yeah, and it and ten bucks'll pay for our dinner," Mac said.

"I'll pay the dinner," Ellis said. "Now that I'm solvent."

"I accept," Mac said.

It was eight thirty when he braked the Cadillac at the MP's signal at the main gate to Fort Bragg.

The MP came around to the window as Mac lowered it.

He took a quick look at Mac and threw a rigid salute.

Mac returned it casually.

"We're reporting in," Mac said.

"May I have your name, Colonel?"

"MacMillan," Mac said. "I'm going to the Special Warfare School."

"Will the colonel please pull his car over to the side?" the MP said, pointing to an area beside the guard shack.

"What the hell?" Mac asked, but the MP was gone.

Mac moved the car.

"What are they doing, searching for booze?" he asked.

The MP came to the window.

"It will be just a minute or two, Colonel," he said.

"What the hell is going on?" Mac asked. The MP walked away without replying.

Mac waited a couple of minutes, time enough to light a cigar and become annoyed. And then he got out of the car.

He was halfway to the MP shack when he saw an MP staff car coming down the highway from the direction of the main post. It had its flashing lights on, but wasn't blowing its siren. It screeched to a stop near him. The door opened, and a very natty MP first john got out.

"Colonel MacMillan?" he asked, saluting crisply.

"That's right," Mac said. "What the hell is this, Lieutenant?"

"Colonel, if you'll be good enough to get back in your car and follow me, sir?" the MP lieutenant said, saluted again, and got back in the MP car.

Mac got behind the wheel of the Cadillac.

"What's going on?" Ellis said.

"I don't know," Mac said. "Maybe we're the ten millionth soldier or something."

The MP car led him down the highway to Post Theatre No. 1, and then turned right onto the main post. Finally, it stopped before Quarters No. 1. The door to Quarters No. 1 opened, and a captain came quickly down the stairs.

"Welcome to Fort Bragg, Colonel," he said. "Will you come with me, please?"

"Come on, Ellis," Mac said. "This may be educational."

He followed the captain up the stairs to Quarters No. 1.

Lieutenant General H. H. "Triple H" Howard came through the door.

"By God, Mac," General Howard said, "it's good to see you."

Mac and Ellis saluted. A flashbulb went off.

Howard took Mac's arm and led him into the house. There was a banner thumbtacked to the wall. On it were representations of the insignia of the XVIII Airborne Corps, the 82nd Airborne Division, a set of Master Parchutist's wings, and the words WELCOME HOME, MAC MACMILLAN.

There were several vaguely familiar officers in the foyer, all of whom offered Mac their hands. Then a photographer arranged all of them before the banner and took several pictures.

Whatever this is all about, Mac thought, *it don't look like the standard reception for somebody on the shit list.*

IX

(One)
The Pentagon
Washington, D.C.
5 Januray 1959

The Vice Chief of Staff of the United States Army received the commandant of the U.S. Army Special Warfare School at 1240 hours, forty minutes after the appointment was scheduled.

"The Vice Chief of Staff will see you now, Colonel," a gray-haired, middle-aged master sergeant said, holding the door open for him.

Hanrahan marched into the office, came to a stop three feet from the large highly polished desk, and saluted.

"Colonel Hanrahan reporting to the Vice Chief of Staff as ordered, sir."

"Hello, Hanrahan, how are you?" General Black responded, with a casual wave of his hand as a returned salute.

"Very well, thank you, sir," Hanrahan said.

"Congratulations on the eagle," Black said.

"Thank you, sir."

"You had lunch?"

"No, sir."

"You have your choice between the official dining room," Black said, "or a submarine sandwich here."

"I'd rather have the submarine, if that would be all right with you," Hanrahan said.

General Black punched his intercom.

"Ask Wesley to make us a couple of sandwiches, please," he said. Then he turned back to Hanrahan. "Lots of goodies with this job. There's a complete kitchen back there. I don't know what kind of a contribution it makes to the national defense, but it's handy if your wife throws you out of the house."

"Is that the same Sergeant Wesley I remember, sir?"

"He's got thirty-six years. I can't throw him out," Black said.

The door opened and the noncommissioned officer in question came through, bearing a tray. He was six feet three inches tall, and weighed nearly 300 pounds. He was wearing one of the new shade 51 uniforms. A dozen hash marks, diagonal stripes each representing three years of service, ran from his wrist to his elbow. He was very black, and had three gold teeth.

"Just happened to have a couple made up, General," he said, and then, spotting Hanrahan: "Well, hello there, and don't you look fine with that gleaming eagle?"

"Hello, Wesley. How are you?" Hanrahan said.

"Older and fatter," Master Sergeant Wesley said. "I guess you'll both have coffee, black, to wash this down?"

"Please," Hanrahan said. General Black nodded. Master Sergeant Wesley laid the tray on a coffee table before a red leather couch. General Black went to it and sat down, then motioned Hanrahan beside him.

"Thank you, sir."

"Have you seen Felter since you've been in Washington?" Black asked.

"Yes, sir. I came here to see him."

"Where'd you spend last night? With him? I was looking all over for you."

It could have been a rebuke.

"General, you understand I'm here on leave?"

"I know why you're here," Black said.

"Yes, sir," Hanrahan said, formally. "Major and Mrs. Felter were kind enough to put me up."

"You're pretty close?"

"Yes, sir. We were in Greece together."

"I have a good deal of respect for *Presidential Counselor* Felter," Black said. "Did he tell you about that?"

"Yes, sir."

Black nodded and lifted an eight-inch-long roll to his mouth and took a delicate bite.

"Trouble with these things is that you dribble Italian dressing on your clothes," he said. "Wes found some old buddy in the District in the business. He sells him the rolls and the filling."

"Yes, sir," Hanrahan said. "They're very good."

"I have so much respect for *Presidential Counselor* Felter," Black went on, "that I have concluded it was a case of *Presidential Counselor* Felter deciding it was in the best interests of the nation and the army to develop a unique asset, not under the control of the airborne establishment, and to arrange for the appointment, DP, of an officer to develop that asset on the basis of that officer's unique qualifications, rather than because *Major* Felter found himself in a position where he could do an old buddy, who was about to fail twice of selection for promotion, some good."

He raised his eyes from his submarine and met Hanrahan's eyes.

"That opinion, Colonel, is not universally held," Black added, levelly.

"I understand, sir," Hanrahan said.

"The situation has been aggravated by several things I have done," Black said. "Things which coincidentally tie in with you. For one thing, I elected not to turn the development of the rocket-armed helicopter over to the air force. It is the opinion of the Chief of Staff that I erred in judgment. More important, that I made this decision not only unilaterally, which was not my privilege, but somewhat disloyally. That I went behind his back, and did something I knew he didn't want done."

Hanrahan was aware that Black was looking at him.

"If the general expects a comment, I'm afraid I have none to make."

"No comment was expected," Black said. "Felter didn't mention any of this to you?"

"You're talking about Lowell, sir?"

Black nodded.

"I decided that my personal annoyance with Major Lowell was not sufficient grounds to force him out of the service," Black said. "Additionally, I thought he was singularly qualified to keep that program on the tracks, rather than have it become yet another empire of the Cincinnati Flying Club."

The Cincinnati Flying Club was much like the West Point Protective Association—at least in the minds of those not members. The club was composed of old-time army aviators, who were—not entirely unfairly—accused of trying to obtain promotions and good assignments for themselves, at the expense of newcomers.

"But when I went to Fort Rucker," General Black went on, "it was the Chief of Staff's understanding that Major Lowell's career was about to be terminated. So it is not surprising that the Chief of Staff believes my decision to retain Major Lowell in the service was another example of action on my part that was both ill-advised, unilateral, and disloyal."

Hanrahan had no idea why Black was telling him all this, and was uncomfortable because he couldn't think of anything to say.

"Finally," Black said, "on New Year's Eve, Mac MacMillan had a few too many drinks, and took a punch at an officer he thought was misbehaving toward Roxy. He knocked him through the railing of the balcony of the Rucker O club. The officer assaulted wanted him court-martialed. Acting unilaterally, disloyally, and perhaps ill-advisedly, I stopped that and ordered that Mac be immediately transferred. I wasn't thinking too clearly, Colonel. I thought that since Mac had so much excess energy, it would do him good to work it off running around the boondocks at Bragg. I ordered him assigned to you."

"I see," Hanrahan said. "General, I've worked with MacMillan before. I think I can handle him."

Black's eyes narrowed.

"The point I had hoped to make, Colonel," he said, coldly, "is this." He paused. "Let me back up a little. I believe that the notion of the United States developing a force of highly trained officers and noncoms to serve as the nucleus of native forces is a sound one. I was impressed with how many German divisions were tied up in Greece and in Russia by guerrillas, and I was impressed with the whipping the Vietminh gave the

French at Dien Bien Phu. I believe, in other words, in Special Forces."

"I'm pleased to hear you say that, sir," Hanrahan said.

"I also agree with Major Felter that you're the man to get it going and that it should not be under airborne," General Black said. "And finally, I believe—but I will not entertain your questions on the subject—that in the very near future it may be necessary to deploy irregular forces such as those I expect you to develop."

That was a bolt out of the blue. Hanrahan had difficulty not asking for amplification.

"Having established that," Black went on after a moment, "I want you to understand that you're standing all alone down there. In your position, you should have influence in high places. You're not going to have it. I can't do anything for you, for the reasons I have just given, and Felter won't be able to do you any good, because he has to keep his hole card. There will be pressure to have you relieved. Felter can stop that, because anybody trying it would have to go to the President and tell him his man was wrong. The only man who could do that would be the Chief of Staff, and I don't think the Chief of Staff is going to go to the President and demand that you be relieved because you persist in wearing a funny hat and are somewhat less than enthusiastic about the role of parachute troops in the army of the future. But Felter cannot use that hole card every time Triple H Howard harasses you."

"I take the general's point," Hanrahan said.

"I hope so, Hanrahan," Black said. He took another bite of his sandwich.

"Colonel Hanrahan," he said. "The military attaché of the U.S. Embassy in Paris is retiring as of 1 February. You have been nominated for the position. It is a stabilized three-year assignment, and carries with it certain prerogatives. There is diplomatic status, a generous per diem, a uniform allowance, an entertainment allowance, and some other things. Would you like to go to Paris?"

"I am perfectly satisfied with my present assignment, sir," Hanrahan said.

"I can only presume that you know what you're doing," Black said. He extended his hand. "Thank you for coming to see me, Colonel."

"Thank you for seeing me, General," Hanrahan said.

"Apropos of nothing whatever, Hanrahan, just to satisfy my curiosity, has Special Forces appealed to our Puerto Rican troops? Do you have many Puerto Rican volunteers? Or, for that matter, any other Hispanics?"

"I don't have any figures, sir," Hanrahan said. "I've seen some black faces, and there are, what's the phrase, 'Latin' sounding names, not many, on the rosters."

"Hmmm," the Vice Chief of Staff said. "Have a nice trip home, Colonel."

"Thank you, sir."

(Two)
Fayetteville, North Carolina
2305 Hours, 7 January 1959

There was no direct air service between Fayetteville and Washington. Hanrahan had to fly first to Atlanta, and wait there two hours for Piedmont Flight 203. When he finally arrived in Fayetteville, a Green Beret, a buck sergeant in fatigues, was standing inside the terminal waiting for him. He saluted snappily.

"Good evening, sir."

"Evening," Hanrahan said, returning the salute.

"Give me your stubs, please, sir, and I'll get your bags," the sergeant said. "The car's out in front."

"My wife's meeting me," Hanrahan said.

"No, sir," the buck sergeant said. "The OD called her and told her we'd be out here anyway and would pick you up."

"Well, fine," Hanrahan said, handing the baggage checks over. "Thank you."

There was another Beret, another buck sergeant, leaning on the highly polished fender of the staff car.

"Good evening, sir," he said, saluting crisply, and then opening the door. "Nice flight?"

"Yes, thank you," Hanrahan said. He got in the back of the car. There was a thermos of coffee, a china mug, and a copy of the semiofficial Fort Bragg newspaper, the *Para-Glide*, on the seat.

"Who are we meeting, Sergeant?" Hanrahan asked.

"Sir?"

"What are you guys doing out here?" Hanrahan asked.

"Meeting you, sir," the sergeant said.

He was on leave, and thus not entitled to offical transportation. They'd somehow learned when he was coming in and met him. With a thermos of coffee. He was touched.

He picked up the *Para-Glide* and glanced at the front page. There were two familiar faces, smiling faces, on it. General Howard's and Mac MacMillan's. Hanrahan read the headline.

82ND A/B DIV MEDAL OF HONOR WINNER
RETURNS TO HOME OF AIRBORNE

Below the picture, which occupied four columns, was the story.

Lt. Gen. H. H. Howard, Commanding General of the XVIII Airborne Corps and Fort Bragg (left) is shown welcoming Lt. Col. Rudolph G. MacMillan back to Fort Bragg. General Howard described Col. MacMillan as one of the "legendary troopers of the 82nd Airborne Division in World War II."

"Col. MacMillan," General Howard related, "was in the 82nd Airborne before it was officially a division. As Pathfinder Platoon Sergeant of the 508th PIR, he made every combat jump the regiment made during the war. He was given a battlefield commission during Operation Market-Basket, shortly before the action during which his exploits against overwhelming enemy forces earned him the Medal of Honor.

"It was only after the last of his men had been killed or wounded, and his ammunition gone, when he had literally nothing left with which to fight that MacMillan fell into enemy hands," General Howard went on, "and that didn't hold him down either. He was awarded the Distinguished Service Cross for his incredibly courageous and resourceful escape from a prisoner-of-war camp."

"Colonel MacMillan also served with great distinction in the Korean War," General Howard went on, "where he twice earned the Silver Star. And more recently, he was invested as a Chevalier in the French Legion of Honor following a special assignment with the 3rd Parachute Regiment of the French Foreign Legion at Dien Bien Phu in French Indochina.

"Col. MacMillan," General Howard said, "is the paratrooper's paratrooper, an inspiration to everyone connected with Airborne, indeed to every soldier. And speaking for everyone at the home of Airborne, it's great to have him home."

"Jesus!" Hanrahan said.

The sergeant turned around at the word, in time to see Hanrahan toss the paper aside.

"What about that guy?" the sergeant said. "John Wayne! Is all that crap true, Colonel?"

"Nothing is ever all true, Sergeant," Hanrahan said. "You'll shortly have a chance to judge Colonel MacMillan for yourself."

"Sir?" the sergeant asked, confused.

"Colonel MacMillan is being assigned to us," Hanrahan said.

"It didn't say that in the paper," the sergeant said.

"No," Hanrahan said, "I noticed."

The other sergeant arrived with the bag and got in the front seat.

"Sorry it took so long, sir," he said.

"Tell me, Sergeant," Hanrahan said, "do any of the sterling troopers of the Special Warfare School ever fall from virtue and visit Blood Alley?"

The sergeant hesitated before replying.

"Not many, Colonel," he said. "Sometimes, if they just miss a bus, they'll go to Clara's for a beer while they're waiting."

"Clara's Cafe? Is that still in business?"

"Yes, sir."

"Take us by Clara's, Sergeant," Hanrahan said. "Let's see if anybody missed the bus."

The two enlisted men exchanged glances with each other.

"Yes, sir," the driver said.

Blood Alley was a street lined with bars, hockshops, Army-Navy stores. Clara's Cafe was in the middle of the second block.

The sergeant in the passenger seat jumped out and opened the door for Hanrahan.

"You guys stay here," Hanrahan said. "I won't be a minute."

The interior of Clara's Cafe was very dark. Smoke hung heavily in the air. There was a strong smell of disinfectant which did not quite overwhelm the sour smell of beer. It was packed tightly with soldiers, in and out of uniform.

Three Green Beret noncoms, two sergeants first class and a master sergeant, all in their late twenties, sat hunched over beers at the bar.

"How's it going?" Hanrahan said.

One of the noncoms turned his head quickly, took in Hanrahan's beret, and returned his glance to his beer bottle.

"Whadayasay?" he said.

And then realization dawned. There was a silver eagle on the Green Beret. He started to get to his feet. Hanrahan pushed him back down.

"You guys need a ride to the post?" he asked.

The other two Berets now looked at him. One jumped up. "Jesus Christ!" he said.

"No. Hanrahan," Hanrahan said. He went on: "Anybody want a ride to the post?" When there was no response, Hanrahan said: "It's a suggestion, not an order. I just happened to be in the neighborhood . . ."

"We missed the bus by five minutes, Colonel."

"Well, if you want a ride, you're welcome," he said.

He turned and began to push his way through the crowd.

The three sergeants straightened their berets and tugged at the skirts of their tunics and followed him outside.

An MP jeep had nosed in before the staff car. Both white-hatted MPs were at the driver's window of the staff car.

One of them spotted Hanrahan and nudged his partner. Then he saluted, trying to conceal his surprise at seeing a full bird colonel coming out of Clara's Cafe.

"Good evening, sir!" he barked. "May we be of assistance to the colonel, sir?"

"Everything's under control, thank you," Hanrahan said. He got in the back of the staff car. The three sergeants came out of Clara's. Two of them got in the back with Hanrahan, the third in the front.

The staff car drove off.

There were giggles in the front seat.

"That's a private joke?" Hanrahan asked.

The giggles stopped. There was silence for a moment, and then the driver said: "Colonel, what the one MP said was, 'May

I see your trip ticket, please?' and what the other one said, was, 'We got your ass for sure.'"

"Didn't you tell him I was inside?" Hanrahan asked.

"No, sir, Colonel," the driver said. "What I did was take my time finding the trip ticket. He just got finished saying, 'What did you do, steal the staff car?' when you came out."

"'May we be of assistance to the colonel, sir?'" the other sergeant mimicked.

"Have you got something against those two personally?" Hanrahan asked. "Or don't you like MPs generally?"

"I don't like MPs," the sergeant said, turning on the seat to look at Hanrahan. "But they've got it in for us. All they have to do is see the beret, and they want to see your pass and ID. Or your trip ticket, like now."

"And maybe you're paranoid," Hanrahan said.

"Colonel," one of the sergeants said, "maybe I'm bombed and shouldn't run off at the mouth..."

"So don't," another of the sergeants said.

"What those bastards do," the first sergeant went on, "when they see you in the airport, is wait until they call the plane, and then they ask for your orders and ID, and they study it long enough so that you miss the plane."

"What *I* think," the third sergeant said, somewhat thickly, "is that that bastard Triple H told them to lean on us. Anybody in a beret is fair fucking game for imaginative chickenshit."

"I'm sure," Hanrahan said, coldly, "that you're mistaken, Sergeant."

"Yes, sir," the sergeant said, quickly. "Sorry, sir."

"While I am running off the mouth, sir," the first sergeant said, "what were you doing in Clara's? Looking for us? If you don't mind me asking?"

"I was just curious to see if it had changed," Hanrahan said. "I used to go to Clara's years ago."

"I thought maybe you were looking for us," the sergeant said. "The word is that we're encouraged not to go there."

"No," Hanrahan said. "I was just curious to see it again, and once I was there, I thought you could use a ride."

The last time he had been in Clara's Cafe, Colonel Paul T. Hanrahan had been a second lieutenant and junior officer of the day. He had gone there with the Military Police when word had come that some crazy bastards from the 508th PIR had gone apeshit. A push and shove had turned into an all-out brawl, which saw a half dozen soldiers hospitalized. The victors were still inside Clara's Cafe when Hanrahan got there, holding off MP reinforcements and the Fayetteville Police Department with thrown whiskey bottles and whatever else they could pick up or tear from the walls.

He had been able to negotiate a reasonably peaceful solution. The crazy bastards from the 508th were the Pathfinder Platoon, whose sergeant, Rudolph G. MacMillan, was a friend of his. Consequently Mac trusted him when Hanrahan had told him he could either give up (and he would see about squaring things with the colonel), or he could keep on fighting and spend the next year in the stockade.

(Three)
Office of the Commanding General
XVIII Airborne Corps
Fort Bragg, North Carolina
0915 Hours, 8 January 1959

"Colonel Hanrahan, sir," the sergeant major announced.

"Come on in, Paul," Lieutenant General H. H. Howard called, cordially.

Colonel Paul Hanrahan, wearing crisply starched fatigues, a Model 1911A1 in a holster suspended from a web belt, jump boots, and a green beret, marched into the room and crisply saluted the commanding general. MacMillan was standing nearby.

"Good morning, General," he said.

"I was about to say to you, 'Look what the cat drug in,'" General Howard said, smiling, returning the salute. "But now I wonder if I shouldn't say that to Mac. Are you running a field exercise, Paul?"

"No, sir," Hanrahan said. "I'm running fatigues as the Special Warfare School's uniform of the day."

"For all hands?" Howard asked, as if greatly surprised. "I thought post regulations prescribed fatigues only for field exercises and work details."

"I believe that is correct, sir," Hanrahan said.

"Then, Paul," General Howard asked, reasonably, "wouldn't that make you out of uniform?"

"As I understand it, sir," Hanrahan said, "post regulations apply only to those personnel under your command, sir."

"I see," General Howard said, icily.

"I'm sure the general understands that no disrespect is intended."

"Of course," General Howard said. "And I'm sure you'll understand that I think Mac here looks more like a senior officer should than you do."

Lt. Colonel MacMillan, like General Howard, was in the army green uniform, and like Howard's his was festooned with ribbons and devices.

General Howard and Colonel Hanrahan smiled artificially at each other a moment.

"Yes, sir," Hanrahan said. "I take the general's point."

He turned to MacMillan and offered his hand.

"Hello, Mac," he said, "it's good to see you."

"Mac's staying with me until we can work something out about his quarters," Howard said. "Technically, I suppose, he's AWOL."

"That's very kind of you, General," Hanrahan said.

"Good to see you, Red," MacMillan said.

"Sergeant Major," General Howard said, raising his voice, "would you get us all some coffee, please?"

He gestured for Hanrahan to sit down.

"How was Washington, Paul?" Howard asked.

"About like it always is, General," Hanrahan said.

"How's that?"

"Never have so few been led by so many," Hanrahan said. Howard laughed politely.

"Did you wear your beret?" General Howard asked.

"Yes, sir," Hanrahan said.

The sergeant major delivered coffee in china mugs. He offered sugar and cream, which was refused, and then he left the room.

"Mac and I have been gaily skipping down memory lane," General Howard said. "You'll never guess where we had breakfast?"

"No, sir," Hanrahan said.

"With Headquarters and Headquarters Company of the 508th PIR," Mac said.

"That must have given the mess sergeant a thrill," Hanrahan said. "How was it?"

"Actually, not bad," General Howard said. "I like to make an unannounced visit to a mess every once in a while."

"The last meal I had with H&H of the 'Eight,'" MacMillan said, "was in Holland."

"And were you wet-eyed with nostalgia, Mac?" Hanrahan asked, dryly.

"It was a funny feeling," MacMillan said, looking at him strangely.

"I made a trip down memory lane myself last night," Hanrahan said. "Blood Alley."

"Really?" Howard asked.

Hanrahan had been watching General Howard's face, and concluded from it that Howard had already heard about his visit to Clara's Cafe.

"I was checking out a rumor that the MPs are extraordinarily zealous in the performance of their duties insofar as my people are concerned," Hanrahan said.

"And what did you find?" Howard asked.

"Nothing that merits an official complaint," Hanrahan said.

"I'm glad to hear that," General Howard said.

He and Hanrahan smiled icily at one another.

"Well, Paul," Howard said finally, "I'm sure Mac's interested to see where he'll be working, and I'm sure you have things to do."

Hanrahan came quickly to his feet.

"With your permission, General?" he said.

"Thank you for coming to see me, Paul," Howard said, and then to MacMillan: "If Paul has no plans for you, Mac, we'll expect you for dinner."

"I have no plans for Mac, General," Hanrahan said.

"Then we'll see you about six, Mac, if not before. Paul, are you and your wife occupied?"

"I'm afraid we are, sir," Hanrahan said.

"Perhaps another time, then," General Howard said.

Hanrahan and MacMillan saluted. It was returned, and they left General Howard's office.

"How do you want me to do this, Red?" MacMillan asked. "About my car, I mean? Leave it here, or what?"

"I'll get you a ride back to it," Hanrahan said. "I've got a jeep out in back."

There were reserved parking spaces behind the brick barracks which had been converted into Headquarters, XVIII Airborne Corps. Three of the spaces had been specifically reserved for unspecified colonels, the spaces being marked with a representation of the eagle insignia. Hanrahan had parked his jeep in one of them. When they got to it, an MP staff car had pulled in behind it, and two MPs in white hats and webbing and army green uniforms were standing in front of the jeep, writing on a clipboard.

"Is something wrong?" Hanrahan asked.

The MPs saluted.

The taller of them asked, "Is this your jeep, sir?" When Hanrahan nodded, he went on, "We're looking for your driver, sir."

"I'm driving it," Hanrahan said.

The announcement surprised them.

"I asked," Hanrahan said, "if something was wrong."

"Sir, post regulations require that drivers stay with their vehicles," one of the MPs said.

"Are you about to issue a citation?" Hanrahan asked.

The MPs looked at each other uncomfortably. And then the taller one had an inspiration.

"Sir, may we please see your trip ticket?"

"It's in the glove compartment," Hanrahan said, and walked around to the back of the jeep and reached into it and came out with the trip ticket. He handed it to the MP, who looked at it to see who the form listed as the driver.

"Your name is Hanrahan, sir?" he asked.

"That's correct."

The MPs looked at one another again, and then the taller one went to the MP car and got on the radio. In a minute he was back.

"You can go, Colonel," he said. "Sorry we had to hold you up, sir."

"No problem," Hanrahan said, and got behind the wheel.

"Get in, Mac," he said. "We're free to go."

The MPs got in their car and backed it out of the way.

"What the hell was that all about?" MacMillan asked.

"You heard it, I broke a post regulation."

"Why the hell don't you have a driver? For that matter, what are you doing driving a jeep? Don't you rate a staff car?"

"Let's just say I like to drive myself in a jeep," Hanrahan said.

"Then you are going out of your way to ruffle Triple H's feathers. What the hell for?"

"Is that what he told you?" Hanrahan asked.

"Several people told me," Mac said.

"We're over in Smokebomb Hill, Mac," Hanrahan said, obviously changing the subject. "It's hardly changed at all."

"We're old friends, Red," MacMillan said. "You and I go back before the beginning of airborne. Let's stop the bullshit. Do you know why I got transferred here?"

"I saw Felter and E. Z. Black in Washington," Hanrahan said. "They both told me."

MacMillan had served under Howard in Sicily, at Anzio, in Normandy, and in the jump across the Rhine during which MacMillan had been captured. He thought of Howard as a friend and as a fine officer, who was a superb commander. Thus he didn't understand, and was made uncomfortable by, the visible friction between him and Paul Hanrahan.

"Triple H was pissed that you didn't tell him you were going to Washington," MacMillan said. "In case you didn't know."

Hanrahan didn't reply.

They reached the Smokebomb Hill area of Fort Bragg, a collection of frame barracks and other buildings built in the early days of World War II to last five years. A somewhat faded sign, a four-by-eight-foot sheet of plywood mounted on two-by-sixes, identified the U.S. Army Special Warfare School.

"I'll give you a tour later," Hanrahan said. "I've got a couple of things to do in the office first."

He drove the jeep up the footpath leading to the front door of the frame headquarters building and stopped. He got out and went up the wooden steps and opened the door. MacMillan, trailing after him, heard someone call "attention" and Hanrahan's immediate reply: "As you were."

When he stepped inside the tired old building, MacMillan found Hanrahan standing in a doorway. He motioned for Mac to follow him. Through the door was an office, holding the desks of the sergeant major and a clerk. Two doors opened off that office. There were signs on each door: cheap, cardboard signs, white letters on a dark blue background, the kind you can find in drugstores advertising the day's bargain on plastic kitchen ware.

One said, on two lines, P. T. HANRAHAN COL INF, and the other said, R. G. MACMILLAN LT COL INF.

"Sergeant Major Taylor," Hanrahan said, "this is Colonel MacMillan."

"How are you, Sergeant?" Mac said, smiling and offering his hand.

"Good to see you again, sir," Sergeant Major Taylor said, and when he saw the surprise on MacMillan's face, he went on. "I used to know the colonel, sir, when the colonel was running the 'Eight's Pathfinders.'"

"You did?" Mac asked, genuinely surprised. "Taylor? The only Taylor I remember was a little guy, a kid, broke his leg going into Sicily."

"If the colonel will forgive me," Sergeant Major Taylor said, "we are all a little older, sir, than we were then."

"Well, Jesus, I'm glad to see you," Mac said, enthusiastically pumping his hand.

"You two can gaily skip down memory lane later," Hanrahan said. He was mockingly quoting General Howard. When Mac looked at him in surprise, Hanrahan motioned with his head for him to enter his office. "I'm in conference," Hanrahan said to Sergeant Major Taylor.

"Yes, sir."

"Sit behind the desk," Hanrahan ordered.

"*Behind* it?" Mac asked, confused. "You mean in your chair?"

"Yeah," Hanrahan said.

"What the hell for?"

"Because I said so, and for the moment at least, I'm in command."

MacMillan did as he was ordered.

"You can have that seat if you want it, Mac," Hanrahan said, pleasantly. "Maybe not for sure, but you've got the best shot at it you'll ever have."

"I don't get any of this, Red," Mac said.

"All you have to do to get my job is keep your eyes open around here, and let the post commander know what's going on."

"I don't want to get in the middle of whatever's going on between you and Howard," Mac said.

"What's going on between me and Howard is that he wants me out of this job, and he wants this school under him; and in the best of all possible worlds he wants it under a commandant he can trust to do exactly what he tells him to do, which, at the moment, I think means you."

"Why does he want you out?" Mac asked.

"Because he knows that Special Forces are going to be important, and he believes they should be under airborne."

"And you don't?"

"If I had my way, this place would be at Camp McCoy, Wisconsin, and the wearing of jump wings would be forbidden," Hanrahan said.

"Camp McCoy?"

"It was used to train a ski-troop division in War II. Now it's a National Guard summer training base."

"Why Camp McCoy?" Mac asked. He saw from the look on Hanrahan's face that he considered that a stupid question.

"Because nobody ever heard of Camp McCoy," Hanrahan said. "Because we could train there with nobody looking over our shoulder."

"Let me make it clear, Red," Mac said. "I'm not after your job."

"Don't be so eager to make a decision. You're a light bird now. There are no time-in-grade requirements to make bird colonel. You do right by Howard, and you could count on that eagle in a year."

"Bullshit, Red."

"No bullshit, Mac. Think about it. Marvelous public relations, among other things. Medal of Honor paratrooper named to head super-troopers."

"Is that what this place is? A school for super-troopers?"

"The point is how the term is defined," Hanrahan said. "Howard sees it as a collection of super-troopers, super-physical specimens honed to a fine edge who can be ordered anywhere in the world to out-marine the marines."

"What's wrong with that?"

"Nothing," Hanrahan said, "except that we already have a Marine Corps, and I don't think a regiment of para-troops...even, for that matter, a company...will ever be dropped into combat again. Certainly not as the spearhead for conventional forces."

"And what do you think you should be doing?"

"Training guerrilla leaders," Hanrahan said. "People who are ordered to stay alive because they're too valuable to get killed. People who speak the language of the people they're teaching how to fight. People we can send anywhere, very quietly, to beef up native forces, so that it won't be necessary to send out regiments and divisions. And if we do find ourselves in a conventional war, people who can really raise hell running around the enemy's rear."

"Well, who's in charge?" MacMillan asked.

"Felter got me my eagle and the command," Hanrahan said. "But that shot his wad. Black told me I can't look to him for protection. Realistically, Mac, I'm outnumbered and about to be overwhelmed."

"Felter thinks this is a good idea?"

"Felter was in Greece with me. And he saw, as you should have, how effective Indochinese irregulars were against conventional French forces . . . paratroops, I have to remind you . . . at Dien Bien Phu. Yes, of course, Felter thinks it's a good idea."

"I meant, your fighting with Howard," MacMillan said.

"He knows I have to do it, or we won't have Special Forces in anything but name."

"Well, then, you've got the clout on your side," MacMillan said. "From what I hear, Felter spends more time with Ike than Mamie."

"He told me he can't go back to the well," Hanrahan said. "He didn't say it, but I had the feeling the President feels Felter slipped one over on him. Take my word for it, Mac, right now I'm that one guy in the live-fire infiltration course who just can't keep from sticking his head up to see if they're *really* using live ammo."

"And Black can't help you, either?"

"Black is really on the upper-echelon shit list. The flak from his decision to keep the armed helicopter away from the air force is just starting."

"Plus Lowell," Mac said.

"Plus Lowell," Hanrahan agreed.

"Why don't you do the smart thing, Red, and go along with Howard? Christ, you *could* be a little easier to get along with, for openers."

"The beret, for example?"

"The beret, for example. That really pisses him off. You can't tell a lieutenant general to go fuck himself about his uniform regulations, and you know it."

"The beret is a symbol, Mac. Of the independence of this place, that airborne is not telling us what to do."

"What do you mean 'we,' white man?"

"What?" Hanrahan asked, not understanding.

"The old joke, Red," MacMillan said. "The Lone Ranger and Tonto are surrounded by ten thousand howling Indians; and the Lone Ranger says, 'What do we do now, faithful Indian companion?' and Tonto says, 'What do you mean, 'we,' white man?'"

"Oh, yeah," Hanrahan said, impatiently.

"Tell me what you want from me, Red," MacMillan said.

"I want you to think this over, and then tell me where you stand," Hanrahan said. "That's all."

"You really want to know what I think, Red?"

"Please."

"I think you're out of your fucking mind," MacMillan said. "With Felter on your side, and Black, maybe you could have gotten away with telling airborne to go piss up a rope. By yourself, no way."

"And you go with winners, right, Mac?"

MacMillan shrugged and nodded.

"OK," Hanrahan said. "I appreciate the honesty, Mac."

"You're entitled," Mac said. "We go back a long way."

"Take a couple of days off to get settled, Mac," Hanrahan said. "A week, if you need it. By the time you report back in, I'll have figured out some way to keep you out of the line of fire."

Jesus, MacMillan thought. *Out of one fucking frying pan right into another. What a fucking choice he asked me to make. I'm up to my ears in crap no matter what I do.*

They looked at each other a moment. Then MacMillan shrugged his shoulders and threw up his hands helplessly.

Then he walked out of Hanrahan's office.

He stopped at the sergeant major's desk.

"You got any friends at quartermaster clothing sales?" he asked.

"What does the colonel need?"

"The colonel needs a set of tailored fatigues yesterday," MacMillan said. "I haven't worn fatigues in years."

Sergeant Major Taylor dialed a number from memory, identified himself, and told the person he called that a Lieutenant Colonel MacMillan would be in to see him, and would appreciate whatever he could do for him.

"Thanks," MacMillan said. "And now I need somebody to take me back to my car."

Sergeant Major Taylor snapped his fingers, loudly, like a rifle shot. A buck sergeant appeared a moment later at the door.

"Take the colonel where he needs to go," Sergeant Major Taylor said.

When he heard the sound of the jeep engine starting, Sergeant Major Taylor went into Colonel Hanrahan's office.

"Colonel MacMillan will report back within the week," Colonel Hanrahan said. "When he is present for duty, put him on Distribution List 'A.'"

There were several distribution lists at the Special Warfare School. Distribution List "A" included everybody. Distribution Lists "B" and "C" were shorter. "B" listed the officers whom Hanrahan partially trusted, and "C" was limited to those whom he believed could be trusted absolutely not to pass on to anyone what they knew about Hanrahan's plans.

"Just 'A,' sir?"

"I'm afraid so," Hanrahan said.

"I'm sorry to hear that, Colonel," Sergeant Major Taylor said.

"Me, too, Taylor," Hanranah said. "But I guess Mac figured he got where he is by going with winners, and now was not the time to change tactics."

Taylor backed out of Hanrahan's office.

An hour later, he was back, knocking at the frame.

"What?" Hanrahan said.

"We've got a Green Beret officer out here, Colonel," he said. "He says he's two days AWOL reporting in."

"Oh, Jesus, that's all I need. Can't he see the exec?"

"He insists on reporting to the colonel, Sir."

"Well, send him in," Hanrahan said, tiredly.

The officer who came into the office was wearing fatigues. They appeared brand new. He marched to within three feet of Hanrahan's desk and saluted crisply.

"Lieutenant Colonel MacMillan, Rudolph G., sir," he barked. "Reporting himself two days AWOL reporting for duty, sir. No excuse, sir."

Hanrahan returned the salute.

"Are you sure, Mac?" he said.

"No excuse, sir," MacMillan said.

"You know what I mean," Hanrahan said.

"Begging the colonel's pardon, sir, I am still somewhat

unsure of the beret. It makes me feel like a girl scout, sir."

"I'm sure, Colonel, that you will grow used to it in time," Hanrahan said. "Sergeant Major?"

"Sir?"

"See that Colonel MacMillan is placed on Distribution List 'C.'"

"Yes, sir."

X

Laird Army Airfield
Fort Rucker, Alabama
1810 Hours, 18 January 1959

Roxy MacMillan smiled fondly at Craig W. Lowell, who was loudly and enthusiastically singing along with George London and the Vienna Philharmonic the sextet from Donizetti's *Lucia di Lammermoor*.

The music was cut off abruptly.

"Commander One Five, Laird."

The voice of the Laird Army Airfield control tower came over the speakers mounted in the ceiling of the Aero Commander's cockpit. It was Lowell's newest gadget from Aircraft Radio Corporation. When there was no ground-to-air or air-to-air communication, the speakers played music from an 8-track tape player.

The chairman of the board of Craig, Powell, Kenyon and Dawes, the investment bankers, had telephoned Major Lowell the previous Thursday.

"I thought you would like to know that we just bought fifty thousand shares of Aircraft Radio Corporation," Porter Craig, Craig Lowell's cousin, announced.

"Really?"

"I thought it a sound move," Porter Craig said. "If they're sending everybody with an airplane bills like the one they sent me, they're going to be able to pay a hundred percent dividend."

"I think you're trying to tell me something, Porter."

"Thirty-six thousand odd dollars," Porter Craig said. "What the hell is 'weather avoidance radar'?"

"It tells you if there are storm clouds ahead," Lowell said. "What is known to the cognoscenti as a 'weather disturbance.'"

"You could, you know, charter a number of airplanes for just what this latest bill represents."

"We all have our toys, Porter," Craig Lowell replied. "You have your mistress, and I have mine. Mine has wings."

"I don't have a mistress!" Porter Craig protested indignantly, before he realized that his leg was being pulled.

"Pity," Lowell said, laughing.

"The reason I called, Craig . . ."

"Was because you hadn't heard from me, and were worried."

"Your butler told me you are now stationed in Alabama," Porter Craig said.

"On that subject, some friends will be in the Georgetown place until the spring."

"So your butler told me."

"Is that why you called?" Lowell asked.

"No," Porter Craig said. "Actually, it's because . . . and hear me out before you start arguing with me . . ."

"All right," Lowell said, reasonably.

"You're familiar with Haymann Freres?"

"Haymann Freres?" Lowell asked, as if greatly puzzled.

"For God's sake," Porter Craig said, in exasperation. "It's our French bank. I mean to say, we own it."

"Oh," Lowell said, *"that* Haymann Freres."

"Yes, that Haymann Freres. And we have on the board a man . . ."

"The Baron de Pildet?" Lowell interrupted.

There was a pause. Porter Craig was confused.

"You know the name?"

"He's my roommate's uncle, actually," Lowell said.

There was another pause.

"I'll be damned," Porter Craig said, finally.

"I normally can't stand frogs," Lowell said. "But I thought it would be good for the firm if I was nice to him."

"Why is it that I don't believe that?"

"He's a friend of friends of mine," Lowell said. "Including the people who will be using the place in Georgetown."

"It would be a business use of your airplane, which is what IRS would like to hear, if you brought him to New York for a weekend, Craig."

"I'll ask him," Lowell said.

"Is there anything I can do for you, Craig?"

"Pay Aircraft Radio," Lowell said. "Say hello to your family."

"Bring him to New York, Craig," Porter said.

"Good-bye, Porter. Thank you for calling."

"Good to talk to you," Porter Craig said. The line went dead.

"Go ahead, Laird," Lowell said to the microphone mounted on a thin boom in front of his lips.

"In-flight advisory, One Five. Ground transportation will be available at the Board parking area."

"Roger, Laird," Lowell said. "Thank you. I should be over the outer marker in a couple of minutes. One Five clear."

He turned to Roxy MacMillan in the copilot's seat beside him.

"One of your kids meeting us?" he asked.

"I don't think so," Roxy said.

He shrugged his shoulders and tapped a switch on the wheel. George London's voice and the Vienna Philharmonic returned to the cockpit.

He saw Laird field before the needles on the radio direction finder reversed.

"Laird, Commander One Five," he said. "Two miles north at fifteen hundred. I have the field in sight. Permission for a straight-in approach to three eight and landing, please."

"One Five, you are cleared for a straight-in to three eight. You are number one after the Beaver on final. The winds are negligible from the north. The altimeter is two niner niner niner."

"I have the Beaver in sight," Lowell said.

He reached forward and eased back on the throttles. There was the sound of hydraulics as the flaps came out of the wing, and a moment later as the wheels dropped down and locked. The Commander touched down a hundred feet past the end of the runway. The engine changed pitch as he reversed the props.

"Laird, One Five on the ground at ten past the hour," he said into the microphone. "Taxi instructions to the Board area, please."

"One Five, take taxiway three north to the Board area."

"Understand three north," Lowell said. Now moving slow enough down the runway to apply the brakes, he slowed and then turned off the runway.

"Well, my lovely, we cheated death again," he said, leering at Roxy.

She shook her head and smiled at him again.

The glistening Aero Commander rolled down the taxiway, first past quadruple lines of Cessna L-19s, single-engine observation aircraft also used for primary flight training, then past rows of high-winged DeHavilland L-20 "Beavers," and then past a half dozen Beechcraft L-23D "Twin Bonanzas." And then past two Aero Commanders, part of the school fleet. A quarter mile beyond, they came to the Army Aviation Board's parking area. There were thirty aircraft of all kinds, including two Sikorsky H-19s in the process of being fitted with rocket launchers. And the black H-19 Lowell had "borrowed" from the school fleet, which was in the process of being restored to the condition it had been in before Lowell had "borrowed" it.

Lowell had been unable to convince Bill Roberts that it would be simpler to keep the one they had, rather than do a double conversion.

"The less I hear about the school's H-19, Lowell, the better. All I want to know about it ever again is your report that it has been restored to them in the condition in which you 'found' it."

Roberts had also made it clear that he wanted no paint scheme on the two H-19s being converted except what was provided for in the regulations. The official test aircraft for the armed helicopter program would not be painted black, would not be labeled "Big Bad Bird," and would not feature a cartoon of Woody Woodpecker throwing beer bottles.

A couple of enlisted men, ground handlers, came out of Board Operations and showed him where to park. As he turned the plane into line, he saw the Cadillac Eldorado parked behind the Board Operations building.

"Jannier," he said to Roxy.

"He's here already?" she asked, surprised.

Not quite forty-eight hours before, they had dropped Captain Jean-Philippe Jannier at Washington National Airport. He had insisted on bringing Lowell's car from Washington. He was not only a superb driver, he announced, but he welcomed the opportunity the drive would give him to see the country.

Lowell and Roxy MacMillan had then flown on to Fort Bragg. Mac, who had originally called Roxy to tell her that he was being assigned quarters on the post, had called again to announce that "something had happened," and they would have to buy a house. Then a week later he'd called again to announce he'd found the house they needed, and wanted her to come look at it and sign the papers.

It would kill three birds with one stone, Lowell had announced when he volunteered to fly Roxy to Bragg: he could drop Jannier in Washington to pick up his car, get Roxy to Bragg to see the house, and have a chance to see Paul Hanrahan.

He'd learned from Paul Hanrahan why the on-post quarters originally offered MacMillan had become "unavailable." Mac was no longer the hero returned to airborne, but another disloyal sonofabitch like Hanrahan. It was Lowell's judgment that Hanrahan was fighting a battle that could not be won, and he was relieved that he had turned down Hanrahan's offer to come to Special Forces.

Hanrahan had not repeated the offer, which meant that he thought he was fighting a losing battle, too, and didn't want to drag anyone else down with him.

Captain Jean-Philippe Jannier walked up to the Aero Commander as Lowell checked the tie-down ropes. He was wearing what must be, Lowell thought, a genuine Andalusian shepherd's jacket, the furry side out. His shirt was open most of the way to his navel, and he had a silk scarf knotted around his neck. He was wearing baggy corduroy trousers and what looked like canvas shoes. He held a long, black cigar in his hand. He was, Lowell thought, a handsome, elegant sonofabitch.

Jannier took Roxy's outstretched hand, bent over it, and kissed it.

"And did he behave, Roxy, when he had you alone in the airplane?"

"How did you get back so quick?" Roxy asked, avoiding the question.

"Très rapidement," Jannier said. "I have to have that car, or one exactly like it, perhaps in yellow."

"You're lucky you didn't go to jail," Lowell said, chuckling.

"There was an incident in Virginia," Jannier said. "Almost on the Tennessee border . . . Did I say that right, 'Tennessee'?"

"You got pinched," Roxy announced.

"Pinched?" Jannier asked. The term was new to him.

"Arrested," Lowell provided, as they walked to the Eldorado.

"I was *detained,*" Jannier said. "Until we found an officer who knew what a diplomatic passport meant."

"You've got a diplomatic passport?" Lowell asked.

"Of course," Jannier said.

"What's that mean?" Roxy asked.

"It means he can thumb his nose at traffic cops," Lowell said. "He's immune to American law."

"You mean it, don't you?" she asked. "How does that work?"

"Not the way he's working it," Lowell said. "How fast were you going?"

"One hundred and ten," Jannier said, proudly. "They put up a roadblock on the highway. I felt like John Dillinger."

"Christ," Lowell chuckled.

"And he got away with it?" Roxy asked.

"I am here," Jannier said, simply. "With the apologies of the Virginia State Police."

"That stinks," Roxy announced.

"The world stinks," Lowell said. "Haven't you noticed?"

He got behind the wheel of the Cadillac and started the engine.

"Do they sell these in Alabama?" Jannier asked, as he slid in beside Roxy. "Or are they special order?"

"I'll sell you this one," Lowell said.

"Done," Jannier said, and reached over Roxy to offer his hand.

"He didn't tell you how much," Roxy said.

"We are gentlemen," Jannier said. "He will make me pay what it is worth."

"As a gentleman," Lowell said, "there is something I should tell you about these cars."

"Which is?"

"They are also admired by *les maquereaux*," Lowell said. "In fact, you can't really consider yourself a *maquereau* in good standing unless you own one."

Jannier laughed.

"What's a what you said?" Roxy MacMillan asked.

"In the American *patois*," Lowell said, "they are known as a 'pimp-mobile.'"

Jannier laughed heartily.

"Then I absolutely have to have it," he said.

"Is what you said the French word for...that?" Roxy asked.

"It's a perfectly proper word, Roxy," Lowell said. "It's where we get the word for 'mackerel.'"

"The fish?" she asked, in disbelief.

"It's true," Lowell said. "The male mackerel provides girl fishes to other boy fishes."

"I don't believe that," she said, firmly.

"It's true, it's true," Jannier said, laughing.

"I'm going to change the subject," Roxy said. "To something safe."

"Like what?"

"Like food, and I don't mean fish. Stop by the A&P in Ozark, Craig, and I'll get us some steaks."

"We are invited for steaks," Jannier said.

"We are?" Roxy asked.

"Chez Parker," Jannier said. "They left a message at the motel to call, and when I called, Madame Parker insisted that we all come."

"Amazing what kissing a woman's hand and calling her 'Madame' will get you," Lowell said.

"She didn't have to do that," Roxy said.

"It'll make Phil happy," Lowell said. "His job is driving him nuts."

There was confirmation of that when they got to the Parker apartment at the hospital. Phil Parker had obviously been at the bottle; and Antoinette Parker took Lowell aside and, as a close friend, gave him hell for not asking Phil to fly along with them.

And then Parker's bitterness came out almost as soon as he'd made them drinks.

"How's Mac doing?"

"Mac is now 'Deputy Commandant for Special Projects,'" Lowell said. "How's that for a title?"

"Maybe that's what I should do," Parker said. "Punch somebody off the balcony."

"Phil!" Toni said, shocked.

"Sorry, Roxy," Parker said.

"Forget it," Roxy said. "And anyway, it's not all sweetness and light over there, is it, Craig?"

"You're asking me?"

"Since Mac won't tell me, yeah, I'm asking you."

"OK," Lowell said, deciding it would be good for Phil to hear what was really going on at Bragg. "What's going on is that airborne thinks it should run Special Forces, as sort of super-paratroops, and Hanrahan doesn't want them to have it. Hanrahan believes Special Forces should be primarily concerned with guerrillas. Or training foreign troops to fight their own wars. Hanrahan's right, of course, but it's David versus Goliath, and guess who David is?"

"How does that affect Mac?" Parker asked.

"Mac was given a choice between being the grand old man of airborne, or standing by Hanrahan. Mac being Mac, he put on the green beret."

"Meaning what?"

"It's a symbol. The airborne, specifically Lieutenant General Howard, forbade the wearing of that silly hat. Hanrahan read the regulations about his authority as commandant of the school . . . it's a Class II activity of DCSOPS . . . and to remind Howard that he's not under him, ordered his troops into the berets."

"What are they really doing over there?" Phil Parker asked.

"Hanrahan's going to train people—experienced noncoms and officers—to run other people's forces. Very much like what we did in Greece. We provide the expertise, and native forces provide the manpower. Guerrillas, in one sense, but more than that."

"What's the fight with airborne?" Phil Parker asked.

"Airborne sees them as Rangers, super-paratroops, like the

guys who climbed the cliffs on the beaches in Normandy."

"I don't get the distinction," Parker confessed.

"Hanrahan explained the difference neatly. Rangers are trained to complete the mission and to disregard casualties. Special Forces are trained to stay alive; they're too valuable to waste."

"Sounds interesting," Parker said. "I wonder how they're fixed for instructor pilots."

"It's not for you, Phil," Lowell said, quickly adding: "Or me. These are nuts-and-bolts guys. The officers are either infantry or signal corps. I don't think they even have any armor officers."

Antoinette decided to change the subject.

"How was the house, Roxy?" she asked. "Do you like it?"

"Not as well as the one here," Roxy said. "But there's nothing wrong with it. I just really hate to leave the house here."

"What are you going to do with your house here?" Jannier said.

"Rent it," Roxy said. "Which means I have to find a light colonel who doesn't have to live in quarters on the post."

"I don't understand," Jannier said.

"I'll have to get three hundred fifty dollars a month for it," Roxy said. "That's a lot of money."

"No," Jannier said.

Roxy and the others looked at him in surprise.

"Craig," Jannier asked. "What are we paying for the motel?"

"Right around five," Lowell said. "A little over five."

"You're paying five hundred a month?" Roxy asked, indignantly. "You're crazy! For a couple of rooms in a motel?"

"Would you rent us your house, Roxy?" Jannier asked.

"I don't know," Roxy said, uneasily.

"I know what you're thinking, Roxy," Antoinette said, laughing. She knew that Roxy was thinking about the problems that would come with renting her house to two bachelors. "But it isn't that way. I used to go to the house Phil and Craig had in Lawton, outside of Fort Sill. Believe it or not, it looked like a page from *Better Homes & Gardens*. There was never anything in the refrigerator but beer and martini onions, of course, but the house was immaculate."

"We had a maid," Phil said. "And of course, men are naturally neater than women."

"I withdraw everything nice I said," Toni said.

"What would you do for furniture?" Roxy asked.

"We could get furniture," Lowell said. The idea appealed to him. He didn't like the motel suite. "It would be better than the motel."

"And they don't have children," Toni said, "to write on the walls with crayons."

"Fine with me," Roxy said, making up her mind.

"When can you move out?" Lowell asked.

"Go to hell, Craig," Roxy said, and then answered the question. "Just as soon as I can get the movers to come. In a couple of days, really."

"You will leave the light bulbs?" Lowell asked, innocently.

Phil Parker collapsed in laughter.

"What's so funny?"

"When we moved into the house in Lawton, the lights didn't go on. So Lowell called the guy who sold him the house and really read him the riot act, and the guy rushed an electrician over. The guy took one look at the fixture and told Craig that you had to have light bulbs in the sockets; otherwise, no lights."

There was laughter, some of it politely forced, for no one else found it as funny as Parker apparently did, and then a new voice came from the doorway.

"I guess I missed the punch line, huh?" Melody Dutton Greer said.

"I was wondering what happened to you," Antoinette said, going to her.

"I was delayed at my mother's," Melody said.

"Don't apologize," Phil Parker said. "If Jean-Philippe hadn't brought it up, you wouldn't have even been invited."

"Phil, for God's sake," Toni said. "If you can't handle it, don't drink!"

Lowell glanced at Roxy. She was looking at him. It was evident that both of them had just realized that Melody Dutton Greer would be Lowell's neighbor . . . more specifically Jean-Philippe Jannier's neighbor, when he and Lowell moved into 227 Melody Lane.

(Two)
The Situation Room
The White House
Washington, D.C.
1430 Hours, 19 January 1959

The meeting to combine and coordinate differing intelligence information about Russian shipment to Cuba was chaired by the Deputy Director, Analysis, the CIA. Major Sanford T. Felter was present officially as an observer, in his role at the President's personal liaison to the intelligence community. In fact, he was responsible for the meeting.

Earlier that day, two Top Secret reports, both marked FOR THE ATTENTION OF THE PRESIDENT, had been delivered by courier to the White House and then to Felter. Among his other duties, Felter was responsible for preparing a one-paragraph synopsis of intelligence reports directed to the President. Both of the reports laid on his desk dealt with the same subject, Soviet military shipments to Cuba. One had been prepared by the CIA, the other by the Office of the Chief of Naval Intelligence. They differed in the assessments of what had already been shipped and what they believed was about to be shipped. They also differed in their assessment of Soviet sealift capabilities. Felter had just finished typing out the one-paragraph synopses (indicating in these that there was a difference of opinion between the two), when a third report arrived, this one from the State Department. It, too, dealt with Soviet military shipments—actual and projected—to Castro's Cuba.

Felter had then telephoned the Deputy Director, Analysis, of the CIA and told him about the other two reports.

"Goddamn it, Felter, they are supposed to route that stuff through me."

"Sir, what would you like me to do about it?"

"I want that material in the President's hands today," the Deputy Director said. "And I suppose that means another goddamned meeting. Will you set one up, Felter? Situation Room at two?"

"Yes, sir," Felter had said.

He had telephoned the State Department (who dispatched an Under Secretary of State for Intelligence) and the Navy (who sent the Deputy Director of Naval Intelligence). Then he had called the Army, the Deputy Chief of Staff for Intelligence (DCSINTEL). He told all of them a meeting was taking place at 1400 in the Situation Room concerning Soviet arms shipments to Cuba.

He had passed the President in the corridor leading from his personal (as opposed to Oval) office. The President had asked if he had anything for him.

"Sometime this afternoon, Mr. President, there will be a report of Soviet arms shipments, actual and projected, to Cuba. The CIA's making a brief of everybody's report at 1400 in the Situation Room."

"OK," the President had said.

When the President walked into the Situation Room at 1405, he gestured with his hand for the Deputy Director, Analysis, of the CIA to keep his seat, and slipped into one of the chairs along the side of the table.

The President, chain-smoking and sipping from a china coffee cup, heard out the differences of opinion between the CIA and the Navy and the State Department without comment. But then, interrupting a discussion involving the Soviet oil tanker capability, he asked DCSINTEL a question that had nothing to do with Soviet sealift capability. He asked DCSINTEL what the Army could offer in the way of unconventional forces—Special Forces in other words—to tie down Cuba's army if an invasion should become necessary.

The Deputy Chief of Staff, Intelligence, very embarrassed, was forced to confess he simply didn't know.

"If we have to do this," the President said, "the less brute force we have to use, the better."

"I'll get the information for you, Mr. President," the DCSINTEL said.

"No," the President said, "you have other things to do." He looked down to the end of the table. "Felter, look into that for me, will you, please?"

"Yes, Mr. President."

"And while you're at it, Felter, get me a report on the availability of those whirlybird tank killers, too."

"Yes, Mr. President," Felter repeated.

"It seems to me that if we don't have the sealift capability to get our tanks to Cuba without requisitioning the Staten Island ferry, then the next best thing we can do is come up with tank-killing helicopters," the President said. "I saw a demonstration on the TV a couple of weeks ago that looked very impressive."

"Yes, Mr. President," Felter said.

"The way things have been going," the President went on, "I should be very surprised to find that we have these assets in place. When you're asking questions, Felter, see if something—I suppose I mean funding—would speed things up."

"Yes, Mr. President," Felter said, again.

The meeting then passed on to other things. When the meeting was over, Felter went to his office, and typing furiously, prepared two extracts of the reports that had just been discussed. One went two and a half pages, and the other was the single-paragraph synopsis the President demanded.

Then he called the Pentagon, and asked General E. Z. Black's executive officer, a full colonel, for an appointment. He hoped, futilely, that Black would be free that afternoon. But the colonel told him he could "slip him in" for half an hour at 1430 tomorrow.

"I'm sorry, sir," Felter said, "but it's necessary that I see the general right away. I'll leave for the Pentagon now. Please make the necessary arrangements."

He was still on the phone to the White House motor pool when one of the other buttons on the telephone lit up. When he was finished with the motor pool dispatcher, he punched it.

"Felter."

"Black," the familiar voice said.

"Good afternoon, sir."

"I understand you insist on seeing me right away."

"Yes, sir."

"Stay where you are, Major," Black said, and hung up.

Felter called the motor pool back and cancelled the car. Then he walked upstairs and down the corridor and gave the President's secretary a large manila envelope with the Soviet war material reports in it.

Then he walked back to his office and waited.

Twenty minutes later, the guard shack called. General E. Z. Black was at the gate. Was he expected?

"Pass him in."

He was furious with his stupidity. He had presumed that Black had a White House pass. Obviously he didn't. Would Black think that he had known all along, and had had him stopped at the gate to show his own importance?

Black was shown into Felter's small office a few minutes later.

Felter stood up.

"Good afternoon, sir," he said.

"Thank you for seeing me, Major," Black said. He handed Felter a large manila envelope. "I believe this is what you're after," he said.

"May I offer the general some coffee?" Felter said.

"That's very kind of you, Major. Thank you," General Black said.

"General," Felter said, "I was instructed by the President to get some information for him. It was necessary that I insist..."

"I believe the information you seek is there," Black said, indicating the envelope.

DCSINTEL, Felter realized, had lost no time in reporting what had happened at the meeting.

Felter pushed a button on his intercom.

"Coffee, please, for two," he said.

"Very interesting," General Black said. "Rumor has it, Felter, that you have one of the ultimate status symbols around here."

"What would that be, General?" Felter asked.

"A telephone that puts you right through to the President."

Felter didn't reply. He opened the envelope.

It contained two memoranda from Black, both addressed to the Chief of Staff. One had HELICOPTERS, ROCKET-ARMED, ANTITANK in the "Subject" block, and the other, SPECIAL FORCES, AUGMENTATION OF W/SPANISH-SPEAKING PERSONNEL. Both were dated 3 January 1959, two days after Fidel Castro had rolled triumphantly into Havana in his jeep.

"The memoranda are apparently being studied," General Black said. "I don't believe the Chief of Staff has had the opportunity to make his decision."

Felter read the helicopter memorandum quickly but carefully. Black had recommended that a provisional company of twenty rocket-armed helicopters be immediately formed at Fort Knox, Kentucky. H-19 aircraft were to be obtained by levy upon those posts and organizations that had them, and pilots and maintenance crews were to come from Fort Rucker, Alabama, and Fort Knox. It recommended the immediate allocation of $2 million for immediate expenses.

The Special Forces memorandum recommended the immediate augmentation of the Special Warfare School with such equipment and funds as were considered necessary to train and equip four companies—each of 214 officers and men—of Spanish-speaking personnel for possible use in the Caribbean area. It would authorize the commandant of the Special Warfare School to recruit such personnel in the Zone of the Interior, and would direct the Adjutant General to order the transfer of such personnel without regard to any objections that might be raised by their present units. It was recommended that $10 million be made available immediately.

"I think the President will be glad to hear this," Felter said. And then he added, "General, I would have been happy to come get this from you. You didn't..."

He stopped in midsentence. He now understood why General Black had come to the White House. And what General Black wanted from him.

He looked at General Black for a moment, and then he picked up his telephone. There was a row of buttons on its base. The extreme right button was protected with a cover against inadvertent use. Felter pushed the cover out of the way and punched the button.

"Yes?"

"Felter, Mr. President. I have the information regarding the rocket helicopters and the Green Berets."

"Good," the President said, obviously puzzled that Felter had telephoned him about it.

"General Black is here, sir," Felter said. "In case you would like to ask him something specific."

There was a pause.

"Bring him up, Felter," the President said, finally. "You have five minutes."

"Thank you, Mr. President," Felter said.

The President's Chief of Staff was visibly annoyed when Felter appeared with General Black.

"You're fouling up the schedule," he said. "You know that."

"I'm sorry," Felter said.

"Is General Black out there?" the President's voice came over the intercom. "And Felter? Send them in."

Black marched into the office and saluted. Felter saw that the President's Chief of Staff had followed them into the room.

"How are you. E. Z.?" the President asked. "Good to see you."

"Very well, Mr. President, thank you," General Black said.

"You have the answers the DCSINTEL didn't have?"

"Yes, sir," Black said, and handed him the memoranda.

"What do they say, Felter?" the President asked.

"General Black, on 3 January, recommended that a provisional company of rocket-armed helicopters be formed at Fort Knox, at initial funding of $2 million, and that four companies of Spanish-speaking Special Forces troops be recruited for training at the Special Warfare School. The money there is $10 million."

"That much money?" the President asked.

"More will be needed, Mr. President," General Black said. "I have sent subsequent memoranda to the Chief of Staff as figures became available to me."

"But you have this money?"

"No, sir," Black said. "Apparently the Chief of Staff has the matter under study."

"In other words, he's sitting on it?" the President asked.

"I didn't say that, sir," General Black said.

"No, but that's why you're here," the President said. "What's the fight, still over who gets to run Special Forces? Or over you putting the rocket choppers under armor?"

"I have not discussed the matter with the Chief of Staff, sir," Black said, uncomfortably.

"I knew it was bad between you two," the President said, not kindly, "but I didn't know you weren't talking."

The President reached into his pocket and took out a plastic ballpoint pen. He wrote, "Approved, DDE," on both memoranda.

"Did I ever tell you you sometimes remind me very much of Georgie Patton, E. Z.?"

"I'm flattered, Mr. President."

"Don't be," the President said. "It wasn't intended that way. In the end, you'll remember, I had to relieve him. When he caused more trouble than he was doing good."

"Mr. President," the President's Chief of Staff said, "we're getting way behind schedule . . ."

(Three)
Bachelor Officer's Quarters No. T-2215
Division Area
Fort Bragg, North Carolina
0245 Hours, 21 January 1959

They had begun playing at shortly after noon, with chips.
The chief warrant officer who organized the game served as
the banker. The white chips were worth a quarter, the red chips
worth fifty cents, and the blue chips a dollar. Everybody bought
chips, and the chief warrant officer put the money in the cardboard box that had held the chips, weighting it down with an
electrician's and carpenter's pocket knife that he had had since
he was a staff sergeant.

At the time everyone antied up he took a blue chip from
each player's pot and put it in the box. He had a refrigerator
full of beer, and there were bottles of Jack Daniel's whiskey
and Dewar's White Label scotch. When they sent out for food
from the PX snack bar, he would pay for that, too. In the
course of an evening, the value of the blue chips taken from
the pots would be worth maybe fifty or seventy dollars more
than what the booze and chow had cost, but it was understood
that the profit was his because he had organized the game, and
it was going to be his ass if the MPs or the officer of the day
came into his room and accused him of running a gambling
operation—or in the quaint language of the *Manual for Courts-
Martial,* "of maintaining gaming tables," which was an offense
against good military order and discipline.

There were six men at the table now. Earlier there had been
as few as three and as many as seven. The chief warrant officer
was now out of the game. It had grown too serious for him.
And although there were still chips on the table, mostly green-
backs were in the pots now—fives and tens.

The chief warrant officer was surprised that the game had
gotten too rich for his blood, because they were three weeks
into the month. On payday, he would not have been surprised
at today's stakes. Now he was.

With the exception of the kid, the officers hunched over the
blanket-covered table were mostly older people. There was
another chief warrant officer (the assistant S-4 of the 505th
Parachute Infantry Regiment); a captain of the Medical Service
Corps (in charge of administering the 82nd's dispensaries); an
artillery captain from Division Artillery; a senior lieutenant

of the Adjutant General's Corps (the 505th's assistant adjutant); the chief warrant who had organized the game (he was OIC of the 505th's parachute riggers), and the kid. The kid was a shiny new shavetail, fresh from OCS, who had a platoon in one of the line companies.

It had been the chief's matter-of-fact belief that the kid was about to lose his ass when he'd joined the game. These people knew how to play poker, and the kid was obviously out of his class. The chief had felt no pity for him. Learning when to play poker—or more importantly, when not to play poker—was an important part of a young officer's education; and the only way to learn that was to get into a game over your head and lose your ass.

But the kid hadn't lost. He was a lot more cautious than the chief thought he would be, and he'd won steadily. Not much at once, no spectacular hands, but the pile of chips in front of him had continued to grow. He was at least smart enough not to try to drink hard stuff in the company of these people. He'd had a couple of beers, was all. And when they'd brought in the fried chicken from the PX snack bar, he'd gotten out of the game instead of eating while he played, and he'd eaten more chicken and french fries and cole slaw than you'd think would go in him.

Then he'd gotten back in the game.

The others didn't like it much. They had figured that they'd take the kid's money in a couple of hours, and he'd leave the game, and then they could play the way they usually did. The way they usually played (they were all pretty well matched) was that nobody ever won or lost more than a hundred bucks— most often something on the order of fifty or sixty.

But there was that much money in each pot now. When the stakes had gone up, it hadn't frightened the kid. He'd stayed right in there, folding usually when somebody opened for ten bucks, but sometimes staying and sometimes winning, and winning enough so that the stack of chips he was using to hold down the folding money looked like it was about to fall over.

"Five games," the kid announced, as he watched the Medical Service Corps captain rake in a pot worth maybe sixty-five bucks.

"Huh?" the artillery captain asked.

"Five games," the kid repeated. "In five games I quit. I've got a field training exercise at 0400."

"Quit now, if you want," the artillery captain said.

"I'll give you five more chances to get your money back," the kid said. "Then I quit."

"Quit now, for all I care," the artillery captain said.

The first hand, the kid folded his cards after looking at them.

The second hand, he stayed until the second raise, but folded after the artillery captain raised the AGC lieutenant twenty bucks.

The third hand, the kid folded again after looking at his cards.

The fourth hand, the kid stayed all the way, losing maybe fifty, fifty-five bucks, when he called the warrant officer who had a full house, tens over threes.

The fifth hand, the kid opened for twenty dollars, and as he dropped the twenty, folded in half lengthwise, onto the blanket, he said: "Last hand. Take a chance."

Everybody but the AGC lieutenant stayed in.

The kid took one card. He looked at it, and then laid it on top of the others.

"Up to you," the artillery captain said.

The kid thought it over.

"Another twenty," he said, and dropped two tens onto the blanket.

That folded the warrant officer. The Medical Service captain dropped a twenty onto the blanket.

"Your twenty and twenty," the artillery captain said, when it came to him.

"And twenty," the kid said, counting out forty bucks in fives and tens and dropping it on the blanket.

That folded the Medical Service Corps captain.

"You're bluffing, Sonny," the artillery captain said.

"I'm giving you a chance to get your money back," the kid said. "This is my last hand."

"You said that before," the artillery captain said. He looked at the kid, and then at his cards.

"Your twenty and fifty," he said.

The kid counted the money in front of him. He had eighteen dollars in folding money. He had twenty-three dollars and change worth of chips. He pushed the chips and folding money, forty-one dollars' worth, into the center of the table. Then he reached in his pocket and threw his wallet after it.

"Call," he said.

"Full house," the artillery captain said, turning over three jacks and a pair of eights.

He looked at the kid.

The kid turned his cards over. Four kings. Three kings, a six, and another king. The way he'd handled his cards, laying them in front of him as he got them, not touching them except to discard one of them, everybody knew he'd been dealt three kings, and gotten the fourth when he'd drawn the one card. He had tried to draw another six.

A real poker player would have drawn two cards, hoping to make either the fourth king, or get a pair.

"I guess that's mine, huh?" the kid said. He started to reach for the pot.

"What's in the wallet?" the artillery captain said.

"For Christ's sake, he was only nine dollars shy," the chief who ran the game said.

"If you're shy, you got to say so," the artillery captain. "He didn't say anything."

"There's enough in the wallet to cover the nine bucks," the kid said.

"I want to see it," the captain said.

"That's the same as calling me a liar," the kid said. "Is that what you're doing?"

The artillery captain, with a sudden move, grabbed the wallet. He opened it.

"The fucking thing is empty!" he said, triumphantly, and tossed the wallet to the chief whose game it was. "That's my pot, and that's the last time you play with us, fuckhead!"

The kid said: "Chief, there's a ten dollar bill folded up in the plastic window with my driver's license."

The chief looked. There was. He unfolded it, snapped it open so everybody could see it, and then dropped it in the pot.

"It's his pot," he pronounced.

The kid pushed his chips to the chief, who counted out twenty-three dollars and seventy-five cents from the bank and gave it to him. He counted the money he had from the pot, put all the twenties together and the tens and the fives and the singles.

"Good night," the kid said.

The chief warrant whose game it was nodded. None of the others said a word. They had watched him count his money, and they were all a little pissed that this dumb little second john was walking out with $320 of their money. He'd played bad poker and bet all but his last fucking dollar, and was still walking out with their money. That wasn't poker, that was bullshit. They would not let him play again.

The kid was pleased. They had not been watching him early in the game, when he had begun to palm a ten dollar bill here, a five there, whenever he had won a pot, and to stick them in his pocket so the others wouldn't notice. He had come in the game with $105, and he had no intention, if the cards went against him, of leaving the game with less than that. After the first two hours, he had been playing with their money. If he lost that, he would have quit. As it turned out, he was walking out with $650 of their money, not $320.

The kid was pleased with himself. He was going to go in the boonies and play boy scout in the morning; but he'd be back on Friday and be given the rest of the day off. There was a used car lot on Bragg Boulevard with a sign that said, "$100 Down on Any Car on the Lot." He would go buy a car, any car, just so he would have wheels. He could get a better car later. But the first thing to do was buy a car, and the second was to drive over to the Special Warfare School and give Colonel MacMillan his two hundred back.

XI

(One)
Hangar No. 4
Laird Army Airfield
Fort Rucker, Alabama
23 January 1959

Mrs. Jane Cassidy sat in Major Lowell's small office at a desk back to back with that of the major. The section's three pilots (one of whom was WOJG William B. Franklin) and two clerks (one a PFC, the other a GS-4 clerk-typist) were installed in half of the larger of the rooms of the two-room "suit." The armorer officer (CWO "Dutch" Cramer and his three enlisted men: two armorers and one aircraft frame mechanic, all senior noncoms in their late twenties) had the other half.

Lowell really hadn't known what to expect the first duty morning after the New Year's party. He would not have been surprised if Jane had not come to work at all, and he would have been equally unsurprised if she had been waiting for him as a mistress waits for her lover.

She had stood up when he walked in. He'd looked at her. She avoided his eyes.

"Good morning, Major Lowell," she said.

"Good morning, Jane," he'd replied.

She had raised her eyes to his.

"I've made coffee," she said. "Would you like a cup?"

"Yes," he said. "I would. Thank you."

She had fetched the coffee from the machine in Dutch Cramer's room, and set it before him on his desk.

Then she had sat down at her typewriter and begun to type. She had been obviously unnerved by the encounter, but Lowell had decided that the ball was in her court. If she wanted a transfer, she would have to bring it up.

She did not bring it up. She acted as if New Year's Eve simply hadn't happened. It was too easy a solution, he thought. Sooner or later, there would be a reference to it. But until there was, he decided, the action indicated for the situation was no action at all.

The next day, she brought a framed photograph of herself with her family and put it on the desk.

The crucifix, he thought, held up in the face of Lucifer to ward him off.

And that was all that happened between them.

Lowell was not unaware, however, of Jane Cassidy's physical charms. The smell of her perfume or simply looking at her triggered a hunger in his groin. And when she reached to answer the telephone they shared, as she did now, he was acutely aware of what her breasts looked like beneath the layers of clothing that modestly restrained and concealed them.

With a little bit of luck (that was already showing up on the horizon), he would shortly leave the Rocket Armed Helicopter Section, Rotary Wing Branch, Aircraft Test Division—and Mrs. Jane Cassidy—and put the whole thing behind him. It would become one of his better memories, he thought. The memory of her in his bed would endure for a long time.

"One moment, please," Jane Cassidy was saying to the telephone, which was mounted on a swinging platform bolted to the wall. She covered the mouthpiece with her hand.

"General Jiggs, Major," she said.

She put the handset on the telephone platform and pushed it over to him, in the process innocently giving him a view down the open collar of her blouse. The cups of her brassiere were stitched in a circular pattern, like a bull's-eye.

"Major Lowell, sir."

"I understand you're about to go over to Knox," Jiggs said.

"Yes, sir," Lowell said. "They've formed a company. I thought I should go see what help I could be."

He desperately wanted command of the rocket-armed helicopter company. He thought that when the time came he could ask for it, and that he would probably be given it. In the meantime, he wanted to be as close to the company as possible.

"Tell me your plans," Jiggs said.

"I'm taking Dutch Cramer, Bill Franklin, and Sergeant Piller, one of the armorers, with me, sir," Lowell said. "We're going over in the morning."

"How are you traveling?"

"In the Commander, sir," Lowell said.

"In order to get everybody TPA, or because no aircraft was available?"

"No aircraft was available, sir," Lowell said. "It was either take my airplane or go commercial, and it's a hell of a roundabout way to get from here to there."

"I just found that out," General Jiggs said. "And concluded that two and a half hours sitting around Atlanta between planes was not a wise expenditure of my time."

"You're going to Knox, sir? Would you like to fly over with us?"

"What I think we should do, Craig, is for you to leave your people behind, then you and I should go over together. Unless there is some objection, I've laid on a school L-23 for 0530 tomorrow morning. We'll spend the night and come back the day after tomorrow. You can send your people over then, if you like."

"Yes, sir," Lowell said. For some reason, Jiggs wanted to go to Knox with him alone. He was very curious about that, but knew he dared not ask. If Jiggs had thought he was entitled to an explanation, he would have given him one.

"Are you checked out in the L-23?" Jiggs asked.

"No, sir. Not at Rucker."

"Is there some reason you couldn't take a check ride this afternoon?"

"No, sir," Lowell said. "But we could take the Commander."

"A school L-23 will be at Laird Operations in thirty minutes

with an instructor pilot," General Jiggs said. "If you bust the
check ride, call me when you get back. Otherwise, I'll see you
at 0530 tomorrow."

"Yes, sir."

Lowell broke the connection with his finger after he heard
General Jiggs hang up, then dialed the number of Colonel
William Roberts.

"What is it, Lowell?"

"General Jiggs just telephoned, sir," Lowell reported. "He
wants me to go to Fort Knox with him in the morning, RON.
And he wants me to leave Mr. Franklin, Mr. Cramer, and
Sergeant Piller behind."

"You'll travel in your aircraft?" Colonel Roberts asked coldly.

"No, sir. The general has laid on an L-23."

"I wasn't aware that you're checked out in the L-23."

"The general has arranged for a check ride in half an hour,
sir."

"I see," Roberts said. "Thank you for keeping me abreast,
Major." Then he hung up.

"Jesus!" Lowell said, as he hung up the phone.

"Something wrong?" Jane Cassidy asked.

"I'm going to Fort Knox with General Jiggs in the morning,"
Lowell said. "And for some reason, this displeases Colonel
Roberts."

"I'm surprised that you're surprised," she said.

"Huh?"

"Colonel Roberts is one of those people who wants to keep
all his puppies in their kennels where he can keep an eye on
them," she said. "And here you are, running off with another
pack."

He chuckled.

"That's a good way to put it, I guess," he said.

"In many ways, you're very innocent," she said. "You don't
really understand why you make people like Colonel Roberts
uncomfortable."

"*Innocent?*" he said, in surprise. He had never been accused
of that before.

"Socially speaking, I mean," Jane Cassidy said. It was
oblique, but it was unmistakably her first reference to what
had happened between them. The proof was in the faint flush
that came to her face.

He ended it quickly. "See if you can find either Mr. Cramer

or Mr. Franklin, will you, please?" he asked.

She nodded and walked out of the office.

Warrant Officer Franklin came in a moment later.

"You wanted to see me, sir?"

Lowell told him what had happened.

"Tell Dutch and Sergeant Piller, will you, Bill?"

"Dutch is on the flight line," Franklin said. "Mrs. Cassidy went after him."

"OK, then I'll tell him. Or she will. But you too. OK?"

"Fly good," Franklin said. "It would be *very, very* embarrassing to bust a check ride under these circumstances."

"Screw you, Bill," Lowell smiled. "And close the door when you leave. I've got to change clothing."

He took off his tunic and laid it on the desk, and then added his necktie. Then he took off his trousers and put them on a hanger, added the tunic and tie, and hung it all on a nail pounded into the concrete blocks.

He had just put on his flight suit when Jane Cassidy came back into the room.

"Mr. Cramer was busy," she said. "So I told him what's happened."

"Thank you," he said.

"Aren't you going to be cold, wearing just that?" she asked.

"There's a heater," he said.

He turned his back to her, and took a zippered nylon flight jacket from another hanger suspended from a nail in the concrete block wall. He thrust his arms into the sleeves, and felt for the zipper.

"That's only cotton," she said. "I should think you'd freeze to death."

"No," he said.

"I guess that some people are just warmer-blooded than others," she said.

There was a meaning beyond the words. He turned to face her.

"When are you coming back?" she asked.

"I'll be at Knox only overnight," he said.

"Tom's leaving tomorrow for St. Louis," she said. "They're having trouble with one of the purifiers."

"Oh," he said.

"He's taking the children with him," she said. "It was his idea. They've never been there before."

"Do you want to go with them?" he asked.

"No," she said.

Without being aware that he was doing it, he reached out and touched her face. She caught his hand in both of hers and held it against her chest. His fingers spread and touched her breast and tightened.

"I was afraid you wouldn't want to," Jane Cassidy said.

"I'm afraid for you."

"You're afraid it will get out of control," she laughed. "It won't. I don't fancy myself falling in love with you."

"That's not beyond possibility," he said.

She pushed his hand off her breast and turned around.

"Then forget it," she said, coldly. "I can't afford that. I won't have it!"

He put his hand out toward her hair, and then withdrew it.

"Where the hell would we go?" he said.

"Moving Jannier in with you wasn't the smartest move you've ever made," she said. "But that isn't the problem. I've arranged for a place to go."

"What is the problem?"

"That dumb remark of yours about love," she said. "And from you, of all people."

"What is it you want from me?" he asked.

She turned to face him again. Her face was calm, but there was excitement in her eyes. Her hand moved to the thin cloth of his flight suit. He was erect. She grasped him firmly.

"This," she said. "Only this. Nothing else. Can you understand that?"

She turned him loose.

"Can you?" she asked.

"Yes," he said.

"We have a place in Panama City," she said. "I told Tom I would drive down there to check on it while he's gone. It's off by itself. Safe, in other words."

(Two)

The pilot of the L-23F waiting for Lowell at Laird Operations was a lieutenant colonel, wearing an army green uniform onto which were pinned the starred wings of a Master Aviator. He was one of the old-timers, the professional pilots, maybe going back as far as War II, an officer who had spent ten years doing nothing but flying single-engine two seaters. A card-carrying member, Lowell knew, of the Cincinnati Flying Club.

Lowell saluted him.

"Good afternoon, sir," he said. "I hope I haven't kept you waiting."

There was no direct reply to this.

The lieutenant colonel pointed at the L-23, which was the military version of the Beechcraft Twin Bonanza, a six-place, twin-engined, low-wing airplane.

"How much L-23 time do you have, Major?" he asked. He did not offer either his name or his hand.

"A couple of hundred hours," Lowell said.

"And how much twin engine time?"

"Counting civilian time, about twelve hundred, sir."

"Most of it in the Commander?"

Charm time having failed, fuck you, colonel.

"Most of it, Colonel. May I proceed with the preflight?"

"How much time in the F model L-23?" the lieutenant colonel pursued.

"When my Commander was in for a 500-hour overhaul," Lowell said, "I rented a Queenaire and put twenty-five, thirty hours on it."

"Then you actually have *no* time in the L-23F?"

"Colonel, it's the same airplane," Lowell said.

"No, Major," the lieutenant colonel said. "It is not."

"Yes, sir."

"Major, you don't seem to have the qualifications to take a check ride in this aircraft."

"Colonel, I was ordered here to take a check ride."

"And does General Jiggs know that you haven't gone through the transition course?"

"I would guess, sir," Lowell said, "that the general has made the same mistake I have."

"I don't understand."

"The general has flown with me in a Queenaire," Lowell said. "And I would hazard the guess that he presumes that if I could fly a Queenaire, I can fly this thing."

"May I ask where you have flown the general?"

"From here to South Dakota, Colonel, and back. We went out there to shoot pheasant."

The colonel looked at him.

"Well, Major, since the general has arranged for me to see

if you're qualified to fly the L-23F, I think we should do just that."

"May I proceed with the preflight?"

"I always give people I'm checking one mistake, Major," the colonel said. "Here's yours: Don't you think it would be a good idea to file a flight plan, first?"

You chickenshit sonofabitch!

"My mistake, sir. I mistakenly presumed the colonel would have filed a local flight plan, sir. I regret my mistake."

(Three)
Laird Army Airfield
Fort Rucker, Alabama
0533 Hours, 24 January 1959

"Laird clears Army 4177 for takeoff on three-eight for VFR direct Birmingham. The time is four zero past the hour. The altimeter is two niner niner eight. The winds are five miles per hour, gusting to fifteen, from the north. Contact Birmingham local control on 127.27."

"Seven Seven rolling," Lowell said to the microphone as the L-23F moved off the threshold and onto runway three eight.

"Have a pleasant flight, General," the tower operator said.

"Thank you," Jiggs said, picking up a microphone.

Jiggs waited until Lowell was on a course for Birmingham—and had contacted Atlanta area and been given an instrument flight rules clearance from Birmingham to Godman Field at Fort Knox—before he said: "Of course, I'm pretty new at this, but for an amateur, you seemed to do that rather smoothly for someone only marginally qualified to pilot this aircraft."

"Is that what the sonofabitch said?" Lowell asked.

"That's what he said, and when I told him that I thought I'd take my chances, I'm sure I left him convinced that I was prepared to make literally any sacrifice for the Armor Protective Association."

Lowell chuckled.

"What are the differences between this plane and the one you used to fly?"

"Aside from the military frequency radios, none that I can find."

"In other words, you really feel that you can safely fly me to Fort Knox?"

"Yes, General, I have that hope."

Jiggs chuckled again.

"Why did you file the IFR after you were airborne?"

"Because with all the training going on at Rucker—people flying from nowhere to nowhere for the practice—Atlanta makes the army wait until they clear people who are really going somewhere. You'll notice there was no wait when I told them we were going to Kentucky."

"And there would have been otherwise?"

"If we had asked to go round-robin to Savannah, there would have."

"You're devious, Lowell," Jiggs said, approvingly. "Very devious."

"It was the leadership I had as a young officer, sir," Lowell said. "I was forced to serve under an officer, sir, who couldn't get me comfort rations. When I politely remonstrated with him, he told me to be devious."

"Did I really use that word?"

"Yes, sir, General, sir, you really did. 'Be devious, Lowell. Think of something,' is exactly what you said."

General Jiggs laughed.

"Well, I paid for that, and dearly," he said. "I wrote reports on you and your damned comfort rations for years after that."

"You mean somebody found out?"

"Oh, sure they found out. And the clear implication was that I'd sold the razor blades and soap on the black market."

"Why didn't you tell them they were lost to enemy action?"

"That's the difference between you and me, Craig," Jiggs said, almost sadly, and no longer jocularly. "I can't do that sort of thing as easily as you can. I won't be a hypocrite and say I didn't know our S-4 was a bit vague about whether some equipment was lost to the enemy—or just lost; but I can't sign a statement I know isn't true."

"So what did you do?"

"I told them the truth, that one of my officers was over-zealous, but that the responsibility was mine."

"You should have given them my name," Lowell said. "I was on the shit list anyhow."

"Was on?"

"I believe that combat troops are entitled to whatever their commander can get for them, even if he has to steal it."

"And that made you a superb combat commander," Jiggs said. "Beloved by his troops."

"But?"

"But what?"

"Wasn't that sarcastic?"

"Not at all."

"I was neither superb nor beloved," Lowell said. "Immodesty compels me to admit that I was good, but let's not go overboard."

"You were both," Jiggs insisted.

"But?" Lowell asked.

He suddenly realized what was happening. He was being given a father-to-son—or, perhaps more accurately, a Dutch uncle—talk prior to the announcement—or even prior to his figuring it out—that he was to have command of the 3087th Aviation Company (Tank Destroyer) (Provisional). He hadn't even had to wait for the appropriate moment to ask for it.

He thought that was a very nice thing, indeed, for Paul Jiggs to do. Unnecessary, but nice. Lowell didn't have to be told that this command was his last chance, that if he fucked this up, he might as well get out of the army. If he fucked this up he just might—some distance down the pike—get a silver leaf. But that would do him about as much good as a gold watch and social security, because *that* promotion would be the kiss good-bye before his forced retirement. He needed that silver leaf, but he needed it pretty damn soon. His time was running out.

But if he handled this command right, he would get the silver leaf, and soon, and he would be back in the competition for promotion: first for an eagle and ultimately for the stars of a general officer. He had every intention of commanding the 3087th Aviation Company (Tank Destroyer) (Provisional) not only to the best of his ability, but with one eye on what was expected of him as a responsible field-grade officer.

It was less a question of his having been forgiven than of his actual qualifications. He *had* been a tank commander of distinction. There was no question about that. He had a Distinguished Service Cross (the second highest decoration for valor), a Distinguished Service Medal, a Silver Star, and a chapter in the textbooks. "Task Force Lowell," named after its youthful commander, was cited as the "classic example" of the proper use of an armored force in the breakthrough and exploitation.

And with Ed Greer in his grave and Mac MacMillan running around in the boondocks of Fort Bragg in a silly green hat, he was *the* expert on this newest tool of war, the tank-killing, rocket-armed chopper. If there was a God of War, ol' Mars had decided to annoint him.

In his mind, Lowell went one step further. He *had* been *admired* by his troops. He had never asked them to do anything that wasn't necessary, and they knew it. And the result had been that when he asked them to do something, they'd given it one hell of a try.

He had not commanded troops since Korea. It was going to be just fine to be "the Old Man" again.

"But nothing, Craig," General Jiggs said. "You were one hell of a commander."

(Four)

"Godman, Army 4177," Lowell said to the microphone.

"4177, Godman."

"Godman, Army 4177, L-23F, five minutes out, due south. Request approach and landing."

"4177, have you a Code Eight aboard?"

Lowell looked at Jiggs. Code Eight made reference to the fact that a major general was in paygrade 0-8.

"No honors," Jiggs said.

That didn't surprise Lowell. Jiggs rarely took advantage of the privileges which he was entitled to as a general officer. He stood in line in the officer's club cafeteria at lunch. It was to be expected that he would not wish the airfield commander to drop whatever he was doing to jump in a jeep and rush out and salute him when he landed in an airplane.

"Godman, affirmative on the Code Eight. No honors, I say again, no honors, are desired. Ground transport will be required."

"Godman clears Army 4177 for landing as number one on one eight. The winds are negligible, the altimeter is two niner niner seven. Report on final."

"Understand number one on one eight," Lowell said, as he dropped the nose of the airplane.

He saw U.S. Highway 31W, leading to Elizabethtown, off

his left wing; and he made his approach over the main post.

"4177 over the outer marker," he reported, and then a moment later, "4177 turning on final."

"4177, hold on the runway for a Follow-Me," Godman tower ordered.

"Roger, Godman," Lowell said, as he lined up with the runway. The landing, he thought somewhat smugly, was a greaser. Just a faint chirp from the tires, no bump. As he reversed the propellors, he saw a jeep painted in a black-and-white checkerboard pattern, with an enormous checked flag flapping in the wind. It was racing the Follow-Me down the taxiway parallel to the runway.

The airplane slowed. He retarded the throttles.

"Well, General, sir," he said, "despite your marginally competent pilot, you'll probably see your wife again."

Jiggs laughed.

He stopped the airplane on the runway, and then turned it around. The Follow-Me drove onto the runway, turned around, and then started down the runway. Lowell opened the throttles enough to follow it.

"Oh, Jesus!" General Jiggs said, pointing out the windshield.

Beyond the Base Operations buildings and the hangars beside it, on an expanse of grass, was a company of troops, a half dozen M48 tanks, a band, and a color guard.

"One would surmise," Lowell said dryly, "that the general's desire for no honors is being gloriously ignored."

"I shouldn't have told him I was coming," Jiggs said.

"If you've got it," Lowell said, "flaunt it."

"Go to hell, Craig," General Jiggs said.

The Follow-Me led them off the runway onto a taxiway, and then toward the troops and the tanks. Two ground handlers in white coveralls ran in front of the aircraft and with snappy signals showed where it was to be stopped. Finally, with their signal wands crossed at their necks, they ordered Lowell to kill the engines.

Lowell turned in his seat and pushed open the curtain separating the cockpit from the cabin.

"Davis," he called to Jiggs's aide-de-camp, "give the general a minute to pull up his tie before you open the door."

Jiggs got out of the copilot's seat, buttoned his tunic, and tugged at the skirt.

He pushed the curtain aside.

"And now we'll wait for Major Lowell to pull up his tie, Davis. I wouldn't *dream* of depriving Major Lowell of the indescribable pleasure of participating in this military panoply."

Lieutenant Davis went down the steps of the fold-down door first. He saluted the five officers standing on the ground, a major general, a brigadier general, a colonel, and two aides-de-camp, and then he stood at attention as General Jiggs climbed off the airplane. Salutes were exchanged.

"Welcome to Fort Knox, General," Major General David Henderson said.

"How good of you to meet me, General," Major General Jiggs replied. They shook hands.

Lowell got off the airplane.

The brigadier general and the colonel shook hands with Jiggs, calling him by name.

The aides introduced each other.

Lowell stood by the plane door, hoping he would be ignored.

"Dave, this is Major Lowell," Jiggs said.

General Henderson looked at Lowell, his eyes dropping to the armored insignia on Lowell's lapels, and above his breast pocket the pilot's wings, and above them the miniature Expert Combat Infantry Badge with a star signifying the second award.

"Another good tanker gone wrong, I see, Major," General Henderson said, offering his hand. "But I'm pleased to see that General Jiggs at least has the good sense to have himself flown around by a tanker."

"How do you do, sir?" Lowell said politely.

"Actually, Dave," General Jiggs said, "Major Lowell is the rocket-armed chopper expert."

"Well, then, Major," General Henderson said, "you're doubly welcome."

"Thank you, sir," Lowell said. The brigadier general and the colonel offered their hands.

"Now we'll officially welcome you, General, to Fort Knox," General Henderson said.

"You didn't have to do this, Dave," Jiggs said. "I never thought I was George Patton."

"I wouldn't have missed this opportunity for the world," General Henderson said. "Who would ever have thought, so to speak, when I first laid eyes on you, then a skinny, freckle-faced callow youth, that one day I would be in a position to render to you the honors of a general officer?"

"You were a prick in Beast Barracks, Dave," Jiggs said, tempering that remark only slightly with a smile. "You've grown more sophisticated, is all."

General Henderson smiled warmly and a bit stiffly. He nodded his head.

The band played ruffles and flourishes. The tank cannon fired the salute prescribed by regulations for a major general. Then the band played the national anthem.

"Would the general do me the honor of trooping the line?" General Henderson asked.

Jiggs nodded.

Trailed by their aides, the general officers marched over to the company of troops. While the troops executed open ranks, they trooped the line. After they had finished and Jiggs had offered the company commander the ritual compliments on his command, the command "March Past" was given, the band struck up "For in Her Hair She Wore a Yellow Ribbon," a "traditional cavalry air," and the company of troops began to march past.

They were followed by the six tanks and finally by the band.

"That was very impressive, Dave," Jiggs said. "Unnecessary, but first class, and I thank you."

"My pleasure, Paul," General Henderson said. He looked at his watch. "And right on schedule, too. We've time for everything."

"What's everything?" Jiggs asked. "I came over here to talk to you . . ."

"'Everything' begins with a quick trip to the museum. Just a short stop. There's something there I think you'll be interested in. And then we're going to have lunch at my quarters. There's someone I want you to meet. This afternoon we can have our talk. I've got the whole afternoon set aside for that. And tonight, I've laid on a dining-in at the main club. I thought it would give you a good opportunity to make your aviation pitch to my officers."

"Major Lowell would be better at that than me."

"They'll pay more attention to you," General Henderson said. "You are the only man who's commanded an armored unit larger than a battalion in combat since War II."

"Am I?" Jiggs said, embarrassed.

"Yes, you are, and you know it. That's the point. And *they* know it." He looked at Lowell. "You know that about the general, don't you, Major?"

"Oh, yes, sir," Lowell said, innocently. "General Jiggs has been kind enough to relate many of his exploits in Korea."

Jiggs gave him a withering look.

"And wouldn't you agree that tankers would rather hear from a tank force commander about aviation than from an aviator?"

"Absolutely, sir," Lowell said, enjoying himself heartily.

"That was a bit insulting to Major Lowell, don't you think, Dave?" Jiggs snapped. "You'll notice he's wearing a CIB above his wings."

"It certainly wasn't intended to be insulting," Henderson said. Sensing that Jiggs for some reason was genuinely annoyed, he changed the subject: "We're going to put Major Lowell and your aide up in the VIP guest quarters. You'll stay with Beth and me, of course. Are you familiar with Knox, Major? Can you find your way from the guest quarters to the main club tonight?"

"If it's still across the street, yes, sir," Lowell said.

"Major, would you like to ride along with General Jiggs and me to the museum? You would probably find it interesting."

It was, Lowell saw, a waving of the peace branch. Jiggs decided to let the subject drop. He nodded his head just perceptibly.

"If I wouldn't be in the way, sir," Lowell said.

A line of olive-drab staff cars rolled up. General Henderson's aide opened both doors of the first one. Jiggs and Henderson got in the back, and Lowell in the front.

"Take General Jiggs's aide to the VIP quarters, show him around, and then bring him to mine," Henderson ordered.

"Yes, sir," the aide said and saluted, and the car drove off.

"We have great plans for the museum," General Henderson said. "We're going to call it 'The Patton Museum,' for one thing. And down the road, we're going to get a new building. We've already got his Cadillac and his jeep, and I finally got authority for a full-time curator."

"It's a good idea," Jiggs said. "I'm glad to hear that."

"We had a hell of a fight getting tanks away from ordnance," Henderson said. "From their museum, I mean. E. Z. Black helped us. At least we're getting their duplicates, and we've got some they don't have."

The car moved slowly from Godman Field around the out-skirts of the main post. They came to a frame building in the row of tank barns at the foot of the hill on which the barracks of Student Officer Company were located. Lowell could see the mess hall where he had eaten as a student.

A lieutenant colonel and a master sergeant were standing on the stairs before a tank barn labeled "The Armored Museum." When they saw the staff car approaching, they walked to the edge of the street.

The sergeant-driver of the car jumped out, ran around the rear, and opened the curbside door.

General Henderson introduced the lieutenant colonel who was the curator and the sergeant who was his assistant, and then said they were "running a little late," and would have to skip "for now" a tour of the museum proper.

"I think it's more important," General Henderson said, "wouldn't you agree, Colonel, that picking General Jiggs's brain on our new acquisition is more important than showing him inside?"

"Absolutely, sir."

They were led down a narrow space between two of the tank barns. Behind the tank barns was what looked like an ordnance junkyard: tracked vehicles, American, German, Russian, English, Japanese; artillery pieces; enormous crates apparently unopened in years, their shipping instructions stenciled on their sides; and four tanks, one of them an M26, to which General Henderson and the curator proudly led them.

"Look familiar, Paul?" General Henderson asked.

"Unless memory fails," Jiggs said, dryly, "that's an M26."

"Is that all you've got to say?"

"How about a beat-up M26?" Jiggs asked, innocently.

"That's one of yours, Paul," General Henderson said, a hint of annoyance in his voice.

"Mine?"

"We checked the hull number," the curator said. "We found the records. That tank was issued to the 73rd Tank Battalion in Pusan on 29 August 1950."

"I'll be damned," Jiggs said.

"The colonel was hoping you could tell us something about it," General Henderson said.

"I don't quite understand," Jiggs said.

"We were hoping we could go beyond saying simply that

this tank served with the 73rd Tank Battalion," the curator said. "For example, did it have any official kills? Did it participate in the breakout from Pusan? What company was it assigned to? That sort of thing. Did it have a name?"

Lowell looked hard at the worn-out M26. He had seen a hundred of them. He had even seen one with a scar in the turret like this one had, the scar left by the impact of a 2.8 inch rocket, captured and in the hands of the North Koreans . . . But none of them had the name this one had on its turret.

"Jesus H. Christ!" he said. He experienced a chill.

Generals Jiggs and Henderson and the curator and the master sergeant looked at him in surprise.

"It was called, 'Ilse' at first," Lowell said, his voice level.

"God, Craig," General Jiggs asked. "Are you sure?"

Major Lowell pointed at the flecking paint on the turret. The letters, 's' and 'e' were faintly visible. They had been painted over several times, but flaking paint had uncovered them again.

"You've found your man, Colonel," Jiggs said. "Major Lowell is familiar with this tank."

The colonel beamed.

"Do you know for sure if it was in the breakout?" the curator asked. "That would be nice to know."

Major Lowell nodded.

"It was in the breakout," he said. "And it went to the Yalu and back."

"Then it would be reasonable to presume that the kills painted on the turret were earned," the curator said. "There're eight."

"I can verify that," Paul Jiggs said.

"Splendid!" General Henderson said. "When we get back to the main post, I'll get my secretary to take a short statement from you. Just a short one, stating that to your personal knowledge the tank 'Elsie' made the breakout, went to the Yalu, and had eight kills."

"Ilse," General Jiggs corrected him. "The name of this tank was 'Ilse.'"

"That sounds German. One of your troops have a German girl friend?"

"Ilse was German," Lowell said, icily. "She was born Ilse von Greiffenberg. Her father is Generalmajor Graf von Greiffenberg, Chief of Intelligence of the Bundeswehr."

"Really?" General Henderson said, pleased. "Put that in

your statement, too, Paul." He chuckled. "So no one will think you went to war with the name of some GI's shack job painted on her turret."

Jiggs saw Lowell's stricken face.

"This has gone quite far enough," Jiggs snapped. He turned to the curator. "For your sign, Colonel, or however you decide to identify this tank, you may state that it was the tank assigned to the commander of the force which led the breakout from the Pusan perimeter. That force was known as Task Force Lowell."

"Task Force *Lowell*," General Henderson said. "Of course. It led the breakout." He looked at Lowell. He thought he had everything explained. "Your brother, Major? Or your father?"

"Let it go, Paul," Major Lowell said, barely audibly.

"The tank was named after Major Lowell's wife," Jiggs went on relentlessly. "Two hours before Task Force Lowell made the link-up with elements of the United States X Corps, it was my unpleasant duty to inform Major Lowell that his wife had been killed by a drunken QM major in an auto accident in Germany."

"I am sure," General Henderson said, upset and contrite, "that Major Lowell understands I had no intention of insulting the memory of the lady. I will be happy to get in touch personally with the officer in question, to tell him how pleased we are to have his tank in our museum."

"You're looking at him, Dave," Jiggs said.

It took General Henderson a moment to collect himself.

"That's my second unintended insult, Major," he said, finally. "I offer you my most sincere apology. In extenuation, I can only say that you just don't look old enough."

"He wasn't old enough, or senior enough, or experienced enough," Jiggs said, still angry. "But somehow he did it anyway."

"God, I wish we had a PIO photographer with us," General Henderson said.

"I'm glad you don't," General Jiggs snapped. "And I'm sure Major Lowell feels the same way. You said something about lunch, Dave?"

(Five)

Someone touched his shoulder. Lowell looked up and saw Paul Jiggs, bending down by the open door of the staff car.

"You all right, Craig?" Jiggs asked.

"Lost in thought," Lowell said. "I'm sorry, sir."

"Don't be ridiculous," Jiggs said.

Lowell got out of the car. They were stopped in front of Quarters No. 1. General Henderson was standing ten feet from the car, looking uncomfortable.

"Sorry to keep you waiting, sir," Lowell said.

General Henderson made a deprecating gesture with his hand.

Lowell followed them into the house, an attractive but not luxurious brick home. Lowell thought that the first time he had seen officer's row at Fort Knox, he thought it looked like a set for a prewar Hollywood musical comedy about a college campus. Mid-American U.

It was, he thought now, far more elegant than Paul Jiggs's official quarters at Fort Rucker. More elegant and much larger.

The aides were inside. Lowell was surprised when General Henderson led them past the living room—where a tray of hors d'ouveres was waiting on a table—into the kitchen. To the obvious surprise of the white-jacketed GIs in the kitchen, Henderson pulled open one of the kitchen cabinet doors and took from it three glasses. Then he stooped and opened another cabinet and took from it a bottle of scotch.

"If you have had the privilege of serving under General Jiggs, Major Lowell," he said, "then I'm sure you have learned that there are times when a commander must violate one of his own orders. This command frowns on drinking before 1700. This is the time to violate that regulation. I hope you'll join me."

He poured whiskey in the glasses and handed one to Jiggs and Lowell.

Lowell took his.

Henderson looked as if he could think of nothing to say.

"Absent comrades," Paul Jiggs said, softly, and tossed down his whiskey straight.

"Right," General Henderson agreed, and drank his at a draught.

"Absent companions," Lowell said, and drank his.

"Make three more of those," General Henderson said to one of the enlisted men, "with ice and water, and bring them into the living room."

He motioned Jiggs and Lowell ahead of him.

"You were stationed here, Lowell?" he asked.

"Yes, sir. I went to Officer's Basic Course, and then I was assigned to the Armor Board for a while."

"You've been here, before? To Quarters 1, I mean?" General Henderson asked.

"Just in the garden, sir."

"A lot of interesting people have lived here," Henderson said. He showed him a plaque on which the names of former residents were listed. It was a long list. The names included Major General G. S. Patton, Jr., who had occupied Quarters No. 1 before the European campaigns of World War II from which he emerged as a four-star general; Major General E. Z. Black, now the four-star Vice Chief of Staff; and Major General I. D. White, who had gone on to command the X Corps (Group) in Korea and was now the four-star Commander in Chief, Pacific.

Lowell was pretty sore that Paul Jiggs's name would never be on the list. Now that he had thrown in his lot with aviation, it was highly unlikely that Jiggs would ever be given command of Knox. He would get more stars, maybe as many as four; but he would never command the Armored Center, and Lowell wondered if that bothered Jiggs.

The door chimes sounded.

"That must be Colonel Warner," General Henderson said. A moment later, the aide confirmed his guess.

"Colonel Warner, General," he announced.

"Come on in, Tom," General Henderson said.

A tall, good-looking lieutenant colonel in fatigues and tanker's boots came into the living room. He was wearing aviator's wings, but there was no Expert Combat Infantry Badge. It was possible that he had the CIB and wasn't wearing it, Lowell thought, but it was unlikely. He was also wearing a West Point ring.

"Hello, Tom," General Jiggs said. "How are you?"

"Very well, thank you, General," Colonel Warner said.

"You shake hands with Major Lowell, Tom," General Henderson said. "And then relax."

"How are you, Major?" Warner said, giving Lowell his hand. His grip was firm. Lowell made an instant judgment that he liked this man.

"Colonel Warner was concerned, Lowell," General Henderson said, "that the expert who's going to help him would turn out to be some wide-eyed dreamer who didn't really understand tanks. You can take it from me, Tom, that won't be a problem with Major Lowell. He served with General Jiggs in Korea."

"I'm envious," Colonel Warner said, smiling. "I sat out that war in Berlin, and then they had me on the staff here."

"We had more tank officers than we needed for Korea," General Jiggs said.

"When did you go to flight school?" Lowell asked. Warner looked vaguely familiar, and he thought he might have encountered him before, somewhere in aviation.

"Last year," Warner said. "The general somehow got wind of what you people were up to, and 'suggested' to me that I should apply. Looks like I made it just in time."

"I don't quite understand," Lowell said.

"I wasn't back here a month before they established the 3087th," Warner said. "If I hadn't been here, they'd have had to give it to someone else."

"You're commanding the 3087th?" Lowell asked. He looked at Jiggs and had his answer from Jiggs's eyes before he got Colonel Warner's reply.

"Uh huh," he said. "And I've got the company on standby for this afternoon. We're hoping you can give us a couple of hours. The list of questions is endless."

Lowell fixed a smile on his face. He wanted to swear, to break something. He felt lightheaded—or maybe as if he wanted to throw up.

You naive sonofabitch, you should have known they wouldn't give you a command.

"I'm at your service, Colonel," he said, smoothly.

He glanced at Jiggs. Jiggs, reading in Lowell's eyes what was in his mind—*You should have told me, goddamn it*—made a slight shrugging movement of his shoulders.

"I will spare Major Lowell the embarrassing recitation of his distinguished service," General Henderson said. "You can get it from him this afternoon. General Jiggs believes, and I agree, that Major Lowell should say a few words at the dining-in, and I think it would appropriate for you to introduce him, Tom."

"Yes, sir."

"Now, let's get something to eat," General Henderson said.

XII

(One)
227 Melody Lane
Ozark, Alabama
1930 Hours, 25 January 1959

When they were about to take off from Fort Knox, Major General Paul T. Jiggs politely asked Major Craig W. Lowell if it would be all right if he sat in the left seat.

The left seat was the pilot's seat—the *captain's* seat. Lowell was amused and a little touched. The glamor of flying had gotten even to Paul T. Jiggs. He wasn't qualified to fly the L-23, but he was not above giving Major General David Henderson the impression that he was.

"It's a good idea, sir," Lowell said, straight-faced. "Might as well take the opportunity to learn about the aircraft."

Later, on the runway, he went further. Making sure General Henderson would hear him, Lowell asked, "If you're going to fly, General, would it be all right if I slept in the back?"

"I would prefer that you work the radios, Lowell," General Jiggs said.

"Yes, sir," Lowell said, disappointment in his voice. He was convinced that General Henderson was now certain that General Jiggs was a fully qualified twin-engine pilot.

General Jiggs saluted General Henderson through the cockpit window, and then said, "OK, get us out of here," to Lowell.

"You wanted to fly, so fly," Lowell said.

"I'm not qualified in this thing . . ." Jiggs protested.

"Just think of all the dummies who are," Lowell said. *"L'audace, l'audace, toujours l'audace, mon Général."*

"Screw you, Craig," Jiggs said; but he took the brakes off, put his hands on the throttle quadrant and taxied the L-23 away from Base Operations.

Lowell watched him carefully on the takeoff, but Jiggs did nothing wrong. Lowell was just about to tell him to lift it off when Jiggs did that himself.

When they were at altitude and on course, General Jiggs brought up the tank-killer chopper company that Lowell had not gotten.

"I understand you did a good job talking to Warner's troops," he said, "and I thought you handled yourself very well at the dining-in."

Lowell didn't reply.

"If General Black asks me, I will tell him that," Jiggs went on. "And if he doesn't ask, I'll work it into the conversation, somehow."

"Don't bother," Lowell said, but then realizing he had snapped, he added: "Thank you just the same, but don't bother."

"I understand your feelings, Craig."

"I'm angry—but primarily with myself—for letting wishful thinking get in the way of reason."

"And with me."

"I didn't say that," Lowell said.

"You think I should have told you; and don't tell me you don't."

"I think a little warning would have been in order," Lowell said.

"You're a clever fellow; if I had told you, you would have found out all about Tom Warner. When you'd learned that he's never heard a shot fired in anger and that he only just got through flight school, you would have hated him before you met him. Understandably."

"Unfortunately, he's both a nice guy, and from what I saw of his troops, a good commanding officer."

"Who should have had your job in Korea," Jiggs said. "Did that thought occur to you?"

"I don't think I follow *that* line of convoluted thought," Lowell said, bluntly.

"What do you think Warner—a West Pointer and an honor graduate of the Armor Advanced Course—would have thought as he sat in Berlin with the two companies of tanks that he got to run every two weeks in a parade, if he had learned that the tanks leading the breakout from Pusan were commanded by a twenty-four-year-old involuntary reservist who'd gotten his captain's bars in the Pennsylvania National Guard?"

"Touché," Lowell said.

"Everybody knocks the West Point Protective Association, Craig, but in this case . . . and you'll notice I'm not pretending the WPPA wasn't hard at work here . . . I think it was remedying an injustice, for the greater benefit of the service. We had a fine young light colonel, who, through no fault of his own, had been denied the opportunity to command in combat. Because of that, and because of his grade, and because officers who had done well in war are available he was not about to be given command of a tank outfit. Command of an experimental tank-killing chopper outfit was the next best thing."

"And since C. Lowell is not a member in good standing of the WPPA, just forget that I was a good commander in combat and that I am singularly well qualified to run rocket-armed choppers?" He waited for an answer.

"Those are the arguments I tried to use in your behalf," Jiggs said.

"I never will get a command, will I?" Lowell said, bitterly.

"You're being damned unreasonable. A month ago, you were being thrown out of the army. The Vice Chief of Staff has been severely criticized for keeping you. How the hell could you expect to be given command of the 3087th?"

"You're right, of course," Lowell said, after a moment. "Seeing that goddamned M26 knocked me off my feet. I just couldn't handle not getting that company, too."

"I told you, you handled it well," Jiggs said. "That must

have been a jolt, the very damned tank."

"I'm over it now," Lowell said. "Just now, I was thinking of my other distinction connected with that tank."

"What was that?"

"I was the only officer who got in trouble with a white woman in Korea," Lowell said. "In that very tank."

"*In* the tank?"

"In the tank," Lowell chuckled. "It's amazing, General, what you can do when you set your mind to something."

"Where'd you find the room?"

"We got very close," Lowell said.

"You ever see her afterward?"

"I saw her once when I came home," Lowell said. "The magic, as they say, was gone." After a moment, he added: "And there's somebody else I haven't seen lately—my son."

"How is he?"

"He's twelve, that's how he is. A regular little kraut. I want to go see him, Paul."

"Can you spare the time?"

"I can spare the time, but I'm not sure Bill Roberts will think I can."

Jiggs fell silent a moment.

"I'll speak to him," he said. "If you feel you can take the time, you can take the time."

"I'm going to send Bill Franklin over there to teach the pilots, and Dutch Cramer to talk to their ordnance people, and one of my sergeants to talk to their airframe mechanics. It'll be three weeks before we get the hardware, and another week, ten days, before they'll be able to get it installed. I'm really not needed at the Board. It works. Ed Greer and Mac saw to that. Now is a good time to go."

"I was sure you had thought it through," Jiggs said. "I'll call Bill in the morning, and tell him I think it's a good idea you take some leave."

"Bottle fatigue," Lowell said, chuckling.

SFC Joe McInerney was waiting with Jiggs's staff car when Lowell parked the L-23F in front of Base Operations at Laird Army Airfield.

"Joe will run you home, Craig," Jiggs said. "After he drops us off."

"Thank you," Lowell said. "I didn't think about getting home."

"I hope that isn't a pointed remark," Jiggs said. "I had hoped that I had explained things to your understanding, if not your satisfaction."

"No, sir," Lowell quickly explained. "I sold my car to Jannier. I mean, he's got it, and I need a ride."

Jiggs looked at his face and saw that was the truth.

"OK," he said.

They dropped Lieutenant Davis at his quarters, and then drove further in to the officer's housing area to Quarters No. 1.

"Not very fancy, by comparison, is it?" Jiggs said, as they started up the driveway.

"I wondered if you noticed," Lowell said.

"I did, but I think I'm more useful here than I would be at Knox," Jiggs said, as he opened the door. "But it would be nice, Craig, wouldn't it, if we were both at Knox?"

"How about Quarters 3 at McNair? You as Vice Chief, and me, say, as Director of Army Aviation?" His voice was light, joking.

"I wouldn't want to be E. Z. Black right now," Jiggs said. "And I don't think you'd want to be Bob Bellmon." He paused a moment, then said, "Good night, Craig," and shut the door.

There were lights on at 227 Melody Lane, and the Eldorado was in the carport, but there was no one in the kitchen or living room when Lowell walked in through the unlocked door. Jannier, Lowell decided, was probably visiting Melody. He went back to the kitchen and opened the refrigerator, looking for a beer. He saw there was Tuborg, and thought it was pleasant living with a Frenchman who took his food and booze seriously.

He went into the living room with the beer and sat down in one of their new armchairs.

Jean-Philippe Jannier came into the living room. Somehow the short silk robe he was wearing seemed to shout that he was naked beneath it. It was a sexy bathrobe; Jean-Philippe Jannier was a robustly sexual male.

"Welcome home," Jannier said. "Are congratulations in order?"

"Oh, was I wrong about that!" Lowell said. "Not only did I not get the company, but I was politely given to understand that now that I have made my little contribution to the rocket-armed helicopter, the best and the brightest would take it from here."

"And you are disappointed?"

"Very, very disappointed, my friend," Lowell confessed. Then, so as not to appear a whiner, he changed the subject.

"How did you do with your first check ride?"

Jannier shrugged his shoulders. It could have meant anything.

"I'm going to go see my son," Lowell said.

"Good," Jannier said. "I envy you a son. A man is not complete without a son."

It was, Lowell thought, an odd remark.

"You have a message," Jannier said. "Your secretary called." *Jesus, I'd forgotten all about her!*

"What did she say?"

"Only that you call her at home." Jannier said. "The number is there."

He pointed to a notepad beside the telephone at Lowell's side. There was nothing Lowell could do but dial the number.

"Hello?"

"Major Lowell, Jane," he said.

"Is someone with you?" Jane Cassidy asked.

"Yes," he said.

"Colonel Roberts's secretary called. You are to be in his office at 0800. She said you are to wear a good uniform."

That was an odd message. It carried with it a suggestion that otherwise he might appear in a shabby or soiled uniform. Lowell was one of those people who looked elegant in a baggy cotton flight suit. His "regular" uniforms were tailored by Brooks Brothers in New York; his "good" uniforms, and his shirts, shoes, and boots, came from London.

"With your ribbons," Jane added.

"I wonder what the hell that's about?" Lowell asked.

"I don't know," Jane said. And then: "Are you free?"

"Yes."

"Can you meet me at the Piggly-Wiggly parking lot in Enterprise in thirty minutes?"

"Yes."

"Good," she said, and hung up.

Lowell turned to Jannier and told him that he had to go out to the post.

And then Melody Dutton Greer came into the living room. She was dressed in a skirt and a sweater, and her hair was combed, but there was no makeup on her face, and Lowell had seen enough women fresh from bed to know that she had not been in Jean-Phillipe Jannier's bedroom to examine the new furniture.

"We didn't think you were coming back tonight," she said.

"Obviously," Lowell said, without thinking.

Melody flushed, but she did not avert her eyes.

"That was thoughtless of me," Lowell said. "I'm sorry."

"We will be married," Jannier said.

"You think I'm a whore," Melody said.

"You don't know what I think," Lowell said.

He was not, he realized, either surprised or outraged.

"What do you think?" Jannier said.

"I was thinking I hope you don't get caught at it," Lowell said. "It would be very awkward."

"And you were thinking Ed isn't dead a month," Melody said.

"I was thinking that Ed and I are probably the only people who would understand," Lowell said.

"Merci, mon vieux," Jean-Philippe Jannier said, emotionally.

"You really want to marry this frog, honey?" Lowell asked.

Melody, tears in her eyes, nodded her head.

"Your father wasn't exactly fond of Ed," Lowell said. "Wait till he hears that you're going to marry a frog and go live in wicked Paree."

Melody, wiping at her eyes with her knuckles, laughed bitterly.

I'm not outraged. I'm jealous. No one has looked at me like she's looking at him since Ilse.

Lowell mockingly blessed them with a sign of the cross.

"Bless you, my children," he said. "Go and sin some more."

"That's terrible," Melody said, but she had to giggle.

"I am hungry," Jannier said.

"I wonder why?" Lowell asked dryly.

"And what we will do," Jannier went on, "is open a bottle of champagne, and I will make an omelet."

"So that's it," Lowell said. "The mystery explained." He looked at Melody. "There is absolutely nothing the American female won't do to get out of the kitchen. Even marry a frog."

Melody, surprising him, came to him. She stood on her tiptoes and kissed him.

"Thank you," she said.

And then she surprised him even more. She put her arms around him, and laid her head on his chest. He put his arm around her, and felt a wave of tenderness for her. Then he bent his head and kissed her hair. He was aware that he was actually on the edge of tears himself.

"I am so *happy*," Jannier announced, his voice breaking.

Lowell drank a glass of champagne with them, and then he got in his car and went to meet Jane Cassidy in the Piggly-Wiggly parking lot.

(Two)
Office of the Deputy Commandant for Special Projects
The U.S. Army Special Warfare School
Fort Bragg, North Carolina
0745 Hours, 26 January 1959

Lieutenant Colonel Rudolph G. MacMillan was aware that he had a problem. Early the previous afternoon, Colonel Paul Hanrahan had given him his first real assignment. He was to develop a plan for the recruitment of 1,000 officers and men, in a ratio of roughly one officer to six men.

The officers were to be lieutenants and captains, although specially qualified majors might be considered. The noncoms were to be in the top three enlisted grades, although specially qualified enlisted men in lower grades might also be considered.

They were to have unblemished records, although in the case of specially qualified enlisted men, this might be waived—so long as the blemish was not enough to prevent the issuance of a Secret or Top Secret security clearance.

At least seventy-five percent of those recruited were to be qualified parachutists. Others had to be willing to volunteer for parachute training, and thus they had to be able to pass a physical examination certifying they were fit for parachute jumping.

At least eighty percent of those recruited had to be able to read and write a foreign language. And of that group, a further eighty percent had to be able to speak, read, and write the Spanish language. At least fifty percent of the officers had be of "combat arms"—that is infantry, armor, or artillery. At least twenty-five percent had to be from the signal corps. At least five percent had to be physicians.

Hanrahan had told him he was not to be concerned with the

objections of commanding officers. The Assistant Chief of Staff, Personnel, had been directed to effect the transfers of people Hanrahan wanted. The only problem was to find them.

There were other qualifications and restrictions. MacMillan had worked late into the night trying to draft a recruiting plan. All he had managed to do, so far, was the basic arithmetic. One thousand officers and men in a 6-to-1 ratio meant 167 officers and 833 men. Eight hundred, total, had to speak a foreign language, and of that 800, 640 had to speak Spanish. He needed eight and a half doctors, six and one quarter of whom had to be qualified parachutists, and six and one half of whom had to speak Spanish.

He had, in other words, a lined tablet page and a half full of meaningless figures, and absolutely no idea how to proceed. He was about to make an ass of himself in front of Hanrahan, which would make it clear that he was a fucking dumbbell who had to be led around by the hand.

There was a knock at his door.

"Come!"

It was Second Lieutenant Thomas J. Ellis, of the 82nd Airborne Division, and right now the last thing MacMillan needed was a second john wet behind the ears.

"What the hell do you want?" he snapped, and was immediately sorry.

Ellis marched into the office and saluted.

"Sir, I'm sorry to bother you," he said, "but I wanted to give you this."

Ellis laid four fifty dollar bills on MacMillan's desk, and then returned to attention.

"Oh, stand at ease," Mac said. "Sit down, as a matter of fact. You want some coffee?"

"I don't want to take up your time, Colonel," Ellis said.

"Sit," MacMillan said, pointing. Then he stood up and turned to his coffee maker and poured some coffee in mugs. "How do you take it?"

"Black, please, sir."

MacMillan handed him the mug.

"Got a partial pay, did you? You got enough left until payday? This one and the next one?"

"It could be considered a partial pay, sir," Ellis said.

"If I didn't know better, I would guess you were playing poker again, Lieutenant," MacMillan said.

"No comment, sir," Ellis said, with a smile.

"Well, if you're sure you've got enough to carry you?"

"More than enough, sir," Ellis said. "I even made the down payment on a car. It's not much, but it's better than walking."

"I'm sorry I snapped at you," MacMillan said. "I've got problems."

"You don't have to waste time with me, sir, to be polite," Ellis said, starting to get to his feet.

"Sit," MacMillan ordered again.

"Yes, sir."

MacMillan looked at him and smiled. He looked, in his immaculate uniform, like a recruiting poster. The brand-new shavetail parachutist, hair closely cropped, nothing on his uniform but his wings and his gold bars.

"What do you think of the division?" Mac asked.

"It's not very interesting," Ellis said. "Not what I thought it would be."

"You have probably been assigned as assistant supply officer, reenlistment officer, army welfare officer, and VD control officer, in addition to your other duties?" Mac asked.

"Yes, sir."

"It'll pass, in time," Mac said. "Standard procedure."

"Yes, sir."

"Tell me, Ellis, how is the division fixed for spics?"

"I don't understand the question, Colonel," Ellis said, a little stiffly.

"How many taco eaters? You know what a spic is, don't you?"

"Yes, sir, I know what a spic is," Ellis said.

"I'm in the market for spics," Mac said. "That's why I asked."

"Sir?"

"My perfect spic is a combat arms officer, jump qualified, who reads, writes, and speaks spic like a spic," Mac said. "I need 167 of them, preferably lieutenants or captains. They have to be volunteers."

"Because of what's happening in Cuba, you mean, Colonel?" Ellis asked. "They're planning to use Green Berets?"

"I didn't say that," MacMillan said.

Ellis stood up, came to attention, and a stream of rapid Spanish came out out of him.

"What the hell was that?" MacMillan said.

"That was Spanish, sir. What I said was that I hoped the colonel will grant me the honor of permitting me to volunteer."

"Where the hell did you learn to speak Spanish?" MacMillan asked.

"From my mother, sir. I'm half Puerto Rican. I suppose you could say that makes me fifty percent spic."

MacMillan's already ruddy face flushed red.

"Ellis, I didn't mean to..."

"I've heard it before, Colonel," Ellis said. "If you live in Spanish Harlem and look like an anglo, you learn pretty quick what the anglos think of the spics—and what the spics think of anglos."

"I didn't mean to say anything..."

"Sir, I'm dead serious about wanting to volunteer," Ellis said.

Hanrahan's voice, distorted but recognizable, came over the intercom: "Mac, how're you coming with the recruiting plan? Can I have a look at it?"

MacMillan looked at his watch. It was 7:55. Hanrahan had said "in the morning." He wanted the plan now, and it wasn't even started.

"I'm interviewing an officer right now, Colonel," Mac-Millan said.

"One meeting the specs, or one you dragged off the street?"

"A Spanish-speaking, jump-qualified infantryman, sir."

"This I've got to see," Hanrahan said. "Bring him in."

"You've got between now and the time we get to the colonel's office to change your mind, Ellis," Mac said.

"Thank you, Colonel," Ellis said.

They marched in side by side, the nearly middle-aged lieutenant colonel—who was the most highly decorated officer on the post—and the teenaged second lieutenant fresh from OCS. They saluted the commandant, and when he had returned it, they stood at attention before his desk. The comparsion was not lost on Paul Hanrahan.

"You two look like 'Before' and 'After,'" he said. He offered his hand to Lieutenant Ellis. "My name is Hanrahan, Lieutenant. Sit down and tell me why you'd like to join Special Forces."

MacMillan was surprised and relieved to hear Ellis's answers. Ellis told Hanrahan he thought that Special Forces would "be interesting," and that it would give him an opportunity to learn skills which would be valuable to him later.

"And you like the glamor, too, I suppose?" Hanrahan said.

"I understand the ladies look on Special Forces that way, sir," Ellis said.

Hanrahan asked him a few questions. He had already made up his mind to take one or two bushy-tailed, virginal shavetails into Special Forces, not for the contribution they could be expected to make, but to see how much training they could absorb in a short period of time. This second lieutenant would serve that purpose. He wondered where MacMillan had found him on such short notice.

He called the sergeant major on the intercom, and asked him to send Master Sergeant Jesus Santana in.

Santana, a swarthy bull of a man, came in a minute or two later.

"Colonel MacMillan tells me this officer is fluent in Spanish, Santana," Hanrahan said. "I don't think he's qualified to judge."

Santa spoke to Ellis for several minutes, then rendered his judgment.

"He's perfectly fluent, sir," he reported. "Actually, he speaks rather Castilian Spanish, as opposed to Puerto Rican or Mexican."

"We had Spanish nuns in school, sir," Ellis said.

"When would you like to come over here, Lieutenant?" Hanrahan asked.

"This afternoon, sir," Ellis replied immediately.

"I'd hoped," MacMillan said, "to use Lieutenant Ellis as my translator. To see that people really speak Spanish."

"That makes sense," Hanrahan said.

In bringing in Ellis, MacMillan was dropping another hot potato in his lap sooner than he had expected. There were going to be howls of rage from the 82nd Airborne, from XVIII Airborne Corps, and from other units at Bragg (because they were mostly paratroops, the majority of his new people would have to come from Bragg). He knew the sooner he got through that fight, the better.

He took the Fort Bragg telephone directory from his desk drawer, and found the number of the XVIII Airborne Corps G-1 (Deputy Chief of Staff, Personnel). He dialed the number, then asked for the G-1.

"Colonel," he said, "this is Colonel Hanrahan of the Special Warfare School. I wondered if you had gotten the TWX about my authority to recruit for Special Forces?"

He listened for a full minute, and when he finally spoke again, his voice was cold and abrupt.

"It is not my understanding, Colonel, that I am to be offered my choice of personnel from rosters prepared by anyone. It is my understanding that I have been given authority to recruit whomever I please. Will it be necessary for me to seek clarification from DCSOPS?"

There was a much shorter reply.

"I am about to put a Lieutenant Ellis on the horn, Colonel. He will give you his serial number and organization. Please see that he is transferred to me, effective today. Thank you very much."

He took the telephone from his ear and extended it to Ellis.

If Hanrahan stays mad, and asks me for my plan, Mac MacMillan thought, my ass is still going to be in a crack. But if he doesn't ask me for it, I'm home free. I can stall for a day. And in a day I can find somebody—maybe even Ellis—who can write a goddamned plan.

(Three)
Office of the President
The Army Aviation Board
Laird Army Airfield
Fort Rucker, Alabama
0815 Hours, 26 January 1959

There were two civilians in Colonel Bill Roberts's office when Major Craig W. Lowell, in an impeccably tailored uniform—but without ribbons—marched in and saluted.

"Good morning, sir," Lowell said. "You wanted to see me?"

"I'd hoped to see you wearing your ribbons, Major," Bill Roberts said coldly, but masking it with a smile. "This gentleman wants to take your picture for *Time-Life*, and I thought you should be wearing your ribbons. Didn't your secretary relay my message?"

"It must have been garbled, sir," Lowell said.

Williams stood up and came around the desk.

"Miss Thomas, Mr. Norton, this is Major Craig Lowell, the officer charged with the testing and development of the rocket-armed helicopter."

Mr. Norton was in his forties, a balding, pudgy, rumpled

little man festooned with Nikon cameras. An enormous leather gadget bag was at his feet. Miss Thomas was in her middle twenties. Her hair was blond and long, parted in the middle and hanging below her shoulders. A pair of sunglasses was stuck on top of her head. She wore a pleated, plaid woolen skirt and a soft woolen sweater that did not conceal her ample bosom.

If I had not just spent a rather exhausting night with Jane Cassidy trying to set a world's screwing record, followed by a prebreakfast encore, I would certainly contemplate jumping your bones, Miss Thomas.

"Pleased to meetcha, Major," Norton said, offering an indifferent hand.

Miss Thomas offered her limp fingers and a dazzling smile. "How are you?" she said.

Lowell thought he had Miss Thomas pegged the moment he'd seen the Peck & Peck sweater and skirt, the single string of real pearls, and the loafers. Confirmation came when she spoke. He smiled, remembering Sandy Felter's remark about people like Miss Thomas: "Is that inbred, genetic, or do they send them to school to learn how to talk with their jaws locked and through their noses?"

Lowell had a lifelong experience with Miss Thomas types, and it had taught him to keep his distance from them.

"I want you to give Mr. Norton and Miss Thomas as much of your time as necessary, Lowell," Bill Roberts ordered. "Show them everything about our rocket-armed helicopter that's not classified. If they'd like, take them for a ride."

"Colonel," Lowell said, "the entire weapons system is classified secret. What should I show them?"

"Then everything but the weapons system," Roberts said, annoyed.

"But we came to see the weapons system," Miss Thomas said, winningly.

"As absurd as it might seem to you," Lowell said, flashing her a dazzling smile, "we have to go on the premise that you're Russian spies."

She was not amused. And there was steel beneath the Peck & Peck smile.

"We're here with the blessing of the Chief of Information," she said. "And it was clearly understood by him why we were coming all the way down here. To see the weapons system on your whirlybirds."

"I'm truly sorry, Mrs. Thomas," Lowell said.

"That's 'Miss,'" she said.

"Right," Lowell said. "But my hands are tied. You'll have to take that up with Colonel Roberts."

Lowell was amused at Roberts's predicament. Roberts had apparently been so dazzled by the appearance of *Time-Life* and/or by the dazzling smile, long legs, and intriguing bosom of Miss Thomas that he had forgotten that the project was mostly classified.

Now that it had been brought to his attention, he made up his mind quickly.

"What I'll do, Miss Thomas, is get on the telephone and see how much of the weapons system can be declassified. I mean, after all, it's been on television. And failing that, I'll be more than happy to provide *Time-Life* with photographs which have been cleared for publication."

"You mean," she said, bitchily, "with the sexy parts air-brushed out?"

Roberts laughed uncomfortably.

"Lowell, why don't you take my car and driver and give these people a tour of the place? Say for an hour? Until I get some answers from Washington."

"My pleasure, sir," Lowell said.

"I would hate to think I'm being given the runaround, Colonel," Miss Thomas said, unpleasantly.

She walked out of the room, past Lowell.

She had a nice, springy, feminine walk, and she smelled of something both very appropriate and very expensive.

Smith, he decided. Not Vassar. Smith. And then the graduate school of journalism at Columbia. And then journalism. Journalism was chic, *Time-Life* even more chic, a perfect place to meet someone of one's own background, someone to marry before establishing a home in Mamaroneck, or Princeton, or Darien, there to breed another generation of teeth-clenchers to be dispatched to Country Day School, Miss Porter's, St. Mark's, and then Harvard, Smith, Yale, and Vassar.

Major Craig W. Lowell had been privately tutored before entering St. Mark's, from which he had been expelled before going on to Harvard, from which he had also been expelled.

He was, he realized, mocking his own, and wondered why. And then he understood. He resented the intrusion of that world into this one. And he understood that it was important that this long-legged blond must not learn any more about him than he had to tell her.

Her questions began as soon as they began the ride from Laird Field through Daleville to the main post.

"Have you been in the army long, Major . . . Lowell, is it?"

"Lowell," he confirmed. He did the arithmetic. "Thirteen years," he said.

"West Point?"

"Oh, no," he said. "I came in the army as an enlisted man."

"Battlefield commission?" she asked, hopefully.

He looked into the back seat. She was scribbling into a notebook. Her legs were crossed and her hair had fallen forward. She looked up at him. Her eyes were light blue, intelligent.

"Nothing as romantic as that," he said. "I was commissioned into the finance corps, and then transferred to armor."

"Oh?"

"I wasn't a very good finance clerk," he said.

"Where are you from?"

"Long Island," he said. "A little village on Long Island. Glen Cove."

"Oh?" she said. "I'm from Scarsdale. You don't sound like a New Yorker."

"I don't suppose I am, anymore," he said.

"Are you married?"

"I have a twelve-year-old son," he said.

"Here?"

"In Germany."

She was clever, and put that together.

"You married a German girl?"

"Yes," Lowell said. "When I was nineteen."

She was too polite—and it was not germane to her story— to probe further into his personal life.

"When did you become a pilot?"

"The army calls us aviators," he said. "In 1954."

"And you're the man responsible for the rocket-armed helicopters?"

"Oh, no," Lowell said. "Get that straight. Two men were responsible for that: Lieutenant Colonel Rudolph G. MacMillan and First Lieutenant Edward C. Greer."

She made him spell the names, and then said: "I'd like to talk to them."

"That'll be difficult," Lowell said. "Lieutenant Greer was killed just before Christmas. And Colonel MacMillan was transferred. I've taken over for them. But the work was already mostly done when I did."

"Greer was killed in that accident we saw on television?"

"Yes."

"And the other one, MacMillan, was the one who shot up the Russian tanks?"

"I don't think it's been determined, officially, who did that," Lowell said.

"But this MacMillan has been transferred, right?" she asked. She had put that together, too.

"It was a *routine* transfer," Lowell said. "As I told you, the development work on the rocket-armed helicopter is about over."

"Huh!" she snorted.

"And I was brought in to take over since it was," he went on.

She closed her reporter's notebook and put it in her purse. Lowell had been ordered by Colonel Roberts to take them on a tour of the post. He pointed out Hanchey Field, the world's largest heliport, and the post hospital, and the dependent housing area.

She asked only one more question.

"Is that where you live, Major Lowell?"

"No, ma'am, I live off post," he said.

When the hour was over, they returned to the Army Aviation Board.

"We'll have to get you another guide, Miss Thomas," Colonel Roberts said. "Major Lowell is going on leave."

"Oh?" she asked.

Roberts looked at Lowell.

"While you were gone," he said, "the post commander telephoned and recommended that Major Lowell be placed on leave. Lowell has been working very hard lately."

"Sir, I can put that off until Miss Thomas and Mr. Norton are through here," Lowell said.

"I wouldn't think of it, Major," Colonel Bill Roberts said, icily. "If the post commander thinks you should go on leave, *I* think you should go on leave."

"Yes, sir," Lowell said.

"Thank you for the cook's tour, Major Lowell," Miss Thomas said, offering her hand.

He took it, and met her eyes. Her hand was warm and soft, and something else. Vibrant, he thought.

"My pleasure, Miss Thomas," Lowell said. Then he shook hands with her photographer, saluted Colonel Roberts, and left the office.

As he got into Bill Franklin's car to leave the field, he thought about what had happened the night before. Sometimes after a really wild session in bed, he was hornier than he would have been after a quickie. And the session with Jane Cassidy had been wild. Once she had let the barrier of fidelity down, all of her suppressed hungers had rushed out.

It had left him with the odd feeling that he was being used. It was not a pleasant feeling, and it occurred to him that women must also often feel that way: Jane Cassidy didn't love him, or even particularly like him. She was just hot for his body.

He laughed at himself: *Oh, you poor, used dear, you!*

He thought then of the very different—and very loving—expression on Melody Dutton Greer's face, when she looked at Jean-Philippe. An expression that reminded him how alone he was. Being with Jane hadn't changed that. But he was sure that this loneliness would pass—and also that he had handled Miss Thomas (he realized he didn't even know her first name) the way she needed to be handled.

(Four)
Conference Room 3-101
The Central Intelligence Agency
McLean, Virginia
1815 Hours, 2 February 1959

The red telephone, one of three instruments at the head of the broad table in front of the Director, both buzzed and flashed. It was the presidential office line—a line whose use was restricted to the President's immediate staff.

The Director said, "Excuse me," picked it up, said, "Hello," listened, said, "He's here; I'll tell him," and hung up.

"The President," he said, "has expressed a desire to see you, Colonel Felter, at seven thirty."

"That's the second time he's done that," Felter said. "Made

me a colonel. I wish he'd put it in writing."

"The President can call you 'colonel' all he wants, Felter," the Deputy Director, Covert Operations, said, chuckling. "But before the army will pay you as a colonel, it will have to have the advice and consent of the Senate."

The men at the table laughed. It was not, Felter realized, the second time, but rather the third or fourth time in the last couple of weeks that the President had called him *"Colonel* Felter." For a long time Ike had referred to him simply as "Felter" . . . calling errand-runners and spear-carriers by their last names was usual.

"Hope springs eternal in the human breast," Felter said.

He wondered what the President wanted. He looked at his watch. The meeting here couldn't last much longer. He would have plenty of time to take the Volkswagen and drive to the White House by half past seven.

The President's military aide was waiting for him in the basement when he got to the White House.

"Let's go get a cup of coffee, Felter," Major General Faye, who was in uniform, said. "You're fifteen minutes early, and fifteen minutes is one of those time frames that doesn't give you many other options."

"Thank you, sir," Felter said.

They went into the executive mess, and white-jacketed navy stewards brought them coffee and doughnuts. There was hardly time to finish the coffee before they had to get on the elevator and ascend to the presidential apartments.

"Have any idea what he wants with you?" General Faye asked, when they were on the elevator.

"No, sir."

The Secret Service agent on duty in the upstairs corridor nodded at them, and then held the door at the end of the corridor open for them.

Felter was not surprised to see the senior senator from California and his wife in the presidential apartments. He was close to the President, and the lady and Mamie Eisenhower were cronies. What really surprised him was that his own wife was there. It wasn't the first time she'd been in the place, but— God knows—Sharon was hardly part of the White House inner circle. All he could figure was that Mrs. Eisenhower had drafted Sharon for some social duty. Sharon smiled nervously at him.

The President came into the room, and on his heels one of the White House butlers carrying a silver tray with silver cups on it.

"Artillery punch," the President said. "Mamie's idea. She thought it was appropriate for the occasion."

Felter quickly searched his mind, wondering if there had been a victory for one of the West Point athletic teams that day. It was the only reason he could imagine for the artillery punch, the army Auld Lang Syne.

"Go on, Senator," the President said.

"Sandy," the senator said, "in its infinite wisdom, the United States Senate, on the recommendation of the President, has granted its advice and consent to your promotion to lieutenant colonel."

"By God, I think he is surprised," the President said, flashing his world-famous grin.

"Flabbergasted, Mr. President," Felter said.

"Good," the President said, taking one of the silver cups from the butler. "I'm pleased to see there is something that can astonish you." He waited until the other cups had been passed out. Then he went on: "Ladies and gentleman, I give you Lieutenant Colonel Felter."

"Hear, hear," General Faye said.

"Thank you very much, Mr. President," Felter said. He looked at Sharon. She was beaming.

My God, he thought, *have we come a long way from the Old Warsaw Bakery on the corner of Aldine Street and Chancellor Avenue in Newark, New Jersey.*

"And his gracious lady," the President went on, raising his cup to Sharon.

"Hear, hear," General Faye said again.

"Sandy, I've got to tell you I got my silver leaf with much more pomp and circumstance," the President said. "In the Malacan Palace in Manila. From General MacArthur. Who was then Marshal of the Philippine Army. Everybody in dress whites. Very grand, indeed."

"I can think of nothing that would be more grand than this, Mr. President," Felter said.

"I promoted you a little early, Felter, because I wanted it understood that you had earned it, and it wasn't something I passed out just before leaving office."

"I don't know what to say, Mr. President," Felter said.

The President smiled at him. Then he raised his silver cup. "Absent comrades," he said.

The others parroted him.

"Get the photographer in here," the President said.

The photographer appeared immediately.

"We want two pictures," the President ordered. "One of all of us, and one with just Mrs. Eisenhower, Mrs. Felter, Colonel Felter, and me."

"Yes, sir," the photographer said.

"I don't think it'll be on the front page of the *Washington Post,* Felter," the President said. "But maybe, when you're as old as I am, it will be kind of fun to take out and look at."

The President of the United States put his arm around Sandy Felter's shoulders.

"Say 'cheese,' Mrs. Felter," the President said.

XIII

(One)
Schloss Greiffenberg
Marburg an der Lahn, West Germany
14 February 1959

There was a 200-meter firing range set up between rows of apple trees in the orchard to the west of the Schloss. When Generalmajor Graf Peter-Paul von Greiffenberg had had it refurbished after the war, he had it equipped with electrical targets. An electric motor and pulley system permitted targets to be fastened to a rack at the firing line, and then moved to the butts. After these had been fired on, they could be returned to the firing line for examination.

The targets today, however—somewhat to the consternation of Generalmajor Graf von Greiffenberg—were four quart cans of Campbell's tomato juice, raised from the ground on bricks.

The marksman was Peter-Paul Lowell, a blond twelve-year-old who was tall for his age and who bore a strong resemblance both to his grandfather and his father. He was wearing a formal

German hunting costume: a green lodencloth jacket, matching green knickers, gray stockings, and a felt hat, the band of which was not ornamented. If he was lucky the next day, he would get his roebuck, a small deer, and thus be privileged to dip the hat feathers in the animal's blood, a symbol of entering the fraternity of hunters.

Peter-Paul Lowell also wore a pair of American shooting muffs over his ears. They didn't fit over the hat, so the headband was down on his neck.

Major Craig W. Lowell, similarly attired, corrected his son's standing position, and then stepped back.

"Go ahead, P.P.," he said in English.

"I do wish you wouldn't call me that," the boy said, in British-accented English.

"Pardon me," Lowell said, smiling. "Go ahead, *Peter*."

The boy took the rifle from his shoulder and worked the action. Then he put it to his shoulder again.

"Take a breath," Major Lowell ordered. "Let half of it out. Hold it. And then squeeze." He put his index fingers in his ears.

The boy took careful aim through the telescopic sight and fired.

There was a sharp crack. The recoil staggered the boy. The can of Campbell's tomato juice exploded.

"Mein Gott!" Peter-Paul Lowell exclaimed.

His father and grandfather applauded. Peter-Paul Lowell turned to them beaming.

"Keep the goddamn muzzle pointed at the ground and down range!" Craig Lowell snapped.

Embarrassed, the boy complied.

"Open the action," Lowell commanded, "and hand it to me. And then run down there and have a look at the can."

The boy did as he was ordered.

"You've made him very happy with that rifle, Craig," the Graf von Greiffenberg said, when he was out of earshot.

"He's making me very happy with it," Lowell said.

"And I see your reasoning with the juice can," the Graf said, nodding down range. The boy was holding up the can, ripped wide open by hydrostatic force, awe on his face.

"My father did that to me," Lowell said. "With a sixteen-bore shotgun. It's something you never forget."

Peter-Paul Lowell ran back from the butts.

"It simply exploded!" he said. "Quite extraordinary."

You're not only half kraut, you're half limey. Which leaves no half for American.

"Beginner's luck, probably," Lowell said. "I'll bet you can't do it again."

"I shall certainly have a go at it, Father," the boy said, miffed, and reached for the rifle.

He fired four more times, missing once.

"What do you say, Grandpa?" Lowell asked, seriously. "You think we can safely take him with us?"

"I'm not sure, Craig," the Graf said, solemnly, going along. "He's still so young."

"Grosspapa!" Peter-Paul Lowell said, in exasperation.

"Well, perhaps we could try," von Greiffenberg said.

"May I shoot some more?"

"You can finish that box of shells," Lowell said. "But we're out of tomato juice."

He had just finished shooting three five-shot groups of about three inches, which made his father extraordinarily proud of his son, when the butler appeared.

"Herr Generalmajor Graf, your guests have arrived."

"We'll be there directly," the Graf said.

"Now comes the dirty part," Lowell said. "First you clean up the mess the tomato juice made, and then you clean the rifle."

"Yes, sir," the boy said.

"Perhaps," the Graf said, tactfully, "Peter-Paul could do that after he's met our guests."

"Of course," Lowell said.

He had understood both the Graf's tactful reluctance to override Lowell's orders to his son and the "our" guests. Lowell knew the primary—perhaps the only—reason the Graf had invited U.S. Army officers on the hunt was to introduce him to them.

"You always make sure the weapon is empty," Lowell said, "and then you leave the action open."

"Very well," Peter-Paul Lowell said.

There were four U.S. Army officers, in uniform, waiting in the sitting room of the Schloss (which was more of a large villa than the term "Schloss," or "castle," implied). The two senior officers were Major General Bryan Ford, the European Command intelligence officer, and Brigadier General John B.

Nesbit, the Seventh Army intelligence officer. They were accompanied by two junior officers, their aides-de-camp. All four stood up as they saw von Greiffenberg stride into the room.

Out the window, Lowell saw they had come in staff cars. An invitation to shoot with the Chief of Intelligence of the Bundeswehr was apparently considered official business.

"I'm so sorry not to have personally greeted you," the Graf said. "We were teaching Peter-Paul how to fire his new rifle. You have, at least, been offered something to drink?"

"We've been well taken care of, Herr Generalmajor Graf," Major General Ford said, in fluent German.

"I don't believe you know these gentlemen, do you, Craig?" von Greiffenberg said. "General Ford, General Nesbit, may I present my son-in-law, Major Lowell?"

"We have mutual friends, Major," General Ford said, in English, as he offered his hand. "Colonel Hanrahan and Lieutenant Colonel Felter."

"*Lieutenant Colonel* Felter, sir?" Lowell asked.

"A couple of weeks ago," General Ford said.

"The best friend," Lowell said, dryly, "is always the last to know."

General Ford wondered if there wasn't a touch of bitterness in Lowell. He knew a good deal about Major Craig W. Lowell. When he'd examined the dossier on Generalmajor Graf von Greiffenberg, he had found it fascinating that the Generalmajor, (who had been one of the very few members of the Colonel Graf von Stauffenberg plot to assassinate Hitler to go undetected and to survive the war) had an American officer for a son-in-law. He had looked into it.

The first information he'd come up with had been promising. Lowell was an aviator—and a very rich man. That had seemed to indicate that he was sort of a playboy, who, not needing to earn a living, found it amusing to be a soldier and a flyboy. Just the sort of man, in other words, that he could arrange to have assigned to Germany to be close to his father-in-law. He probably wouldn't learn much from the close-mouthed Graf. But he just might. Getting Lowell close to the Graf was worth whatever effort it might require.

But then he'd learned more about Craig W. Lowell, and why he was an aviator. Lowell had performed brilliantly as a tank force commander in Korea; his performance had earned him a Distinguished Service Cross and a major's gold leaf at twenty-four. And then he'd had a run-in with a general officer, ostensibly for something silly, taking a visiting movie actress to the front line, but actually for standing up in a court-martial in defense of a black officer accused of shooting down a cowardly infantry officer. The result had been the same, Paul Hanrahan had told him: an efficiency report accusing him of immaturity, of lacking the qualities required of a commanding officer.

And Mr. Spook himself, Presidential Counselor (and then Major) Sanford T. Felter, had told General Ford that in his opinion the assignment of Major Lowell to a position where he "could keep an eye on von Greiffenberg" would be "ill advised."

"I'd actually hoped, Major, that you would talk to him. Perhaps appeal to his sense of duty."

"And his patriotism?" Felter had replied.

"That, too," General Ford had said, with a smile.

"General," Felter had said, very coldly, "when this officer was nineteen years old, he elected to assume command of a company of Greek mountain infantry when its officers were killed. The prudent thing for him to have done—what he was authorized to do—was evacuate himself when he was in any kind of danger. At the time he was rather severely wounded. I would not presume to lecture him on duty. Neither would I suggest to him that he involve himself in something I regard as both shoddy and counterproductive."

"We're in a shoddy business, Major," General Ford had replied. He did not like being lectured to by a Jewish major.

"If Major Lowell were given such an assignment, he would resign; and in the process you would alienate Generalmajor Graf von Greiffenberg," Felter said. "To reiterate, I consider it ill-advised."

"I had frankly hoped to have your cooperation, Major," General Ford had said.

"I'm sorry, sir, you have my opposition," Felter had replied.

Felter's opposition had proven to be more than philosophical. General Ford had put the wheels in motion; after there had been no action in two months, and during a time when he had been in Washington, he'd asked the Deputy Chief of Staff, Intelligence, about the case.

"You can't have Lowell, Bryan," The DCSINTEL said. "I'm surprised that you asked."

"May I ask why, sir?"

"Because Major Felter thinks it would be counterproductive," the DCSINTEL said. "He told me so, personally."

"And you agree with him, sir?"

"As a matter of fact, I do," the DCSINTEL said. "But that isn't really the point. The point is that Major Felter meets privately with the President of the United States for fifteen minutes every day. I haven't seen the President at all in three months. He didn't mention that, of course, when he called me about this."

"He called you about this?"

"Yes, he did. He said that he was very sorry that he had to disagree with you about it, and asked me if I thought he was wrong."

"I just can't believe that you jump when a major says to," General Ford said.

"It didn't get to that, Charley," the DCSINTEL said. "I think he's right and you're wrong. It was therefore unnecessary to find out for sure who has more influence with the President, me or his personal representative to the intelligence community."

"You think Felter would have taken it to the President?"

"I don't know," the DCSINTEL said. "But I do know that when he does go to the President, he generally gets what he wants. He had Paul Hanrahan put in charge of the Green Berets over the violent protests of airborne establishment."

"A man with a lot of clout, who takes care of his buddies?"

"I'm not getting through to you, Bryan," the DCSINTEL said, somewhat sharply. "That's disappointing. The reason Major Felter has influence with the President is because the President knows his advice is not influenced by any personal considerations. The only axe Felter grinds is the President's. If you like, the country's."

General Ford thought of that conversation with the DCSINTEL as he watched Major Craig Lowell, dressed up like a German aristocrat, shaking hands with the aides-de-camp.

"General Ford is my counterpart in the EVCOM, Craig," the Graf said. "And General Nesbit is the Seventh Army G-2."

"How are you, young man?" General Ford said to Peter-Paul.

"I am very pleased to meet you, General," Peter-Paul

Lowell said, in his British-accented English, as he offered his hand.

He holds out his hand like the Prince of Wales meeting a faithful lackey, Lowell thought, and sounds like him, too.

General Ford was visibly surprised at the boy's adult behavior.

"And that's a new rifle?" Ford asked. "May I see it?"

"Father brought it to me from America," Peter-Paul said, handing it over.

General Ford looked first in the breech, and then examined the rifle carefully.

"Very nice, indeed," he said, handing it to General Nesbit. He looked at Lowell and repeated it, and then asked, "Two-fifty-three thousand, isn't it?"

"I don't know what that is," General Nesbit said, as he handed the rifle to Ford's aide.

"It was the first of the high velocity cartridges," Lowell said. "It fires an 87-grain hollowpoint at a little over 3,000 feet per second."

"And without much recoil, is that it?" Ford asked.

"That was how it was sold to me," Lowell said. "Griffin and Howe made it up for P.P. in New York. They said it would be ideal for roebuck."

"I'm sure it will be," Ford said. "That's really a fine rifle, young man. You can be proud of it."

"I am," Peter-Paul said. "Quite."

The butler extended a tray with glasses on it to Lowell.

"The scotch is to the right, Herr Major," he said, in German.

Lowell took the drink.

"We have our cultures mixed here," the Graf said. "The European drinks bourbon, and the American drinks scotch."

"That isn't the only way the cultures are mixed," Lowell said, without thinking.

"To a good hunt," the Graf said, raising his glass.

Lowell saw a stout envelope on one of the tables. It looked familiar, and when he went to it, he saw that it was addressed to him at Schloss Greiffenberg, c/o the Dresdener Bank in Frankfurt and bore the return address of Craig, Powell, Kenyon and Dawes. It was marked "Personal—By Courier."

"How long has that been here?" he asked the butler.

"It came forty minutes ago, Herr Major," the Butler said. "A messenger from the Dresdener Bank brought it."

Lowell was aware that General Ford's ears had picked up
on that.

"It's probably nothing more than my officer's club bill, sir,"
he said, "but I arranged to have my mail, official and otherwise,
forwarded to me here. I suppose I'd better look at it."

"Go right ahead, Major," General Ford said.

Lowell sat down and ripped open the envelope.

He was glad he had. In addition to his bill from the officer's
club, which he waved triumphantly over his head for General
Ford to see ("What did I say, sir?"), there were three memos
from Bill Franklin at the Board requiring his decisions, and
two letters from Porter Craig, one asking what sort of a bill
for rent he was supposed to send General Bellmon for his use
of the town house in Georgetown, another dealing with the
place in Glen Cove. Both letters required immediate answers.

And then he saw the other envelope. It bore the imprint of
the Daleville Inn and was addressed to him at the Board. The
handwriting was unfamiliar. He opened it.

THE DALEVILLE INN
Daleville, Alabama 36367
180 Air-Conditioned Rooms + Restaurant

Lowell, you smart-ass sonofabitch!

I can't imagine what was running through your
perverted mind, except that you concluded I was
so dumb that I would never find out that it was
you flying the helicopter that blew up the tanks on
television, or that you were the youngest major in
the army with as many decorations as Patton. I am
sure only that it wasn't modesty.

Why a bunch of very nice guys (Franklin, Cramer, et al.) think you're Mr. Nice Guy baffles me.

It is lucky for you, and you will doubtless be
surprised to learn, that I am not one of those jour-
nalists who get their revenge with a poison pen,
but I could not pass the opportunity by to tell you
that I think you stink in spades!

You had no reason at all to make a fool of me!
Screw you, Lowell!

Cynthia Thomas

So that was her name. Cynthia. It was a real jaw-clencher's name.

"Gentlemen," Lowell said, "will you excuse me? The barn is burning down and nobody can find the fire hose."

He called Fort Rucker first and put out those fires, and then he called Porter Craig at the firm.

"You are not to send the Bellmons any kind of a bill, Porter," he said, when he reached him. "What the hell's the matter with you? I told you they're friends of mine."

"I'm fine, Craig," Porter Craig said. "Thank you for asking. And how are you? How's the littlest Lowell?"

"And I don't care if it takes half the lawyers in New York, I want that 'public domain' bullshit about the beach in Glen Cove fought all the way."

"You should read more carefully, Craig," Porter Craig said. "The property in question is not contiguous to the estate. It's half a mile down the beach. And, as I thought I explained rather clearly in the letter, it is my humble judgment that (a) there are some very interesting tax advantages; (b) they are going to clarify the position of the estate, in other words, admit the grandfather clause is applicable, which will preserve it for you until the country goes communist; and (c) there's nothing we can do about it. It has been used as a public beach for eighty years, and they could, if they wanted to, claim it as abandoned."

"Oh," Lowell said, lamely.

"You're welcome, Craig," Porter Craig said.

"I'm sorry, Porter," Lowell said. "I really am a little upset."

"About what?"

"The littlest Lowell is half kraut, half limey, and no percent American."

"Oh," Porter Craig said, sympathetically. "Craig, if I have to say this, we'd love to have him here."

"Which is worse?" Lowell said. "Half kraut and Half limey? Or one hundred percent jaw-clencher?"

"I wouldn't hazard a guess about what that means," Porter Craig said.

"Speaking of jaw-clenchers," Lowell said.

"I'm sorry, I don't know that means, Craig."

"He said, speaking from between clenched jaws," Lowell said. "Porter, we have a public relations guy, don't we?"

"We have a Vice President for Public Relations, yes," Porter Craig said.

"I want him to do something for me," Lowell said.

"I don't think I'm going to like this," Porter Craig said. "Why do you suppose that is, Craig?"

"I want him to get an address for me, and then send some flowers."

"I knew it. Another actress, Craig?"

"No. This one is a reporter for *Time-Life*. Send her a couple of dozen roses..."

"A couple of dozen roses? Do you have any idea what roses cost this time of year?"

"No," Lowell confessed. Porter Craig told him. "That much? Jesus! That would be a bit much. Send her something cheaper. With a card reading, 'No offense intended, Craig Lowell.' Will you do that for me, Porter?"

"What did you do to her, Craig? Perhaps a couple of dozen roses might not be enough."

"Send her a dozen roses," Lowell said. "And the card with that message."

"I presume the lady has a name? And that you're going to tell me what it is?"

"Her name is Cynthia Thomas," Lowell said.

"Very interesting," Porter Craig said. "How do you spell 'Thomas'?"

Lowell spelled it for him.

"I have to tell you, Craig," Porter said, "I find this very interesting..."

"Don't make a production of this, Porter," Lowell said. "She's just a girl I met in passing..."

"I know... like two ships, passing in the night..."

"And she got the wrong idea about me," Lowell said.

"You had your hands up her skirt looking for mushrooms, right?"

"Fuck you, Porter, just send the goddamned flowers," Lowell said, and hung up.

(Two)
Fort Rucker, Alabama
15 February 1959

C O N F I D E N T I A L

HEADQUARTERS

The Army Aviation Center & Fort Rucker, Ala.

Fort Rucker, Alabama 36361

15 October 1959

SUBJECT: Personnel Interviews
TO: Commanders, Subordinate Units
INFO: Commanders
U.S. Army Aviation Board
U.S. Army Aviation Combat
Developments Office
U.S. Army Signal Aviation Test &
Support Acitivy
U.S. Army Transportation Test &
Support Activity
U.S. Army Aviation Accident Board

1. Reference is made to TWX, Hq DA, Subj: "USASWS Recruiting Team," dated 11 Oct 59 and to DA Circular 23–103, "Special Forces Requirements and Qualifications."

2. A USASWS Personnel Recruiting Team is presently at Fort Rucker. Certain personnel have been selected for interview by Lt. Col. R. G. MacMillan of the USASWS. Commanders will insure that personnel selected will be available at the time and place directed. No requests for waiver of this DA mandated personnel action will be entertained.

3. Other personnel, meeting the criteria outlined in DA Circular 23–103, who wish to be interviewed by the USASWS Personnel Recruiting Team are encouraged and will be released from duty to do so. Appointments

may be obtained by contacting Lt. Davis or M/Sgt Wojinski at Ext. 2408 or 2440.
     BY COMMAND OF MAJOR GENERAL JIGGS
     Charles M. Scott, Jr.
     Lt. Colonel, AGC
     Adjutant General

CONFIDENTIAL

(Three)
The U.S. Army Special Warfare School
Fort Bragg, North Carolina
21 February 1959
    The commandant of the U.S. Army Special Warfare School
was up over his ass in paper, and Sergeant Major Taylor had
to wait at the open door for a full minute before Colonel Hanrahan sensed his presence and looked up.
    "The building's on fire?" Hanrahan asked. "How long have
you been standing there, Taylor?"
    "Not long, sir," Sergeant Major Taylor said. "You looked
busy, Colonel."
    "What's up?"
    "There's an officer, an aviator, out here asking to see you,
sir," Taylor said.
    "What's he want?"
    "He said he wants to enlist," Taylor said.
    "Send him to the adjutant," Jiggs said.
    "He asked to see you, sir."
    "Tell him to see the adjutant," Hanrahan said.
    "Yes, sir," Taylor said, and backed away from the open
door.
    A minute later, he was back.
    Hanrahan looked up impatiently.
    "He said that I was to say he's a friend of Major Lowell,
sir," Sergeant Major Taylor said.
    "Tell him 'hooray for you' and send him to the adjutant,"
Hanrahan snapped. Taylor turned. "Wait a minute," Hanrahan
called. "Send him in."
    A very large, very black captain in a sweat-stained flight
suit marched into Hanrahan's office, saluted crisply, and said:

"Captain Parker, Philip S., sir, requesting an audience with the colonel, sir."

"An *audience*, Parker? I'm not the Pope," Hanrahan said. "Stand easy and tell me what trouble Lowell's in now."

"None that I know of, sir," Parker said. "He's in Germany, visiting his son."

"What's on your mind, Parker? I'm not trying to get rid of you, but I am busy as hell."

"I'd like to join up," Parker said.

"Then you apply," Hanrahan said. "You must know that, Captain."

"Sir, Colonel MacMillan turned me down."

"Then you're turned down," Hanrahan said. "Surely Mac gave you his reasons."

"Only that it wasn't for me, sir."

"When did all this happen?"

"Two days ago, sir, at Rucker."

"They pulled your records, Mac interviewed you, and turned you down? Is that it?"

"I was not selected for interview, sir," Parker said. "And I technically don't meet the requirements of DA Circular 23–103, sir."

"Then you've wasted your time coming here, and are wasting my time standing here," Hanrahan said.

"Mac admitted to me at lunch, sir," Captain Parker said, "that the provisions of DA 23–103 can be waived. That he had that authority, from you."

"If you're a friend of Mac's, then you know Mac sometimes talks too much," Hanrahan said.

"May I make my pitch, Colonel?" Parker asked.

"You've got 120 seconds," Hanrahan said, after a pause.

"Sir, I'm a regular army officer out of Norwich. My family..."

"You can skip all that," Hanrahan said. "Our friend Lowell has told me all about you."

"Sir," Parker went on, "I have been a captain more than eight years. I am not on the new major's list. I am currently an instructor pilot. I am apparently in as much of a dead-end job in aviation as I was before I went to aviation."

"And you see us as a path to promotion?"

"I think I could make a contribution here, sir."

"How?"

"I'm a good combat commander, sir," Parker said.

"I understand you have a habit of shooting people who don't behave the way you think they should," Hanrahan said.

"I was acquitted of that charge, sir," Parker said.

You were acquitted of it, but you know as well as I do that's why you haven't been promoted, why you won't be promoted.

"Do you regret having shot that officer?"

"I was accused of murdering two officers, sir. There were two incidents."

"I asked you if you were sorry about that?"

"I am sorry it was necessary, sir," Parker said.

"You're not parachute qualified?" Hanrahan asked.

"No, sir."

"If you're flying, you've passed a tougher physical than ours," Hanrahan said. "But no foreign languages?"

"Just what I got in college, sir. I can read and write German, but I can't say I'm fluent."

"And you're over twenty-nine, which is our maximum age for an officer in your grade?"

"I'm thirty, sir."

"You're fixed and rotary wing qualified?"

"Yes, sir."

"And you want to throw that away? What I mean by that is that it's fairly obvious that army aviation is going to grow, and you're an old-timer, so to speak. You're asking the army to simply throw away the fortune it's cost to train you, so that you can come here."

"I repeat, sir, I think I could make a contribution here."

"And also maybe get promoted?" Hanrahan asked, sarcastically.

"Yes, sir," Parker said. "That's my motivation. I can see no future for myself as an aviator. If they haven't promoted me, they obviously aren't going to give me an aviation command."

"You seem pretty sure of that," Hanrahan said, coldly. "Are you feeling sorry for yourself? Taking your ball and going home?"

Parker came to attention.

"I beg the colonel's pardon for wasting his time, sir. With the colonel's permission, I will withdraw, sir."

"Sergeant Major!" Hanrahan called.

Taylor came into the office.

"Sir?"

"Take this officer with you," Hanrahan said. "Get him a cup of coffee. And then get his serial number and so on, and arrange to have him transferred."

"Yes, sir."

"Thank you, sir," Parker said.

When they stand you in the door of the airplane and tell you to jump," Hanrahan said, "or when we run your ass off around here, trying to change a flabby flyboy into a Green Beret, you may have second thoughts."

"I hope not, sir," Parker said.

"You ever watch Groucho Marx on television, Captain?" Hanrahan asked.

The question obviously surprised Parker.

"I've seen him, sir. Yes, sir."

"You know the part when somebody says the magic words, and the rubber duck comes down?"

"Yes, sir."

"You said the magic words, Captain Parker. What you said should be the motto of this outfit. 'We do a lot of nasty things we regret are necessary.'"

Parker didn't reply.

"You are dismissed, Captain," Colonel Hanrahan said.

(Four)
New York City
1235 Hours, 2 March 1959

When Lowell had called Porter Craig from the Rhine-Main airport in Frankfurt to ask for a letter of credit, he had refused Porter's offer to send a car to meet him at Kennedy.

"It's quicker, I've learned, to catch a cab," he had said. "I get in at 11:05, so figure half past twelve."

"Half past twelve for where?"

"I'd really rather not go downtown, Porter," Lowell had said. "All I'm asking is that you meet me someplace with the letter of credit. How about the Century?"

"What are you going to buy now?"

"The Graf came through where you failed me, Porter. I have a car waiting for me at the Mercedes place, at Park and 58th Street."

"The showroom's there. I think the garage is on Eighth," Porter Craig said.

"I was told to go to the place on Park Avenue."

"You want to have lunch up there?"

"At the Mercedes place?"

"Actually, I was thinking of the Plaza," Porter Craig said.

"God, no," Lowell said. "We'd look like a gigolo and his pimp."

"Where, then?"

"The Century," Lowell said. "There are no women in the bar there."

"I sent the flowers, by the way, to your lady friend," Porter said.

"The Century," Lowell said, "at half past twelve."

And then he'd hung up and walked into the boarding area at Rhine-Main in Frankfurt, where they were calling his name.

When he got out of the cab at the Century, he was wearing a trench coat with a black Persian lamb collar and a matching hat, which was shaped something like an overseas cap, but several inches taller. The Graf had a similar outfit, and to Lowell—with several drinks in him after a lunch in Frankfurt am Main—buying such a coat and hat for himself seemed like a splendid idea. Now, he wasn't so sure.

He was paying the cabbie when a chauffeur appeared at his elbow.

"I'll take care of those for you, Mr. Lowell," he said.

Lowell smiled automatically and looked beyond him. There was a Lincoln limousine at the curb. The passenger compartment windows and the divider were of dark glass and he couldn't see in.

"Mr. Craig's car?" Lowell asked.

As if in answer, the curbside door swung open, and there was a glimpse of Porter Craig beckoning to him.

He walked to the car and leaned down to look in.

"Aren't we going in?"

"Kitchen's closed today for some reason," Porter said. "I just found out."

Lowell got in the car and closed the door.

"This thing looks like a hearse," he said.

"And I was so hoping you'd be pleased," Porter Craig said, lightly sarcastic.

"I am, I am," Lowell said.

"Nice flight?" Porter asked. He was a large, pudgy man, balding, in a nearly black gray suit. Lowell had often thought that Porter Craig looked like what a banker should look like. He looked respectable, honest, trustworthy, and smart.

"Ugly stewardess," Lowell said. "I thought they had a rule they had to be young and good looking?"

"I thought your heart was spoken for," Porter said, obviously pleased with himself. "After all, you did send her a dozen long-stemmed roses."

"Good God, I told you there was nothing to that," Lowell said.

"So you did."

"Where are we going to eat? All I had on the plane was a couple of rolls and coffee."

"I thought Jack and Charlie's," Porter said.

"21? I thought that responsible bankers should not be seen in there during business hours."

"It's on 52nd Street. You're going to 58th. It's on the way."

"I don't mind if you don't," Lowell said. *"My* appearance there won't cause a run on the banks."

The chauffeur slammed the trunk, and then got behind the wheel. Lowell picked up the telephone.

"Will you lower that divider, please? I feel like a corpse back here."

The divider whooshed down.

"I like your hat," Porter said. *"Très chic!"*

"You're in a jolly mood today, aren't you, wise-ass?" Lowell said.

"It's because I'm so thrilled to see you, cousin."

"It's because I didn't go to the office and check the cash," Lowell said.

A doorman came out from the cast-iron fence at 21 and opened the door.

"Good afternoon, sir," he said to Lowell, and then spotted Porter Craig. "How are you, Mr. Craig?"

"Give us an hour or so, Tom," Porter said to the chauffeur and looked at his watch.

"If you're on a first-name basis here," Lowell said, "I think I will check the cash drawer."

A maître d'hotel Lowell did not recognize greeted Porter Craig warmly and showed them to a table set for four. A waiter and a wine steward appeared immediately, but no busboy to take away the extra two place settings.

"I would like a Bloody Mary," Lowell ordered. "With lots of tomato juice and no Worcestershire."

"Yes, sir," the waiter said.

Porter ordered a martini.

"They announce they make the best Bloody Mary in the world here," Porter said.

"If I get one with Worcestershire, it goes back," Lowell said. "What's with you and the martini? I thought you drank those only when you'd just dispossessed a really needy widow."

"Oh, this is rather an occasion for me," Porter said, gaily.

Lowell was as good as his word. His Bloody Mary came with Worcestershire, and he called over the maître d' and handed it to him.

"I ordered this without Worcestershire," he said.

"Oh, I'm terribly sorry," the maître d' said.

"Good," Lowell said.

The maître d'hotel hurried away.

"My," Porter said, "you certainly know what you want, don't you?"

"Porter, this surplus bonhomie of yours is making me suspicious. What have you set me up for?"

"I have no idea what you're talking about," Porter said.

Lowell looked at him and snorted. And then Porter stood up.

"Clem," he called, "over here!"

"Who the hell is Clem?" Lowell demanded.

Porter was beaming. Someone approached the table. A hand came over Lowell's shoulder to shake Porter Craig's.

"Clem, I don't think you've met my cousin Craig Lowell, have you?" Porter said "Craig, this is my old friend, Clemens Thomas."

Lowell got to his feet and put out his hand and found himself looking into the surprised and angry face of Cynthia Thomas.

"I believe you *do* know Miss Thomas, Clem's sister?" Porter Craig said. His pudgy face was a map of delight.

"We're old pen pals," Lowell said.

"I'm going," Cynthia Thomas said, furiously. "This was a shitty thing for you to do, Clem."

Heads turned.

"Very funny, Lowell," Cynthia went on. "Screw you again!"

She turned on her heel and stormed to the door.

Lowell went after her. He caught her at the hatcheck counter and spun her around.

"I didn't want you to go away thinking I set this up, lady," he said. "My asshole of a cousin has got a sick sense of humor."

She shook free of his hand and then looked into his face. Her eyes were even bluer than he remembered.

Her brother rushed up.

"My God, Cyn," he said. "He did send flowers, after all. Come on back."

"Did you send the flowers?" she asked Lowell. "Or was that something these two thought was clever?"

"I sent the flowers," Lowell said. "Or I had Porter send them."

"So your wife wouldn't see the bill?" she asked.

"My wife is dead, Miss Thomas," Lowell said.

"Oh, Jesus," she said. "I'm sorry, Lowell."

She reached out and found his hand. It *was* vibrant, he thought. He caught himself caressing it, and let it go.

"Let's go eat," Cynthia said, reaching for it again. "They say you can order anything you want in here. Let's see if they have some arsenic for these two."

"Now that you're here," Lowell said, without thinking, "I'll even spring for lunch."

She looked at his face and blushed, then averted her eyes.

"No," she said. "My asshole of a brother will pay. But thank you for the thought."

She did not let go of his hand until they were back at the table.

He had, he thought, been chaste since the session with Jane Cassidy at her beach place. That was some time back. Was that why he now found Cynthia Thomas an absolutely fascinating female?

(Five)
Mercedes-Benz of America Showroom
Park Avenue at 58th Street
New York City
1540 Hours, 2 March 1959

"God!" Cynthia Thomas said when she saw the car. "It's *gorgeous!*"

She looked at Lowell and smiled.

"So are you," he said.

She shook her head at him, as if to indicate he was crazy.

What was crazy was that she was here with him. He couldn't remember much about lunch, except that he couldn't keep his eyes off her, and that it had somehow not seemed at all important that her brother and his cousin were visibly smug that they had 'carried it off.'

Normally, he would have left Porter sitting with whatever 'nice young woman' his cousin was trying to palm off on him. And he somehow knew that the same was true of Cynthia. But he hadn't left and neither had she.

Finally, they had left together. They had walked. He had taken her arm crossing the street, and the soft warmth of it had been delightful. And then he had taken her hand, and despite the glove, it had been warm and soft, too. And she had seemed to welcome the touch. They had walked over to Park Avenue, and then up, holding hands like teenagers.

The two-passenger Mercedes convertible, top down, was sitting in the center of the showroom, where it could best be seen from the street. It was the first thing walk-in customers would see when they came in off Park Avenue.

"We had rather hoped to have it on display for several weeks," the sales manager said.

"But why baby blue?" Cynthia asked.

"That is Capri blue, Madame," the sales manager corrected her.

"It was the only color they had," Lowell said.

"You do understand, don't you, Mr. Lowell, that this is the very first of this model to be sent to the United States?"

"Then there's a discount?" Lowell asked, as if he were serious.

"We were given to understand that we were not to deliver this car until others were available," the sales manager said, not amused. "We don't even have the winter season top."

"The what? You mean it doesn't have a roof?" Lowell asked.

"It has, of course, the *folding* top," the salesmanager said. "The *winter season* top—which does not retract, but rather is fastened in place—is recommended for use in the winter season."

"This top does go up?" Lowell asked. "It would be a long,

cold ride to Alabama with the roof down."

"It would be a long, cold ride to Central Park West with the roof down," Cynthia said.

She got in the car and tried some switches. When nothing worked, she tried the ignition.

"The battery's dead," she chortled.

"The battery has been *disconnected*," the sales manager said, "against untoward incidents. You would be amazed to hear what I could tell you about what people do to cars on display."

"Well, let's get the battery hooked up, and the roof up, and let me pay you for it and whatever," Lowell said.

"The documentation is in my office, Mr. Lowell," the sales manager said. "If you'll be good enough to come with me?"

Lowell got a good look at Cynthia Thomas's long legs as she got out of the Mercedes.

He managed to touch her shoulder as he motioned her after the sales manager. She turned and looked at him, and smiled as if she somehow understood, perhaps felt the same hunger to touch him that he had to touch her.

The manager began a long speech about breaking the car in and bringing it in for service.

"I'll read the book," Lowell said, impatiently. He took a purchase order from his pocket. Porter Craig said that if the IRS hadn't put them all in jail for the airplane, the firm might as well own the car, too.

"Tell me how much," he said. "I presume you'll honor a purchase order?"

"The financial arrangements have been taken care of, Mr. Lowell," the sales manager said, a hint of suspicion in his voice. "I would have presumed you knew that."

"Are you sure?" Lowell said.

The sales manager handed him an envelope.

"I presume this is the title," he said. "It was delivered by a man from Mercedes three days ago."

Lowell tore the envelope open. There were two sheets of paper in it, one from Mercedes-Benz/Daimler G.m.b.H., a shipping invoice, paid in full, for one Mercedes coupe. And the other was a folded sheet of paper with an embossed crest.

My dear Craig,

Permit me to offer this small token of appreciation for my life, and for my grandson.

v.G.

"Jesus H. Christ!" Lowell said.

"What is it?" Cynthia Thomas asked, concerned. He handed her the note.

"Who's 'v.G'?"

"My father-in-law," Lowell said.

"Nice father-in-law," she said. "What did he mean 'for his life'?"

"In other words," Lowell said, avoiding the question, "we're through here?"

"It will take just a moment to have the battery connected," the sales manager said.

Minutes later, the double glass doors were opened, and Lowell drove the coupe across the sidewalk and onto Park Avenue.

"What did he mean 'for his life'?" Cynthia asked again, as they started downtown. Before he had a chance to reply, she said, "Go crosstown on 49th."

"Where are we going?" Lowell asked, as he made the corner.

"What about his life?" she persisted.

"He was in Siberia," Lowell said. "A friend of mine got him out. I had nothing to do with it."

"Siberia, as in Russian Siberia?" she asked.

"That's the one. Lots of snow. That Siberia."

"We want to come out onto Central Park West at 64th," she ordered.

"Your place?"

"I've got something to pick up," she said. "It won't take a minute. And then you can take me for a ride in your nice new car."

"I'd like that," he said.

A doorman opened the door for her.

"I won't be a moment," she said.

Ten minutes later, as he was growing impatient, the doorman tapped on the window. Lowell found the window control switch and lowered the window.

"Miss Thomas asks that you go up, sir," he said.

"What do I do with the car?"

"I'll park it for you, sir," the doorman said.

"Be careful with it," Lowell said. "It's brand new."

"I will try, sir."

The elevator took him to the penthouse. There were two doors in the elevator landing. One of them was open.

He went to it and called her name.

"I'll be right out," she called. "Go in the living room and make yourself a drink."

Lowell saw that there were two penthouses in the building. Cynthia had what he thought was the better of them. She had views from three sides, to Central Park, across the street; west to the Hudson River; and downtown.

He found the bar, and made himself a drink. He hadn't been in an apartment like this in years. He had forgotten what a spectacular view there was from the top of a building like this.

He took a pull at his drink. He was not going to blow this one. He knew he and Cynthia would make love all right. But he wanted it to happen very carefully, very slowly. He wasn't going to grab at her and scare her off.

"I'm sorry to have kept you waiting," she said, and he turned to face her.

She was standing in the door to a bedroom, wearing a negligee that revealed more than it concealed.

"I had to get rid of the help," she said. "And I wanted to take a bath."

Oh, shit. I was right the first time. An independent female. I should have guessed from the way she swore. From the way she let me touch her. Goddamnit!

He made no immediate move to go to her.

"Is something the matter?" she asked. "Don't I pass muster?"

"You're good looking," he said. "As a matter of fact, you're beautiful. But I just got off an airplane, and I'd like to get to Washington before it's too late."

"You sonofabitch!" she screamed, which he had more or less expected, and then she pulled off her shoe and threw it at him, which he had also more or less expected. And then she did something he didn't expect at all. All of a sudden, she sort of collapsed against the door and started to weep.

Lowell started for the door.

She was moaning now, repeating, "Oh, God! Oh, *God!*" over and over.

Something is expected of me, required of me, as a gentleman.

He walked to her.

"Look," he said, "if you're worried that I'm going to say something, don't be. I'm not."

She put her hand, the fist balled, into her mouth and looked at him out of horrified eyes. Tears streamed down her cheeks. Her breasts heaved with the effort of weeping.

"I really am tired," he said. "And I'm just not interested in a casual roll in the hay. No offense. It has nothing to do with you."

"I thought," she blubbered, "that was all you were interested in."

"What?"

"You sonofabitch," she said, half weeping, "Do you really think I play the whore every time I meet a new man?"

"I didn't say that," he said.

"But that's what you think, isn't it?" she challenged.

"No," he said.

"It is," she said. "It is. Oh, *God!* I can see it in your eyes. That's just what you think!"

"Even if I did, so what? What possible importance can that be to you?" he asked, believing it to be a reasonable question.

She spat in his face, and then, before he could recover, hit him with her fist, just above his ear. He was shaken a little, but managed to grab her wrists. She kicked at his crotch. He ducked, but her knee painfully struck his thigh.

He put his foot behind her leg, then pushed. She fell backward, and he allowed himself to fall on top of her. He sat on her legs, far enough down so that she couldn't flail them, then pinned her hands to the carpet. His face was six inches from hers.

"Jesus Christ, what kind of a nut are you, anyway?" he asked. "Now behave."

"The kind of a nut that fell in love with you the minute I saw you," she said.

"Don't be absurd," he said, softly.

"I didn't *want* to, you sonofabitch!" she said. "It just *happened*."

"Jesus!"

"I came on like a whore, because I thought that's what you wanted," she said. "And you know something? I liked it, because I thought that's what you wanted."

He laughed. It infuriated her. She struggled and failed to get free.

"Before you came out of the bedroom in your see-through negligee," he said, "I vowed to keep my hands off you. I was thinking that whatever I did, I would have to play this very coolly. That I really didn't want to blow it with you."

"And now what do you think?" she asked, very softly.

"The strange beating of my heart is only partially because you're under me with that exquisite genuine blond pubic tuft exposed," he said.

She looked into his eyes for a long moment.

"Since we've both lost our minds," she said, "do you want to do it right here on the carpet? Or would you rather get into bed?"

He got to his feet, and offered her his hand. He pulled her to her feet. As a reflex action, she closed the gown over her exposed breast. She looked up at him. He bent and kissed her. Without taking her mouth from his, she shrugged out of the gown, so that by the time he had carried her to the bed, she would be naked.

XIV

(One)
The Office of the Secretary of the Army
The Pentagon
Washington, D.C.
1230 Hours, 6 March 1959

The Secretary of the Army is provided with a private dining room, adjacent to his suite of offices. It comes with a complete kitchen, staffed with a chef and two waiters. The chef and the waiters are army enlisted men.

The Secretary's mess can be viewed either as a shameless waste of the taxpayer's money or as an important management tool. Which is cheaper in the long run: operating a mess where the Secretary and his assistants can have their meals in a secure room, where they can work as they eat, or sending them from their office to eat somewhere where they cannot, for security reasons, discuss anything more classified than the weather?

The mess today had one table set up for lunch; and the word had been passed that the room would not be available for lunch to the staff. The table was set up with place settings for five people. The chef prepared a simple tossed green salad with a blue cheese dressing; vichyssoise; a small pork roast, with glazed carrots and French green beans; French bread; and for dessert, a crème caramel. The Secretary of Defense, who would be present, was known to like crème caramel. Two bottles of a very pleasant Napa Valley California Cabernet Sauvignon were opened to breathe.

The wine was for the Secretaries coming, not the brass. So far as the brass was concerned a glass of wine at lunch in the Pentagon was drinking on duty. Glasses would be set before them, and they would turn the glasses over.

The Secretary of Defense and the Secretary of the Army arrived together from a meeting in the Secretary of Defense's small conference room. The Chairman of the Joint Chiefs of Staff (it was the Army's turn to hold that position, and the CJCS was an Army four-star general) and the Army Chief of Staff were waiting for them, standing up at the buffet sipping coffee.

One luncheon guest, the Vice Chief of Staff of the U.S. Army, was not yet present, but this was not mentioned in the belief that he would be along in a moment.

As expected, he entered the room not two minutes later.

"Mr. Secretary," General E. Z. Black said, shaking the hand of the Secretary of Defense, "I apologize for being late."

"Don't be silly," the SECDEF said. "We just got here."

"Mr. Secretary," General Black said, nodding at the Secretary of the Army. He nodded at the two other four-star generals, and twice said, "General."

There was, E. Z. Black thought wryly, a hole in the protocol. There were only two verbal forms of adddress for the five people in the room. Despite great differences in grade, the only titles available were "General" and "Mr. Secretary." There was no practical alternative, except possibly to address the Chairman of the Joint Chiefs of Staff as "Mr. Chairman," which would sound as if he had his office in the Kremlin.

He wondered why he was in such a flippant mood. The odds, he calculated, were about even that he would walk out of this dining room into retirement.

"I'm hungry," the SECDEF announced. "Can we eat?"

They took their places around the octagonal table.

The SECDEF bowed his head.

"For the bounty we are about to receive, dear Lord, we thank You," he prayed, almost conversationally, as if he were on close personal terms with the Almighty, "and ask Thy blessing upon our labor in your service. Through Jesus Christ, Thy Son, our Saviour. Amen."

"Amen," the others mumbled, and reached for their napkins.

The white-jacketed mess attendants appeared. One skillfully balanced five plates of salad, which he laid before them; the other carried a bottle of the California Cabernet Sauvignon. The CJCS and the Chief of Staff turned their glasses over. The SECARMY tasted the wine and nodded his head. The mess attendant half filled his glass, and then the glass of the SEC-DEF. He then put the bottle in a basket on a small table within reach of both.

"I'll have a little of that, if I may, Sergeant," General Black said. What the Chief of Staff was about to use against him made drinking a glass seem an inconsequential sin.

"Excuse me, sir," the sergeant said, smoothly.

The CJCS raised his eyebrows. The Chief of Staff pursed his lips.

"Very nice," the SECDEF said. "This the stuff you get from California?"

"A guy I went to college with," the SECARMY said, "decided one day he didn't want to spend the rest of his life in the stock market; he sold out, went to California, and bought a vineyard. He sends it to me."

"I'm glad he did. This is very good. Can you buy it in stores?"

"I'll get you a case."

"You like that, E. Z.?" the SECDEF asked.

"Very good," General Black replied.

"You've been at Knox, I understand," the SECDEF asked.

"Just got back," General Black said. "That's why I was late. I told the pilot to allow for an hour and a half in the stack over Washington-National. I should have told him an hour forty-five."

"How's the rocket whirlybird project coming? That's why you went down there, isn't it? To see it demonstrated?"

"I saw it demonstrated at Rucker, Mr. Secretary," General Black said. "I had other things to do at Knox, but I checked on their progress. They have ten percent of their authorized equipment up and running."

"That was quick," the SECDEF said. He was not surprised. The quicker they got an operational unit running, the better. There was still a chance—as long as it was only a "provisional" unit—that they might still lose it to the air force.

"Yes, Mr. Secretary," Black said. "I thought so."

One of the waiters began to lay plates with thick slices of pork before them, while the other laid out bowls of French green beans and glazed carrots.

"You didn't happen to stop by Bragg on the way home, did you, General?" the Chief of Staff asked.

"I decided not to, General," Black said. "I think the best way to handle that situation is to leave it alone."

"I was led to believe you were going there."

"No," Black said, picking up his knife and fork.

Ths mess attendants placed two large silver coffee pots, a bowl of cream, and a bowl of sugar on the table and then left the room.

"Very nice pork," the SECDEF said.

"It's from the A&P in Alexandria, believe it or not," the SECARMY said.

"Very nice," the SECDEF repeated.

The SECARMY looked at General Black.

"Just for the sake of conversation, E. Z.," he said, "what would you think of CINCPAC?" (Commander in Chief, Pacific)

"In what context, Mr. Secretary?"

"Of taking it over?"

The SECARMY did not like General E. Z. Black, personally or professionally. If he had his way, Black would be retired as soon as possible and replaced by someone who took orders from him and the Chief of Staff and who carried them out without question, without making as many waves as E. Z. Black made.

"I go where I'm sent and do what I'm ordered to do, Mr. Secretary," General Black said.

"For that matter, E. Z.," the CJCS said, "what would you think of NATO?"

The SECARMY gave him a dirty look. The civilian control of the military broke down with the Chairman of the Joint Chiefs of Staff. He was an Army officer, but he was not really subordinate to SECARMY. He took his orders—what orders he took—from SECDEF. And he was an old buddy of the

Commander in Chief, the President. He also knew that there was nothing anybody, including the commander in Chief, could do to him but fire him. And—no fool—he knew that firing (actually, retiring) the CJCS was politically inflammable.

General Black took a swallow of his wine.

"Are those my choices, Mr. Secretary?" General Black asked the SECARMY.

"I didn't say that, General."

"There's a third option, E. Z.," the SECDEF said, "since this bad blood between you and the Chief of Staff seems to be getting worse, and the Air Force is still howling for your scalp."

"Mr. Secretary," General Black said to the SECDEF, aware that he was lightheaded, "if it is your pleasure, I will submit my application for retirement this afternoon."

"That's your option, E. Z. If I wanted your resignation, I would have asked for it."

"And so would I," the CJCS said.

Those sonsofbitches sandbagged me, the SECARMY thought.

He said: "No one's asking you to leave, General."

E. Z. Black looked at the Chief of Staff. Their eyes locked for a moment.

"I would consider it a great privilege," General Black said, "to be named CINCPAC."

"You've got it," the SECDEF said.

"Presuming the concurrence of the President, of course," the SECARMY said.

"The President told me he would go along with whatever we decided," the SECDEF said.

"You're a little old, and a little too fat for a surfboard, E. Z.," the CJCS said. It was less a dry remark than a question: *Why CINCPAC? NATO's more prestigious.*

"Maybe," E. Z. Black said, "I could learn how to ride one anyway, before the balloon goes up over there."

"You think that's where it's going up?" the SECDEF asked, very seriously.

"Yes, sir," General Black said. "I'm very much afraid of Vietnam."

"Most everybody else thinks that situation can be stabilized," the Chief of Staff said, "that Cuba is the immediate problem."

"I'm talking about a non-nuclear war," Black said.

"You think Cuba is a nuclear war situation?" the Chief of Staff asked, levelly.

"I think we're going to go eyeball with the Russians over Cuba. Something like Berlin. And one side or the other will back away, or there will be a nuclear war."

"God forbid!" the SECDEF said, softly, fervently.

"And what's going to happen in Vietnam, in your opinion, General?" the SECARMY asked.

"We've already got advisors there," Black said. "We'll keep sending in more and more advisors. And we'll be in a war. We'll have slid into a war...a conventional, more or less, war."

"In other words, you don't agree with the Chief of Staff that it can be contained?" the SECDEF asked.

"That," the Chief of Staff added, "if it got down to it, we couldn't pacify the country with a couple of divisions?"

"No, I don't," Black said.

"For Christ's sake," the Chief of Staff said, forgetting the SECDEF did not like anyone taking the Lord's name in vain, "all they've got is people in black pajamas, no match for modern forces. We functioned successfully in Greece, you know."

"Greece was different," Black said. "Vietnam is going to be a lot harder. That's going to be a different ball game."

"I'd like to know where you get your information," the Chief of Staff said. When there was no reply from Black, he asked: "Your friend Felter been telling you things he hasn't told me?"

"Unless I was asked, General," Black said. "I would not presume to offer my views to, or seek information from, a Counselor to the President."

The Chief of Staff snorted.

"Then where did you get your background?"

"I got my information from a sergeant," General Black said, his eyes icy, his smile cold. "He told me that an army scared hell out of him that was so well disciplined that they manhandled 105 mm howizers up mountainsides by hand, and then supplied them two rounds at a time, by people pushing them on a bicycle."

"Is that where you get information on which to base your decisions? From sergeants?" the Chief of Staff asked. He had intended to be droll. It came out contemptuous.

" 'Wisdom from the mouth of babes,' it says in the Bible," the SECDEF said.

He thought: *I separated these two just in time.*

(Two)
227 Melody Lane
Ozark, Alabama
1630 Hours, 6 March 1959

Lowell turned sharply into the driveway. Because there was a two-car carport, there would be room for the Mercedes beside the Cadillac he had sold to Jean-Philippe Jannier. But there was another car in the driveway, a Buick station wagon. The tires squealed. Cynthia Thomas was thrown against Craig Lowell.

"Jesus," she said, in complaint, but she did not move away from him.

He bent his head and kissed her forehead.

"Well," he said, "here we are."

"I'm surprised we made it," she chuckled.

Right after the first time, as she lay with her breasts on his abdomen toying with the hair on his chest, she had announced flatly that she was sorry, but that it was absolutely out of the question for her to come to Alabama with him. She had a job, obligations. She just couldn't drop everything and run halfway across the country with him just because he was the best screw she had ever had in her entire life.

"If you're going to be an officer's lady," he said, "you're going to have to learn not to swear like a tank company first sergeant."

"Who said anything about me becoming an officer's lady?" she asked.

"You wouldn't want to disappoint your brother, would you?" he said. "Not to mention the other asshole?"

She chuckled and moved her head and nibbled at his nipple until he yelped.

"I'm disappointed," she said. "Folklore has it that soldiers can screw all day and then all night."

"I'll make a deal with you," he said. "Once more here, and then once more in Washington. Then you can catch the shuttle back here."

"Where would we do it in Washington?" she asked. "In the Lincoln Memorial?"

"We'll take a motel room," he said.

"That's wicked," she said. "I love it."

When they got to Washington, just before nine, he told her that he wanted her to meet some lady friends of his. One of whom would probably feed them, and then they could get the motel and later she could catch the shuttle.

The visit with the Bellmons in Lowell's town house in Georgetown lasted longer than Cynthia thought it would. She and Barbara Bellmon liked each other from the moment they met. Then a very nice, very shy Jewish woman appeared, and Cynthia was very touched by her. She was apparently very, very fond and protective of Craig Lowell. Her husband showed up a half hour later, and Cynthia was really surprised when he was introduced as a lieutenant colonel. He was the last man in the world she would have suspected of being an army officer.

The officer barely had time to eat the hash Barbara Bellmon made of leftover roast beef before he was called to the telephone and had to leave. But his wife stayed, and there were several bottles of wine, and then it was midnight, and Barbara said it was silly to go back to New York in the middle of the night.

"The idea of Craig sleeping on a couch in his own house amuses me," Barbara said. "And if you stay, I'll tell you everything you want to know about him and were afraid to ask . . . and I know *everything*."

"I can't pass that up," Cynthia said.

She was surprised and touched when the Jewish woman, whose name was Sharon, kissed her when she left. Cynthia was not a kisser, and she suspected that Sharon wasn't either. She had been examined, she knew, and been judged satisfactory.

Lowell and Bellmon vanished into the bar. Then she helped Barbara clear the table, and Barbara told her about Lowell's first wife and the circumstances of her death.

In the morning, on the way to the shuttle terminal at Washington National, Cynthia said: "I was awake half the night waiting for you to sneak into my room and steal my virtue."

"Don't think I didn't think about it," he said.

"Well?"

"I didn't want Barbara to get the right idea about you," he quipped, and then corrected himself. "Barbara is a straight arrow. You don't sleep under her roof with people you're not married to. She wouldn't understand us."

Cynthia thought he was wrong, but didn't press the point.

"I would really like to stop somewhere and get a change of underwear," she said.

"Why don't we stop somewhere and get you some underwear," he said. "And then go to the airport? The Atlanta airport?"

"That's crazy," she said.

But they both knew that's what would happen, and it did. They didn't even stop at the airport in Atlanta. It was only a "couple of hours" further down the road to Ozark, and there were some other people he wanted to her to meet.

"Boy Scout's honor, I'll fly you to Atlanta in the morning," he said. "It'll only be a couple of hours more."

As they approached Ozark, he told her about Jannier and Melody.

"She's either going to be at the house," he said, "or we'll ask her over. I want you to meet her."

Cynthia was not anxious to meet a woman who had begun an affair with a man less than a month after her husband had been killed, but there didn't seem to be anything she could do about it.

And Melody *was* at the house. The Buick station wagon had been a gift from her father. "You'll need the room for the baby's things. And you'll be safer in a big car. I read that in *Time*," he had said.

When she heard the screeching tires of the Mercedes, Melody came to the kitchen door, with her son in her arms. She smiled when she saw Lowell, but then the smile vanished when Cynthia appeared. She was grossly embarrassed, Cynthia saw, and that was because she was a good person.

I don't know how I'm going to do it, Cynthia vowed, *but I'm going to make her understand that I understand.*

"God, I'm glad you're here, Melody," Craig said after the introductions had been made. "Is there someplace around here where Cynthia can buy some clothing?"

"No," Melody said. "I thought you knew, Craig, we all make our own clothes here, from homespun cotton."

"Don't be a wise-ass," Lowell said, fondly.

"Move your new toy out of the driveway," Melody said, and then to Cynthia: "What do you need?"

"A sweater and a skirt, some underthings, enough to get back to New York."

Jean-Philippe Jannier came out of the house. He had obviously been sleeping, Cynthia saw. She also thought that he was almost as sexy as Craig Lowell. He got in the Mercedes, backed it out of the drive, and with a squeal of tires, raced down the street.

He was back in a minute, obviously having only driven around the block. Wearing a wide smile, he parked the car on the street.

Melody handed Cynthia the baby and got into the Buick.

"If all you want is a sweater and a skirt," she said, "it'll be cheaper in the PX."

"Can I buy things in the PX?" Cynthia asked, uncomfortably.

"Officer's widows can," Melody said. "I'm an officer's widow."

Cynthia didn't reply.

"Did Craig tell you?" Melody asked.

"He told me he's very fond of you, too," Cynthia said.

"If I'm in this house," Melody said, "with Jean-Philippe, or even if we're at my own house and we're alone, it doesn't seem to matter. It's only when the outside comes in . . . Do you know what I mean?"

"You mean, I make you uncomfortable?" Cynthia asked.

"No. Just the opposite," Melody said. "If Craig brought you here, you must be somebody special."

"I came without so much as a toothbrush," Cynthia said. "I know what you must be thinking."

"Only that it was important to you that you come," Melody said.

"I thought that handsome bastard was only interested in a quick lay," Cynthia said. "So I took him to my apartment, drank four ounces of brandy, and took all my clothes off. I did everything but grope him . . . and I almost lost him."

"But it worked out all right in the end, right? You're here. That makes you special to him."

"I hope," Cynthia said, "as the girl prayed waiting to see if the rabbit died."

"If he thought you were nothing but . . . what you suggested . . . he wouldn't have brought you here."

"I've been shown off all along the East Coast," Cynthia said. "A general and his wife, and then a Jewish colonel and *his* wife..."

"Then he *really* must like you," Melody said. "Sandy Felter is his best friend. Sharon told me that Craig wept like a baby, when they thought Sandy had bought the farm in Indochina, and she and the kids wound up comforting him."

"'Bought the farm'?" Cynthia asked.

"Sandy, another officer named MacMillan, and my husband got themselves shot down going into Dien Bien Phu. For five days, everyone thought they were dead. That was before I met Ed."

"That's an odd phrase," Cynthia said.

"I understand it's an old army saying," Melody said. "Old soldiers used to dream of retiring and buying a farm."

"Are they afraid of saying the words, 'getting killed'?"

"Getting killed is what happens to other women's husbands," Melody said. "If you can't convince yourself of that, you'd go crazy."

"That was very thoughtless of me," Cynthia said. "I'm sorry."

"That's the way it is," Melody said.

"And now you have Jean-Philippe. He's also a soldier!"

"Until he decides to quit," Melody said.

"You think he will?"

"I tell myself that very soon—since he's rich—he will realize that there is more to life than the army."

"Is he rich?"

"Almost as rich as Craig," Melody said. "Nobody's as rich as Craig."

"I am," Cynthia said. "My brother sees this little romance as a chance for a sound corporate merger."

Melody looked at her.

"And you must be, too," Cynthia said, "or you wouldn't be talking about it."

"My father's well-off," Melody said. "Not in the same league as Jean-Philippe and Craig, but rich. And I'm his only child."

"Is that the attraction? We recognize each other? Sort of a rich people's Masonic organization? With a secret recognition signal?"

"Why do you say that?"

"I was immediately pals with Barbara Bellmon," Cynthia

said. "Not with Sharon. Sharon was very suspicious of me. But Barbara and I understood each other from the very first. Now I think I know why."

"I don't understand," Melody confessed.

"There was something about Barbara that I couldn't quite figure out. Until just now. Have you been to Craig's place in Washington?"

"I've heard about it," Melody said. "Jean-Philippe stayed there when he was in Washington."

"Very elegant. With a staff," Cynthia said. "I don't know what they pay generals, but I do know it's not enough to afford a place like that. After we ate, Barbara cleaned off the table and carried the dishes into the sink. I thought it was odd. Then I thought it was because she was a middle-class housewife and not used to servants. But now I understand it. If she was a middle-class housewife, enjoying somebody else's help, she would have left it there for them to clean up. But that isn't it at all. She was perfectly at home in Craig's house; that means she's used to money."

"Ed told me they have a big place, several hundred acres, in Virginia," Melody said. "I think they've got some money. They don't show it the way Craig does, with his airplane and his cars; but they've got it. Not like his, more like mine."

"Then what the hell are they doing in the army?" Cynthia asked.

"I don't know," Melody said. "The men want to do it, and I guess the women want to do whatever the men want."

"'Whither thou goest'? Even to the dark recesses of Alabama?" She realized what she had said. "That was rude of me."

"We were in Texas," Melody said. "Ed and me, I mean. That was really awful. I know what you mean."

"You're quite a woman," Cynthia said. "I know why Craig likes you."

"And I can see what he sees in you," Cynthia said.

They went to the PX, where Cynthia picked out a skirt and a sweater, underwear and hose, and then, on impulse, an orange nylon zipper bag with "The Army Aviation Center, Fort Rucker, Ala." painted on it. Then they drove back to Ozark.

There was another car in the driveway at 227 Melody Lane, a Cadillac Coupe de Ville.

"Another rich one?" Cynthia asked. "Aren't you afraid the lower classes will rebel?"

The door of the Cadillac opened as they turned into the driveway.

"Wrong," Cynthia said. "She's colored."

"Right," Melody said. "That's Antoinette. You're really being shown off."

The colored woman waited for them to get out of the car.

"Dr. Parker," Melody said, "Miss Thomas."

"Well, I can see what he sees in you," Antoinette Parker said, offering her hand. "The question is, what do you see in him?"

"Hello," Cynthia said.

"You seem like an intelligent young woman," Antoinette said. "Why are you considering joining us camp followers?"

"What's the matter with you?" Melody asked.

"You mean you haven't heard?" Antoinette said.

"Heard what?"

"Wait till we get in the house," Antoinette said. "Then I won't have to tell the story twice."

The men were in the kitchen doing something with a large piece of meat.

Craig, smiling broadly, put his arms around Antoinette's shoulders.

"You two have met?" he asked. And then without waiting for a reply, "You get what you needed?"

"Yes, and yes," Cynthia said.

"Ask me when Phil is coming over, Craig," Toni Parker said.

He looked at her curiously.

"OK," he said, agreeably. "When is Phil coming over?"

"I don't think he will be," Toni said.

"Why not?" Lowell asked.

"I thought you would never ask," Toni said. "The reason Phil's not likely to come over, Craig, is because he's at Fort Benning."

"Oh? What's he doing at Benning?"

"Would you believe jumping out of airplanes?" Toni said.

"What the hell's that all about?"

"And when he knows how to jump out of airplanes, he's going to learn how to make fire by rubbing two sticks together and all that sort of thing. He's a little old to be an eagle scout; so when he finishes, they're going to let him wear a green beret."

"Oh, Jesus H. Christ!" Lowell said.

"A pied piper appeared," Toni said, bitterly, "by the name of MacMillan—and you have to see Mac in one of those hats to believe it. MacMillan piped away on his pipe, which I think is filled with what they call a controlled substance, and little Philip skipped gaily along after him."

"Spare me the allegory," Lowell said, sharply. "Tell me what happened."

"Could I have a drink, first?" Toni said. "I'm aware I'm playing the bitch, but I can't help it. I'm so goddamned mad!"

Lowell reached under the sink and came up with a half gallon of scotch.

"I was bitchy to you, too," Toni said, to Cynthia, "and I'm sorry. It's just that I'm a little upset because my husband has lost his mind. Or else he's suffering from premature Cloud's Syndrome."

"What's that?" Lowell asked.

"Male menopause," Toni said. "Manifested by a desire to act youthful to the point of . . . oh, hell, there I go again. Sorry."

Lowell handed her a drink.

"Now tell me what's happened," he said.

"Well, first the pied piper appeared," Toni Parker said. "He's recruiting people for Special Forces. Phil told me he was going to see him, just to see Mac in a green beret. At first, I thought he thought it was just funny. It never entered my mind that he would volunteer."

"Didn't he talk it over with you?" Lowell asked.

"Oh, yeah," she said, bitterly. "A couple of days later. He had a cross-country RON to Bragg . . ."

"What does that mean?" Cynthia said. Everybody looked at her.

"You have your own language," Cynthia said. "I don't understand half of what you're saying. Or am I intruding?"

"Phil's a flight instructor," Lowell explained. "What Toni said was that he took a group of student pilots on a cross-country training flight to Fort Bragg. RON means Remain Over Night. He went along to make sure they didn't get lost, in other words. The students take turns navigating. They spend the night someplace—in this case, Bragg—and then come back."

"And when he came back," Toni Parker said, obviously anxious to tell her story, "he told me that he had been thinking about how much nicer Bragg was than Rucker, how the hospital was much larger, and how I could easily get a job there. I said that if he was thinking of volunteering for the Green Berets, he was out of his mind."

"Green Berets?" Cynthia asked, and immediately regretted it. Toni gave her a dirty look, Lowell an impatient one.

"They're sort of super-paratroops," Lowell said. "What they do is train native forces. Guerrillas, in other words."

"Then Phil said," Toni Parker said, angrily, "that as a matter of fact, he had already volunteered, and his orders would probably be along in a day or two."

"Jesus!" Lowell said. "What the hell was he thinking of?"

"He was thinking, Craig," Toni said, "that if they didn't give you command of that rocket-armed helicopter company, his chances of getting a command had dropped from remote to nonexistent."

Cynthia desperately wanted to know what that was all about, since it was the first suggestion she'd heard that Lowell wasn't the fair-haired boy of the U.S. Army, but she knew she couldn't interrupt again.

"Maybe," Lowell said, "he's right."

"Of course, he's right," Toni said. "Forgive me, Craig, but to use that delightful army expression, both of you are pissing into the wind. The army will keep you around and squeeze what they can from you, but so far as promotions or meaningful assignments are concerned, forget it."

"Running the rocket chopper program is hardly the same thing as garbage disposal officer," Lowell said, a bit angrily.

"They took that away from you, didn't they? For all practical purposes, they took that away from you."

"Something will turn up," Lowell said; and Cynthia saw that he was embarrassed, because of her. "It always has."

"How long have you been a major, Craig?" Toni asked. "Phil has been a captain since September 1950. And he's not even on the major's list!"

"I've been a major as long as Phil has been a captain," Lowell said.

"The two of you make me sick," Toni said. "Why don't you face facts?"

"What's Phil supposed to do, Toni?" Lowell said. "Become the 'doctor's husband'? What would I do outside? The army is our life."

"That's why you make me sick," Toni said. She looked at Cynthia. "I'm really sorry you walked into this."

"It's all right," Cynthia said.

"The only reason I can talk to Craig this way," Toni said, "is because he knows I love him. He wouldn't take it from somebody else."

"I'll talk to Jiggs," Lowell said. "Maybe something can be done."

"I've already talked to him," Toni said, tiredly. "I talked to him ten minutes after Phil dropped his little bomb on me."

"What did he say?"

"He said he would look into it. He called me back the next day and said there was nothing that could be done. Whoever Hanrahan wants, Hanrahan gets. He has clout running up to the White House. And we know who that means, don't we? The ACLU must be ecstatic. A Jew in a position to take care of a nigger."

"Hey, *Toni!*" Craig said.

"I didn't mean that," Toni said. "And you know it. I'm just so goddamned mad. At Phil. At you. At the *goddamned army!*"

She set her glass down on the sink, knocking it over, and ran from the room.

Lowell looked at Melody Dutton Greer. He made a movement of his head, a suggestion that Melody go after her. Melody handed the baby to Cynthia and left the kitchen.

"Shit!" Lowell said.

Cynthia looked at him. Then she handed him the baby and went after the other women.

(Three)
The Pentagon
Washington, D.C.
1045 Hours, 20 March 1959

Mrs. Dorothy Washington Thomas, Personnel Officer, GS-15, Deputy Chief of the Special Assignments Branch, Commissioned Personnel Division, Office of the Deputy Chief of Staff, Personnel, Headquarters, Department of the Army, had been an employee of the army since 1945.

The same year, in a night-school class in business law, she met Theron Thomas, who was then employed by Piggly-Wiggly Supermarkets, Inc., as a stock boy. Mr. Thomas had passed the entrance examination for the Washington, D.C. police force and was waiting for an appointment. Dorothy Washington and Theron Thomas were married in February 1948, in St. Matthew's African Methodist Episcopal Church by the Rev. Jerome Fortin Keyes, D.D., a week after Mr. Thomas had entered upon an appointment as a probationary patrolman on the Metropolitan Police Force.

A couple of years later the Deputy Provost Marshal General of the United States Army personally sought out Mrs. Thomas—then assigned to the Office of the Chief of Transportation in the Pentagon—to inform her that her husband had been wounded in action in Korea.

Sergeant Thomas had been struck by artillery fragments. He had suffered wounds to the head, the right arm, and the left leg. When Sergeant Thomas was airlifted to the United States, a silver plate had been implanted in his skull; and, while it had been impossible to repair the damage to his left eye, his right eye was intact. He still retained use of his right hand and fingers, although it had been necessary to repair his shattered elbow in such a manner that movement was restricted to thirty percent of normal. It had been necessary to surgically remove his left leg at a point three inches above the knee.

Sergeant Theron Thomas was honorably discharged from the U.S. Army in 1952, after having been adjudged to have sustained in the line of duty permanent damage entitling him to a one hundred percent disability pension.

Civil Service Regulations provide that spouses of veterans who are either deceased or disabled in military service are entitled to "veteran's preference," as if they themselves were veterans.

Mrs. Thomas believed that it was her veteran's preference that saw her selected as a "management intern" in an interior management development program established by the Deputy Chief of Staff for Personnel. She had not then completed her undergraduate work; and management interns, as a general rule of thumb, had to have one or more college degrees before being hired.

Theron Thomas tried to work, but his vision and his mobility were limited; and he suffered headaches, aches in his elbow, and "phantom pain" in the knee and lower leg that had been removed.

He and his wife decided that there was no reason for him

to try to work. He had his pension, she had her job, and they didn't really need the money. Theron became the housekeeper and Dorothy the breadwinner.

The built a house just over the district line in Maryland. Having nothing better to do, Theron watched the builders work, and was not at all impressed with the carpenters, the finishers, and the roofers. Though he could no longer wield a hammer, he knew how one should be wielded. So he backed into the contracting business, which within four years became the Thomas Construction Company.

There was enough money for Dorothy to quit. But she didn't want to quit, and it wasn't only the money. She liked what she was doing, she was good at it, and she thought it was important. She was in charge of people's lives—of picking or rejecting them for important assignments. She privately and proudly believed she was making a bona fide contribution to the national security.

As a GS–15, whenever she traveled to a military base, she was entitled to the same accommodations and privileges as a colonel. She was proud of that, too. She had no intention of giving that up to sit around playing cards or run white elephant sales for the church, she told Theron.

There was no major fight about it. Both Theron and Dorothy were convinced that they had more to be grateful for than tney had to regret.

"Mrs. Thomas asks if you have a minute, General," the secretary to the Deputy Chief of Staff for Personnel (DCSPERS) said through the intercom.

"Come on in, Dorothy," he called.

He thought her appearing now was a fortuitous happenstance. The day before he had had an unofficial, out-of-channels request that he had decided he could not ignore. Paul Jiggs had called him from Rucker and asked him to find out—unofficially, out of school—exactly what there was in the records of one of his captains that had kept him off the major's list.

He had been tempted at the time to tell Jiggs to bug off. Jiggs had no right to get involved. You simply couldn't afford to permit every general to get on the horn to Washington and foul up the smoothly operating system.

The trouble with Jiggs—and the reason the DCSPERS had decided not to tell him to please stay within channels—was that Jiggs was one of those post commanders thought of as *influential*. As it had been so aptly phrased by that English writer, "Some pigs are more equal than others."

For years—thirty, forty of them—the commanding generals of four posts—Fort Benning (infantry), Fort Sill (artillery), Fort Knox (armor), and Fort Bragg (airborne)—had been more equal than the commanding generals of, say, Fort Dix, which was a basic training center. It was perfectly clear to DCSPERS that very recently Fort Rucker (aviation) had become important.

The commanding generals of, say, Fort Dix, N.J., or Fort Polk, La., were responsible to their army commanders and then Continental Army Command. That wasn't true of Benning, Sill, Knox, Bragg, and now Rucker. Their commanders spent at least two days a month in Washington, and while they were nominally under the command of the army commanders and CONARC, *de facto* they were not. They worked for DCSOPS and the Vice Chief of Staff; and when they didn't like something, they were all skilled at putting a polite word in the ears of those luminaries.

And they couldn't be stepped on; for the commanders of the combat arms posts had a long tradition of being further—and rapidly—promoted. The Chairman of the Joint Chiefs was once a commander of Sill; the Chief of Staff a commander of Benning; and the incumbent Vice Chief who had once commanded Knox, was about to be replaced by a former commander of Bragg.

Thus the DCSPERS had decided that discretion dictated that he find out what Paul Jiggs wanted to know about that captain of his. The person who had that answer was Mrs. Dorothy W. Thomas, the Deputy Chief, Special Assignments Branch, Commissioned Personnel Division.

Dorothy Thomas gave him an icy smile. She was angry. Her eyes showed it.

"Sit down, Dorothy," the DCSPERS said, with a smile. "Would you like some coffee?"

She deposited a five-inch-thick stack of records on his desk.

"Yes, thank, you, I would like some coffee," she said. "Then look at this file. You won't believe what you'll read in it."

He glanced at the tab on the file she had laid before him. It was neatly lettered with an officer's name, branch of service, and serial number: *PARKER, Philip Sheridan IV, Armor 0–230471.*

"We have a problem," Mrs. Thomas said. "We have to figure out how to right the wrong done to this officer."

"I see," the DCSPERS said. He opened the top file. There was a 4 × 5 inch color photograph of the officer whose record it was. Captain Philip Sheridan Parker IV was a Negro. Mrs. Thomas was obviously as mad as a wet hornet, and that could mean that whatever was wrong had racial overtones.

"How has Captain Parker been wronged?" the DCSPERS asked.

She looked at him a moment, and then nodded her head.

"The officer in question is regular army," she said. "Norwich. He was promoted to captain under AR 615–399, after having performed satisfactorily in a higher grade in combat, the exigencies of the service having required such service. His promotion was justified by subparagraphs *(a)* and *(b)*: *(a)* stipulates that such performance of duties be for any period of time during combat for which the promoted officer was decorated for valor and/or personally observed by a general officer; *(b)* stipulates that such assumption of brevet rank or command be over a period of no less than ninety days, at least forty-five of which were in combat. In other words, he got an unquestionably legal battlefield promotion in Korea. Subsequently he went to aviation, where he has been until now. He has just been selected, after volunteering, for Special Forces. At the moment, he's at Benning, going to jump school."

"What's his date of rank?"

"September 1950."

"That's more than eight years ago," the DCSPERS said.

"He was court-martialed in Korea," Mrs. Thomas said. "And acquitted."

"What for?"

She didn't reply to the question. Instead, she said, "When an officer is acquitted by a court-martial, all references to that court-martial must be expunged from his record. There is no indication on his record that he was ever court-martialed," she said.

"Then how do you know?"

"I took the time and trouble to find out," she said. "You can tell when a new service record has been made up. He was tried for murder, two counts, and acquitted."

"I see," the DCSPERS said.

"He has subsequently been rated quarterly and annually. He has never been in trouble of any kind since; and his efficiency ratings generally place him in the 'Excellent' to 'Outstanding' categories. I would not have been surprised to see that he had been on the five percent list in any of the past three years."

(Promotion boards are given a specific number of officers to promote from a pool of officers eligible by virtue of their having completed a specified period of service, a specified period of time in grade, requisite formal schools, and other qualifications. Provision is also made, however, for the promotion of no more than five percent of the total officers to be promoted "outside the zone of consideration." These officers are those not meeting the established criteria, but who have nevertheless demonstrated unusual talent meriting their promotion. Officers so promoted are said to have been promoted "on the five percent list.")

"Why hasn't he been?" the DSCPERS asked.

"Because, at the time the charges were made against him, his records were flagged to delay any personnel actions, advantageous or detrimental, until the resolution of the charges made against him."

"That's standard procedure," the DSCPERS said.

"The flags were never taken off, General," Mrs. Thomas said. "This officer has not been promoted because his records were never sent before a promotion board."

"The flags never came off?"

"That seems to be the situation," she said.

"I find it hard to believe," the DCSPERS said. "He just slipped through the cracks, huh?"

"You could put it that way, I suppose," she said, icily.

"Well," he said. "Let's see what we can do to make things right with this officer. When does the next promotion board meet?"

"Next month."

"Then he should head the list," the DCSPERS said. "I was afraid that it wasn't until next year."

"You really think that promoting this officer, say in nine months, will make things right?"

"It would open a large can of worms to do anything else," the DCSPERS said. "Are you suggesting that we do that?"

"I am suggesting to you that you seek permission from the Chief of Staff and SECDEF to convene a promotion board immediately, to consider the promotion of this officer, who because of our error was not considered by previous promotion boards."

"That's going to make us look rather sloppy, isn't it?"

"I am prepared to make that recommendation in writing," Mrs. Thomas said.

"And if I turned the recommendation down?"

"I don't really know what I would do in that circumstance, General," she said. "But I would suggest that now that our error has been uncovered, questions are liable to be asked when this officer's name, as it must be, is submitted for consideration by the next major's board. Someone is certain to ask why this officer's name was not previously submitted."

"Can we go off the record, Dorothy?" the DCSPERS asked.

"Certainly."

"Just between us, Dorothy, would you be so upset if the officer in question were not what he is?"

He knew the moment he saw the look on her face that he had made a mistake. First there was genuine confusion, then annoyance and anger. She stood up and went to his desk and picked up the file. She saw the photograph of Captain Philip Sheridan Parker IV.

"Nigger, isn't he?" she asked, bitterly.

She looked at him witheringly.

He knew she had not known.

He buzzed for his secretary.

"Yes, sir?" his secretary asked, as she entered the room with her stenographer's notebook.

"Prepare a DF for SECARMY, via the Chief of Staff, stating that without objection it is my intention to immediately convene a promotion board to consider Captain P. S. Parker IV. Say that through inexcusable error, for which I hold myself responsible, Captain Parker's name has not been previously submitted for consideration, and that in my opinion a grave injustice has been done to him."

(A DF, or distribution form, is a letter-sized Department of Defense form used for internal communication.)

"Yes, sir."

The DCSPERS dismissed his secretary with a nod of his head.

"I apologize, Dorothy," he said.

She walked out of his office without response.

XV

(One)
Fort Rucker, Alabama
1705 Hours, 12 April 1959

"Laird, Army Two Two One, turning on final," Craig Lowell said to the microphone he held in front of his face.

He hung the microphone in its hook, lined the Cessna L-19 up with runway 28, and put it on the ground. It had been a very long haul in the single-engine, high-wing, two-seater observation airplane from the Lexington (Ky.) Signal Depot. The L-19 was not designed for cross-country flight. The trip had taken him more than twice as long as it would have in his Aero Commander, and the L-19's seats were far less comfortable than the padded leather seats in the Aero Commander.

But he'd had a fuel-pump problem in the left engine of the Commander, and he had had to go to the Signal Depot. Because there had been an inexplicable (and he had learned, inexcusable) delay in the delivery of a van-mounted avionic maintenance facility to Colonel Tom Warner's 3087th Aviation

Company (Armed Helicopter) at Fort Knox, it had been necessary for him to go to Lexington to kick a little lead out of dead asses. But with the Aero Commander down, it was either the L-19 or a day up and and a day back on commercial airlines. No faster aircraft were available to him from the Board fleet.

He taxied the little airplane to the end of the parked aircraft line, turned it into line, and shut it down. He got stiffly out and leaned against the fuselage as he filled out the forms and handed them to a waiting sergeant.

"Long flight, Major?" the sergeant said, sympathetically.

"My ass has been asleep for two hours," Lowell said, smiled, and walked toward the parking lot.

He glanced toward Hangar No. 4, and saw Jane Cassidy walking to the parking lot. She raised her hand in a greeting that was also a signal for him to wait for her.

He unlocked the Mercedes, and got in and waited for her.

"Hi," he said, when she walked up to the car.

She handed him a telephone message form.

"Major Lowell," it read, "if you get back before 8:00 P.M., please call me at home. Jane."

He smiled at her, then mimicked looking at his watch and picking up a telephone call.

"I have to see you," she said, very seriously.

"Here I am," he said, trying to keep it light.

"Not here," she said. "We have to talk."

"Oh?"

"Meet me at the beach place at eight," she can. "Can you?"

The beach place was in Panama City, which was an hour and a half's drive. The thought of the drive itself would have been displeasing, even if it hadn't been to the place where he had bedded Jane.

"Can't we talk here?" he asked. "Or go get a cup of coffee in the snack bar?"

"No," she said, firmly. "I'm sorry, but I have to talk to you."

"Something's wrong?"

"Of course something's wrong," she said. "And I don't want to talk about it in a parking lot or a snack bar."

"OK," he said, forcing a smile. "Eight o'clock."

"Thank you, Craig," she said, and then she walked away toward her Buick station wagon.

He went to his office and spent a little more than an hour

trying to work down the mountain of paper on his desk, and then he got in the Mercedes and started toward Panama City.

He had just crossed the Alabama-Florida line when he suddenly understood what was up, what was bothering Jane.

He cursed himself for not thinking of it instantly. He should have known that ending that relationship had gone entirely too easily to be real.

A couple weeks before, Tom Cassidy had called him at the office shortly after Cynthia had gone back to New York.

"It's my husband," Jane had said, confused and uncomfortable, "and he wants to talk to you."

It turned out that Tom had just come in from Kansas City and had brought with him some of the most beautifully marbled steaks he had ever seen. He wanted Craig Lowell to come to supper—and would take no excuse short of nuclear war for his not coming. He was grateful, Tom had said, for all Lowell had done for Jane.

There had been no way to get out of going. But it had gone well, incredibly well. Or so, in his innocence, he had thought at the time.

In response to Tom Cassidy's question, "Well, what have you been up to lately?" Lowell had replied, looking right at Jane, "As a matter of fact, I've been falling in love."

Her smile had vanished for a moment, and then returned as he went on.

"It turned out that the *Time-Life* reporter who was here is the sister of a friend of my cousin Porter Craig's. I met her in New York, almost by coincidence, and, well, one thing led to another."

"Well," Tom Cassidy had said, enthusiastically, "good for you!"

"I'm happy for you, Craig," Jane Cassidy had said. "Tell us all about her."

He had, he thought, come out of that one smelling like roses—and mildly astonished at how skilled a hypocrite he could be when the occasion demanded.

Now he knew he had been a fool.

He banged his fist, hard, against the horn of the Mercedes.

"Jesus Christ, she's pregnant!" he said, aloud.

That was the only possible explanation. She had to "talk" to him. Of course, "something is wrong." What the hell else could it be?

The question was what to do about it?

"For Christ's sake," he said aloud again as he approached the beach house, his headlights catching the reflection of the Buick's tail lights, "why the hell didn't she take care of herself?"

When he went in the house, she was standing at the bamboo bar.

"Right on time," she said. "Thank you. Scotch?"

"Please," he said.

She had changed clothing since he'd seen her in the parking lot. She was now wearing a skirt and sweater. And, he noticed, nothing under the sweater.

She handed him the drink.

"Thank you," he said.

She tapped rims with him.

"I've missed you," she said.

"I've missed you, too," he said.

You are a sonofabitch, Lowell. You would like to jump/her bones, Cynthia or no Cynthia. Then he pardoned himself./*You wouldn't do it, of course. Thinking about it is not the same thing as doing it. That was just a perfectly normal reaction to a woman walking about with her boobs unrestrained under a sweater.*

"Then why have you been avoiding me?" Jane Cassidy asked.

"Have I been avoiding you?" he asked, aware that it was an inane answer.

"You know very well you have," she accused.

"If I have," he said, aware he was making no sense, because he didn't known what was going on, "it's been unintentional."

"Huh!" she snorted.

He decided to get the conversation to the point.

"How long have you known?" he asked, gently.

"How long have I known what? That you've been avoiding me?"

"That you're pregnant," Lowell said.

"Pregnant? You think I'm pregnant? What gave you that idea?"

"You're not pregnant?"

"Of course I'm not pregnant."

"Thank God!" he said. Elated, he drained his drink and walked around her to the bamboo bar and fixed himself another.

"You can't do this to me, Craig," she said to his back. "It's not fair!"

Now what the hell?

"I don't understand what you mean," he said.

"You just can't drop me where I am," she said. "You got me into this, and you're just not going to abandon me until I get things figured out."

"I got you into what?" he asked, turning to face her.

"Facing my sexuality," she said, and he could tell by her face that she was perfectly serious. He wasn't sure what she meant, but whatever it was, she was dead serious.

"Oh," he said.

"Don't act as if you don't understand what I'm talking about," she snapped.

"To tell you the truth, Jane," Lowell said, "I don't."

"Before I started this affair with you, I didn't have any problems in that regard," she said. "Or rather, I had them, but I didn't know it."

He nodded his head, as if agreeing with her. He still didn't know what she was talking about.

"If I have to spell it out for you," she said, nastily, "I never really came until you."

"Jane!"

"I didn't miss it, because I didn't know what it was," she said. "But now I do."

"If I taught you something, Jane," Lowell said, carefully, "that's all to the good."

"You taught me something all right," she said.

"But why don't we do the smart thing, and quit while we're ahead?"

"Damn you!" she said. "You selfish bastard!"

"Look," he said, "we had a wonderful time. We didn't get caught. If I taught you something, that's all to the good. Your husband is a nice guy."

"Yes, he is," she said. "You just don't understand, do you?"

"No," he said, "I don't."

She colored and looked away.

"If I . . . took Tom in my mouth . . . or the other way around, if I asked him to do that to me . . . my God, he'd leave me."

"I think you would probably make him the happiest man in the world," Lowell said.

"He would think I'm depraved," she said.

"No believe me, he wouldn't," Lowell said.

I don't believe that; he just might.

"Yes, he *would!*" she said, in almost a wail.

"You could teach him," Lowell said. "If you wanted to."

"I'm going to try," she said.

"Good," he said.

"And what am I supposed to do in the meantime?" she snapped.

"For Christ's sake, Jane. I'm in love with somebody. I think I'm going to marry her."

"Huh," she snorted. "*I'm* married. What has that got to do with this?"

"If I have be crude, Jane, I don't think I could get it up with you," Lowell said. "Not anymore."

"Because you're in love?" she asked.

"Yes, of course," he said.

"You taught me different," she said, her voice low. "You taught me that fucking has nothing to do with love."

"I didn't teach you that, because it's not true," Lowell said.

"Until I can straighten my life out—and I will—you're not just going to drop me," she said. "You got me into this, and you're going to stick with me. I need sex, and I'm going to get it, and I'm not going to risk a scandal by getting it from somebody else."

"I understand what you're saying, Jane," Lowell said, uncomfortably. "But it just wouldn't work. I don't think I would be able to."

She looked at him. Then she crossed her arms in front of her, putting her hands on the hem of her sweater. Then she pulled it over her head.

"You'll think of some way to help me," she said.

He felt himself stirring.

It's absolutely true, he thought, mildly surprised. *The sun always comes up in the morning, and a stiff prick has no conscience.*

(Two)
Broadlawns
Glen Cove, Long Island, New York
1845 Hours, 1 May 1959

"Where the hell have you been?" Cynthia Thomas asked

Craig Lowell as he came into the foyer of the house. "You were expected at half past three!"

"I got hung up in Boonton, New Jersey," he said. "Sorry."

He kissed her lightly, even chastely, but managed to get a little squeeze of her tail.

"Boonton, New Jersey?" she asked. He nodded. "What's in Boonton?"

"ARC," he said.

"All right, I'll bite," she said. "What's ARC?"

"It's Craig's favorite charity," Porter Craig said, walking up and offering his hand. "The Aircraft Radio Corporation."

"Both of my ADFs quit working," Lowell said. "I called up and they said they would fix them right away, if I brought them to the plant."

"How did you get here?" Porter Craig asked.

"They loaned me a car," Lowell said.

"They should have given you one," Porter said. "As much business as you give them."

"How did lunch go?"

"I've heard of brides being left at the church," Cynthia said. "But never before at a garden party where the engagement was to be announced."

"How did the garden party go?" Lowell asked. "Has everybody gone, I hope?"

"You *bastard*," Cynthia said, but she smiled.

"I shouldn't even be here," he said. "Technically, I'm AWOL."

"I hope they catch you," she said. "Maybe they'll throw you out of the army."

She said it jokingly, but she was serious. So long as he was in the army, she would not have a husband who could ever be where she wanted him to be. The ultimate solution to that problem would be to get Major Craig W. Lowell out of uniform.

"Everybody's down at the boathouse," Porter said. "It's beautiful there, so I made them move the buffet out."

"Let me get a little liquid courage, and then I'll go face them," Lowell said. "God knows, I can use something to eat."

"I had them set up a bar out there, too," Porter Craig said. "You can have a drink there."

"I'll have a drink here," Lowell said. He put his arms around Cynthia's shoulders and led her into the bar. A maid and a barman were cleaning up the room. He didn't recognize either of them and decided they were working for the caterer. Broadlawns was well staffed, but there were not enough servants to handle a garden party for forty without help.

"Put a little scotch in a large glass, please, and fill it with soda," Lowell ordered. "No ice."

"I believe the other guests have gone to the boathouse, sir," the barman said.

"I didn't ask for information," Lowell said, somewhat nastily. "I asked for a drink."

"This bar has been closed, sir," the barman said.

"Not as long as I own this house it hasn't," Lowell said sharply. He walked behind the the bar and picked up a bottle of scotch and a soda water siphon. The barman shrugged at the bad manners of the rich and handed him a glass.

"You do insist on your way, don't you?" Cynthia said. "People are waiting to see you."

He gave her a withering look.

He had been up since half past three and had flown over two thousand miles to get here. It was 1620 before he had been able to go into the dirt field at the Aircraft Radio Corporation at Boonton. He was met there by a salesman with the keys to a loaner car. He had then had to drive through New Jersey to the Lincoln Tunnel, arriving there just in time for the regular traffic jam. It was bad going into Manhattan, worse in Manhattan, and absolutely maddening on Long Island.

It took him five minutes longer to drive from Boonton to Glen Cove than it had taken him to fly from Alabama to the Lexington Signal Depot earlier in the day. But he was finally here for this goddamned party of Porter Craig's and Cynthia's family; and if he wanted a drink before facing them, it seemed to him a perfectly reasonable thing to ask for.

Cynthia backed down.

"Give me a little soda, please, with a slice of lime," she said to the barman.

A balding man of about Lowell's age, wearing a three-piece, gray pinstripe suit, appeared in the doorway to the bar. Porter Craig motioned him to come in.

"Craig," he said, "this is Stevens DePaul, who handles our public relations."

"How do you do, Mr. Lowell?" Stevens said, offering his hand.

"You could say that Stevens is cupid's helper," Porter Craig said, playfully. "It was he who found out that *your* Cynthia was *our* Cynthia, and sent the flowers."

Lowell flashed a quick smile.

"How do you do?" he said.

"Mr. Craig thought you should see this before we release it, Mr. Lowell," Stevens DePaul said, handing him a sheet of paper. "The Thomases and the Peltons have already approved of it."

Lowell took it from him and read it:

CRAIG, POWELL, KENYON AND DAWES, INC.

17 Wall Street, New York City, New York

Stevens DePaul
Vice President, Public Affairs
Tel: 742–1177, 742–1178

FOR IMMEDIATE RELEASE TO THE NEW YORK TIMES:
...........................THE WALL STREET JOURNAL:

New York City, May 2—Mrs. John Schuyler Pelton of New York and Palm Springs, Cal., and Mr. Clemens Thomas of New York have announced the engagement of Mrs. Pelton's niece, and Mr. Thomas's sister, Miss Cynthia Thomas, of New York and Palm Beach, to Mr. Craig W. Lowell, of Glen Cove.

Miss Thomas is the daughter of the late Mr. and Mrs. Edward T. Thomas. Mr. Thomas was Chairman of the Board and Chief Executive Officer of Thomas & MacNeil, Inc., the investment bankers, a position now held by his son Mr. Clemens Thomas. Mr. Lowell is the son of Mrs. Andre Pretier of Glen Cove and Palm Beach, and the late Mr. Porter Lowell, who was Executive Vice President of Craig, Powell, Kenyon and Dawes, Inc., the investment bankers.

A graduate of Miss Porter's School and Smith, Miss Thomas is a reporter for *Time* magazine. Mr. Lowell, who attended St. Mark's School and Harvard, is a graduate of the Wharton School of Business of the University of Pennsylvania. He is presently on military leave from Craig, Powell, Kenyon and Dawes, of which he is Vice Chairman of the Board.

The upcoming nuptials were announced at a garden

party today at Broadlawns, Mr. Lowell's estate in Glen
Cove. A June wedding is planned.
   (Note to Editor: Guest list attached.)

"Jesus Christ!" Lowell said, handing the sheet of paper to
Cynthia. "Is that really necessary?"

"Is there something wrong with it, Mr. Lowell?" Stevens
DePaul asked.

"Well, I realize this is tantamount to confessing that the
store is being minded by a convicted embezzler," Lowell said,
"but it's *Major* Lowell."

"Oh, for God's sake, Craig!" Porter Craig said.

"As odd as the notion may strike you, Porter," Lowell said,
"some of my friends read the *Times* and the *WSJ*, and I don't
want them to think I'm somehow embarrassed about being a
major in the army."

"There are reasons for that," Porter said.

"Please change this thing, Mr. DePaul," Lowell said, "making me a major, and drop that absurd statement that I'm on
military leave from the firm."

"Is this really important, Craig?" Cynthia asked.

"Under the law, Craig," Porter Craig said, "it is considered
a patriotic gesture for us to continue your salary while you are
off in the army. So far, no questions have been raised about
your regular status. If you are not, however, on military leave,
your salary would become a nondeductible charitable contribution."

"Then kill the salary," Lowell snapped. "I will not have it
suggested that I am a part-time soldier."

"Then we would not be able to provide you with the airplane,
or the use of the house in Georgetown, or a long list of other
things to which you are entitled by virtue of your title, no
matter how absurd you think it is."

"You're being foolish, Craig," Cynthia said.

"You've noticed?" Porter Craig asked sarcastically.

"You can leave the military leave in," Lowell said to Stevens
DePaul. "But if that story appears without reference to my
military rank, I'll break both your arms."

"Oh, my God!" Cynthia said. "Sometimes you're impossible."

"I'm sure Major Lowell was joking," Stevens DePaul said.
"I understand how he feels."

"Don't bank on it, Stevens," Porter Craig said.

Lowell gulped down his drink, and extended it for a refill.

"OK," he said. "I would rather face a thousand deaths, but let's go."

"Now, what does that mean?" Cynthia asked, somewhat sharply.

"It's what Lee said at Appomattox Courthouse, when he was getting ready to surrender to Grant."

"Is that what you think this is?" Cynthia snapped. "A surrender?"

He had taken her arm. She jerked free of him, and went to the French doors in the bar, opened them, and walked briskly down the long verdant lawn to the party that Suzie Knickerbocker's "Society" column two days later would refer to as "the largest gathering of the oh, so quietly, and oh, so longtime, and oh, so *very* rich in years."

(Three)
Above Camp McCall, North Carolina
1430 Hours, 20 May 1959

Captain Philip Sheridan Parker IV's fatigues were soaking wet. Around his armpits and his buttocks were roughly circular patches, lined with white: salt. He had been taking salt tablets, a tablet every time he drank water to replace the fluids lost through perspiration. Because he had been sweating a lot, he had had to drink a lot of water, and a lot of the salt he'd taken had passed out again as sweat. The resulting residue had caked here and there on his clothes . . . a lot of it.

At the moment he was genuinely frightened. He was no stranger to fear or terror. He had spent 397 days—over a year—in combat, according to his records, and maybe 45 days of what he thought of as *real* combat, days when logic had told him that he would be incredibly lucky if the worst he got was wounded. During those times, he had lost control of his bowels, he had literally shaken with fear, he had been soaked in cold sweat. But he had never lost control of himself; he had always been able to do what his sense of duty had told him it was necessary to do.

He had also experienced fear as an aviator any number of times. Once he had lost an engine on takeoff and for a horrifying thirty seconds he'd been absolutely certain he was about to crash. He had been lost in a snowstorm in Alaska in a Beaver, and for an hour certain that if he descended through the clouds, he'd fly into a mountain or crash the Beaver into a forest. On a dozen occasions, it had seemed entirely likely that one or another of his student pilots would kill the both of them. But he had never lost control of his emotions in a cockpit.

Until Fort Benning he had believed that he had learned how to conquer fear—to reason his way through it.

As a thirty-year-old, out-of-shape aviator what he had feared before going to Benning was that he would not be able to keep up with the kids, the seventeen and eighteen and nineteen-year-old enlisted men, and the twenty-one and twenty-two-year-old lieutenants fresh from basic training or OCS. They would be in first-class physical shape, and he would be unable to keep up with them in the rigid physical conditioning program. He had feared he would not be able to run five miles or do 100 pushups or whatever other physical torture was expected of him. And thus he would fall out, thereby humiliating and disgracing himself as a regular army officer, a Norwich graduate, and a black man.

That flabby nigger aviator just can't hack it. What did you expect?

But what actually almost stopped him at Benning was the forty-foot tower. He had run with the kids, and he'd kept up with them, his heart beating painfully, his throat on fire, his muscles throbbing and his chest heaving. He had done 127 pushups and paid for it with a night of agony. He had done 56 pull-ups, a creditable accomplishment for anyone who weighed 220 pounds.

But now he was on the goddamned forty-foot tower. The tower was a training device, and it was built of telephone poles, with a platform forty feet off the ground. Trainees climbed a ladder to the platform, where they were strapped in a parachute harness. The harness was connected to a steel cable. The trainees then exited the platform as they would exit an aircraft when they made an actual parachute jump.

There were instructors who watched the trainees exit the platform, other instructors who watched them slide down the cable, and still other instructors who watched them strike the ground. The instructors would criticize—in a more or less friendly way—the trainees. It must be said that the usual courtesy which enlisted men paid to officers was placed in limbo during training. If an officer looked like a fucking pregnant duck (which was often the case), the instructor corporals would not be hesitant to tell him so in a voice loud enough so that other trainees could also profit from the expert advice.

Now, halfway up the ladder to the platform, Parker was stricken with terror. He had an almost irresistible urge to wrap both arms around the ladder and stay there. He was suddenly soaked with a clammy sweat. He felt dizzy. Never as an aviator had he experienced vertigo like this—never terror like this.

Get your ass moving! Whatsamatter? Afraid of heights?
Precisely.

There was a word for it, although he could not now for the life of him come up with it. *Aerophobia?* No, that wasn't it. Whatever it was called, he had it, and he had it bad. It took him more determination than he had ever summoned before to climb that last fifteen or twenty feet to the forty-foot platform.

When he was strapped into the harness and ordered to stand at the edge of the platform, he knew it was going to take even more strength of will to jump off. Other men had done it, he told himself—a hundred thousand? two hundred thousand? The vast majority of those men had not blessed with his own innate advantages—or so at least logic told him. He was smarter than most, with an unusually large and muscular body recently whipped into superb shape by a rigid regimen of exercise.

The reason the others had not been terrified, he concluded, was that they were too dumb to be scared. They had no idea what they were doing.

He jumped.

Afterward the instructor did not tell him he looked like a pregnant duck. He described him as having all the grace of a cow on ice . . . and ordered him back up the ladder to the forty-foot platform.

It took him four jumps before his performance was judged satisfactory.

He could not eat supper that night until he'd had half a bottle of scotch in the privacy of his BOQ. He was grateful that his railroad tracks gave him a private room. He didn't know what he would have done if there had been another officer with him to witness the signs of his cowardice. After he drank the scotch, he went to the officer's club and had a steak. And threw it up in the men's room.

He had his first real jump from an airplane the next morning—

without a breakfast he knew he would throw up, and probably very publicly. He was third in the stick and went out the door with his eyes closed, so terrified that he was numb. He was only vaguely aware of the opening shock when the canopy filled with air, and was genuinely surprised when another, far more violent, shock told him that he was again on the ground.

"You can't daydream coming down, Captain," a sergeant instructor told him, not unkindly. "That was really a bad landing you made."

He wasn't at all sure that he would be able to force himself to get back into the airplane, but he made his second jump that afternoon. Aware that he had to eat, he had two PX hamburgers for supper, then went to the BOQ and drank the rest of the scotch. Then he called Toni. She could tell by his voice that he was drunk, which made her hurt and angry.

The next day, he made his third and fourth jumps, and that night the fifth, qualifying jump. His prayers that doing it at night would somehow be easier went unanswered. Actually, it was worse at night. He didn't think it was possible that it could be worse, but it was.

There was a party later that night. In the morning, there would be a parade. After the parade, the commandant of the Parachute School would pin the silver wings on their chests. Thereafter they would be entitled to refer to themselves as parachutists. It was an occasion to tie one on.

He had one drink, went to the BOQ, and called Toni. When he told her he wasn't sure he was going to get through it, he realized she thought he was trying to gain a little undeserved sympathy. Which was not unreasonable of her, he thought. After all, he was a perfect physical specimen and an aviator, and there were a lot of really stupid people around wearing jump rings. Becoming a parachutist was no big deal.

He did not discuss the Parachute School when he went home over that weekend. There were other things to discuss, friends to see, arrangements to make for the transfer to Bragg.

His orders required that he report for duty at the U.S. Army Special Warfare School not later than 0900. He thought that was a reasonable hour, and he thought it was a pleasant indication of what the school would be like when a qualified Green Beret officer saw that he and the five other officers reporting in were comfortably settled into a BOQ. The orders of the day were to appear in fatigues after lunch. There was an officer's section in a GI mess hall, separated from the enlisted men's part by a plywood partition. Lunch was nothing to rave about, but it was cheap.

When they assembled after lunch, there were thirty-five enlisted men along with the six officers. He was the ranking officer, and he was politely asked to take over the formation, call roll, and load everybody onto a GI bus which sat nearby.

No member of the faculty got on the bus, and when one of the other officers asked the driver where they were headed, all the driver knew was that he was supposed to follow the jeep. In the jeep was a Green Beret master sergeant.

They were driven to Pope Field, and then onto an unusually large aircraft parking area. Parker noticed that the air force transports were parked rather further apart than he would have expected. He imagined this was because the aircraft were used to transport personnel of the 82nd Airborne Division, and that extra space was required for trucks and supplies.

Then the bus stopped behind a Lockheed C–130 "Hercules." The large rear door of the air force transport was open, and a bored-looking air force master sergeant, the crew chief (or loadmaster), looked out at them.

The Green Beret master sergeant came onto the bus.

"Will you unload your people, please, Captain?" he asked.

Parker wondered why they were being shown a C–130. Everybody was a qualified parachutist; everyone knew what a C–130 looked like.

When he got out of the bus and saw the parachutes and equipment, he knew what was going on, although he didn't want to believe it.

The Green Beret master sergeant made a "form on me" signal, and when everybody had gathered arouund him, he said: "Gentlemen, you will find field gear, weapons, and parachutes labeled with your name beside the aircraft. Please put your parachutes on and form yourselves in two ranks."

The equipment was complete. There was a full set of web equipment, knapsack, shelter half, blanket, harness, and everything else from helmets to .45 pistols in holsters. There was an M14 rifle and magazines for it (loaded with blanks) in pouches on the web belt. There was even water in the canteen, Parker saw with surprise.

Putting the equipment on took some time. All the straps had to be adjusted, as did the harness on the parachute. Parker, having no idea how to carry an M14 on a parachute jump, had to be shown.

In ten minutes, they were ready.

"Gentlemen," the Green Beret master sergeant said, "herewith the First Commandment of the Special Warfare School: 'Be prepared for anything.' The Second Commandment is not 'like unto the first.' The Second Commandment is to forget anything you think you know about parachute jumping except that it is, like the bicycle, a means for getting from one place to another. Now, please board the aircraft."

"Jesus!" somebody said.

"Mary and Joseph," somebody added, and there was nervous laughter. Then everybody went up the ramp and got on the C–130, including the Green Beret master sergeant, who walked casually up the ramp with his main chute over one shoulder, and carrying his spare chute and all the other equipment in his hands.

The aircraft engines started immediately, even before the last man was aboard; and as they started to taxi, the rear door closed. It had been bright on the parking stand, but with the door closed, it was dark in the cavernous interior of the airplane. Parker felt fear build up in him again. He forced himself to think of other things. He remembered, for instance, that the C–130 could carry sixty-four parachutists or ninety-two troops. Which meant it was only two-thirds full. Then the pilot in him made him evaluate the C–130's pilot's takeoff skill. His takeoff roll was short, and he banked to the north immediately, leveling off and changing to cruising power at no more than 3,500 feet . . . not bad.

The Green Beret master sergeant had an electric bull horn, to which a line was attached that let him carry it when he jumped. He put it to his mouth.

"We won't be up here long," he said. "So make sure you're ready to go."

Five minutes later, he gave the order: "Stand up!"

Everybody stood up.

"We're going to go out the back door," he said. "It's easier that way."

The rear cabin door opened down and became an extension of the floor. The noise level increased. Parker prayed that he would not throw up and shame himself on his first day.

The Green Beret master sergeant held up his right hand, the

index finger crooked. It was unmistakable: "Hook up!"

Everybody hooked the static line hook to a stainless steel wire.

The Green Beret master sergeant balled his fists and held them in front of his chest, then made a shaking movement as if he was trying to shake something loose. The miming was clear: "Check your equipment."

Each member of the incoming class turned to the man nearest him and checked his equipment.

The Green Beret master sergeant motioned for Parker and one other man to walk to the rear of the cabin, signaling with his hand where he wanted them to stop. Parker refused to look beyond the ledge the door had become. If he looked, he knew he would never be able to force himself to take that step. He saw the others fall in line behind him, and then—at the instructor's gesture—close up.

Holding onto the fuselage wall, the instructor walked out on the open door, then motioned for Parker and the other man (a sergeant) to go to the edge.

Parker felt faint and nauseous.

And then the instructor made a violent pointing movement with his left hand, finger extended, as clear an order as the others had been: "Go!"

Parker couldn't move. He saw the other line of parachutists begin to move. The instructor appeared beside him and made the signal again—not unkindly—as if Parker had somehow missed it. Parker was prepared for anger, contempt, scorn, even for an attempt to shove him over the edge—and he was not going to go. The friendly reminder overcame that. He stepped over the edge, was aware of the blast of the slipstream, then that he was upside down; and then he felt the tug of the static line as it pulled the drogue chute. A moment later the parachute slipped from its container. It filled with air, and there came the opening jolt.

As he floated toward the earth, faster than the others (for he was heavier than they were), he noticed several other things. They were much higher than he had thought. Seven, eight thousand feet, maybe higher. They must have been in a shallow climb all the way here, and he had been too terrified to notice. And then a body hurtled past him, arms and legs spread wide. Had someone's main and spare chutes failed to open? Was he going to crash? Was the parachutist's ultimate nightmare happening? . . . No. A drogue chute and then the main canopy came out of the falling man's back and filled. Parker just had time to realize that the falling man—who he now recognized as the Green Beret master sergeant—had made a "free fall" (opening his parachute himself, rather than having it opened automatically by a static line connected to the airplane), when he felt a strange warmth at his crotch. He had wet his pants.

They came to earth in an enormous field. He had time before he landed to realize that the people running the jump had known what they were doing. Hitting a field even this huge from the altitude they had jumped from had required a skilled judgment of prevailing winds by the pilot. Parker had no idea how it had been done.

He came down close to one end of the field. And he was out of his harness and had gathered up his chute before the last of the other jumpers touched down. There was a pathfinder team two hundred yards away, smoke still rising from the bomb that had given the C–130 pilot "winds on the ground." He walked to it, awkwardly, in all the equipment, carrying his chute in his arms. If anyone noticed the wetness at his crotch, no one said anything about it.

During the next—and very busy—seventy-two hours, they had been broken down into nine-man teams, shown where to pitch their shelter halves, where to dig latrines, and then they had entered what Parker thought of as a basic training program gone wild. They had alternately been given instruction (how to camouflage the face; how to butcher and cook a small pig, how to come down a tower—and later a cliff—using ropes, a mountain-climber's technique called "rappeling") and small infantry unit tactics.

The third morning, there had been an informal class in free-fall parachute jumping. The Green Beret master sergeant who had jumped into Camp McCall with them simply brought it up informally, almost casually mentioning that those who felt up to it would be provided with the opportunity to try it that afternoon.

Parker, in his naiveté, had concluded that he would have the opportunity to decide whether or not he could face up to that ordeal at some later date, after this frenzied version of basic training in small unit tactics was over. The opportunity came much sooner than he thought.

After lunch (10-in-1 rations cooked by the trainees themselves), they were shown their next problem. They would proceed from Point A to Point B by infiltration, making the twenty-six-mile trip on foot. They would have twelve hours to do it, starting at about 1500. People would be looking for them. But they were expected to move undetected. And they would reach' Point A by free-fall parachute jump. Those who didn't wish to attempt a free-fall parachute jump at this time would please stand up.

They are not going to shoot me if I stand up; not cut the buttons off my uniform and march me past ranks of troops while the band plays "The Rogue's March." The worst that can happen is that they will mark my records, "Unsuited for Special Forces Duty" and reassign me elsewhere, most probably back to aviation.

On the other hand, it is entirely likely that I will freeze going out of the airplane, and be unable to pull on the D-ring, and smash myself into pulp on the ground. Or that I will manage to open the chute and land in a tree somewhere, and break my leg, or my back.

And furthermore, he has made it plain that this is a volunteer thing; I am not being ordered to jump. He has made it easy to say, "No, thank you, not just yet."

He realized that he was being tested. They were making it easy to say no, because that would give them a better idea of his balls factor than ordering him to jump. They might not throw him out for refusing now; it was likely they would give him (and anyone else who declined) another chance, but he suspected that note would be taken of his response.

Two men, an officer and a sergeant, stood up and said they would really feel more comfortable making a free fall after some additional training. The Green Beret master sergeant seemed neither surprised nor disapproving, and the temptation to stand up himself was terrible.

He was again wrong in what he expected. He expected a bus ride back to Pope Field at Fort Bragg, and then another Air Force C–130 for the jump. Instead, they were route-marched back to the huge field where they had first landed. They traveled light, having been given permission to leave behind any equipment they didn't consider necessary to their infiltration man-uever. They had left behind everything but the harness of the field equipment. They were wearing brimmed fatigue caps instead of helmets. Rather than put up with its weight, Parker had also left his shelter-half behind. He had one blanket. Either it would not rain and he could stay warm with the blanket, or it would rain and he would be miserable. He had the .45 pistol in its holster and the M14 rifle and six magazines. He had a carbine bayonet, a canteen, a compass, a map, and enough dehydrated food for supper and breakfast.

At the field he expected some sort of inspection of equipment, a review of the problem, "constructive criticism" by the instructor of his planned route of infiltration.

Instead, a moment after the Green Beret master sergeant glanced at his watch and then at the sky, a familiar aircraft (an Otter) appeared low on the horizon, its flaps already down for landing.

The DeHavilland of Canada U–1A "Otter" was the largest single-engine aircraft then in military service. It was a high-wing monoplane powered by a 600-horsepower Pratt & Whitney engine with a maximum gross weight of 8,000 pounds; and it was capable of carrying eleven troops. Philip Sheridan Parker IV knew all about the Otter. He had nearly a thousand hours of Otter time. Most of it was in Alaska; a lot of it was on floats, some of it on skis.

He was unabashedly jealous of the pilot of this Otter as it taxied up to them, turned around, and gave them a blast of its propeller. The pilot would do his job here, let the idiots jump, and then fly back to Bragg for a cold beer before going to the club for the steak special.

The pilot was an old-time chief warrant officer. He looked familiar to Parker, and Parker hoped the reverse was not true.

"Who's senior?" the warrant asked.

Parker raised his hand.

"The way we do this, Captain," the chief warrant said, "is my crew chief, who's got a set of headphones, will tell you when to go. Understand?"

Parker nodded.

"I'm going to put you out at 4,000 feet," the warrant went on. "That doesn't give you much time if your main chute fails to open. On the other hand, you don't want two canopies open. Be careful."

He motioned them into the airplane's rear door as he climbed up the landing gear strut to the cockpit.

Since he was to be first out, Parker boarded last. There was not room enough in the Otter cabin to move around very much.

It was only when he got into the airplane that he noticed the seats had been removed. The crew chief had lined up the jumpers on the floor of the cabin, facing the rear, one man sitting within the spread knees of the man behind him.

It's a violation of flight safety regulations to transport personnel without seat belts, much less sitting unrestrained on the cabin floor.

Jesus, Parker, this is not the Army Aviation School!

The door had been removed. As soon as the Otter began to roll, there was a howl of wind, and where Parker sat it whipped at him.

The crew chief, a young sergeant, looked at Parker and pointed at his head. It was only after a moment that Parker realized the sergeant was telling him he had his fatigue cap on. If he jumped with it on, he would lose it. Parker took it off and put it inside his fatigue shirt.

A few minutes later, the crew chief motioned them to their feet.

Belatedly, Parker wondered about checking equipment. Who was to give that order?

Jesus, dummy, you're "senior."

He turned around awkwardly and checked the equipment of the sergeant behind him. He realized, shamefully, that the crew chief would not have jumped them if they had not checked their equipment. He would have given the order himself, and then reported:

That dinge captain, remember the one who wouldn't go? I knew we were going to have trouble with that one. He was so scared he forgot to check equipment!

The crew chief motioned him to the door.

He stood on the threshold, holding on to to each side of the door jamb, forcing himself to look straight ahead until the ache in his neck became so painful he could no longer maintain the awkward position.

When he did look down, he felt fear first, then nausea, then dizziness, and then—recognizing the symptoms—vertigo. He was disoriented, sick, and terrified.

The crew chief touched his shoulder.

He didn't move. He couldn't move.

The crew chief gave him a shove, not hard enough to push him out the door, but so there could be no mistaking the order. Parker looked at him and saw contempt in his eyes.

He pushed himself out the door. The horizontal stabilizer flashed past his face, and then he was turned over somehow and the world was turning around him, first sky, then earth, then sky again.

The D-ring! The fucking D-ring!

He put his hand to his chest, found the D-ring, and pulled. It came off in his hand, which somehow surprised him. He was aware of something moving behind him. Then there was a jolt and a gentle popping sound as the canopy filled with air.

There was a tugging at his right leg. He looked down and saw the M14 dangling from a web cord. It had been strapped to his leg and had torn loose somehow. He wondered if he was supposed to try to pull it up and strap it in place again. There wasn't going to be time for that. The ground, a much smaller field than before, was coming up to meet him. He noticed for the first time that an H-19 was sitting on the ground, and to judge from its slowly spinning rotors, hadn't been there very long.

Surprise, surprise! Now that you've jumped from an Otter, you're going to do it all over again from an H-19.

He landed badly, knocking the wind out of him, frightening him badly for a moment.

"You all right, Captain?" a voice asked. What he saw was highly shined boots and above them stiffly starched fatigue trousers. He looked further up and saw Colonel Paul Hanrahan. That explained the H-19.

"I'm all right, sir," he said, struggling to his feet.

"Got something for you," Hanrahan said. He held something in front of Parker's face. It was a brand-new major's gold oak leaf.

(Four)
The Office of the Commandant
U.S. Army Special Warfare School
Fort Bragg, North Carolina
1645 Hours, 20 May 1959

"Go right in, Major," Sergeant Major Taylor said when Parker appeared in his office. "The colonel's waiting for you. May I offer the major a cup of coffee in addition to my congratulations?"

"Yes, indeed, Sergeant, you certainly can," Parker said. He

was a coffee snob. In the Olden Days, before he lost his mind and joined Special Forces, every morning he had ground the beans of coffee Toni's father sent them from Boston and brewed coffee which he then carried around all day in a thermos. There was no way he would drink a lesser brew. "For the last four days, I have been drinking a black liquid made from a mysterious black powder and water laced with a purifier that smelled like horse piss," he said.

Taylor laughed.

Parker knocked at Hanrahan's open door and was motioned in.

"Major Parker reporting as ordered, sir," he said, as he saluted.

"My, don't you look spiffy?" Paul Hanrahan said. He had flown Parker back to Fort Bragg with him, and ordered him to get a bath and a shave and into army greens before coming to his office.

"Thank you, sir," Parker said.

Hanrahan handed him a box.

"This is no present," he said. "I expect to be reimbursed, but if there is anything faster in the army than a newly promoted corporal getting his stripes sewn on, it is a newly promoted major putting on his first hat with the scrambled eggs."

Parker took the cap from the box and put it on. It fit. Hanrahan had gone to the trouble of going to his records for his hat size.

"Thank you, sir."

"Take a look at yourself in the mirror," Hanrahan said, indicating the door to his latrine, "and when you come back, give me $42.55."

"Yes, sir," Parker said.

"I gather you approve," Hanrahan said, dryly, when Parker came back into the office.

"I was a captain a long time, Colonel," Parker said. "I was about to give up hope."

"I know," Hanrahan said, seriously.

Sergeant Major Taylor delivered the coffee.

"In case the colonel hasn't noticed, sir," Taylor said, "duty hours are over."

"He wants to offer you an intoxicant, Major," Hanrahan said. "Isn't that shocking?"

"I'm not shocked, sir," Parker said.

334 *W.E.B. Griffin*

"I need about five minutes of Major Parker's time, Taylor," Hanrahan said, "before we get into the booze. If you want to get home, leave the file drawer unlocked."

"I'd like to have a drink with the major, sir," Taylor said.

"Give us five minutes," Hanrahan said. "And make sure that photographer doesn't get away."

"Yes, sir," Taylor said. He left the office and closed the door after him.

"The reason I don't have a copy of your promotion orders to give you, Phil," Hanrahan said, "is because they haven't been cut."

"Sir?"

"Oh, don't worry. It's official. I got the word from DCSPERS."

That deserved an explanation, and Parker waited for it.

"DCSPERS has asked me to counsel you, Major," Hanrahan said.

"I don't quite understand, sir."

"You have been wronged by the system, Phil. The reason you were not selected for promotion a lot sooner was because your name was never presented to a board."

"I don't understand, sir."

"It was a fuck-up," Hanrahan said. "A simple fuck-up, for which somebody is responsible. DCSPERS is concerned that you may decide that the fuck-up was intentional, and based on the color of your skin. For what it's worth, I don't think that's the case."

"That's good enough for me, sir," Parker said, immediately.

"In any event, they're trying to make amends. Your date of rank will be about two years ago. He didn't know for sure, but he guesstimated two years."

"That's very nice," Parker said.

"No back pay, unfortunately, but I had the feeling talking to him that if that had been possible, you'd have gotten it."

"I'm perfectly happy with the gold leaf, Colonel," Parker said.

"There's something else, probably more important than the pay," Hanrahan said. "Speaking bluntly, I'm well aware that you came here because you thought you were never going anywhere in aviation; and this was your last, desperate hope to get promoted."

"Yes, sir," Parker said.

"You're not really the super-trooper type, Parker, and we both know it."

"Yes, sir."

"Technically, I was not authorized to recruit field-grade officers," Hanrahan said. "And technically, you have been a major for two years. DCSPERS is therefore willing to reassign you to aviation, in a position not only commensurate with your grade and experience, but taking into consideration the wrong that has been done to you."

Parker didn't reply.

"I suppose there is in the back of his mind the hope that this action will keep you from running to the NAACP," Hanrahan said. "I told him I thought that was unlikely, but I didn't feel he believed me."

"There is no question of that, sir," Parker said. "It never entered my mind."

"I have the feeling that if you were to make your views known about where you would like to be assigned, that could be worked out within the army's personnel requirements."

"Sir, I believe that an officer is responsible for his actions. I volunteered for Special Forces, and I would like to stay here. But..."

"Phil, if I were you, I'd go back to aviation," Hanrahan said.

"Colonel, I don't think I have any choice," Parker said.

"Great! Where do you want to go?"

"Please let me explain, sir," Parker said.

"That's absolutely unnecessary, Phil."

"When I stand in the door of an airplane, Colonel," Parker said, "I'm terrified."

"But you've jumped."

"When I jumped into McCall, I wet my pants," Parker said, quickly. "And today when I went out of the Otter, I had vertigo."

"And that's why you 'have no choice'?"

"Yes, sir. I've been able to do it so far, but one day I just won't be able to hack it."

It was a moment before Hanrahan spoke.

"I'm familiar with that," he said, finally. "Years ago, there was a bright and bushy-tailed second lieutenant from the Point who volunteered for parachute duty when they were just thinking of paratroops. You know the phrase, 'when Christ was a corporal'?"

"Yes, sir."

"MacMillan was a sergeant in those days," Hanrahan said. "Anyway, one time, before they came up with the idea of spare chutes, the young lieutenant went out the door and it didn't open. He fell maybe two thousand feet before he could get it out of the bag. From then on he had nightmares. Everybody thought he was tough, and he knew that anybody who quit jumping was a craven coward, that real men weren't frightened. And he had a wife before whom he did not wish to appear a coward. So what to do? He knew he was eventually going to collapse. In this particular case, he prayed for a broken leg—broken just bad enough to keep him off jump status, but not too bad to invalid him out of the service.

"But he kept jumping and jumping, and kept on having plenty of nightmares—but no injuries. So one day, all the officers were called in to meet a strange civilian from Washington who was recruiting brave and heroic paratroopers for something even more dangerous. They planned to drop these people behind enemy lines, where they would annoy the enemy and tie down lots of troops looking for them. The man from Washington told them they had no more than a twenty-five percent chance of surviving the war. The lieutenant I'm talking about, and by now you know I'm talking about Paul Hanrahan, volunteered on the spot. The way he saw it, that meant only one more jump. No more twice a week onto Bragg or Benning. With a little bit of luck, he could stay behind enemy lines—*on the ground*—until the war was over. As it happened, I made two more jumps, both into Greece. I awe people because I have combat stars on my jump wings. But I haven't jumped since, and I pray to God I never have to again."

"Would you, if you had to?" Parker asked.

"That question is the one I should be asking you," Hanrahan said. "But I'll answer it. If I had to, I think I could. But I don't *know*."

"What could I do around here and not jump?"

"Oh, I think we could find somewhere you could earn your pay, Major," Hanrahan said. "I seem to recall you know how to fly airplanes."

"I'd like to stay, sir, if you'll have me," Parker said.

"I'd like to have you, Phil," Hanrahan said.

They shook hands, as if they had just completed some business deal.

"I took the liberty, Phil, of telephoning your wife to inform her that the army had somewhat belatedly recognized your sterling qualities."

"Thank you, sir."

I would rather have done that myself.

"I had to tell her, to explain why Lowell Airlines was flying her and the kids to Bragg," Hanrahan said. he looked at his watch. "They should be here in about an hour, which will give us time to have a drink with Sergeant Major Taylor, and then another drink at the club."

"Lowell's flying them over, sir?"

"He's happy for you," Hanrahan said.

They looked at each other.

"Since I had the DCSPERS in a weakened condition," Hanrahan said, "I asked him to inquire if Major Lowell had also been the victim of an error. He telephoned thirty minutes ago to report that Major Lowell's name has been twice times presented to a board for promotion. He has not been selected."

"If he doesn't make it soon," Parker said, "he'll be thrown out."

"He would have been so notified this month. But because of the Cuban situation, officers who would have been involuntarily separated because of failure of selection for promotion are being temporarily retained."

"Jesus!"

"He doesn't know, and I am faced with the dilemma of whether or not I should tell him."

"Are you going to tell him?"

"Not tonight," Hanrahan said.

"I wish you hadn't told me," Parker said.

"I don't suppose I should have," Hanrahan said. "But you and I are in that very small group who feel Lowell is a fine officer."

They looked at each other, and then—as if on command—shrugged their shoulders in gestures of helplessness.

"Your house apes will be fed with my house apes at my quarters," Hanrahan said, "while the big people eat at the club."

"That's very kind of you, sir," Parker said.

"My pleasure," Hanrahan said. He raised his voice. "Taylor! The booze! And the photographer."

He opened his desk drawer and tossed Parker a green beret. "Put that on," he said.

"I'm not entitled to it, am I?"

"I'm still working on the regulations as to just who is a Green Beret and who isn't. Right now, all I have down for sure is that the individual be parachute qualified, and either go through the school or have previous combat experience leading native troops. You had Koreans attached to you. That makes you qualified."

Sergeant Major Taylor handed Parker a glass of bourbon, then handed one to Hanrahan, and then took one himself. They touched glasses and drank them down. Later they posed for the official picture, pretending that the sergeant major and the commandant were pinning gold leaves to the epaulets of newly promoted Green Beret Major Philip Sheridan Parker IV.

XVI

(One)

PRIORITY

HQ DEPT OF THE ARMY
WASH DC 2000 ZULU, 11 MAY 59

COMMANDING GENERAL ARMY THREE FT MACPHERSON GA
COMMANDING GENERAL ARMY FOUR FT SAM HOUSTON TEX

INFO: COMMGEN CONARC FT MONROE VA
     COMMGEN FT KNOX KY
     COMMGEN FT RUCKER ALA
     COMMGEN 2ARMDDIV FT HOOD TEX
     PRES USA AVN BD FT RUCKER ALA
     CO USA AVN COMBAT DEVELOPMENTS OFFICE FT RUCKER
     ALA

1. FOLLOWING FOR INFORMATION AND APPROPRIATE ACTION.
2. DA WILL SHORTLY ISSUE ORDERS REDESIGNATING 3087TH AVI-

ATION CO (TANK DESTROYER) (PROVISIONAL) TO BE 3087TH AVI-
ATION BN, AND ASSIGNING 3087TH AVIATION BN TO 2ND ARMORED
DIVISION, FT HOOD, WITH DY STATION FT KNOX.

3. DA WILL SHORTLY ISSUE ORDERS CONSTITUTING 3088TH AVI-
ATION CO (ARMED HELICOPTER) (PROVISIONAL), 3089TH AVIATION
CO (ARMED HELICOPTER) (PROVISIONAL), AND 3090TH AVIATION
CO (RECONNAISSANCE) (PROVISIONAL) ASSIGNED TO 3087TH AVI-
ATION BN.

4. PERSONNEL AND EQUIPMENT PRESENTLY ASSIGNED 3087TH
AVIATION CO WILL BE TRANSFERRED TO 3087TH AVIATION BN. NO
CHANGE IN COMMAND IS ANTICIPATED AND COMMANDING OF-
FICER 3087TH AVIATION BN IS DIRECTED TO MAINTAIN LIAISON
WITH USA AVN BD AND USA AVN COMBAT DEVEL OFC WHO WILL
CONTINUE TO MAKE RECOMMENDATIONS REGARDING EQUIP-
MENT AND PERSONNEL TO DCSOPS.

                FOR THE DEPUTY CHIEF OF STAFF, OPERATIONS
                BELLMON, BRIG GEN
                DIRECTOR, ARMY AVIATION

(Two)
The Rod, Reel and Gun Club
Fort Knox, Kentucky
12 May 1959

Lieutenant Colonel Thomas B. Warner, commanding officer
of the 3087th Aviation Company (Tank Destroyer) (Provisional) had two visitors on 12 May 1959. The first didn't
surprise him at all, although he was made a little uncomfortable
by his presence.

He had not been at all surprised when he had received word
at 0830 from Godman Field that a Major Lowell would land
in fifteen minutes and had requested ground transportation.
They had a lot to talk about, regarding equipment for another
rocket chopper company and an aviation reconnaissance company, and he welcomed what Lowell would have to say.

He also worried that Lowell would put him on the spot about
his taking command of one of the companies. The armed chopper was really Lowell's baby, and he was of the right grade.
It would be natural for him to expect command of one of the
companies . . . but he wasn't going to get it. The commanders
had already been picked, and Lowell wasn't one of them.

Warner really couldn't figure Lowell out. He was at once

a terribly bright, very efficient officer with a distinguished record, and he was on somebody's fuck-up list. Warner had heard stories, some of them incredible, but so far had been unable to get any straight poop.

He sent a jeep to fetch Lowell from the airfield to Moving Target Range No. 3, which had, for all practical purposes, been turned over to him for the rocket chopper program.

To Warner's relief, Lowell didn't bring up the subject of his being given a command. Apparently he already had the word that he wouldn't be given one of the companies. Warner, who had come to like Lowell, hoped that the word had been broken to him gently and that they had thrown him some kind of a decent bone. It was more than possible that Lowell was about to be promoted and had been denied a command for that reason. It had already been decided that aviation companies should be commanded by majors, and there would be little sense in giving Lowell a company if his promotion made it necessary to transfer him soon afterward.

It was also possible, Warner thought, that when Lowell was promoted, he would either be assigned to Washington (he spent a lot of time with General Bellmon) or maybe to Aviation Combat Developments.

They had spent the morning alternately watching the progress of the training program and making changes in the provisional company's TO&E, in order to set up a battalion headquarters and headquarters company, and to provide aircraft (including fixed wing) for the new provisional reconnaissance company. The morning had gone quickly.

"Let's go get something to eat," Warner suggested at 1200.

He motioned his jeep driver into the back seat and drove them himself to the Fort Knox Rod, Reel & Gun Club. It served a really nice hamburger and cole slaw and was a much more convenient place than the club or the snack bar on the post would have been.

"Have you ever been here before, Lowell?" Warner asked, as they pulled up outside the building.

"I used to practically live here," Lowell said.

"Oh?" Warner replied. It was a request for information, and after obviously thinking about it, Lowell provided it.

"When I was a second lieutenant, I was assigned to the Armor Board," he said. "I was an assistant project officer on the M46 with the 90 mm tube. I put at least ten percent of the total scrap metal on your range there myself."

Another mystery, Warner thought. Second lieutenants were rarely assigned to the Armor Board. The Board wanted personnel with experience, and second lieutenants—almost by definition—don't have experience.

"My son was born at Knox," Lowell added.

"I didn't know you were married," Warner said. He was surprised. Many of the fantastic tales he'd heard about Lowell dealt with his expertise in the bedroom. He'd even heard that he had been involved with a senator's wife.

"My wife is dead," Lowell said.

"I'm sorry."

"She's been dead a long time," Lowell said. "As a matter of fact, I'm about to try it again."

"Well, congratulations," Warner said.

"It's getting to be a real pain in the ass," Lowell said. "What I would like to do is just go away somewhere and get married. That is not proving possible."

"Big weddings mean something to women," Warner said.

"The goddamned tribal instinct is what it is," Lowell said.

Warner laughed, and they went inside. Lowell bought lunch for the three of them, taking from his pants pocket a fifty dollar bill from a folded stack that looked as if it had nine brothers.

They had eaten their hamburgers and slaw and were having a second cup of coffee when the two women appeared. Few women patronized the Rod, Reel and Gun Club, and the appearance of any female caused raised eyebrows. In this case, highly raised, for one of the two ladies who walked into the room was Mrs. David Henderson, the wife of the post commander. Lowell knew the other.

Warner had quickly decided that the general's lady and the lady with her were on some do-good mission, Save the Squirrels or something, when it became apparent that they were headed right for his table.

He and Lowell stood up; and in a moment, the driver also remembered his manners.

"We're going to have to stop meeting this way," Lowell said to the woman with Mrs. Henderson, "People will begin to ask questions."

"You know Phyllis, I think, Craig?" the woman said.

"Oh, yes. How are you, Mrs. Henderson?"

"It's nice to see you, Major," Mrs. Henderson said.

"This is Sergeant Walters," Lowell said, introducing the driver. "And I'm sure you know Colonel Warner."

"Hello, Tom," Mrs. Henderson said.

"I don't," the other woman said. "How do you do, Colonel? I'm Barbara Bellmon."

Bellmon's wife. What do you know?

She offered her hand to the sergeant too, and spoke to him.

"Could I ask you to entertain Mrs. Henderson while I have a word with the reluctant groom here, Sergeant?"

"Yes, ma'am," the sergeant said, less uncomfortable than Warner would have thought he would be. "Can I get you a burger? Or something else?"

"I was about to say 'no, thank you,'" Mrs. Henderson said. "But I really would like a hamburger."

Before Warner could reach in his pocket for money, Sergeant Walters had gone to the counter. It was an interesting question: Should a general's wife accept a hamburger from a sergeant? Or should she make him uncomfortable by refusing his offer? A hamburger wasn't going to break the sergeant, Warner concluded, and buying it for the general's wife would probably make him feel good.

"I am led to believe," Mrs. Henderson said, nodding to where Barbara Bellmon had led Lowell, "that that'll be either a quick surrender, or a long and bloody battle."

(Three)

"Your move," Lowell said to Barbara Bellmon.

"I beg your pardon?"

"I would ordinarily ask what I can do for you," Lowell said. "And I would mean it. Today, however, I am slightly suspicious of your presence here. You're liable to ask me for something I won't deliver."

"Bob sent me," she said. "Think that over while you get me a hamburger and a Coke."

"Sorry," he said, getting to his feet. "I didn't think."

"That happens with you, doesn't it, Romeo?" Barbara replied, smiling sweetly at him.

He got her a hamburger and a Coke, had his coffee mug refilled, and went back to the table.

"You say Bob sent you?"

"And Cynthia, and your cousin Porter."

"Ah ha, the plot thickens."

"I understand you were a naughty boy at your engagement party," Barbara said.

"I was a little late getting there, if that's what you mean."

"That's not what I mean, and you know it. You threatened to break somebody's arm."

"Figure of speech," he said. "Under the circumstances, I thought my behavior was impeccable."

"That's not what I heard," she said, "and I'm not talking just about what you said to the press agent. I understand you had words with Mrs. Schuyler Pelton, too."

Lowell gave her a dirty look.

"But, letting bygones be bygones," Barbara Belmon said, "shall we stop the crap and get down to business?"

"By all means," Lowell said.

"You and Cynthia will be married at the Farm," she said.

"We will?"

"You will have your bachelor dinner at the Army-Navy Club the night before. And there will be no naked ladies jumping out of cakes, either."

"Anything else?"

"Have you given any thought to a best man?"

"No," he said. "I haven't. Have you pressured Bob into volunteering? Is that what this is all about?"

"I have a much better idea," Barbara said.

"This has gone far enough," he said. "I'm not having any of this."

"Graf Peter-Paul von Greiffenberg," Barbara said.

"Jesus!" he said.

"You haven't even told him, have you?" Barbara asked. "Or your son?" Her tone was mingled annoyance and resignation.

"No," he said. "I haven't."

"Well, you can do that today," she said. "There's still time. I should have put my nose into this sooner."

"I'll call the Graf and I'll tell him, and I'll tell P.P., too."

"You'll call him and ask him to be your best man. And you'll ask him to make sure that P.P. has something suitable to wear for a garden wedding."

"I don't really think he'd want to come," Lowell said.

"Sometimes your stupidity amazes me," Barbara said.

"It's a long way to come for canapés," Lowell said.

"We will of course put the Graf up," Barbara said, "from the moment he and P.P. get off the plane until they get back on. That's very important to Bob, Craig. You can't tell him no."

"Have you got the room?" he asked.

"You know better than that," Barbara said. "The only reason we stayed in your house in Georgetown was because Bob can't stand my brother. There is plenty of room at the Farm—eight bedrooms, I think, or maybe nine."

"Goddamn it!"

"You're welcome," Barbara said.

"Oh, I don't mean you, you know that," Lowell said. "I wish that we could just go find a justice of the peace, or something."

"Well, you can't, so get your show on the road," she said. "Among other things, I'll need your guest list within the next day or two."

"What guest list?"

"That's names of people written on a piece of paper," she said. "So they can get invitations."

"Who the hell am I supposed to invite?" he asked.

"I thought you would never ask," Barbara said and took a typewritten list from her purse and handed it to him. "Go over this in the next twenty-four hours, add some, and delete only those whose arms you are liable to threaten to break."

"I told you that was just a figure of speech," he said. She met his eyes but didn't reply. "I'll pay for all this, of course," he said.

"No," she said. "Despite her having heard you saying she looked and talked like a character in a *New Yorker* cartoon, Mrs. Pelton insists on paying for the reception. That's the bride's family's responsibility, anyway. Everything else, Bob and I are paying for, and that's not open to debate. You know how Bob feels about the Graf. And, luckily, we can afford it."

Lowell took a pen from his pocket and wrote a name on the guest list.

"Who did I forget?"

He nodded his head toward Lt. Colonel Tom Warner.

"Since you have on here the name of every other sonofabitch who ever wore a uniform," he said, "might as well include him. He's both a nice guy and a comer."

It had been a surrender, Barbara Bellmon thought, rather

than a long and bloody battle. In his own way, she knew, Craig Lowell was grateful to her.

(Four)
Walter Reed U.S. Army Medical Center
Washington, D.C.
0830 Hours, 20 June 1959

The commanding general of the Walter Reed U.S. Army Medical Center, a physician and a major general, was more than a little surprised by the telephone call he received from the major general commanding the Military District of Washington.

"Are you sure you've got the right woman, Ernie?" he asked. Ernie was sure.

"I'll take care of it," the commanding general of Walter Reed said. He buzzed for his secretary.

"Will you ask Colonel Horter to come see me right away?" he directed. "And arrange for a car... no, tell my driver to stand by."

"Yes, sir."

Lieutenant Colonel Florence Horter, Army Nurse Corps, reported to the Medical Center commander in operating theater greens. He noticed that there was a spot of blood on her lower sleeve. Colonel Horter might not be awed enough by his summons to change into a uniform, but he didn't think she would purposely show up in bloody greens.

"You wanted to see me, sir?"

Lt. Colonel Horter was a plump, plain-faced woman of fifty-five. She had been an army nurse for eighteen years, and now had a number of highly placed friends in the army medical establishment. The commander had been told by two distinguished surgeons—one in the service and one now teaching at Johns Hopkins—that they preferred Florence Horter as a gas-passer over anyone else they knew, including all the doctors of medicine who chose to specialize in that branch of hhe healing arts.

Her record had seen her assigned to Walter Reed, where she was carried on the TO&E as a senior operating room nurse. She functioned, in fact, as a gas-passer, unless she honored some distinguished cutter by volunteering to assist him. She had recently developed the unfortunate habit of referring to

interns and some residents as "Sonny," which offended their
sense of dignity enough so that official complaints had been
raised. She was also feuding with the Chief of Nursing Services, whom she had described as a "company clerk in a skirt."

But while she enjoyed the respect of some eminent physicians, she was not the sort of woman who traveled in high
places, and she was about to travel in about the highest Washington had to offer.

"Colonel," the Medical Center commander said, "it is the
desire of the commanding general of the Military District of
Washington that you present yourself at the VIP waiting room
of the Air Force Special Missions Squadron at Andrews Air
Force Base not later than 1100 hours. Dress is optional, which
I take to mean you can either wear what my wife would call
a dressy dress, or army blue."

"What's going on?"

"The Military District commander—if indeed he knew—
did not elect to take me into his confidence. You will return
to Washington later this afternoon. My driver will take you out
there."

"And you don't know what it's all about?"

"I haven't the faintest," he confessed.

(Five)
Andrews Air Force Base
Washington, D.C.
1105 Hours, 20 June 1959

The dispatch of Air Force Special Missions Flight 6–20–
09, a VIP configured C-131 (that is, an air force Convair
originally configured to serve as Air Force Two when the Vice
President did not require a larger aircraft) was delayed five
minutes by the failure of Major Sanford T. Felter to appear.

He was brought by a yellow-and-black checkered pickup
truck out to the aircraft as it sat just off the threshold to the
active runway. The stair to the rear door was lowered and Felter
and an army nurse (of all things) in full uniform, her hair blown
out of place by the prop blast of the idling engines, came up
the stairs.

The DCSINTEL was aboard the plane with several assistants, as was the Deputy Chief of Naval Intelligence. And so
were two (of four) Deputy Directors of the Central Intelligence

Agency; a Deputy Director of the Defense Intelligence Agency; and Spires I. Ranaldo, an assistant Secretary of State with some kind of vague, high-level intelligence function. None of these officials were used to being kept waiting, and especially not by a light bird. But no one asked Felter where he had been. They were afraid that the simple question, "Where the hell have you been?" would get the same answer Felter had often given before: "I was with the President."

The flight to Idlewild International on Long Island took about forty minutes, but they were in the stack over New York for nearly an hour, until the pilot demanded a landing priority. The glistening Convair taxied up to the terminal at almost the same moment as Lufthansa Flight 606 (inbound from Frankfurt am Main) did.

"Perhaps," Felter announced loudly, "it would be best if Colonel Horter and I went to meet the Graf."

It wasn't a command, certainly, but it was a reminder that there was a chance one or more of them would be recognized.

"I'll come, Felter," Spires I. Ranaldo announced, "and get them through customs."

"I didn't think about that," Felter confessed.

The three of them went down the stairs of the rear door, and came to a metal door leading to the terminal from the parking ramp under the passenger ramp. The door was normally locked, but an officer in the uniform of a Customs and Immigration Service captain was waiting for them, holding it open.

Spires I. Ranaldo had not really gone with Felter and the nurse to get Generalmajor Graf von Greiffenberg through customs. He went along to make sure the orders he had issued from Washington were smoothly carried out.

When Lufthansa 606 had contacted New York Approach Control, there had been an inflight advisory: Generalmajor Graf von Greiffenberg and party were to exit the aircraft before other passengers; they would be met by officials who would clear their baggage through customs as it was taken from the airplane.

The pilot of Lufthansa 606 was not surprised. Before the passengers had been boarded at Frankfurt, the aircraft and all luggage loaded aboard had been subjected to a minute inspection. The Graf and his party had been the last to board the aircraft, and they had come to the airplane on the ground, alone and by car, rather than through the terminal and on the bus.

And when he'd taken off and was passing through 20,000 feet, there had been a "coincidental" meeting of a flight of Luftwaffe fighter planes on a "training mission" that had headed on the same course, two thousand feet higher, until they were out over the Atlantic.

The Graf was preceded off the aircraft into the terminal by two well-dressed, burly young men, and by his grandson, a twelve-year-old blond boy already starting to turn gawky.

"My dear Felter," the Graf said, pushing past his escorts to offer his hand to Felter. "What a pleasant surprise!"

His English was flawless, as much American as British.

"Uncle Sandy," the boy said, offering Felter his hand. Felter hugged him, which seemed to make the boy uncomfortable— not at the affection, but because he thought it made him look like a child.

And then the Graf saw Florence Horter.

"My dear Colonel," he said, and took the hand she offered as a handshake and bent over it instead and kissed it.

Lt. Colonel Horter blushed.

"Nice to see you, General," she said.

"What do you think?" the Graf said, pushing the boy toward her proudly.

"He's beautiful!" Florence Horter said. She blurted: "He looks like both of them!"

"Yes," the Graf said. "I've often thought so. Peter, this is Colonel Horter. She's a friend of your father's, and she was a very good friend to your mother when your mother really needed a friend."

"How do you do?" Peter-Paul Lowell said, formally, offering his hand. She took the hand, and then hugged the boy to her.

"Your mother would be very proud of you," she said. After she let him go, she turned away and fished in her purse. She came out with a handkerchief and blew her nose loudly.

The Graf by then had been introduced to Spires I. Ranaldo, who took the opportunity to express his hope that while the Graf was in Washington, he could find an hour or so for a talk with the Secretary of State. When the Graf, graciously, said that he was honored by the invitation and would make every effort to find the time, Ranaldo was smugly pleased that he had outfoxed the others on the plane, all of whom wanted a private conversation with the Graf.

They went down the stairs to the parking ramp, and up into the Convair. Right on their heels came three Customs and Immigration officers bearing the luggage.

"Idlewild ground control, Air Force Four at TWA six for taxi and takeoff."

"Air Force Four is cleared to taxi from TWA six via taxiway three two to the threshold of the active, one zero."

And three minutes later, after the Convair had traveled down a taxiway parallel to the one on which twenty-three other aircraft waited for their turn to take off: "Idlewild departure control clears Air Force Four as number one for takeoff on one zero. New York area control clears Air Force Four direct Washington Vector Three. Report passing through one zero thousand."

"Air Force Four rolling."

Forty-six pilots in twenty-three airplanes either cursed the goddamned bureaucrats jumping ahead of them in line, or wondered who the hell Air Force Four was.

In Air Force Four, Generalmajor Graf von Greiffenberg took Lt. Colonel Florence Horter's hand in his.

"Tell me, Florence," he said. "I may call you Florence?"

"Sure."

"Have you met the lady?"

"Yeah. Craig brought her over to my apartment a couple of nights ago."

"And?"

"She's all right, General. She's a lot like him. I suppose that comes with having all that money. Good looking. Well stacked. I think they'll be able to make it all right."

"Good," the Graf said, squeezing her hand. "Good!"

(Six)
The Farm
Fairfax County, Virginia
1130 Hours, 21 June 1959

Barbara Bellmon finally stopped Craig Lowell's nonsense by going out onto the middle of the unpaved road leading to the farm and holding up her arms like a traffic cop—devoutly praying that Craig had taught P.P. how to drive well enough to stop the Mercedes before he ran into her.

She thought she alone understood what Craig was up to. Everyone else—Bob, the Graf, Sharon, her own kids—thought it was another manifestation of Lowell's irresponsibility, to teach a twelve-year-old to drive...in a Mercedes, for God's sake! And on the day when he was to be married!

"I learned how to drive when I was twelve," Lowell had answered. "And I need something to do, anyway."

It wasn't that, Barbara thought, or it wasn't *only* that. Lowell was delighting in his son, which was a perfectly normal thing for a father to do—and especially understandable for a father who saw his son as rarely as Lowell saw his.

The Mercedes skidded to a stop four feet from her.

"I hate to do to this to you, P. P.," Barbara said, walking to the boy at the wheel. "But the sheriff is sending some people to control the traffic, and if they catch you doing this, they're going to put your father in jail."

"I see," he said.

"Balls," Lowell said.

"Would they really take him to jail?" Peter-Paul Lowell asked.

"Yes, I'm afraid they would," she said, as much to Lowell as to his son.

"We'll take one more lap around the block," Lowell announced. "And then we'll quit. OK?"

"Please," the boy said.

The "block" Lowell referred to was the dirt road running around the Farm. Each leg was a mile long.

"Once more, Craig," Barbara Bellmon said, and stepped aside.

Spinning its wheels, the Mercedes roared off. Lowell turned around in his seat and thumbed his nose at her, a wide smile on his face.

She went through the gate in the stone fence. There had been no place to erect the caterer's tent except on the tennis courts, because all the fields had been sown. That meant that the tennis courts would have to be resurfaced after three hundred people—half of them women in high heels—had walked all over them for five or six hours. They would have to pay for that. Cynthia's aunt was paying for the reception, but Barbara could hardly send her a bill for Repairs to Two Damaged Tennis Courts.

Not that she minded; but there were going to be still other expenses involved in getting Craig to the altar. Bob had insisted that they pick up the bill for the bachelor party the night before:

one hundred men—eighty percent of them officers—at the Army and Navy Club. One hundred dinners at $11.50 each plus whatever the bar bill would be was quite a bit of money.

And the simple little lunch she had planned to have for the "family" before the other guests arrived had gotten out of hand. She had originally thought it would be just her family, plus Craig, the Graf, and P.P., and maybe the Felters. But the two characters with the Graf, while they looked and acted like bodyguards, had turned out to be captains in the Bundeswehr, which meant they could not be handed a couple of sandwiches. And then Bob had told her that Sandy had called and said he was sending "some people" over—six of them—who had to "look like" guests. That meant they would have to be fed, too. When the number of people to be fed at the small, informal, "just family" lunch had passed twenty, she had called the caterer and ordered luncheon for thirty, with a reserve.

The guests would start arriving about half past one. Craig's stepfather, and his cousin Porter Craig and his family, had been originally scheduled to be put up in Craig's town house. But Porter Craig had telephoned to tell her that they had decided to turn the town house over to Mrs. Pelton and her party. They would be in the Hay-Adams Hotel instead.

"Are you sure you can get rooms?" Barbara had asked. The Hay-Adams was across Lafayette Square from the White House. It was expensive, chic, and sometimes hard to get in.

"Oh, I'm sure they'll take care of us," Porter said, with such easy certainty that she had wondered if Lowell's family owned that, too. Perhaps not the hotel, she had corrected herself, but the holding company which owned the holding company which owned the bank which owned the hotel.

Lowell and P.P. had spent the night with the Felters, in Felter's small house in a subdivision of Alexandria. They had driven out to the Farm in the morning in the roof-down Mercedes, which had been what triggered P.P.'s driving lesson.

At ten the night before, all the Macmillans but Roxy had shown up at the Farm by auto from North Carolina. They had to be put up at the Farm, too, of course. Mac and Bob had been in the stalag the Graf had presided over. At nine that morning, Lowell's airplane, flown by Warrant Officer Bill Franklin, had landed at Washington National. He had aboard Jane Jiggs and Melody Greer from Rucker, and Toni Parker, Roxy MacMillan, and Patricia Hanrahan from Bragg.

In what was obviously a fortunate coincidence, both the commanding general of Fort Rucker and the president of the Army Aviation Board had to visit Washington. They shared the piloting of an aircraft to get there, on which there was room to carry Captain Jean-Philippe Jannier, whose presence at the French Embassy in Washington had been requested by the French Military Attaché. They had refueled en route at Pope Air Force Base and at Fort Bragg, where, by a fortunate co-incidence, Colonel Paul Hanrahan and a M/Sgt Wojinski just happened to be at Base Operations, hoping to hitch a ride to Washington.

Barbara Bellmon wasn't all that close to Phil and Toni Parker, but she had insisted that they and Warrant Officer Franklin stay at the Farm. They were all very close to Lowell, and besides, she would never give them the slightest impression that their color could bar them from the Farm.

The house was full. If anyone else arrived, they would have to double up in the motel.

Barbara had wondered about transportation from Washington to the Farm. The question had also occurred to Mrs. Pelton, who announced that they had brought cars with them from "the city" and suggested that her chauffeur "serve as sort of a head waiter," to see that the cars were dispatched when and where needed.

"How many cars are there?" Barbara had asked.

"There's two from New York, mine and Porter's, and Porter is sending three from Broadlawns. Do you think that will be enough, or should I arrange to hire some? I always hate to ride in a hired car. It always make me think it's just come from a cemetery."

The cars—and by cars she meant of course limousines— were back-up transportation. Two Greyhound buses had been chartered to carry those who were not immediate family. The limousines were for the family, and the bride, and for those who missed the buses.

"I'm sure that will be enough," Barbara had told Mrs. Pelton.

Lowell and P.P. returned from their last lap at the moment the Reverend Dr. Thomas Grey Edwards, rector of St. Peter's Episcopal Church, who would unite the couple in the bonds of holy matrimony, arrived for lunch. The Reverend Doctor had sternly announced that he would not, could not, conduct the nuptial ceremony unless and until the bridal couple had been "counseled."

He had had a thirty-minute meeting with Cynthia, terminated when Lowell had called from Kentucky to announce he was unavailable. It had not been possible to get Craig any closer to him than that, so Barbara had scratched the Reverend and recruited the Chief of Chaplains. The Reverend Doctor had telephoned two days later (she suspected after the wedding plans had been revealed in the *Washington Post*) and announced that there were, of course, exceptions, and he was looking forward to performing the marriage.

Craig Lowell was to be married by a Reverend Doctor and a Reverend General.

The Reverend Doctor raised his eyebrows at the sight of the boy behind the wheel of the Mercedes, lowered them and smiled when he saw the genuinely touching sight of a father and son, and then raised them again when a waiter offered champagne, and P.P. reached for a glass without incurring parental correction.

(Seven)

Luncheon was very nice—quail. Barbara had not thought to specify what would be served (she recalled now that she had not been asked), and the caterer naturally had decided to provide what was most expensive—save Iranian caviar—in his repertoire. And there was a lot of wine.

The luncheon tables were under the tent at the tennis courts. When luncheon was over, they would be cleared and reset with the buffet for the reception. The wedding itself would be held behind the house, where an in-place rose arbor provided a suitable and lovely setting.

Barbara had been just about to tell her husband to tell Craig to get dressed (which would get him away with the table and the champagne) when she saw Mrs. Pelton's butler go to the table, catch Craig's attention, and then lead him from the table to a corner of the tent. There the butler handed him an envelope.

Barbara got up and walked to Lowell.

He looked at her from very bright eyes, and she could not tell if he was angry or sad.

"I'm very sorry to have done this to you," he said.

"Done what to me?"

He handed her the letter and walked away. She started to go after him, but stopped. It would be better to know what had so upset him, before trying to set it right. She read the note.

Dearest Craig,

I am truly sorry to do it this way, but there is no other way to do it.

If I came out there and faced you, I know that one look at you and I would be willing to take the chance, just so that I could be with you one more night. But that would be the cruellest thing I could do to the man I love.

This just wouldn't work. When I'm with you, I can fool myself. When I'm alone, I see things as they are. I see us, either in some terrible little place like Ozark, Alabama, with me trying be nice to people who bore me and hating you for making me be there, or in Palm Beach, with you fighting valiantly to keep yourself busy playing polo and hating me for making you give up your army.

That's another reason I didn't come out to face you with this. I think you would, given the choice, take me over the army and resign. And six months later, you would hate me for having forced you to make the choice. And I would hate myself for what I had made you do.

If I haven't made myself clear so far: I won't marry you, not today, not next week, not next month, not ever. *Because* I love you. Can you understand, my darling?

Cyn

"Oh, *shit!*" Barbara Bellmon said, so loudly that half of the thirty-odd people at the luncheon tables, the half that hadn't already been stealing curious glances at her anyway, turned their heads to her.

Barbara ran after Craig. But she was not surprised when she failed to catch up with him, or when—as she looked around the living room of the house—she heard the unmistakable sound of a Mercedes engine winding up in low gear. When she ran outside and through the gate to the road, she was able to catch only a fleeting glance of the baby blue Mercedes doing at least seventy and accelerating down the dirt road toward the highway.

Craig Lowell wasn't going to accept the letter as the last word. But he didn't think he was going to find Cynthia Thomas. Nor did he think that if he did find her, he would be able to change her mind. Cynthia Thomas was an intelligent, strong-willed woman who saw things clearly. It was for those reasons that Barbara Bellmon had liked her, and thought she would make a good army wife.

Barbara walked back under the tent on the tennis courts. Not unlike a corporal selecting volunteers to mow the grass before the orderly room, she pointed her finger first at her husband and then at Generalmajor Graf von Greiffenburg, and crooked it, summoning them to her.

(Eight)
The Marquis de Lafayette Suite
The Park-Sheraton Hotel
Washington, D.C.
1015 Hours, 22 June 1959

Captain Jean-Philippe Jannier sat with his back against the headboard of the double bed. A corner of the sheet covered his crotch, and a glass of champagne, which he had informed Melody Dutton Greer was the best thing in the world for a hangover, rested on his stomach.

There had been a party—not a wedding reception, to be sure, but a party. And everyone, from Mrs. Schuyler Pelton to Lt. Colonel Rudolph G. MacMillan, had gotten—in whatever their patois—bombed, plastered, blind, or tiddly.

At half past nine, Captain Jannier had led Mrs. Greer outside.

"Where have you been?" Melody had asked. "Where are we going?"

"I've been packing your things," he said.

A chauffeured Cadillac with a CD tag sat in the driveway. "What's this?"

"Bill," he said, referring to Warrant Officer Franklin, "is a charming fellow, but I would prefer to sleep with you."

Barbara Bellmon had apologized for having to put the two bachelors up together.

"Where could we go?"

"Oh, we should be able to find a motel someplace," he said.

"Where did the car come from?"

"The same place the motel did," he said, and gently pushed her into the car.

It wasn't a motel, of course, but the apartment the French Embassy maintained in the Park-Sheraton for very important visitors.

Melody Dutton Greer was standing by the window. She had opened the heavy velvet drape wide enough to see out, and that let enough light in to silhouette her body. She was wearing a simple cotton nightdress, and the sunlight made it translucent.

Captain Jean-Philippe Jannier had just decided that she had the most exquisite breasts he had ever seen—and he had seen a good many breasts in his day—when one of the two telephones on the bedside table rang.

One of them, he recalled from a previous stay in the Marquis de Lafayette Suite, was a direct line to the Embassy switchboard. The other was connected to the hotel switchboard. He had to wait for the second ring to see which was ringing, and then he made a mistake and picked up the wrong one.

"Jannier," he said, finally getting it right.

"Bill, Philippe," Warrant Officer Franklin reported.

"Have you learned anything?" Jannier asked. Melody left the window and sat on the bed.

"He left Teterboro at half past ten last night. He filed IFR to Atlanta, but he closed out his flight plan over Richmond, Virginia, ninety minutes later. He didn't land at Richmond. Christ only knows where he did land. There have been no reports of crashes."

"Don't be absurd," Jannier said, "if you're suggesting what it sounds like."

"Mac has a buddy at the FAA," Franklin went on. "Sooner or later, we're going to find out where he did land. They're checking."

"Well, at least he's not drinking," Jannier said.

"No," Franklin agreed.

Jannier thought of something. Since Franklin had flown to Washington in Lowell's airplane, he had to have a way to get back to the base.

"How are you going to go back to Rucker?"

"The women are going this afternoon, commercial," Franklin said. "I thought I'd stick around."

"Where are you?"

"At the Farm."

"Can you come here?" Jannier asked. "We can go back together."

"I'm going to have to hitch a ride," Franklin said. "I don't have enough money for an airplane ticket."

"Come here, right away," Jannier said. "Make sure everybody has this number, and then come here."

"Did you hear what I said about being broke?"

"I heard," Jannier said. "It should take you about an hour, if you leave now."

He hung up the telephone, smiled at Melody, and reached out and tenderly touched her cheek. Then he gave into the temptation and let the balls of his fingers slide down to touch her breast through the cotton nightdress.

"Well?" she demanded, catching his hand in hers.

"Well, when he left here, he must have gone to New York to look for her. Bill has found out that he left Teterboro last night. He filed an instrument flight plan to Atlanta, but closed it out over Richmond ninety minutes later."

"Which means he could be anywhere," she said.

He thought that there were few women who understood the intricacies of flying. It was another charming trait of his American.

"It also means he didn't rush out and get drunk," Jean-Philippe said. "He would not fly if he was drinking."

"He'll wait until he lands," she said, and chuckled. "And then . . ."

He nodded.

And then he saw tears in her eyes.

"You are his good friend," he said, "to weep for a friend."

Her face lost its smile.

"I am his friend," she said. "But I'm not crying for him."

"Oh?" he asked.

She let loose of his hand and stood up.

"I have something to say to you," she said. "And since you told Bill to come here, I have to say it now."

"Anything," he said.

"You stay where you are," she said.

"Huh?"

"Don't you come after me," she said.

She looked at him until he shrugged, accepting her odd command, and then she went back to the window. The sun turned her nightdress translucent again.

"You are going to have to get rid of Bill when he comes," she said. "Give him money to go back to Alabama, and get rid of him."

"I am flattered," he said.

"And then we are going to have to find a doctor," she said.

"Is something wrong? Are you sick, ma petite?"

"Not sick," she said. "Pregnant."

There was a pause.

"Are you sure?"

"Of course, I'm sure," she said, furiously. "This isn't the first time. What did you think I was doing in the bathroom when I woke up? Brushing my teeth?"

"I thought it was the alcohol," he said, truthfully.

"They call it morning sickness," she said, bitterly. "I'll pay for the abortion, of course," she went on. "It's my fault, not yours. I didn't do it on purpose, but it's still my fault. I brought a thousand dollars with me. But I don't know where to go."

She looked out the window, and he suspected she was crying. He wanted to go comfort her, but first things first.

He swung his legs out of the bed and picked up the Embassy telephone.

She heard him ask for an extension, and then she heard him say, and understood: *"Bonjour. Ici est Jannier. J'ai besoin d'une service privée."*

Good day. This is Jannier. I need a private service.

Then she put her index finger knuckle between her teeth and bit hard, so that it would hurt, so that she could think of that, the pain, and nothing else.

And then he was standing behind her. His hand gently touched her shoulder, and she allowed him to turn her around and put his arms around her.

"It's all arranged," he said. "He will telephone within the hour with the details."

"I'm so very sorry, Jean-Philippe," she said, fighting down sobs.

"I'm not," he said, tenderly and smugly.

What the hell was that supposed to mean?

"I said I was *sorry,*" Melody said.

"It seems that the problem," he said, his voice drolly amused as only a Frenchman reflecting on the customs of barbarians can be drolly amused, "even with a diplomatic passport, is not in getting a license, or an official, but in obtaining a certificate that one does not have a social disease. I told the manager to tell the Embassy physician that he has my word as an officer and a gentleman that neither of us are so afflicted, and that I would take it as a personal affront if he refused to issue the necessary documents."

She finally understood.

"You're talking about getting *married?*"

"What else?" Jean-Philippe Jannier asked, kissing the top of her head.

When Warrant Officer Junior Grade William B. Franklin came into the Marquis de Lafayette Suite of the Park-Sheraton fifty-five minutes later, he found Captain Jean-Philippe Jannier with a towel wrapped around his waist, sitting on one of the couches in the sitting room, talking to someone on the telephone. Franklin had learned French in Algeria. He understood what Jannier said.

"We shall expect you within the hour, then."

Jannier broke the connection with his finger and asked for the concierge. When he was informed that there was no concierge he asked for the manager. When the manager came on the line, he identified himself and said he would be grateful if the suite could be immediately cleaned up, and that he would require champagne and hors d'oeuvres for eight in an hour.

"And if there is a florist, would you have him send up some flowers? Roses, I think, would be nice. Some in vases, and a bouquet for a lady."

Then he hung up again and looked at Franklin.

"Wipe that look of moral outrage from your face, Bill, and go in the bath and have a shave, then change back into your dress uniform. In an hour, Melody and I are to be married, and I would be honored if you would be my best man."

XVII

(One)
Eglin Air Force Base, Florida
1615 Hours, 22 June 1959

"A" Team 59–23 (Training) had been jumped from an Otter
into a field on the Eglin Reservation ten days earlier.

Eglin was an enormous base, and the reason for that became
immediately clear once the team was on the ground. The vast
majority of it was swamp, useable only for the torment of Super
Boy Scouts in training.

Second Lieutenant Thomas J. Ellis, commanding "A" Team
59–23 (Training), had been issued seven maps. Six of the
seven were sealed in envelopes which were not to be opened
before the instructions on the envelopes told him to—except
in case "one or more members of the team suffers an injury of
a nature requiring medical evacuation." If that happened, they
would have to go back to step one. In other words, they'd have
to start all over again on the two-week problem.

The team was provided with sufficient rations for fourteen days. Unfortunately, no one—not even SFC Eaglebury (who could have been a linebacker for the Green Bay Packers)—could have carried fourteen days worth of rations, in addition to his other equipment, more than 2,000 yards across the swamp.

So, when they were on the ground in the swamp, the first thing Ellis had had to do was supervise the repacking of everybody's gear. Ninety percent of the "good" food (that is to say, "ham chunks w/raisin sauce" and "beef chunks w/gravy" and "chicken w/dumplings," canned during World War II) had to be left behind because of their weight and bulk. They carried with them foil envelopes of powdered eggs and soup; foil-wrapped "high protein" bars; powdered milk, tea, and coffee.

Plus, of course, radios, rifles, pistols, canteens, demolition kits, medical kits, and real (as opposed to dummy and blank) hand grenades and ammunition. In addition to their personal weapons, Training "A" Team 59–23 was equipped with a light Browning .30 caliber machine gun and ammunition for it and two .30 caliber Browning automatic rifles.

Lieutenant Ellis had first crossed swords with SFC Eaglebury over leaving those fucking BARs behind. The sonsofbitches weighed twenty pounds apiece, and they had to be fed with heavy magazines, each holding twenty rounds of .30–06 rifle cartridges. SFC Eaglebury had immediately expressed general disapproval of Ellis's repacking of their rations and other supplies, annoyance that he was ordered to leave his shelter half behind, and outright contempt when Ellis had announced they were going to leave the BARs behind with their chutes, discarded rations, and other equipment.

When they were gone, instructors would pick up what was left behind.

"Lieutenant," Eaglebury had told him, "you know what's going to happen if you leave the BARs behind?"

"Why don't you tell me, Sergeant?"

"We'll be a mile or so in the jungle, and they'll find the BARs. And they'll say that without them we can't accomplish our mission, and they'll make us start all over again."

"I don't think we can accomplish our mission carrying them with us," Ellis had replied. "We'll have to take that chance."

"And the next thing they'll decide," Eaglebury said, as if talking to a backward child, "is that a very good way to teach us *not* to leave our weapons behind is to let us run through the whole fucking program, and *then* tell us we had to have BARs, and *then* tell us to start all over."

It was possible that Eaglebury was right Ellis had decided. But it was certain that they couldn't carry the extra weight of two twenty-pound Browning automatic rifles and ten magazines through the swamp. The BARs had stayed.

All of Lieutenant Ellis's stalwart troops were older than he was. The youngest of them, a sergeant, was twenty-three—with five years' service already. It was not surprising that the rest had come to think of him (and to refer to him behind his back) as "the Boy Wonder." Or else, because of his recent grauation from Officer Candidate School (which had a six months' training program) they called him "the Six Months' Wonder."

All of them were either sergeants first class or master sergeants; members, therefore, of the two highest enlisted grades. Some of them had been nice guys, perfectly willing to play the game that their second lieutenant was an officer and therefore presumed to have the correct answers. Several of them had not. And one in particular, SFC Eaglebury, Edward B., was a real sonofabitch. From the moment they had first been out of sight of their superiors, SFC Eaglebury had made it quite plain that he thought his commanding officer was straight from the Beetle Bailey comic strip. As far as he was concerned, Ellis was absolutely incapable of finding his ass with both hands, much less of leading eight men across thirty miles of cypress swamp from Point A to Point B, in what was euphemistically described as a "map problem."

The map problems that Second Lieutenant Ellis had had trouble with in OCS at Benning now seemed child's play in comparison to this exercise, the sort of thing cub scouts did. What the Super Boy Scouts under his wise and mature command had been expected to do seemed on its face just about impossible. But their execution had proved to be more difficult than that.

The first map, the one issued just before the jump, had a blank spot in the middle. It was marked "uncharted." Among other things they had to do was fill in the blanks with paths, "geological features" (in the swamp, there were none), and "creeks and rivers" (the swamp was mostly water).

On the morning of the third day, he was permitted to open the first sealed map. The blank space was slightly smaller on

Map No. 2 than it had been on Map No. 1, and it showed the approximate location of a stream and a bridge they were to rig for demolition (but not actually blow). They didn't find the sonofabitch for thirty-six hours, during which SFC Eaglebury kept morale up by amusing the others with his impersonation of Lieutenant Ellis as a blind man—complete with a cypress pole cane.

By day ten their food was essentially exhausted, save for some high energy bars. They were obviously going to have to catch something to eat—"game" or "reptile" or "fowl."

The Super Boy Scout Rules, as the "Guidelines" were somewhat irreverently called, proscribed the use of "standard service weapons in the taking of game," but it was permitted to take game (including reptiles) by the "use of locally constructed snares, traps, etc." No instructions concerning the building of a snare or trap, et cetera, had been furnished; and none of the eight enlisted men on Ellis's team of budding Green Berets had even seen a snare or trap, or had any idea how to build and/or use one.

Eaglebury loudly announced that he didn't have the vaguest fucking idea how to find something wild in the swamp, much less kill it, and was happy to leave that little problem to Lieutenant Ellis. However, after they had failed to catch anything with snares or traps, he had a helpful suggestion.

"Grenade the bastards, Ellis," Eaglebury said.

"And how would I explain what happened to the grenades, Sergeant?"

"Just tell them you lost the bastards, Lieutenant. Who'd ever know?"

Ellis refused, although the temptation was great. His reasoning was that his "A" Team was unusual in that none of his troops was a country boy with hunting experience. Ordinarily, an "A" team would have somebody on it who could go out and "snare" or "trap" a turkey or shoot a wild pig with the .22 pistol as easily as going to the A&P and buying a frozen turkey. If he allowed the use of a grenade to kill something, the troops would get the idea it was all right. And it wasn't, for reasons having nothing to do with sportsmanship. Grenades would (a) be needed for a real mission and (b) make a hell of a noise, which would call attention to them.

Ellis's refusal to use grenades, in Eaglebury's opinion, made him chickenshit as well as stupid.

Ellis had done the only thing he could think of. He found some wild pig tracks on an island in the swamp. If pigs had been there before, it seemed to him, they would come back. But not if they saw somebody waiting for them. The solution to that was to hide someone by immersing him in the cruddy fucking water, so that he wouldn't be seen.

He toyed with the idea of having one of his men (Eaglebury came immediately to mind) do the hiding. There were two things wrong with that. He had heard somewhere that an officer should never order his men to do something he was unwilling to do himself (and he was pretty goddamned unwilling to play submarine in the swamp) and he was afraid that if he ordered Eaglebury to do it, Eaglebury would tell him to go fuck himself.

Ellis thus had to play Daniel Boone himself. He left the team on a small, semidry island and waded into the swamp toward the tracks. Despite the heat, he had just begun to shake from the water's chill when he heard a faint grunting sound that could be a pig. So he stayed there. And fifteen minutes later, a wild pig not much larger than a medium-size dog, came into sight, trotting along on thin legs.

It was the first time he had ever had a good look at a wild animal, and it was fascinating.

What is going to happen now, he thought, as he steadied the pistol against the cypress stump beside which he was nearly submerged, is that the fucking sights will be off. Among two thousand other things he had forgotten to do was zero in the pistol.

He could barely see the front sight over the silencer, which was a thick black cylinder and mounted to the .22's muzzle.

He fired when he thought he had the best shot he was going to get, and the wild pig looked only as if something had surprised it. Ellis was sure he had missed. But then the pig just crumpled to the dirt.

Ellis came out of the swamp water steadying the pistol with both hands, aiming at the animal as if it was a dangerous criminal capable of returning his fire. When he kicked it with his foot he was genuinely surprised to learn that it was dead.

When Ellis returned with the dead pig, he knew he had earned the admiration of everybody—except of course Eaglebury. Eaglebury announced that the pig hadn't been cleaned immediately, and was liable to poison them all. Besides, exactly how did Ellis plan to cook the fucking thing? Unless that was done right, they were all going to catch trichinosis.

"Fuck you, Eaglebury," M/Sgt Dessler suddenly snapped.

"*What* did you say?" Eaglebury growled.

"I said 'fuck you,'" Dessler said. "Leave the fucking lieutenant alone."

"Or what?"

"Or I'll shove that fucking dead pig up your ass!"

"You and who else?"

"Him and me, Eaglebury," SFC Talbot said. "The lieutenant got us something to eat. All you're giving us is a pain in the ass."

(Two)
The Office of the Commanding General
Fort Rucker, Alabama
1530 Hours, 3 July 1959

Major General Paul T. Jiggs answered one of the three telephones on his office desk, then handed it to Colonel William R. Roberts, with whom Jiggs had been having a serious talk.

"For you, Bill," Jiggs said.

"Colonel Roberts," he said, wishing that whoever was calling had waited until he was in his own office.

"Sergeant Kowalski, sir. You said I was to let you know the minute Major Lowell showed up."

"Has he?"

"The tower just called, sir. He ought to be on the ground in five minutes."

"Hold on, Sergeant," Roberts said. He covered the microphone with his hand.

"Lowell's five minutes out," he said to General Jiggs.

Jiggs shrugged, then asked: "Who's that?"

"Sergeant Kowalski," Roberts said.

"Tell him to meet Lowell and ask him to come here," Jiggs said.

Roberts nodded, relayed the message, and hung the telephone up.

"Well," Roberts said, "he did come back."

"I expected him back, Bill," Jiggs said. "But I was afraid it would be at 2350."

That was not quite the truth. Until now, Jiggs had not been sure what Lowell was liable to do. But now that he was back,

Jiggs felt more than a little disloyal to Lowell, and was not about to agree with Roberts's insinuation that Craig had gone on a binge.

As Jiggs should have known, Lowell was reporting in just before the end of duty hours on the last day of his leave. The day of departure (no matter what the hour) is a day of leave. The day of return (no matter what the hour) is a day of duty. It was like Lowell to report in during duty hours, not at two minutes to midnight.

When Lowell walked into Jiggs's office, he was wearing a tropical worsted uniform with creases indicating that he had been flying in it for some hours.

"Sir," Lowell said. "Major Lowell reporting as ordered."

"Sit down, Craig," Jiggs said. "Can I get you some coffee?"

"Please, sir," Lowell said, taking one of the armchairs.

Jiggs got on the intercom and ordered coffee.

"A lot of people have been wondering where you were," Colonel Roberts said. It was a reproof.

"I was not aware, sir, that I was required to make my whereabouts known," Lowell said, adding, "Colonel Felter knew where I was."

"He did not elect to share that information," Roberts said, icily. "You might be interested to know that a rather elaborate search was unable to trace you beyond Los Angeles."

"I was in Las Vegas, sir," Lowell said.

"I thought we checked Vegas," Jiggs said to Roberts.

"I put into a private field out of town," Lowell said.

"Have you been on a bender, Craig?" Jiggs asked.

"I don't think it could fairly called a 'bender,' sir," Lowell said.

"I'll rephrase," Jiggs said. "Have you been up to anything that is going to come to my attention officially?"

"No, sir," Lowell said, flatly.

"For what it's worth, Craig, I'm sorry about what happened."

"Thank you."

"And with that, should we close the subject?"

"I would be grateful if we could," Lowell said.

"So how was Las Vegas?" Jiggs asked playfully.

"An awful lot of neon lights," Lowell said.

"Your car is here," Roberts said. He would have liked to have stood Lowell tall for his disappearing act. Jiggs, however, had obviously decided that since Lowell was back from leave on time, the matter should be dropped. Though technically Jiggs was not Lowell's commanding officer, he *was* a major general.

"Mr. Franklin called from Washington and asked for leave to drive it down. I thought it the thing to do."

"That was very kind, sir," Lowell said, "of you and Mr. Franklin."

"And Mr. Franklin has been baby-sitting your house," Colonel Roberts said.

"Sir?"

"I guess you don't know about that, do you?" Jiggs asked. When he saw confirmation on Lowell's face, he explained: "Captain Jannier and Mrs. Greer... eloped, I suppose is the word... while they were in Washington. They are now living in her house. Mr. Franklin asked Colonel Roberts's permission to stay in your house, and he thought it was a good idea."

"I am indebted to Mr. Franklin and you, sir," Lowell said.

The coffee was delivered.

"Is there anything I can do for you, Lowell?" Jiggs asked. He hoped Lowell would say something glib, something about being given tomorrow off. He had a job for Lowell, an important one, but talking to him about it would wait a day or two.

The day of the "wedding," Jiggs and Bellmon had removed themselves to a field three hundred yards from the house to talk privately. Their primary concern at the time was to keep Lowell out of trouble; for there was more than a good chance that he would do something stupid.

But they also had very much on their minds a meeting held that morning in DCSOPS. Invasion of Cuba was under serious consideration, and Jiggs was to have a number of responsibilities in that connection. Bellmon and Jiggs agreed that the one thing Jiggs needed now was someone to help him discharge his new responsibilities. Though the obvious candidate was Colonel Bill Roberts, the conversation turned from Roberts to Lowell.

Bellmon confessed to Jiggs that he was astonished at Lowell's performance in forming, activating, and equipping the armed helicopter companies at Bragg. Bellmon was specifically surprised at Lowell's TO&E for the provisional battalion. He had thought it would take Lowell at least ninety days to prepare the first draft; and he had delivered it twenty-four days after authorization had been received. The draft was approved— with only minor changes—almost as Lowell had presented it. None of this, of course, surprised Jiggs. As Jiggs's operations officer in Korea, Lowell's performance had been brilliant, "more valuable really," he said to Bellmon, "than his saber waving."

"In two weeks, Bob," Jiggs went on, "from the day it was authorized, he turned the 73rd Medium Tank Battalion, with M4A3s, into what was really a combat command, with M48s; and he had it up and running, too."

"Is that why you let him command the task force?" Bellmon asked. He had wondered for years how *that* had come about. He and Jiggs were longtime friends—friends since the Point— but they were officers; and one officer did not ask another the question in Bellmon's mind.

What the hell were you thinking of, giving command of a battalion-size force to a twenty-four year-old who had earned his captaincy in the National Guard?

"No, it wasn't," Jiggs confessed. "If I had taken that command, I would have had six hundred and eighty-four pissed off and surly troops, *bitter* troops, to lead. They called him 'the Duke' and kidded around with him. But if they were going to ride into Balaclava, they wanted 'the Duke' to be leading the charge."

"Balaclava? *'Into the valley of death rode the four hundred'?*" Bellmon asked, softly. It sounded like an exaggeration.

"Yeah," Jiggs said. "But this Duke knew what he was doing. He didn't ride straight into the guns, he sent flying columns to flank them. Flying columns? What they were was four troops in a three-quarter-ton with a .50 caliber machine gun and a couple of .30s. 'What I want you guys to do is sneak around the rear of that hill and blow away the bad guys at the cannons,' Lowell told them. And off they went, no questions and no hesitation, and blew away the bad guys at the cannons. That left me with two nagging questions, Bob."

"Oh?" Bellmon had a strange feeling that this was the first time Jiggs had ever discussed Task Force Lowell with a peer in complete honesty.

"Would they have gone if I had ordered them to go? And

if they had gone, would they have stopped just out of sight and waited for some other sonofabitch to put himself in the line of fire?"

Bellmon didn't reply.

"I know the answer, of course," Jiggs said, softly. "And the answer is that if I had sent them where he sent them, they would have been on the radio in five minutes saying they were pinned down."

"I don't think that's true," Bellmon said. "Did that ever happen to you?"

"Yes," Jiggs said. "It happened to me during the Bulge."

"I was at Kasserine," Bellmon said. "I was captured at Kasserine because troops just evaporated, refused to fight. It happens."

"It never happened to Lowell," Jiggs said. "He's a hell of a combat commander. and now the sonofabitch is passed over for promotion again."

"Have you told him?"

"No. And I don't want you to, either. We need him. I realize what a prick that makes me."

"My father-in-law," Bellmon said, "here at the Farm, as a matter of fact, just before he went back to Germany after the war, told me I should never forget that most soldiers hate warriors. At the time, I didn't really understand what he meant."

"By extension, then, most paper-pushers hate good paper-pushers," Jiggs had replied. "So Lowell has two strikes against him."

Bellmon chuckled.

"He also gets laid a lot," Jiggs added. "That really makes people jealous. Three strikes, Lowell, you're out."

"He's not going to get laid tonight, is he?" Bellmon replied, and was immediately ashamed of himself.

Jiggs flashed him an angry glance, and then smiled.

"Well, maybe working for us on this will keep his mind off that," he said.

"You've decided on him?" Bellmon asked.

Jiggs nodded.

"How are you going to handle Roberts? He's liable to resent it."

"I'll explain the situation to him," Jiggs had said. "He'll understand."

* * *

Jiggs was explaining that situation to Roberts when word came that Lowell had shown up at Rucker. Now he was going to have to explain it all over again to Lowell.

The moment General Jiggs asked him what he could do for him, Lowell brightened and smiled. "How odd that you should ask what *you* can do for *me!*" he quipped.

"Uh oh," Jiggs said, chuckling.

"I'm glad Colonel Roberts is here," Lowell said. "We can go through channels right now."

"What's on your mind, Lowell?" Roberts asked.

"Sir, I am no longer required for the rocket chopper program. Colonel Warner is perfectly capable of taking over what's left to be done."

"And?"

"It would like a transfer to Special Forces, sir. Colonel Hanrahan has twice asked me if I would come over."

Roberts shook his head.

"I would be grateful for anything that could be done to expedite the paperwork, sir," Lowell went on.

"You can't go to Special Forces, Craig," Jiggs said.

"Paul Hanrahan wants me," Lowell said. "He's asked me twice."

"He can't have you," Jiggs said.

"He's led me to believe that he can recruit anybody he wants," Lowell said.

"He's wrong," Jiggs said. "At least in your case." Lowell looked at him for an expalantion. "I really did have official business in Wahsington, despite rumor to the contrary," Jiggs went on. "DSCOPS sent for me."

"Well, then, *your* trip wasn't wasted, was it?" Lowell said.

"Neither has yours coming to my office, Major," Jiggs said. "I had something on my mind beyond your calamitous personal affairs."

His voice was firm and he had used Lowell's rank. He had Lowell's attention.

"What follows is Secret and Top Secret," Jiggs said.

Lowell's eyebrows went up.

"Item one," Jiggs said. "It is considered possible that an augmentation of the advisors currently in Vietnam will be necessary. That much is Top Secret. As part of that, I have been directed—in a document classified Secret—to coordinate the efforts of Aviation Combat Developments, the Aviation Board,

TATSA, and SCATSA in the development of a provisional aviation battalion for possible deployment to Vietnam."

(Transportation Corps Aviation Test & Support Activity; Signal Corps Aviation Test & Support Activity)

"Interesting," Lowell said.

"Item two," Jiggs went on, "classified Secret. SECARMY is going to convene a board to determine the feasibility of developing a division that will be airmobile. That board will be chaired by whoever is the senior of the three post commanders involved, Benning, Bragg, and here."

"It will be either Bragg or Benning, and they will view army aviation as another means of transporting parachutists," Lowell said.

Jiggs ignored the comment.

"Item three, classified Top Secret," he went on. "I have been directed to prepare plans for army aviation and MATS participation in an invasion of Cuba, from Florida."

"And MATS?" Lowell asked, surprised.

(The Military Air Transport Service had started as the Air Transport Service of the air force. Later they won a political battle to strip the navy of their own independent air transport service, and the two had been combined into the Military Air Transport Service, to serve the army, navy and marine corps— as well as the air force—under an air force commanding general.)

Colonel Roberts was aware that Lowell was not behaving the way a major was expected to behave when talking to a general officer. After long service with a general officer, a full colonel might offer unsolicited comments the way Lowell was, but never a major. But then Roberts recalled that Lowell was Jiggs's S-3 in the 73rd Heavy Tank Battalion. He was acting as if that were still the case. Roberts was offended, but since Jiggs didn't object, he could not correct Lowell.

"And MATS," Jiggs repeated. Then he went on: "To accomplish these tasks, I will be provided with a number of staff officers. My recommendations regarding which experts I would prefer to have have not been solicited. If I didn't know better, I would suspect that there are political considerations involved. However, I *was* thrown a bone: I was told that if there was anybody in particular I wanted, I could, of course, have him."

"What was it, a swap? Airborne gets aviation, and you get to tell MATS when and where you want their airplanes?"

"I don't think it was quite that simple," Jiggs said. "But I haven't finished."

"Sorry."

"You came immediately to mind, of course," Jiggs said. "All bullshit aside, you're one hell of a planner; and you've had experience dealing with the establishment of aviation companies."

"And that's why I can't go to Bragg?"

"Just shut up a minute, Craig," Jiggs said, impatiently.

Roberts was pleased to see there was a line Lowell could not cross with impunity.

"Sorry, sir," Lowell said, contritely.

"It further occurred to me that if I assigned you to any of these activities, you would find yourself in one of two impossible situations. You would either be under the command of someone who would be prone to ignore the advice of a major; or you would be a liaison officer, and you know how little attention is paid to the opinions of liaison officers."

He let that sink in a moment, and then went on.

"So I'm going to leave you right where you are," Jiggs said.

"The idea being," Lowell asked, instantly catching on, "that since I have nothing to do, I can work for you out of school."

Jiggs nodded his head. Despite himself, Roberts was impressed with Lowell's grasp. He believed that a staff officer's efficiency was in direct proportion to how well the staff officer understood the commander.

"And General Bellmon and Colonel Roberts, of course," Jiggs said, throwing Roberts a bone. "We'll see you're kept abreast of what's going on. And when your ideas are presented, they will be the sound reasoning of either me or General Bellmon or Colonel Roberts."

Lowell nodded his understanding and agreement.

"I didn't really want to be a Green Beret, anyway," Lowell said, with a smile. "When do I start?"

(Three)
227 Melody Lane
Ozark, Alabama
2030 Hours, 7 July 1959

The Oldsmobile 98 four-door hardtop with Fort Rucker sticker No. 1 turned onto Melody Lane. The commanding general's

lady was about to make an unannounced and uninvited call
upon one of her husband's officers—aware that if her husband
knew about the call, he would make it quite plain to her that
it was ill advised.

At first she had told him that she was going to have Craig
to supper, but her husband had shot that idea down.

"I think the one thing Craig doesn't need right now is domestic bliss on display," he said. "Leave him alone for a while,
Jane, so he can lick his wounds."

"He's probably lonely as hell," she argued.

"He's working. That's the therapy he needs," Paul Jiggs
said.

"He's probably sitting around with a bottle," she replied.

"I don't think so," Paul said.

Paul was now off at Fort Monroe, CONARC headquarters
in Virginia. Jane Jiggs had been to a fashion show at the Ozark
Country Club. Now was the time to call on Craig.

In absolute honesty, she thought she could walk in and tell
Craig that she desperately needed a drink. When she was Mrs.
Commanding General at a female social function, she limited
herself to two glasses of white wine. What Mrs. Commanding
General did, the other officers' ladies did. Some officers' ladies
could not handle liquor. Since Jane Jiggs thought there was
nothing more disgusting than a drunken woman, she was going
to do nothing whatever to encourage women to drink.

When she pulled into the driveway, she saw that Craig was
not alone. There was a Buick station wagon in the carport with
a green, civilian post sticker on the bumper. She stopped, put
the Olds in reverse, and backed down the driveway. And then
she stopped again.

She knew who the Buick belonged to. Craig's secretary,
the tall, good-looking blond who was married to the man who
ran the peanut oil company in Enterprise. A nice woman, Jane
thought, who was doubtless at Lowell's house in order to combine business with a little compassion. Jane Jiggs had met Jane
Cassidy, and, as far as Jane Jiggs was concerned, Jane Cassidy
was the kind of woman who would feel as bad about what that
woman had done to Craig as she herself did.

She stopped the Olds, backed it up to the edge of lawn, and
got out. She cut across the lawn to the carport. The house was
on a little hill, and you couldn't see into the windows from the
street. But you could from the lawn. Inside, for the second

time in her life (the first being an "exhibition" she and Paul had gone to years before, off the Rue de Pigalle in Paris) Jane saw a woman performing the act of fellatio.

After she'd gotten the Olds started up again, the first thing she thought was that she should have listened to Paul. She'd put her nose in where it was neither wanted nor needed.

The second thing she thought was that if word of this affair got to Paul, he would be outraged. She was married, she often thought with pleasure, to the last decent, moral male. Paul had stormed out of the exhibition in Paris in genuine disgust and undisguised contempt for the officer, a classmate, who had taken them to see it.

In other words, Paul would understand if Craig Lowell had found solace in the arms of an exotic dancer—providing that she was not married.

Jane realized that she was going to have to do something. She was going to have to end the relationship before Paul got word of it. And word would certainly get out sooner or later, and then things would be terribly messy.

She was going to have to do something, but she had no idea what.

"God*damn* it!" she said aloud, as she ran the stop sign and turned onto Rucker Boulevard.

She had gone no more than 200 yards when she became aware of flashing red lights in her rearview mirror.

The cops had been watching the intersection for people to run the stop sign. Now, to put a cap on everything, she was going to get a ticket. The fine, she recalled, was $35 plus court costs of $27.50.

Being a good Samaritan, she thought, was going to be expensive.

She pulled to the curb. The police car pulled in behind her, and she saw a cop open the door. She opened her purse and took out her driver's license and the registration. She rolled down the window and looked for the cop. He was nowhere in sight. And then she saw that the cop was back in his car, which was now, making a U-turn back toward Ozark.

They're not rushing off to stop a robbery at the Bank of Ozark, she thought. They'd seen the No. 1 sticker on the bumper. They were not about to risk the rage of Mayor Howard Dutton for having given his good friend the general's wife a ticket for running a stop sign.

She was ashamed at her relief.
And that put Howard Dutton into her mind.

(Four)
Bachelor Officer's Quarters, Bldg. T-2204
The U.S. Army Special Warfare School
Fort Bragg, North Carolina
1200 Hours, 9 July 1959

Second Lieutenant Thomas J. Ellis pinned gold second lieutenant's bars to the epaulets of a tropical worsted blouse, reflecting angrily that the bars were gold and not silver.

Regulations authorized the promotion of second lieutenants to first lieutenant after completion of six months' satisfactory service. Satisfactory service was usually defined as service during which the second lieutenant did not desert; steal the inventories he had been assigned to verify; make a pass at the commanding officer's wife; or commit some other outrage against good military order and discipline.

Second Lieutenant Ellis had been a commissioned officer since 15 December 1958. He should have been promoted first lieutenant, therefore, on 16 June 1959; and he had not been. On 16 June he had been sitting in a swamp on Eglin Air Force Base, roasting pieces of a small and incredibly tough wild pig on a fire built on the stump of a cypress tree.

He finished pinning his insignia to his tropical worsted blouse, then put it on his bed. He put his trousers on, and carefully pulled them high on his thighs so as not to ruin the crease while he was putting on and lacing up his glossy jump boots. Then he hitched the trousers down and bloused them with rolled and tied Sheik condoms.

After he'd finished dressing, he left the BOQ and went to the barracks housing Training "A" Team 59–23. They were all waiting for him. He felt a little silly with only his jump wings and nothing else on his breasts. The others all wore the ribbons that anywhere from five to ten years of service had earned them. Most of them had been to Korea. Many also had Combat Infantry Badges and Silver Stars and Bronze Stars and Purple Hearts. If these guys wanted to call him the Boy Wonder, that seemed all too understandable.

When it was time, he formed his troops into two ranks in front of the barracks, called them to attention, and marched them to the open area in front of headquarters. Seven training teams would be graduated today. Five of them were already there, and the last was behind him.

There was a band—not the whole thing, Ellis noticed, but maybe half-strength.

When the brass came out the front door of headquarters, Ellis saw that the little Jew light bird he'd seen around a couple of times was with Colonel Hanrahan and Lt. Colonel Mac-Millan. He was curious about the little guy to begin with, and now that he saw him in tropical worsteds, he was even more curious. He was wearing a brass's hat with scrambled eggs on the leather brim, so he wasn't a Green Beret. But he was sure loaded down with medals and crap. He had a gold rope hanging from his epaulets that looked liked it weighed two pounds, and he had the CIB and jump wings, and at the shoulder seam was a Ranger patch.

And the Jew didn't stand with Colonel Hanrahan and the sergeant major and the other brass, but walked over to where the trainees were standing. The senior officer among them, a captain, was serving as company commander of the "company" made up of the seven training teams. It looked as if the Jew was taking over from him, and that's what happened. The captain went back to his team, and the little Jew with all the crap hanging on his uniform stood where the company commander was supposed to stand.

The band played, and they went through the first part of the graduation ceremony. And then Colonel Hanrahan gave a speech.

"I always try to say a few words about our heritage," he said. "Today that seems especially appropriate. We trace our beginnings to the first Special Service Force—which was joint Canadian-American—during World War II. But we also trace ourselves back to the Office of Strategic Services—in its guerrilla function. And to units of Americans training and leading the native forces of our allies.

"Some of those people are still around in the service. And we had one hell of a time, frankly, coming up with criteria by which past service could qualify an individual as worthy of the green beret. It was finally decided that an individual would be considered qualified if he had had experience operating behind enemy lines, or if he had served as an advisor to allied forces engaged in combat, and preferably both.

"I sort of jumped the gun when Colonel MacMillan joined us. I just decided on my own that he was entitled to a beret. I thought that anyone who had won the Medal of Honor could be said to have sufficient on-the-job training."

There was laughter.

"But I want to say that Colonel MacMillan is fully qualified under the new criteria. After he won the Medal, he led forty other escaped prisoners of war across Poland to safety. That earned him the Distinguished Service Cross. In Korea, Colonel MacMillan operated behind enemy lines in an operation that's still classified. And on yet another mission, this one closely related to what we're doing, he found himself at Dien Bien Phu in Indochina shortly before it fell. And he did so well there that the French took him into the Legion of Honor in the grade of Chevalier. They also gave him the Croix de geurre. And, what should really impress our friends across the post, the professional parachutists, he was made an honorary member of the Third Parachute Regiment of the French Foreign Legion."

Colonel Mac, Lieutenant Ellis thought, looked distinctly uncomfortable.

"And we have another officer here today, who by the authority invested in me by God and the Deputy Chief of Staff for Operations, will henceforth and forevermore be entitled to wear the green beret, having qualified for it by on-the-job training. Not only was he was with Colonel Mac in Korea and Indochina, and decorated with roughly the same fruit salad for it, but he has one far greater distinction. When he was but a young officer, wet behind the ears, he had the privilege of serving with that great warrior, your modest beloved commandant, in Greece."

There was laughter.

"Now *there* was a war," Hanrahan said. "You must remind me to tell you about it sometime."

More laughter.

Colonel Hanrahan turned to his sergeant major.

"Bring the box, Sergeant Major," he said, loud enough for everybody to hear. Then he raised his voice: "Atten-hut!"

The troops popped to attention.

"And now, our own private command," Hanrahan said, smiling broadly, on the edge of laughter. "Prepare to discard hats! Dis-card, hats!"

Fifty-six hats went sailing into the air.

Ellis saw that the little Jew very carefully set his cap with the scrambled eggs on the brim on the grass beside him.

Hanrahan, Mac, and Taylor marched over to the little Jew. Mac turned to the cardboard carton and took a hat from it. It had a slip of paper pinned to it, the name, Ellis realized. Mac removed the pin, and handed the beret to Felter.

Felter put it on. They shook hands.

"Thank you, Paul," Felter said.

Hanrahan stepped around him, and his foot squashed Felter's brimmed cap. There were titters of laughter.

"Colonel!" Colonel Mac said. "Shame on you! You stepped on his hat!"

"I did not!" Hanrahan said.

Felter looked down at his hat. It was squashed.

The titters were turning to giggles.

"You did too!" Colonel Mac said loudly. "You stepped on his hat just like this!"

Whereupon he stepped on Felter's hat and ground it with his heel.

The titters and giggles turned to guffaws and laughter, loud, but not loud enough to drown out what Lt. Col. Felter said.

"You bastards! I should have known you'd do something like that!"

"Colonel," Hanrahan said, reasonably, "you won't need it anymore anyway."

Then Colonel Mac looked at the assembled hatless troops.

"I didn't give any command to laugh," he said. "The only time you get to laugh is when I give the command, 'Prepare to laugh; laugh!'"

The troops were divided between those who tried to stop laughing and those who came close to hysterics.

Then the three officers and the sergeant major walked down the line of graduating troopers and passed out the green berets they were now entitled to wear. There were a handshake and a word of congratulations for each new Green Beret.

The band had been playing all the time, and now it began to play "The Washington Post March." The March Past began. The band segued to "So Long, It's Been Good To Know You!" and the seven "A" Teams marched off the field.

"Detail, halt!" Ellis ordered. "Huh-right, face!"

They stood at attention, looking at him.

"You guys had to put up with a lot from me," Ellis said. "Thank you." He looked at each one of them for a moment. Then: "Dis-missed!"

They came to him and shook his hand. After it looked as if he couldn't make up his mind to do the right thing or not, Eaglebury walked to him.

"So long, Ellis," he said. "Try to remember a little of what I tried to teach you."

"I'll do my best, Sergeant," Ellis said, coldly.

Sonofabitch won't let up on me, even now.

Ellis started to walk back to his BOQ. One of the sergeants from headquarters ran after him.

"Colonel Mac wants to see you, Lieutenant," he said. "Right away."

There was nobody he liked more than Colonel Mac, but what he had to do right then was take a leak; and he wanted to get out of the hot uniform, and Colonel Mac had already congratulated him, so Ellis was something less than thrilled. Still, he had been summoned, so he went.

Colonel Mac, Sergeant Major Taylor told him, was in Colonel Hanrahan's office, and he was to go there.

He knocked at the door and was told to enter.

"Lieutenant Ellis reporting as ordered, sir," Ellis said, saluting Hanrahan, who was behind his desk. There were several others in the room, off to the side.

"Stand at ease, Lieutenant," Hanrahan said.

He looked at him thoughtfully.

"First things first," he said. "Lieutenant, you are now authorized access to certain Top Secret material. You will consider everything you hear in this room as Top Secret. Clear?"

"Yes, sir."

"I have been getting reports on your behavior in the swamp from Eaglebury," Hanrahan said.

There was a chuckle, and Ellis looked in the direction of it. SFC Eaglebury was sitting on the colonel's couch, drinking a beer.

There had been a rumor, one he had discounted, that the school sometimes sent somebody through training who was not a trainee, but an observer. The rumor was apparently true. He had been evaluated—by Eaglebury—and he was not SFC Eaglebury. A noncom would not have been so relaxed.

"May I presume that SFC Eaglebury is really an officer, sir?" Ellis said.

Hanrahan nodded.

"Then as one officer and gentleman to another, Eaglebury," Ellis said, with surprising anger, "you're a genuinely skilled prick."

Eaglebury laughed.

"And Commander Eaglebury has just been telling us such nice things about you," Hanrahan said.

"*Commander* Eaglebury?" Ellis blurted.

"Lieutenant Commander," Eaglebury said. He got up and handed Ellis a can of beer. "I really hope there's no hard feelings."

"You're a sailor?"

"No," Eaglebury said. "I'm a lieutenant commander. The sailors are the guys in the round white hats."

"Well, sir, I was out of line. I apologize."

"Forget it," Eaglebury said. "I was doing my best to make you lose control. You didn't."

"I won't have to tell you, will I, Ellis, that the commander's status goes no further than the people in this room. Sergeant Major Taylor knows, that's it."

"I understand, sir."

"I don't believe you've formally met Colonel Felter, have you, Ellis?" Hanrahan said.

They shook hands.

"I'll explain what this is all about," Felter said. "The specifics are not your concern, but what is planned is to mount a mission to Cuba. The mission is of greater importance than it must appear. To clarify that: In the event you are captured, we hope that they will be content with having captured a Green Beret team and will limit their interrogation accordingly."

"Yes, sir."

"Would you be willing to lead such a team, with Commander Eaglebury going along as an SFC?"

"Yes, sir," Ellis said without hesitation. But as the realization of what was going on sank in, he felt lightheaded.

"Well, you're OK with the commander," Felter said. "And Mac thinks you're unusual, so it's OK with me."

"Thank you," Ellis said.

"We don't have a time yet, or a place . . ." Felter began.

"So what we thought we'd do," Colonel Mac said, "is run you through Eglin a couple of more times."

"Mac, please shut up!" Felter snapped. Then he continued to address Ellis: "In the meantime, you'll just stay here at Bragg, forming an "A" team. *If* it is decided to field this mission, your commo sergeant will be told he's sick, and he will be replaced by the commander."

"Yes, sir."

"OK," Felter said.

"There's just one more thing," Colonel Hanrahan said.

"Sir?" Ellis said, turning to face him just in time to catch a small piece of cardboard to which two of the silver bars identifying a first lieutenant were pinned.

"It's official as of 16 June," Hanrahan said. "But Eaglebury said he didn't want anything to improve your morale, so we didn't tell you."

"Wait until I get the commander in Cuba, sir," Ellis said, and smiled broadly at SFC/Lt. Commander Eaglebury.

XVIII

(One)
Laird Army Airfield
Fort Rucker, Alabama
1330 Hours, 2 September 1959

Whenever the door to Major Craig Lowell's office in the hangar was closed, it was clearly understood by his people that he was not to be disturbed. His people joked that what was going on behind the closed door was that he was jumping Jane Cassidy on the desk.

Lowell was a good boss. He helped his people. But since the rocket-armed helicopter program really had very little to do anymore, its pilots had little to do. All the same, the rocket-armed helicopter project still had a high priority, thus no one questioned how many pilots were assigned to it. Other Board projects, however—ones with lower priority—had shortages of personnel.

What had happened was that Lowell and Colonel Roberts had beat the system: pilots assigned to rocket-armed helicopters were "made available" to fly test missions for other, pilot-short Board projects.

Lowell and Roberts were playing the game, and they were good at it.

Working for Lowell was the best of all possible worlds. His pilots got to fly a lot. They stayed out of his way, and he stayed out of theirs.

If he was a little weird about keeping his office door closed, that was his business. No one actually thought that Lowell was banging Mrs. Cassidy. Major Lowell was too smart to run the risk of banging his secretary—in the unlikely event that she was willing. Anyway, he kept the door closed even when Mrs. Cassidy wasn't there. Like now, when Mrs. Cassidy had been flown to the Air University Library at Montgomery to pick something up for him.

Mrs. Cassidy had been gone all day, and the door had been closed all day, and it would probably stay closed for the rest of the day. Whatever the hell he was doing in there—maybe writing the Great American Novel (the sound of a typewriter was often heard) or maybe just sleeping—Major Lowell did not like to be disturbed when he was doing it.

The only officer in the outer room when the little light bird walked in was Lieutenant George B. Simmons, a fixed-wing aviator just back from an Initial Utilization Tour. It was his turn to watch the store.

The little light bird, Simmons was startled to see, was a Green Beret. You thought of Green Berets as looking like football players. This light bird looked like a badminton player.

Simmons stood up.

"May I help you, Colonel?"

"I'm looking for Major Lowell," the light bird said. "Have I got the right place?"

"Yes, sir," Simmons said. "He's working, sir, but I'll tell him you're here. May I have you name, sir?"

"Felter."

Simmons went to the door and knocked. It was a moment before Lowell replied, and then all he said was, "Well?"

"There's a Colonel Felter to see you, sir," Simmons said.

"Who?" Lowell asked, incredulous.

"Felter, sir."

"Ask the colonel to wait a moment," Lowell said.

It was more than a moment. It was more like two minutes

before the door opened, and the little light bird was getting visibly annoyed.

Lowell was smiling when he came out, a friendly smile. It almost immediately widened, became one of amusement. Then he laughed, heartily, out loud.

"When did you get that fucking green beret?" he chortled. "Mouse, you look like a mushroom!"

Then he moved with quick grace across the room, grabbed the little light bird by his upper arms, and lifted him effortlessly off the floor. The little light bird struggled uselessly. Major Lowell kissed him wetly on the forehead, and then set him down.

"Sometimes, Craig," the little light bird snapped, coldly furious, "you can be a real pain in the ass."

"What the hell are you doing down here?" Lowell said, blandly ignoring the furious little man. "You should have let me know you were coming."

"I want you to take a ride with me for a couple of hours," Felter said.

"Where?"

"Not far," Felter said.

"Well, I'd have to ask Roberts," Lowell said.

"He knows," Felter said.

"Oh?"

"We're parked right outside," Felter said. "Is there some reason you can't come right away?"

"No," Lowell said. He turned to Simmons. "If anyone asks where I am, Lieutenant, you refer them to Colonel Roberts and you stay here and mind the store."

"Yes, sir," Simmons said.

He had hoped to be introduced to the little light bird, but no introductions were offered.

Lowell followed the little officer back through the hangar. Simmons watched. There was an Aero Commander sitting with engines idling on the parking stand between the hangars. Felter ducked into it, and Lowell followed him. The Commander began to taxi immediately.

Lowell strapped himself into one of the seats in the back.

"I never get a chance to ride in back," he said, with a smile.

Felter was still angry with Lowell for mocking his green beret and kissing him. He hated being kissed. Lowell knew it, and that was why he did it.

"That was a hell of an example you set for that young lieutenant of yours," he said.

Lowell's smile flickered.

"Did that occur to you?" Felter asked, bitterly sarcastic.

"What's this, Mouse? Do you think that a little affection is beneath the dignity of a West Point Colonel—especially one in a green mushroom?"

Felter glowered at him, aware that he had lost his temper and was liable to make things worse.

"Where the hell did you get that thing, anyhow?" Lowell asked. "Are you entitled to it?"

"I'm goddamned well entitled to it," Felter said, angrily. "And you've got no goddamned right to mock it."

The pilot tested the engines on the threshold of the active runway, the sound prohibiting conversation. And then they took off.

"OK," Lowell said, when then pilot throttled back the engines. "If I pissed you off, I'm sorry. I apologize."

Felter glowered at him again, saw that Lowell was genuinely contrite, and softened. Craig Lowell was his oldest, his best, and one of his very few friends.

"I'm wearing the beret because Hanrahan and MacMillan stamped all over my hat," he said, forcing a smile.

That was true. He had changed back into civilian clothes before he had left Fort Bragg, and had forgotten the crushed visored cap until he had taken it from the bag to put it on this morning. It was too torn to wear. But he was honest enough with himself to realize that in a sense he was pleased; it gave him the chance to wear the green beret. He was not at all unhappy at having officially qualified as a Green Beret.

"They did what?"

"I was at Bragg," Felter said, "When they gave me this. People in civilian clothes attract more attention than people in uniforms. So I wore a uniform, and Hanrahan was having a graduation ceremony, and he insisted I get my beret officially. Which was very nice."

"I wasn't mocking you for being entitled," Lowell said, seriously.

"What they do is give you the beret in a ceremony. The troops throw their caps in the air. I had a nearly new $54.95 felt cap, so I put it carefully on the ground beside me. First

Hanrahan stepped on it, and then Mac ground a hole in the top with his heel."

Lowell chuckled. He was genuinely sorry that he had mocked the beret. He still thought the beret was ridiculous, but he knew that when he could arrange for it, Sanford T. Felter liked to be in uniform with his medals and qualification badges on display.

"Just for the hell of it, Craig," Felter said, "you're also entitled to wear one of these."

"How come?"

"For Greece," Felter said. "Command of foreign troops in combat qualifies you for it."

Lowell bit off what came to his lips: *I wouldn't be seen dead in one.*

"I don't think I am, Mouse," he said. "I think you have to be a jumper, too."

"You're not jump qualified, are you?" Felter said, as if he had just remembered that.

"No," Lowell said. "I'm sane."

"Screw you," Felter said, fondly.

"What were you doing at Bragg? Or is that Top Secret?"

"Yes, it is," Felter said, "as a matter of fact."

He reached across the aisle and took a briefcase from the seat. He worked a combination lock, opened it, and handed Lowell two sheets of paper.

"This is only Confidential," Lowell said.

"Read it anyway," Felter said.

CONFIDENTIAL

DEPARTMENT OF DEFENSE

OFFICE OF THE ASSISTANT SECRETARY OF DEFENSE FOR LOGISTICS

WASHINGTON, D.C.

INTERAGENCY MEMORANDUM

17 August 1959

FROM: Deputy Secretary of Defense, Logistics

TO: Secretary of the Navy

ATTN: Chief Bureau of Aircraft
        Secretary of the Army

            ATTN: Deputy Chief of Staff, Logistics

1. Reference is made to:
            a. Letter, Chief of Naval Operations,
Subject: "Aircraft Surplus to Present and Anticipated
Needs," dated 2 August 1959.
            b. Letter, Chief of Staff, Subject:
"Request for Assignment of Military Air Transport
Command Airlift Capability," dated 3 August 1959.
            c. DOD Policy Letter, Subject: "Intra
Agency Transfer of Surplus Property," dated 14
February 1958.

2. The Department of the Navy has eight (8)
Douglas R4D aircraft surplus to present and
anticipated needs. Seven (7) of subject aircraft are
cargo configured. One (1) aircraft is VIP passenger
configured, providing seven passenger spaces, plus
office workspace. It is presently planned to transfer
subject aircraft to U.S. Air Force control for
nonpreserved storage at Davis-Monthan Air Force
Base.

3. The Secretary of the Army is directed to
determine if the surplus Navy R4D aircraft may be
utilized to provide the airlift capability outlined in
paragraph 1.b. above, thereby utilizing surplus
property and effecting a procurement and operational
economy.

4. In the event it is determined that subject aircraft
may be so utilized, this memorandum constitutes
authority for SECNAVY to transfer, on a loan basis,
subject aircraft to Department of the Army control,
pending ultimate transfer to Davis-Monthan Air Force
Base.

5. It is believed that such temporary use by the
U.S. Army of subject aircraft would not violate the
terms of the Interservice Roles & Missions Agreement
(commonly called the "Key West Agreement") of 23
May 1948. However, inasmuch as the presence of

U.S. Navy marked aircraft engaged in airlift operations for the U.S. Army might attract inordinate attention of the part of the press, and others, in the event such aircraft are placed under control, this memorandum further may be cited as authority to remove U.S. Navy markings from subject aircraft. While such aircraft are under U.S. Army control, they will NOT bear U.S. Army markings. Aircraft markings will be limited to aircraft procurement number, on the vertical stabilizer, and the letters "U.S.A." on the lower surface of the left wing, and on the upper surface of the right wing.

C. James Picell
Asst. Secretary for Logistics

CONFIDENTIAL

CONFIDENTIAL

HEADQUARTERS

DEPARTMENT OF THE ARMY

OFFICE OF THE DEPUTY CHIEF OF STAFF FOR OPERATIONS

Washington, D.C.

22 August 1959

SUBJECT: Utilization of Surplus Aircraft

TO: Commandant
U.S. Army Special Warfare School
Fort Bragg, N.C.

1. The Department of the Army has been granted the temporary use of eight (8) U.S. Navy R4D aircraft surplus to navy needs, pending their ultimate transfer to nonpreserved storage at Davis-Monthan Air Force Base. The Deputy Chief of Operations has determined that

USASWS is the U.S. Army activity which can best utilize subject aircraft in the execution of its mission, and this letter assigns subject aircraft to USASWS for temporary use.

2. The aircraft are presently located at the U.S. Naval Air Station, Pensacola, Florida, which has been directed to effect transfer, and to train four (4) army aviators in their operation to a level of skill at which they may serve as instructor pilots. USASWS will designate two (2) aviators to undergo such training, and USAAB and USASATSA will each designate one (1) aviator. USASWS will coordinate.

3. Inasmuch as the temporary use of these aircraft might be miscontrued as a violation of the "Key West Agreement" of 1948, certain restrictions apply to their use:

a. SECDEF concurring, Commanding General, Pope U.S. Air Force Base, Fort Bragg, N.C., has been directed to service subject aircraft within his capabilities. With the exception of Pope AFB, subject aircraft will NOT land at, or request any services from, any other USAF installation.

b. Subject aircraft will be marked only with the letters "U.S.A." on the wings, and with the procurement number on the vertical stabilizer.

c. Only the aviators designated in paragraph 2, above, plus those aviators subsequently designated by the undersigned, will be permitted to operate subject aircraft.

d. The aircraft are NOT to be considered as available for any airlift requirement except that of the USASWS.

e. Any questions concerning this interservice utilization of surplus aircraft are to be referred to the undersigned.

FOR THE DEPUTY CHIEF OF STAFF, OPERATIONS
Robert F. Bellmon
Brigadier General
Director, Army Aviation.

CONFIDENTIAL

"What the hell is all this about?" Lowell asked, looking up from the sheets of paper. "If you're involved, Super Spook, there's more to this than getting the last ounce of use out of worn-out airplanes before sending them to the bone yard."

"Hanrahan has a transportation problem," Felter said. "I thought I could help him, and this looked like a good solution."

"You offered that explanation too quickly," Lowell said. "Bullshit, in other words."

Felter was surprised at the ease with which Lowell had seen through the "official" story: that that sonofabitch Felter was using his influence to get his old pal, the head of the Green Berets, some surplus navy airplanes.

"OK," Felter said, after a minute. "You'd make dangerous guesses anyway, if you weren't told."

"Told what?"

"We are going to assist some Cubans who have been forced out of the country and wish to go back and overthrow Castro," Felter said.

Lowell considered that for a moment before he replied.

"Fascinating," he said. "Where are you going to stage them? Panama?"

"I said you'd make dangerous guesses," Felter said. "Nicaragua."

"Why not lower Florida?" Lowell asked. "Wouldn't that be closer?"

"Nicaragua," Felter repeated. "General Somoza is making available what space we need."

"What's that going to cost us?"

"He gets to keep everything, the airfields, whatever else we build; but aside from that, nothing. He's doing it as his contribution to the Monroe Doctrine, and because he sees Castro as a threat to him."

"And is he?"

"Oh, yes. He's a dangerous man."

"So how does Hanrahan fit in? More important, how do I fit in?"

"He's going to send some Berets down to Nicaragua, very quietly, to do the training. And we're going to funnel the support—the weapons, that sort of thing—through him."

"And fly it down there on old Gooney-birds? Wouldn't it be easier to give them fewer but bigger airplanes?"

"We're going to maintain a very low profile."

"You don't think you can hide something like this from the Russians, do you?" Lowell asked.

"Who mentioned the Russians?"

"Come on, Mouse," Lowell said.

"I suppose," Felter said, "that the President had to take into account certain domestic political considerations. There's a 'Fair Play For Cuba' committee among other things. Kennedy could use it against Nixon, too, I suppose."

"Kennedy against Nixon? What's that supposed to mean?"

"Kennedy's going to run against Nixon; don't you know that?"

"Jesus, that's all we need, a bleeding-heart Harvard liberal in the White House."

"That's one of the things the President is trying to avoid," Felter said.

"Getting back to question number one, where do I fit into this?"

"Not very far, Craig," Felter said. "And that's not subject to negotiation, so don't even ask. With Hanrahan's approval, Bellmon and Jiggs decided that you are in a good position to handle the Gooney-Bird logistics."

"Meaning what?"

"Meaning just what I said," Felter replied. "For one thing, we're going to need pilots for these airplanes. We're going to hide them in your rocket-armed helicopter project. You're going to be in charge of having them trained, of handling their pay, and of any other personnel problems. And then, right away, we're going to have to equip these airplanes with air-to-ground tactical radios . . . the AN/ARC-44 . . . and LORAN over-the-water navigation gear, and that'll be done at Rucker by SATSA. You'll handle the procurement."

"That's pushing paper," Lowell said.

"I know. You're very good at that, I understand."

"Jesus!"

"And you're a good chess player, moving pieces around. That'll come in handy."

"Meaning what?"

"I don't want more than one—and I will not *tolerate* more than two—of these Gooney-birds on one field at one time."

" '*I* don't want'?"

"Yeah," Felter said, after a minute. "*I* don't want. Any other questions, Major?"

"How can I get transferred out of this chickenshit outfit?"

Felter laughed.

"Hanrahan's going to meet us at Pensacola," he said. "You have been deputized by Jiggs and Roberts to represent them at the meeting with the Action Officer."

"'The 'Action Officer'? Who the hell is he?"

"I thought I made that pretty clear," Felter said.

"I thought you were running errands for the President," Lowell said.

"This is in addition to my other duties," Felter said, his voice light. And then he grew serious. "If you—and by 'you' I mean Hanrahan and Jiggs and Bellmon—can do this without making waves, then I can keep running it. If I have to keep putting out fires, Craig, they'll put somebody else in charge."

"I don't see where there will be a problem, Sandy," Lowell said.

Felter nodded.

"What happens to you when Eisenhower leaves office?" Lowell asked.

"I want to go back to the army," Felter said.

"You don't really think they'll let you, do you?" Lowell said. "I think you're dreaming."

"Why do you say that?"

"I think there's a shit list in the Pentagon," Lowell said. "With two names written on it in gold. The two names are Felter, S., and Lowell, C. A lot of big brass, Little Buddy, hates your ass and is just waiting for a chance to stick it in you."

"The day I met you, you were on a shit list," Felter said. "Subsequently, you have done very well."

"The mongrels are nipping at my heels," Lowell said. "Getting braver and braver by the minute. And as soon as you're stripped of that Counselor to the President business, they'll take out after you."

"I have officially requested assignment to Special Forces at the conclusion of my present assignment," Felter said.

"Good luck, Mouse," Lowell said.

He looked out the window. The Commander had begun its approach. They were coming in over the Gulf of Mexico. The sun was high, and the beaches seemed incredibly bright.

Two minutes later, they were on the ground at Pensacola Naval Air Station.

They taxied past Base Operations to a corner of the field. There were a number of R4Ds parked there, fifteen or twenty of them, a fire truck and several utility trucks, two navy staff cars, and an Otter.

A navy officer in a gray flight suit and a brimmed cap with a blue cover walked up the Aero Commander as the pilot shut down its engines.

"Commander Eaglebury," Felter made the introductions, "Major Lowell."

The two officers sized each other up and approved of what they saw.

"What did you do to make the navy mad, Commander?" Lowell asked. "And get yourself shanghaied into this?"

Eaglebury laughed out loud.

A large man, even larger than Lt. Commander Eaglebury, came running up. He wore a green beret and the six stripes of a master sergeant.

He saluted crisply.

"Jesus," he said, enthusiastically. "Just like old times. The Mouse and the Duke and the Polack."

"How the hell are you, Wojinski?" Lowell said, warmly.

"I gather you and the sergeant have met before?" Eaglebury said.

"This sailor's all right," Wojinski said. "He went through the whole damned Super Boy Scout course with sergeant's stripes on his sleeve."

"I *wallow* in your admiration, Ski," Eaglebury said, dryly.

"I was with the Colonel and the Duke and the Mouse in Greece," Wojinski said, proudly.

"I seem to have heard that before, somewhere," Eaglebury said.

"It'll be like old times," Wojinski repeated.

"I don't think so, Ski," Lowell said.

MacMillan and Phil Parker, in flight suits, came up. It was the first Lowell had seen them since the Wedding That Wasn't, and there was a moment's awkwardness.

"If you don't mention my being left at the altar," Lowell said, "I will refrain from telling the commander that you both have the clap, all right?"

There was laughter.

"I was just saying," Wojinski said, doggedly, "that it's going to be like old times."

"And I said I don't think so," Lowell repeated.

"Why not, Duke?" Wojinski asked.

"Because I am here as a simple paper-pusher, Ski," Lowell said. "Officer in charge of the staple gun and the Avgas credit cards, in addition to my other paper-pushing duties. Isn't that so, Colonel Felter?"

"Yes, Major Lowell," Felter said, "that's the way it is."

(Two)
The Law Offices of Howard Dutton
Ozark, Alabama
1430 Hours, 3 September 1959

"Mrs. Jiggs," Howard Dutton said, getting up from behind his desk to walk across the room to shake her hand. "It's a pleasure to see you, ma'am."

Dutton was stocky and ruddy faced. His hair was thin, and he was just beginning to get jowly. He was wearing a seersucker suit.

"It's very good of you to see me on such short notice," she said. "And I know how busy you must be."

"I've always got time for you, ma'am," he said. "Can I offer you something? Iced tea? Coffee? A soft drink?"

She hesitated. He took the chance.

"Maybe something with a little bite in it?"

She smiled at him.

"By a strange coincidence," he said, "I just have some vodka that's about to go stale. Would you like it with tonic water—that seems to cut the thirst—but I've got both tomato and orange juice."

"The tonic, please," Jane Jiggs said.

Dutton tugged at a bookcase against the wall. The whole thing swung open to reveal a wet bar.

"That's very nice," Jane said, impressed.

"Costs a bunch of money to give the impression you wouldn't think of having a nip in your office," Dutton said. "But in a town like this..."

"I understand," Jane Jiggs said.

He made drinks and handed one to her.

"To Melody and Jean-Philippe," Jane said.

"Thank you, ma'am," he said.

"And how are they?"

"They're just fine," Howard Dutton said. "Just fine."

"Craig Lowell told me Jean-Philippe called him one day last week," Jane said.

"Ma'am?"

"Craig Lowell," Jane said, "Jean-Philippe's friend."

"Oh, yes, ma'am," Howard Dutton said. "The one with his own airplane."

"And the one who flew the helicopter at Ed Greer's funeral," Jane said.

"That's right, isn't it?" Howard Dutton said. *"He* was the one."

"He was a good friend of Ed's, and he's a good friend of Jean-Philippe and Melody's," Jane Jiggs said.

"Yes, ma'am, I guess you could say he is," Howard Dutton said. He had decided that whatever Mrs. Jiggs wanted, it had something to do with Craig Lowell. And she certainly wanted something.

Lowell was the sonofabitch who was at least partially responsible for Melody marrying her Frenchman and going off to France. Howard Dutton wasn't at all sure that he wanted to do any favors for Major Craig Lowell, even if General Jiggs's wife asked for them.

"How was France?" Jane Greer asked.

"Well, I'll tell you it's a good thing Melody married a rich man," Howard Dutton said. "I couldn't believe the prices."

"I hear they're outrageous," Jane Jiggs agreed.

"Lucky for us, the Janniers wouldn't let us spend hardly anything. They even tried to pay the hotel bill the day we got there. And I don't mind telling you that they really understand hospitality. All we had to do is look like maybe we wanted something, and there it was, held out on a tray by some servant or another."

"I'm happy for Melody," Jane said. "I think everybody is."

"There are some who wish that she'd waited a decent interval," he said.

"They're just jealous," Jane said, and then: "And that wasn't possible, was it?"

He looked at her, as if surprised she knew that Melody was pregnant, and even more surprised that she had brought it up. He was annoyed.

"What exactly can I do for you, Mrs. Jiggs?" he asked, smiling, but somewhat coldly.

"We have a small problem," she said.

"'We' do?"

"One of our officers is involved with one of your married women," Jane Jiggs said.

"Lowell?" he asked, chuckling at the way she put it.

"The woman is Jane Cassidy," Jane Jiggs said.

"Tom Cassidy's wife?" he blurted. She saw that she had surprised him. She nodded. "Well, I'm right sorry to hear that," he said. "She has two kids, I think."

"So I understand," Jane said.

"Tom Cassidy's a fine fellow," Dutton said.

"I think they're all nice people," Jane said. "That's why I'm trying to help. Why I came to you."

"Well, I'm not much of a marriage counselor," Dutton said. "And I don't handle divorces."

"It's a long way from a divorce," Jane said. "And I want to keep it that way."

"Then Tom Cassidy doesn't know?"

"Nobody knows, yet." Jane said. "Not even my husband. Just Craig and Jane, and you and me."

"Why are you telling me this?" he asked.

"Because Melody once told me that if I ever needed anything fixed, I should see her Daddy," Jane Jiggs said. "And I need this fixed, Mr. Dutton, before some very nice people, including two young kids, get hurt in a scandal."

"I guess you better tell me all you know," Howard Dutton said, draining his vodka tonic. "And then we'll see what can be done."

"I'm very grateful to you, Mayor Dutton," Jane Jiggs said.

"My pleasure, ma'am," he said.

In the end it was a simple thing to take care of. He had a word with the chief of police. He told the chief he wanted him to handle it personally. The chief understood.

Three days later, as Mrs. Jane Cassidy turned onto Highway 27 to return from Ozark to Enterprise, she was stopped for having a faulty taillight. The policeman was the chief of police himself. He seemed genuinely sorry to tell her that he smelled liquor on her breath and was going to have to ask her to leave her car by the side of the road and come to the police station with him, so that she could blow up a balloon which would tell exactly how much she had to drink.

She was taken to the police station, given the balloon test, and then put into a room.

An hour later, Major Howard Dutton came into the room.

"Jane," he said, "I'm sure as God sorry to see you in here."

"I'm not drunk, Howard," Jane protested. "No matter what that damn balloon test says."

"I don't think you're drunk, either," he said. "And I wouldn't be surprised if there was nothing wrong with your taillight."

"I don't understand," she said, confused.

"Chief Scott got born again last year," he said.

"What's that got to do with anything?" she asked, angrily.

"Well, I don't know exactly," he said. "But it's probably got something to do with finding his wife once upon a time where she shouldn't have been, if you take my meaning."

"What's that got to do with me?"

"He told me that he's seen your car where he thinks it doesn't have a good reason to be."

"This is outrageous!"

"Now *I* know—and *you* know—that you haven't been doing anything wrong," he said. "I'll talk to the judge about this drunk driving business, and you probably won't even have to go to court. But I'd very careful where I parked my car in the future. It isn't what people know for sure that counts, Jane, it's what people think they know."

"Did he tell you where he thought he saw my car?"

"I didn't ask him," Howard Dutton said. "I don't want to know anything I don't have to."

"Of course, he didn't," Jane Cassidy protested. "Because I've done nothing wrong."

"I know that, Jane," Howard Dutton said. "And, none of this will go any further than it has to. I'll speak to the judge . . ."

"I appreciate that, Howard."

"But I'm going to have to tell you, between us, that the judge and the chief are two of a kind. I don't know how much influence I would have the second time around. Or if something like this happened again when I was out of town."

"Well," she said, coldly, "since nothing happened this time, there is no chance of anything happening again."

"I'm glad to hear that, Jane," Mayor Howard Dutton said. "I would surely be sad to hear that anything was wrong with a fine marriage like yours and Tom's."

He looked into her eyes to let her know he knew. Then he left her. On the way out, he told the chief of police to leave her alone for an hour and then drive her back to her car and let her go.

(Three)
Davis-Monthan Air Force Base, Arizona
1415 Hours, 24 December 1959

"Davis-Monthan," Lieutenant Commander Edward B. Eaglebury said to the old-fashioned hand-held microphone in the cockpit, "Navy Eight Twenty, an R4D aircraft, ten miles south of your station for landing."

He turned to his copilot, a tall, brown young man, dressed like Lt. Commander Eaglebury in a gray flight suit and a brown horsehide, fur-collared jacket. A patch, bearing gold-stamped naval aviator's wings and the legend "HORNE, ALEXANDER W. LT., USN," had been sewn to the jacket.

"Here we go, Franklin," Eaglebury said, "into the mouth of death. Will you please advise our passengers?"

Bill Franklin spoke into another microphone, addressing the passenger compartment via the public address system.

"We just contacted the tower," he said.

"Aircraft calling Davis-Monthan, say again," Davis-Monthan's tower replied.

It was not surprising that the Davis-Monthan tower was a little slow getting on the horn. It was after all a quarter after four on Christmas Eve. Little traffic was expected by the tower operators, who were to a man questioning the wisdom of a military career which saw them sitting in a glass box eighty feet above the ground on Christmas Eve—while regular people were gathered around Christmas trees, listening to Perry Como sing Christmas carols on the television.

"Davis-Monthan," Lt. Commander Edward B. Eaglebury repeated, "Navy Eight Twenty, an R4D aircraft, ten miles south of your station for landing."

As Commander Eaglebury spoke, CWO(2) Franklin jiggled the connection of his radio transmitter microphone in quick twisting motions. This served to introduce spurious electronic impulses into the circuit.

"Aircraft calling Davis-Monthan," the tower operator said.

"Your transmission is garbled. Say again. I say again, you are garbled."

There were four passengers in the passenger compartment of the R4D. One of them—a very large, Slavic-appearing individual—was asleep and snoring loudly on a leather couch with which Navy Eight Twenty had been equipped for service as a VIP transport aircraft. He wore no insignia of rank on his flight suit, which had been dyed black; but he was a U.S. Army Special Forces master sergeant, and his name was Stefan Wojinski.

The other three passengers were field-grade officers. They were Lt. Col. Rudolph G. MacMillan, Deputy Commandant for Special Projects of the U.S. Army Special Warfare School, Fort Bragg, N.C.; Lt. Colonel Augustus Charles, Commanding Officer of the U.S. Army Signal Aviation Test and Support Activity, Fort Rucker, Ala.; and Major C. W. Lowell, Chief, Rocket Armed Helicopter Branch, Aircraft Test Division, U.S. Army Aviation Board, Fort Rucker, Ala.

Major Lowell and Colonel Charles were seated in leather chairs, so configured that when pressure was applied to the back of the seat, a foot rest unfolded from the base. Colonel MacMillan was sitting on a couch immediately across the cabin from the one on which M/Sgt Wojinski snored.

They were looking out the windows when the air base appeared in view.

Lt. Col. MacMillan, who had reconnoitered the objective three days before from a Beaver, was displeased with what he saw. He picked up a telephone which was actually an intercom device connected to a loudspeaker in the cabin.

"Do a 180," he ordered, "and then come in from the *south*."

"I am coming in from the south," Lt. Commander Eaglebury objected.

"You're not south enough," MacMillan replied. "Try southwest."

"Yes, sir, Colonel, sir," Lt. Commander Eaglebury replied.

The old, but well maintained ex-VIP transport began a slow turn toward the south.

M/Sgt Wojinski grumbled in his sleep, snorted, and then resumed his snoring.

Lt. Col. MacMillan picked up the telephone again.

"How steep can you bank one of these things?"

Lt. Commander Eaglebury demonstrated, standing the Gooney-bird on its right wing tip.

The remnants of the passenger's and crew's dinner (provided by Executive Aircraft Catering, Inc., of Love Field, Dallas, Texas—their Number Seven, "Deluxe Assortment of cold cuts, turkey, ham, roast beef, salami, cheeses, fresh fruits, *and* Beluga caviar, $15.95 per person"—which had been Major Lowell's little Christmas gift to the expedition) slid off the table onto the floor.

In the rear of the cabin, two forty-pound, 24-volt nickel-cadmium aircraft batteries, equipped with a web harness for easy handling, slid from one side of the cabin to the other. And a moment later, at the low point of the incline, a Winchester Model 1897 12-gauge trench and riot gun, w/bayonet attachment, slid after the batteries.

The aircraft straightened up. The degree of bank and the rapidity with which the aircraft had reached it was impressive, but it was not precisely what Lt. Col. MacMillan had had in mind.

"Now do it the other way," he ordered.

"The United States Navy strives to please," Lt. Commander Eaglebury replied, and this time stood the Gooney-bird on its left wing tip.

In obedience to the immutable laws of physics M/Sgt Wojinski began to move the instant the effect of gravity overcame the friction which held his 230-pound body to the smooth leather of the couch.

A moment later, he landed on the floor and woke with a somewhat profane expression of surprise and annoyance.

The aircraft straightened up.

"Wojinski," Lt. Col. MacMillan said, innocently. "We're getting ready to land. Would you mind getting off the floor?"

Biting their lips, Colonel Charles and Major Lowell looked out the windows.

They were approaching the base again. There were literally thousands of aircraft parked on the desert: Davis-Monthan was the military service's aviation graveyard. The year-round temperature and atmosphere of the base was such that virtually no deterioration to aircraft or their on-board equipment occurred. All the military services sent aircraft to Davis-Monthan for disposal: they were flown in and taxied for miles to a parking space; the engines were shut down, the batteries disconnected, and the fuel was drained; and then the aircraft were just left where they had stopped.

Some aircraft were kept more or less in a state of readiness, and "cannibalizing" then was forbidden. Other aircraft were stripped as needed of whatever parts were functional. Only when it became absolutely certain that no military service or other governmental agency would ever have use for them (the State Department, for example, often gave them to friendly foreign powers) were they scrapped.

The R4D flew over row after row of B-29 "Super Fortress" bombers, perhaps three hundred of them, parked in a group next to perhaps twice that number of twin-engined B-26s; then a hundred or more B-25s. Next came more modern bombers, then a vast array of piston-engined fighter planes, then obsolete jets, air force and navy. There were trainers, observation aircraft, everything in the post-War II military aircraft inventory that had either completed its useful life or was considered obsolete or surplus to needs.

And transports, which is what Lt. Col. MacMillan was looking for.

"I see them, Mac," Eaglebury reported, his voice serious now. Mac reached for the intercom telephone.

"Put us right in the middle of the C-54s," MacMillan ordered.

"I'll do my best," Eaglebury reported. And then he picked up the transmitter microphone.

"Davis-Monthan, Navy Eight Twenty."

"Go ahead, Navy Eight Twenty."

"Davis-Monthan, Navy Eight Twenty is apparently above your station, on a course of just about due north. I'm over a bunch of airplanes. Request landing instructions, please."

"Navy Eight Twenty, we have you on radar," the tower operator reported, somewhat tartly. "You are approximately three miles from the active."

"Roger. Request winds and landing."

"Navy Eight Twenty, what is the nature of your business at this station?"

"Require fuel and someone to look at my radios."

"You are not on a ferry flight?"

"Negative, this is not, I say again, not, a ferry flight."

"Navy Eight Twenty, this station is not open to transient aircraft without prior approval."

"Davis, I can't help that. I need gas and someone to look at my radios."

"Navy Eight Twenty, are you declaring an emergency?"

"Davis, negative. I will wait until I run out of gas, and then I will declare an emergency. For Christ's sake, it's Christmas Eve."

"Navy Eight Twenty, stand by."

"Navy Eight Twenty advises I have thirty minutes' fuel on board."

"Stand by, Navy Eight Twenty."

Eaglebury put his flaps and his wheels down, slowed the Gooney-bird as much as he could, and moved in a serpentine pattern over the field. MacMillan came to the cockpit and stood between the seats, while they decided what they would do when he got it on the ground.

"Navy Eight Twenty," the radio called.

"Eight Twenty."

"Navy Eight Twenty is cleared as number one to land on runway eight four. The winds are negligible. The altimeter is three zero zero zero."

"Understand eight four," Franklin said to his microphone as Eaglebury turned the aircraft.

"Navy Eight Twenty, suggest you land long," the tower went on. "There is no Follow-Me available at this time. Take taxiway zero two right, which is at the extreme west end of the active."

Franklin, Eaglebury, and MacMillan looked at each other and beamed. If there was no Follow-Me, it would be considerably easier for them to get lost. If there had been one, Contingency Plan B—which was both a royal pain in the ass and much riskier—would have had to have been put into play.

"Roger," Eaglebury said to the microphone. He looked at Bill Franklin and made a twisting gesture with his fingers. Franklin nodded.

When Navy Eight Twenty reported turning on final, his transmission was garbled.

Navy Eight Twenty landed short, very short; and then, damned near standing the Gooney-bird on its nose, Eaglebury braked hard and turned onto taxiway two eight left. Taxiway two eight left was at the opposite end of the runway, which had been built to accommodate B-52 aircraft and was 3.2 miles long. It led in the opposite direction from taxiway zero two right.

Navy Eight Twenty proceeded down taxiway two eight left at a very high rate of speed, far in excess of good taxiing procedure.

It passed long lines of dead aircraft, Navy biplane trainers first, a flock of them giving way to some old air force Ryans, and then at least one hundred Beechcraft C-45 twin-engine navigation trainers.

"Navy Eight Twenty, we do not have you in sight. Are you on the ground?"

Lt. Commander Eaglebury made the twisting motion with his fingers, and then spoke to his microphone.

"Eight Twenty," the tower responded, in disgust. "You're garbled."

Eaglebury made a cutting motion with his hand. Franklin stopped twisting the microphone connector.

"Davis-Monthan," Lt. Commander Eaglebury said, "say again your last transmission, you are garbled."

They were in the graveyard for transports now. There were at least a hundred Gooney-birds, either R4Ds or the air force version of the Douglas DC-3, the C-47.

Eaglebury taxied past them, then past a fleet of Lockheed Constellations, some of them long-range reconnaissance aircraft equipped with grotesque radar domes sprouting out of the top of the fuselage.

And then they were among the C-54s—known as the R6D in the navy and as the DC-4 by its manufacturer, Douglas, and by the airlines that had flown them immeidately after World War II. The C-54 was essentially a bigger version of the DC-3/C-47/R4D. It had four engines instead of two. The fuselage was larger, longer, and wider. It sat on a tricycle gear, rather than main gear and a tail wheel. But there was no mistaking it for what it was, the Gooney-bird's big brother.

"OK?" Eaglebury asked.

"Good enough," MacMillan said, turned and went back into the cabin.

Eaglebury let the Gooney-bird slow, and then braked it to a stop and killed the right engine.

Master Sergeant Wojinski lowered the stair-door. Then he

easily picked up the two forty-pound aircraft batteries, one in each hand, and went down the steps. He began to trot, holding the heavy batteries away from his body so that, swinging, they would not hit him.

He trotted three rows deep into the parked C-54s and put the batteries behind the ladning gear of one of them. Lt. Colonels Charles and MacMillan ran after him. Charles had a large avionic technician's tool kit, a metal box two feet long and a foot high, cradled in his arms. Colonel MacMillan had a large cardboard carton holding several thermos bottles and jugs. Major Lowell was nearly hidden under the four down-filled sleeping bags he was carrying.

When Wojinksi had dropped off the batteries, he ran back to the Gooney-bird. CWO(2) Franklin was sitting in the door.

"Remember where you left us, Franklin," Wojinksi said. "A guy could starve to death out here before anybody found him."

Franklin handed him another cardboard box. Wojinksi ran off between the parked aircraft and disappeared from sight.

Franklin leaned out the door, looking toward where Lt. Commander Eaglebury was staring out of the sliding window. He made a tugging gesture, like a train conductor ordering a commuter train into motion.

The running engine revved, and the Gooney-bird turned around and taxied a half mile down the taxiway back toward the runway. There it stopped. Franklin went down the stairs carrying the Winchester riot gun. He walked in front of the left wing, faced rear, and put one shell into the magazine. Then he worked the action, chambering the shell. Taking careful aim, he blew a hole in the Gooney-bird's tire.

Then Lt. Commander Eaglebury got on the radio (which seemed to be working now) and informed the Davis-Monthan tower that not only did he seem to be lost, but he had blown a tire, and would somebody come help him?

(Four)

Operation Fearless had been born two weeks before on the 15th tee of the Fort Rucker golf course. Major Lowell had been invited to go a round with Lt. Col. Charles. At first Lowell had turned down the invitation; but Charles had insisted, and Lowell had concluded that Charles had something on his mind besides hitting a small white ball with a variety of steel and wood implements.

The problem was the AN/ARC-55 radio. AN stood for Army-Navy. ARC stood for Aircraft Radio Communications. The number 55 identified the model. The ARC-55 was a high-frequency, long-range, radio transmitter-receiver. The Gooneybirds were going to need such radios to fly to Nicaragua from Florida.

There were none in army stocks, because the army had no requirement for radios with a long-distance capability; and the navy had long ago declared the model obsolescent and transferred its stock of them to the air force. The air force was "regrettably unable to comply" with Lt. Col. Augustus Charles's request for the interservice transfer of any AN/ARC-55 radios.

Both Lt. Col. Charles and Major Lowell were extraordinarily good golfers, and they played quickly. They talked about the ARC-55 problem only as they walked together down the fairways, never on the tees or greens, where only Sunday golfers profaned the noble sport by idle conversation.

By the 15th tee, however, Lt. Col. Charles had gone through his problems with finding the ARC-55.

"The air force is screwing us," he said. "I know goddamned well they have ARC-55s in warehouses. But they want us to set up a large howl about not having any, whereupon they can ask what we want them for. And that opens a large can of worms."

"Felter can get them for us," Lowell said.

"I look at Felter as a too easily expendable asset," Charles said. "I'd rather keep his clout in reserve until we really need it. And God knows, I don't want to see him lose his job and have it taken over by those lunatics in the CIA."

"I've got just about a blank check," Lowell said. "Can we buy them?"

"I looked into that, too. Unless we go to the trouble of getting a special exemption for a classified project, we would have to put acquisition up for bids. That would take too long for one thing. And for another, even if we had the time—and we don't—to put it up for bids, that would give the air force a chance to ask what we wanted long-range aviation radios for."

"You tell me. What do we do?"

"You ever been to Leavenworth?" Lt. Col. Charles asked.

"Fort Leavenworth, or the prison?"

"The prison."

"When I was at Command and General Staff," Lowell said, "they took us on a tour of the prison."

"What did you think of it?"

There was a reason for the question, Lowell sensed, so he answered it.

"The prisoners live better than GIs," he said.

"That's what I was thinking," Charles said. "I mean, going there wouldn't be all that bad, if you got right down to it. Not that I plan to get caught, of course. Just thinking about the worst possible scenario."

"Get caught doing what?"

"Stealing ARC-55s from the air force graveyard at Davis-Monthan," Charles said.

"Have they got them out there?"

"All C-54s were equipped with them," Charles said. "I'll bet I could come back with a couple of dozen of them."

"You couldn't do it by yourself," Lowell said.

"No. I figure it would take at least three people."

"You got anybody in mind?"

"You can't ask people to take a risk like that," Charles said.

"Aside from you and me, I mean?"

"Funny," Charles said. "I thought you just might volunteer."

"Not only will I volunteer, but I have an ace in the hole who owes me a favor."

"A professional thief, I hope?"

"Better than that, a Medal of Honor winner. They never get court-martialed. Think of the bad publicity."

"MacMillan?"

"Why not? He's going to use the damned radios."

"OK," Charles said. "I will not offer the comment that while Medal winners can commit murder and get away with it, their partners in crime go to jail just like ordinary people."

"Colonel," Lowell said, "why don't we finish this round quickly, then repair to my home, where we can get down to some serious planning?"

Colonel Charles hustled Major Lowell for one hundred and fifty dollars on the last three holes of their game. Major Lowell was impressed with Colonel Charles. There were few people able to hustle him—either on the golf course or on a caper that was very likely to melt the thin ice on which his chances of promotion were already skidding.

Lowell told himself that he should have known something crazy like this would come up. That very morning (when Jane Cassidy's transfer to the Department of Publications at the Army Aviation School had at last come through) he had permitted himself to think that he had escaped for a while from crazy situations. He should have realized that he, of all people, couldn't be that lucky.

Three months ago, Jane had come up to him in a rage and accused him of being just like every other man: "You just have to boast about your conquest, don't you?" she screamed.

He had no idea what she was talking about—and said so.

"If you hadn't boasted, if there had been no talk, the chief of police would have never found out," she said.

"What chief of police?" he asked.

"The Ozark chief of police," she hissed. "He knows."

"Oh, I don't think so," he said, without thinking. He immediately regretted his comment. If she thought the chief of police knew, she just might decide the whole thing was too risky.

"It's over, of course," she said. "You've left me where I thought you would."

He could think of no reply to that, so he said nothing.

"You're going to have to get me a transfer," she said.

"If you think I should," he said, "I'll see what I can do."

"You won't 'see what you can do!'" she snapped. "You'll do it! You owe me that much! My marriage is at stake!"

The wheels of bureaucracy moved with their usual slowness. Even after he found her another job, it took a couple months for the transfer to be made official. During that time, she treated him with icy courtesy.

His relief when the transfer came through was enormous. Jane was replaced by a plain, pleasant woman in her late forties. An absolutely undangerous woman, delighted with the promotion the transfer had meant for her and determined to make good.

Once again, Craig now realized, he was jumping from one frying pan into—if not the fire—then another frying pan. If they were caught stealing radios at Davis-Monthan, he would

be in as much trouble as if he had been caught with Jane Cassidy
in his bed.

He consoled himself with the thought that at least there was
a noble purpose in stealing the radios. Jiggs would understand
that. But Jiggs would have been shocked and dismayed if he'd
known about Craig's connection with Jane Cassidy.

The first thing Major Craig Lowell and Colonel Augustus
Charles realized when they got down to specifics was that they
could not execute Operation Fearless with only three people.
At least one more was needed.

That led them to Lieutenant Commander Eaglebury. As a
navy pilot, he could fly the VIP Gooney-bird, which he could
identify as a navy airplane. To save him from potential trouble,
they tried at first to keep him in the dark about what they were
up to. But Lieutenant Commander Eaglebury took only two
days to figure out that they were going to do something in
Arizona besides look at the desert flora and fauna. He demanded in on the whole picture, or they could get somebody
else to fly their airplane.

Lieutenant Commander Eaglebury also pointed out that regulations prescribed that a Gooney-bird be driven by two chauf-
feurs. Another getaway driver was needed: CWO (2) William
B. Franklin (whose promotion from Warrant Officer Junior
Grade had come the week he had been qualified as pilot-in-
command of R4D aircraft). Not only could Franklin be trusted
to keep his mouth shut; but if they were caught, he told them,
he would just play the dumb nigger warrant officer who didn't
even know he was in Arizona.

The sixth co-conspirator joined up when Lt. Col. MacMillan
asked Master Sergeant Wojinski to get him a riot gun from the
arms room and to keep his mouth shut about it. When Wojinski
had demanded specifics, MacMillan told him Lowell wanted
it, but he didn't know what for.

M/Sgt Wojinski showed up at Fort Rucker with the shotgun
in a golf bag, and announced that whither Lowell was going
with it, so was he.

In order to discourage the sergeant from sticking his ass in
a crack where it would very likely get nipped off, Wojinski
was given the rough outline of the plan.

"No disrespect, Major," Wojinski said. "But if you guys
are going to get away with this, you're going to need a professional. You're, excuse me, just a bunch of fucking amateurs."

He thereupon proceeded to point out several flaws in the operations plan. Wojinski was in.

(Five)

Immediately upon entering into Phase II of Operation Fearless—infiltration of the target area—it became apparent that there was a flaw in the operations plan that even Wojinski had overlooked. There was no way to get inside the airplanes from which the radios would be stolen; their doors were too high off the ground. Even with Lowell (six feet two) standing on Wojinski's (six feet three) shoulders, he was at least four feet from a latch that might—or might not—gain them access to the aircraft.

"There is only one thing to do," Wojinski said.

"Surrender, and throw ourselves on the mercy of the air force."

"No," Wojinski said. "I'll go steal one of those pickup trucks with a stairs on it."

"A what?" MacMillan asked.

"You *know*," Wojinski said, patiently. "One of those things they drive up to airplanes so people can get on and off. There must be a couple of them around here."

"If there is, it would be at Base Operations," Lowell said. "That must be five miles from here."

"I can go catty-corner," M/Sgt Wojinski said. "I figure three, maybe three and a half miles."

He took a compass from the knee pocket of his flight suit, consulted it a moment, replaced it, and then trotted off into the massed, parked airplanes, his forearms pumping parallel to the ground, his fists balled, his back straight—the jogger out for his daily physical conditioning.

Lt. Col. Charles, Lt. Col. MacMillan, and Major Lowell then went up and down the lines of parked C-54 aircraft, picking out aircraft which seemed most likely to have AN/ARC-55 radios aboard in good condition. The aircraft in nonpreserved storage ranged from skeletonized derelicts, not much more than stripped airframes, to aircraft which appeared ready for takeoff. There was no problem finding a dozen likely candidates for their midnight requisition.

Then, curiosity aroused, they moved out of the C-54 area. There came a loud shout from Charles.

Lowell first thought that Lt. Col. Augustus Charles had lost his marbles, calling attention to them. But then he realized that the chances of anybody else but himself or Mac hearing a shout were just about nonexistent. He went in the direction of the shout, and a minute of two later found Charles and Mac, beaming with delight, standing under a Lockheed Constellation. He didn't know the air force nonmenclature for it.

"Look at this!" Charles said, pointing up at the narrow nose. There was a legend painted on the nose, the word "Bataan" superimposed on a map of the Bataan peninsula.

"I thought he had a C-54," Lowell said, remembering newsreels of General of the Army Douglas MacArthur regally descending from his personal transport aircraft.

"So did I," Charles said. "But it says 'Bataan.'"

"I'll bet there's beds on that sonofabitch," Major Lowell said, thoughtfully.

Thirty minutes later, they heard the sound of a vehicle in the distance. It was possible that the air police patrolled the area, so they hid themselves behind landing gear and watched.

It was M/Sgt Wojinksi at the wheel of an air force pickup truck. He was driving with his elbow out the window. The pickup truck was equipped with a stairway, and behind it was something else—a trailer holding a ground auxiliary power unit.

"The whole fucking operation almost went down the tube," M/Sgt Wojinski announced.

"They saw you?" Lowell asked.

"Nah," Wojinski said, offended at the suggestion. "What happened was that the base commander come by Base Ops to wish the troops stuck with the duty Merry Christmas. And he felt so sorry for Eaglebury and Franklin getting stuck here on Christmas Eve that he wanted to have the flat fixed right away."

"How do you know?" MacMillan asked.

"I was looking in the window," Wojinski said.

"So what happened?" Mac asked.

"Eaglebury said that he would rather not have the general ask enlisted men to work on Christmas Eve. He said that he would hate to have a work crew remember that they had to work on Christmas Eve because of some damned naval officer."

"So they're not coming tonight?" Charles asked.

"No. And the general was so touched by Eaglebury's speech that he gave one of his own. He said *he* would hate to have two naval officers remember that they had spent Christmas Eve in a BOQ in Arizona, with the club closed, and that he would be honored if they would accept the hospitality of his quarters."

"He took them home with him?" Lowell asked, incredulously.

"I hope to Christ he don't ask Franklin anything about the navy," Wojinski said. "For a moment, I thought he was going to turn white."

"You're sure nobody saw you steal this?" MacMillan asked.

"Nah," Wojinski said, deprecatingly. "They had four of them in a motor pool."

"How'd you get it out of the motor pool without being seen?" Lowell asked.

"There's generally two gates to a motor pool," Wojinski explained. "All I had to do was go to the back one and pick the padlock."

"What about the ground power unit?" Lt. Col. Charles asked.

"That was on the transient parking lot," Wojinski explained.

"Aren't they going to miss it?"

"Not before we're long gone," Wojinski said.

(Six)

Phase III of Operation Fearless went very smoothly. They drove the pickup truck with the stairway to the door of the first C-54 they'd selected, opened the door, and Lt. Col. Charles and Major Lowell entered the aircraft. Major Lowell carried one of the nickel-cadmium batteries, and Lt. Col. Charles and Lt. Col. MacMillan carried between them the tool kit.

Five minutes later, the dials of the AN/ARC-55 radio aboard glowed, Lt. Col. Charles having powered it up by disconnecting it from the 24-volt major buss and to the nickel-cadmium battery. He set a frequency he thought was unlikely to be monitored by the Davis-Monthan tower, closed his tool box, and then he and MacMillan went down the stairs.

Lowell was left alone in the aircraft. It was an eerie feeling. He wondered how long it had been since anyone had sat on the radio operator's stool.

Ten minutes later, there was a voice in his earphones.

"Air Force Six Thirteen, Air Force Fourteen Ten."

"Go ahead, Fourteen Ten," Lowell said to the microphone. "How do you read?"

"Five by five," Lowell replied.

"Six Thirteen, give me a long count, please."

"Ten, Niner, Eight, Seven, Six, Fiver, Four, Three, Two, One."

"Six Thirteen, I read you five by five. Fourteen Ten, clear."

They now had two functioning radios.

Ten minutes later, having removed an ARC-55 and its immediate wiring and power supply from Donor Aircraft No. 2, Lt. Col. Charles went on the air using the ARC-55 in Donor Aircraft No. 3. There was no reply. He checked his connections and found nothing wrong, which meant that particular radio was not working. So he closed his tool kit, went down the stairs, and was driven to Donor Aircraft No. 4.

By 2045 hours, the bed of the pickup truck held twelve AN/ARC-55 radios, four more than Operations Fearless called for, plus so much other "excess to air force requirements" aviation communications and electronic equipment that it was impossible to lower the hydraulically operated stairway.

A thirteenth ("for good luck," Lt. Col. Charles said) AN/ARC-55 and its ancillary equipment was removed from Donor Aircraft No. 1, and Major Lowell was able to evacuate the radio operator's stool in that aircraft as he joined the others. Then M/Sgt Wojinski drove the pickup truck onto the runway to their own R4D aircraft, tilted to one side on its flat tire.

The avionics equipment was loaded aboard the aircraft: in the baggage compartment in the nose, in the radio compartment between the passenger compartment and the cockpit, and in the toilet in the rear of the cabin.

The operations plan for Operation Fearless next required that they reload the food and sleeping bags aboard the Gooney-bird. They had been off-loaded against the contingency that the air force would either move the Gooney-bird to Base Operations or place a guard on it.

"If you'll go get our crap and load it, I'll put the truck back," M/Sgt Wojinski said.

"Sergeant Wojinski," Major Lowell said, "far be it from a 'fucking amateur' such as myself to offer a suggestion to a fucking professional such as yourself, but how would you like to sleep in General of the Army Douglas MacArthur's very own bed?"

"Come on, Lowell," Lt. Col. Charles said. "We'd need the stair-truck to get in it."

"And you, Lt. Col. Charles, how would you like to sleep in a bed previously occupied by Mrs. MacArthur, or at the very least by Major General Willoughby? Or some other member of the Imperial Guard?"

"What do we do with the truck?" Lt. Col. MacMillan asked. Lowell's suggestion had struck a chord.

"If Ski tries to take it back, he's liable to get caught."

"Bullshit," M/Sgt Wojinski said, flatly.

"He'd have to use headlights, and there would be a risk. However, in two or three days, after the air force finally misses their truck and the ground power supply, and after they start looking for it, if they were to find it parked against the "Bataan" with the power supply plugged into it, they would probably decide that several of their own people had used the Christmas holidays to view an historic aircraft."

Lt. Colonel Charles thought that over a moment.

"Lowell," he said, "I hate to admit it, but you are one smart sonofabitch."

"Thank you, sir."

When they got aboard the "Bataan," they found that it had one permanently installed double bed. Lt. Colonel Charles claimed the privilege of rank and shared it with M/Sgt Wojinski. Lowell and MacMillan spent the night in their sleeping bags on couches made up from folding seats.

They also found that with the ground power supply plugged in, it was possible to close the curtains over the windows, thus permitting the cabin lights and a broadcast band radio to be turned on. The electric galley worked, and thus they were able to warm their rations and heat water for powdered coffee. This, to mark the successful completion of Phase IV of Operation Fearless, they laced with cognac that Major Lowell had included with the rations against the chance one of the team might suffer snakebite.

(Seven)

Phase V of Operation Fearless went smoothly. At first light, they left the "Bataan" and walked to the Gooney-bird. M/Sgt Wojinski sat in the cockpit and served as lookout.

When an air force caravan (two pickup trucks; a staff car; a huge, bright yellow truck equipped with a derrick and sling; and a fuel truck) appeared on the taxiway shortly after 0800 hours, Lt. Col. Charles and Major Lowell secreted themselves in the radio-navigator's compartment, and M/Sgt Wojinski and Lt. Col. MacMillan in the toilet.

Air force technicians quickly arranged a sling around the left wing, and the derrick raised the aircraft off the ground. The blown tire was quickly removed, replaced, and the aircraft lowered to the ground.

Lt. Commander Eaglebury profusely thanked the aerodrome officer for all his courtesies, and told him that if he was ever in the vicinity of the Anacostia Naval Air Station to be sure to look him up.

Greetings for the holiday season were exchanged. The pilots boarded the aircraft.

"Davis-Monthan clears Navy Eight Twenty for taxi to the active. You may use the taxiway as the threshold. There are no winds. The altimeter is two niner eight. The time is forty-five past the hour. You are cleared for takeoff when ready."

Five minutes later, Bill Franklin spoke to his microphone: "Davis-Monthan, Navy Eight Twenty rolling. Thank you, Davis-Monthan."

"Merry Christmas, Navy Eight Twenty."

(Eight)

Major Lowell offered to spring for the Christmas Day buffet at the Dallas Country Club when they landed at Love Field for fuel, but the others were anxious to get home, so they took aboard more in-flight meals from Executive Air Catering and flew on to Laird Field at Fort Rucker.

MacMillan, Eaglebury, and Wojinski took off again as soon as the ARC-55s and other equipment had been off-loaded. Franklin announced he had "plans," and Lowell told him to go ahead.

"I think we've earned ourselves a drink," Lt. Col. Charles said. "Can I buy you one?"

They went to the officer's club. There were few wives, for it was Christmas Day, but it was fairly crowded with bachelors. They spent ten minutes trying to play the devil's advocate... *what could go wrong now?*

They came up with a number of possibilities—that someone at Davis-Monthan would have noticed that the tail number of "Navy Eight Twenty" did not include those numbers, or that the stolen truck would be discovered missing in time to make the connection with them—but it seemed as if Operation Fearless had been flawlessly executed.

"You really are a pretty smart fellow, Lowell," Lt. Colonel Augustus Charles said.

Lowell suspected that there was a hooker in the compliment even before Charles asked, "Can I ask you a personal question?"

"Sure."

"How come a smart fellow like you is fucking his secretary?"

"What makes you think I am?"

"His married secretary," Charles went on.

"Where did you get that idea?"

"My wife told me," Charles said. "She's a regular FBI."

"Your wife is in error, Colonel," Lowell said.

"Sure she is," Charles said. "And at this very moment, she is a very pissed-off woman. She has the odd notion that I should have been home over Christmas."

He tossed money on the bar.

"'Keep your indiscretions a hundred miles from the flag-pole,'" he said. "You ever hear that, Lowell?"

He walked away without waiting for Lowell's answer.

Jesus, Lowell thought, shaken by Colonel Charles's announcement, *I did get out of that business with Jane Cassidy just in time. If Mrs. Augustus Charles knew, it was amazing that neither Bill Roberts or Paul Jiggs had heard from the wives' grapevine.*

And then calm returned. He *was* out of the affair with Jane Cassidy. *And* they had carried off Operation Fearless without a hitch.

God was in his heaven, all was right with the world.

"You want another drink, Major?" the bartender asked.

"No, thanks," Lowell said. "I really didn't want this one."

He left it unfinished on the bar and walked out. He had a lot of work to do.

And that, too, was a good thing, he thought. It would give him something to do on Christmas Day. No matter how often he told himself that Christmas was just one more day of the year to someone like him, that just wasn't true.

XIX

(One)
The Skyclub
National Airport
Washington, D.C.
1715 Hours, 19 May 1960

The Skyclub was maintained by American Airlines so that its frequent first-class passengers would not have to mingle with the riffraff. Nevertheless, it was crowded. It was a Friday afternoon, and people were leaving Washington for the weekend. There were senators and congressmen in the Skyclub, lobbyists, lawyers, a half-dozen executive directors of various national organizations, wives, one lady congressperson, and assorted girl friends. And about a dozen army officers, including an army major whose Skyclub card was made out in the name of C. W. Lowell, Vice Chairman of the Board, Craig, Powell, Kenyon and Dawes.

Major Lowell was in the Skyclub because when he had announced he was going to Washington, Colonel Bill Roberts had pointedly suggested that he "go commercial with the others," in other words leave the Commander parked at Laird Field.

The others were a dozen officers from various departments of the Army Aviation School. With one exception—a newly promoted major—they were all senior to Lowell. They had come to Washington for a conference which had dealt with several draft reports concerning the formation and organization of the airmobile division. The conference was intended to resolve objections to the reports raised by the Infantry Center, the Armor Center, the Airborne Center, and the Artillery Center, each of whom had also dispatched a dozen officers. The conference had been chaired by the Deputy Assistant Chief of Staff, Operations, who had also decided to hold the conference in Washington (which was neutral ground) rather than at one of the posts of the involved combat arms.

The first meeting had been called to order at 0830 on Monday; the last had been adjourned (two hours late) at 1515 on Friday. For a solid week, there had been argument—often at length—over very minor recommendations. A phalanx of typists would now prepare a report that would summarize the agreements (very few) and detail opposing views on those points (most) that had not been resolved. This document would then be circulated among the various participants to insure that their views were correctly reflected. Then it would be corrected, typed yet again, and submitted through the Deputy Assistant Chief of Staff, Operations, and then through the Assistant Chief of Staff, Operations, and finally to the DCSOPS, for his decision.

The whole thing, which could have been handled in two hours on the telephone, would take at least a month, Lowell thought. He was by nature cynical insofar as army procedures were concerned. And a solid week of conference had made him bitter.

Not a few comments, he was sure, were made not for their validity but because the commentor felt obliged to say something—anything at all—in order to prove that he was making a contribution. Some of the comments had been silly, foolish, and even absurd. For example, the decision over whether to pool chaplains in a Chaplain's Section of the Division Headquarters Company or to assign them on the basis of one per so many officers and men throughout the division had taken two hours of discussion before tentative resolution.

When they got to the important things (how many gas trucks would be required to fuel the division's aircraft, and where and to whom they should be assigned, for example), the decision-making process had been even slower.

And in the end, Lowell knew, the decisions would be made by the Deputy Chief of Staff, Operations, in about ten seconds. The DCSOPS would base *his* decision on what *he* thought and wouldn't even look at the supporting arguments in the voluminous reports.

He might decide, for example, that chaplains belonged with the troops, and so order. Or that the only way to keep a handle on religion was to have the chaplains gathered together in one spot under a senior officer charged with keeping them in line. And so order.

After the final meeting had broken up, Lowell took a cab to the Hay-Adams Hotel, where he was staying, and quickly packed his bag. Then he was driven in the Hay-Adams Rolls-Royce to Washington National, where he missed the 1650 Southern Airways flight to Atlanta by five minutes.

Major Lowell turned his bags over to Southern, then went to the Skyclub and told the hostess of his problem. She assured him that American Airlines would do everything possible to get him on the very first available seat to Atlanta and that American would be delighted to call ahead and arrange a charter flight for him if there was nothing available on Southern to take him from Atlanta to Dothan. If the Vice Chairman of the Board of Craig, Powell, Kenyon and Dawes (who had a Sky-club Card with a discreet symbol that he was to be treated as a Very Very Important Person—as opposed to a frequent traveler who was a salesman, for example) wanted to go to Dothan, Alabama, she was being paid to see that he got there in the smoothest possible way.

She escorted Lowell to a red leather couch (none of the small tables was free) and got him a scotch and soda and a bowl of cashews. She handed him a copy of the *Wall Street Journal*, and told him she'd give him the word about his flight the moment she had it.

The woman who came into the Skyclub had three large leather bags suspended from her shoulders. She had just flown ten thousand miles. In thirty minutes, she would catch the New York shuttle. In the meantime, she wanted a drink, and she wanted to sit down.

There was no place she could sit alone, as she had hoped. So she decided the best vacancy available was on a couch beside a man behind a *Wall Street Journal*. As she walked to the couch she decided she would put her bags on the cushion between them, just to make sure.

She did so. She dumped the heavy bags on the center cushion, more than a little embarrassed that she bounced the whole couch when she did it. Averting her eyes in embarrassment, she sat down. Then she stole a look at the man. If he was glowering at her, she would apologize. She had been wrong.

"Oh, Jesus!" Cynthia Thomas said.

"We're going to have to stop meeting this way," Craig Lowell said. "People will talk."

"Oh, my God!" Cynthia said.

"I'm fine, thank you," Lowell said. "And you?"

"I just got in from Moscow," she said. "I'm going catch the shuttle..."

"Moscow in the spring!" Lowell said. "How *chic!"*

"Don't, Craig," she said.

"Don't what?"

"Don't be cleverly bitter," she said.

"Me? Bitter? Perish the *thought!"*

"What are you doing in Washington?"

"Leaving," he said.

The hostess brought Cynthia a drink.

"So how have you been?" Lowell asked, sarcastically.

"I've been busy," she replied. "And I've been lonely and miserable."

"No new love?"

"That was a cheap shot!"

"Sorry."

"But on the other hand, I haven't been in Fort Rucker, Alabama, either," she said, "making the both of us miserable."

"So where does that leave us?" Lowell asked.

"Nowhere," she said. "But we never were really anywhere, really."

"I'd forgotten how beautiful you really are," Lowell said softly, almost to himself.

"Damn you," she said.

"I think I'd better change seats," he said.

"No!" she said, immediately, so loudly that heads turned.

"Now everyone will think I've made a pass at you," he said.

"Why don't you, Craig?" Cynthia asked, very softly.

He looked at her in disbelief.

"Will they stand you before a firing squad if you don't get to where you're going by the dawn's early light?" she asked.

"I have the weekend free," he said.

"Isn't a weekend better than nothing?" Cynthia asked.

"What if it's not enough?" he asked.

"It's all we've got," she said.

There was a telephone on the coffee table. An operator answered.

"This is C. W. Lowell," he said. "Call the Hay-Adams and tell them my plans have changed, and I'll require my suite through the weekend."

(Two)
Above Tallahassee, Florida
1730 ZULU, 14 October 1960

Major Craig W. Lowell watched the ADF needles reverse as he passed over the Tallahassee omni, and then picked up his microphone.

"Tallahassee, Trans-Caribbean Four Oh Two over the omni at ten thousand at thirty past the hour."

"Roger, Trans-Caribbean, radar has you at one zero thousand, ground speed two one zero, on three ten true."

"Trans-Caribbean Four Oh Two leaving 125.2 at this time," Lowell said.

He leaned back in the pilot's seat of the Gooney-bird, craned his neck further back to get a good look at the dial, and changed his transceiver frequency.

"Valdosta area control, Trans-Caribbean Four Oh Two."

"Four Oh Two, Valdosta."

"Valdosta, will you close me out, please?"

There was a moment's pause, then: "Valdosta area control closes Trans-Caribbean Four Oh Two over Tallahassee at one zero thousand at three two past the hour."

"Thank you, Valdosta," Lowell said. "Four Oh Two switching to Tallahassee approach control at this time."

He changed the transceiver and ADF frequencies again, but not to those utilized by Tallahassee.

He got the Laird omni.

Dah dah dah, dah dah dit dit, dit dah dit.

The international Morse code in his earphones spelled out OZR. Why the hell the Laird Omni didn't spell out dit dah dit dit, dit dah dit, dah dit dit, for LRD, as in *LaiRD*, or dit dah dit, dah dit dah, dit dah dit, for RKR, as in *RucKeR*, was a mystery whose solution was known only to the FAA. The FAA assigned omni codes and persisted in using dah dah dah, dah dah dit dit, dit dah dit for *OZaR*k, which had never had an omnidirectional navigation aid, even before Fort Rucker.

He made a slight course correction, so that the needles were where they were supposed to be, and then went on the horn.

"Laird, Army Four Oh Two."

"Aircraft calling Laird, say again."

He was a bit far out, but what the hell.

"Laird, Army Four Oh Two," he said again.

"Four Oh Two, Laird. You are weak but readable."

"Four Oh Two, visual, seventy miles southeast at ten thousand. Estimate Laird in twenty minutes."

"Understand seven zero southeast, one zero thousand, two zero minutes."

"Affirmative," Lowell said. "Laird, Code Eleven. Capacity eight. Confirm."

"Understand Code Eleven, capacity eight."

"Affirmative."

"Capacity is eight? Confirm?"

"Affirmative, capacity is eight."

He had just announced that he had personnel aboard requiring medical attention, including transport by ambulance. He had, he thought, just given the boys in the tower—and for that matter the boys in the hospital, and probably even Major General Paul T. Jiggs—something to liven up an otherwise dull day.

One of the hush-hush airplanes will land in twenty minutes, and requires ambulances for eight people!

They would probably be just a little disappointed when he landed and they learned that what he had aboard was just one wounded man (a *Cubano* had surprised hell out of a Green Beret hand-to-hand combat instructor by stabbing the Beret in the groin with a bayonet the instructor had planned to take away from him with skill and élan) and seven others, including five Rucker pilots, suffering from semiterminal cases of the running shits.

Lowell reached over his head again and adjusted the trim

control, a four-inch diameter wheel. The nose of the Gooney-bird dropped just perceptibly.

He turned to the man in the copilot's seat.

"Almost home," Lowell said.

The man in the copilot's seat was not an aviator. He was a Green Beret sergeant first class, an instructor in radio communication. He was riding in the right seat because there were no pilots available, and Lowell thought that if needed, the sergeant could be pressed into service to work the radios.

He had not been needed. It had been a long, slow, uneventful flight.

In addition to the eight passengers in the compartment of the Gooney-bird were a number of crates (Lowell had taken off considerably over the specified maximum gross weight). These crates contained items of equipment which, having been sent by a very circuitous route to Nicaragua, had not worked when they arrived there.

There was a good deal fucked up in this operation, fuck-ups which sorely tried the patience of the Action Officer, one Sanford T. Felter. Felter had been nearly as furious about the failure to properly treat the water, which had laid low eighty-five Americans and several hundred *Cubanos*, as he had been to learn that the medicine on hand to deal with this unfortunate contingency was out of date and useless.

But not as furious as he had been when the Gooney-bird delivering fresh medicine had landed at Nicaragua with Major Craig W. Lowell at the controls.

"What the hell are you doing here?" he had snapped. "I told you you were not to come down here."

"Somebody, Little Man, had to drive the airplane."

"You are Category I, goddamnit!" Sandy had fumed, genuinely angry.

Category I was that small list of persons who had knowledge of the entire operation. Category I personnel were not to be placed in a position where they might fall into the wrong hands, and thus compromise the security of the operation.

"Sandy," Lowell had tried to reason, "there was nobody else available to fly it. I had two choices: delay shipment from thirty-six to forty-eight hours (and you wanted this stuff immediately) or come down here myself."

He was tempted to add, but didn't, that his presence was proof positive of his noble self-sacrifice in the name of duty:

Cynthia Thomas, just back from London, had suggested that she was free to spend a few days with him. He was at the humiliating point with her where he was willing to settle for a couple of days, anywhere, anytime, at her pleasure.

"You should have waited however long it took," Felter said, coldly furious.

"Forgive me, Generalissimo, I have erred," Lowell said.

"It's more than an error, Major Lowell," Felter said, his voice as cold as Lowell had ever heard it. "It's direct disobedience of an order."

"Forgive me, Colonel Felter," Lowell said, "you won't be able to make that stick. It may be an error of judgment, but I was responding to an emergency situation to the best of my ability."

"This *is* an order," Felter said. "I will try to phrase it so that even you cannot misunderstand or misinterpret it. You will not leave the airfield. You will get whatever sleep you feel you need, you will service that aircraft, and you will immediately return to Fort Rucker. You are never to come here again unless I expressly order you to do so. I hope, Craig, for your sake, that you understand how serious I am about this."

"Yes, sir," Lowell said.

Felter had glowered at him and stalked off, and he had not seen him again.

Lowell had napped for a sweat-soaked four hours on a blanket spread out under the wing. He had been bitten awake by a swarm of insects, feasting at his crotch and armpits. He had stripped and sprayed himself with a stinging DDT aerosol bomb, and then gone to Base Ops, a tent, and announced he was ready to go back.

The surgeon had met him there, asking that he take as many people as he could in addition to the priority cargo and the two priority passengers: the Green Beret radio sergeant and the sergeant stabbed by the *Cubano*.

"I think the priority, doctor, would be my pilots," Lowell said. "The sooner I can get them cured of the GIs, the sooner they can be back at work."

The surgeon had thought that over and nodded agreement.

Thirty minutes later, a thousand pounds over max gross, Lowell had finally managed to get the Gooney-bird airborne. He had cleared the rain forest at the end of the runway by no more than twenty feet, and it had been a long time before he had been able to pick up either airspeed or altitude.

The Gooney-bird did not have the range to fly over the Gulf of Mexico directly to the States. There had been two options: flying up the coast and refueling at least once in Mexico, or going the long way (which would, it was hoped, make the Gooney-bird flights much less suspicious and conspicuous).

The long way was from the field in Nicaragua to Grand Inagua Island in the Bahamas, where they'd refuel. This was the longest leg—close to the maximum distance the Gooney-bird could fly. The greatest risk occurred on the way down from Grand Inagua to Nicaragua. The last five hundred miles on that leg were over water. Lowell had been willing to take the chance of flying over max gross on that leg because his route to Grand Inagua would take him over Jamaica and then through the Windward Passage between the southern tip of Cuba and Haiti. If he ran low on fuel, he planned to put in to Port-au-Prince, Haiti, or if necessary, Kingston, Jamaica—or, in a genuine emergency, into Guantanamo, the U.S. Navy base on the tip of Cuba.

There were (someone had made a list) seventy-odd "airlines" operating in the area, most of them one or two-plane operations. Of course, there was no Trans-Caribbean, but an "airline" by that name flying an old DC-3 would not cause undue attention. Lowell had devised the basic flight plans he himself was using on this flight.

The R4Ds took off from Rucker or Bragg bound for Nicaragua on visual flight rules. Once airborne, they contacted either Atlanta or Valdosta area control, identifying themselves as Trans-Caribbean aircraft, and filed an instrument flight plan to Miami. One more unpainted DC-3 cargo plane at Miami raised no eyebrows. At Miami the planes cleared U.S. Customs. And then they left Miami on IFR flight plans to anywhere: the Bahamas, or Haiti, or the British West Indies. Later they closed out the flight plans in the air, and flew on to Nicaragua, homing in first on a radio station in Bluefields, and when close, on an omni set up at the jungle field.

On the return, the second leg was from Great Inagua to Miami, a 550-mile leg. The third leg was from Miami to Rucker (or from Miami to Bragg, with a fuel stop in Savannah). Somewhere over Florida, "Trans-Carribbean" closed out its IFR flight plan, and the R4D became an army aircraft flying on visual flight rules again.

It had been a long flight, the Gooney-bird cruising along at no more than 190 knots, and Lowell was glad to see Dothan, Alabama, under his wing.

"Laird, Army Four Oh, five miles southeast for landing."

He made a very shallow approach over Clayhatchee; and as he turned on final, he saw two ambulances with red lights flashing coming down the road from the post to Laird Field. As he touched down, he could see out of the corner of his eye two ambulances and two staff cars parked on the ramp at the Board area.

They were probably prepared to conduct emergency surgery on the spot, he thought somewhat nastily, and what they were going to get was an epidemic of loose bowels.

As he taxied up to the Board area, he saw that another two ambulances had arrived, and that one of the staff cars had a Collins antenna mounted on its roof. The antenna, even more than the red plate with two stars, identified it as Paul Jiggs's staff car. That made him feel bad. Jiggs, a commander who could not sit at a desk when there were "injured troops," really had no cause to be here.

Lowell turned the Gooney-bird into line, killed the engines, and stuck his head out the window.

"We need only one stretcher," he called out to the sixteen medics and that many nurses and doctors waiting to attend the "injured" and carry them off the plane to the ambulances.

And then he chuckled as he thought that *no* stretchers were needed. The Beret the Cubano had stabbed was so embarrassed that he would have walked off the airplane on his hands before they carried him on a stretcher.

Lowell sat in the pilot's seat and did the paperwork, then walked down the sloping cabin floor as ground crewman began to unlash the cargo. When he got off the airplane, Major General Paul T. Jiggs was standing there.

Lowell saluted.

"I'm sorry you had to come out here, sir," he said. "But I didn't think I should go on the air with the announcement that the walking wounded were suffering from the GIs."

"It's all right," Jiggs said. "I wanted to see you, anyway."

From the tone of his voice, it was clear that his visit was official. Lowell wondered then—for the first time—if Sandy had been so angry that he'd gotten in touch with Jiggs.

Jiggs handed him a TWX:

HQ DEPT OF THE ARMY
WASH DC 1456 ZULU 13 OCTOBER 1960

TO COMMANDING GENERAL FT RUCKER ALA

FOR PRES USA AVIATION BOARD

1. THIS TWX CONFIRMS TELECON 1800 ZULU 12 OCT 60 BETWEEN BRIG GEN BELLMON DCSOPS AND MAJ GEN JIGGS.

2. COMGEN FT RUCKER IS AUTH AND DIRECTED TO ISSUE LETTER ORDERS ASAP PLACING MAJ LOWELL, CRAIG W 0–366901 ARMOR USA AVN BOARD ON TEMP DY WITH HQ US ARMY PACIFIC, HONOLULU HAWAII, FOR A PERIOD OF 180 DAYS UNLESS SOONER RELEASED BY CINCPAC.

3. OFF IS AUTH TVL BY MIL OR CIV AIR TRANS TO HAWAII. THIS TWX CONSTITUTES AUTHORITY FOR AAA PRIORITY IN EVENT MIL AIR TRANS IS UTILIZED.

4. OFF IS NOT AUTH TRANS OF PRIVATE VEHICLE, HOUSEHOLD, OR PROFESSIONAL BOOKS AND PAPERS. OFF IS AUTH 250 POUNDS EXCESS BAGGAGE ALLOW.

5. OFF WILL BE EXPECTED TO HAVE SUITABLE CIVILIAN CLOTHING IN ADDITION TO COMPLETE SET TROPICAL CLIMATE MIL UNIFORMS. THIS TWX CONSTITUTES AUTH FOR PAYMENT OF $300 SPECIAL ALLOWANCE FOR PURCHASE OF SUITABLE CIV CLOTHING AND PAYMENT OF $225 FOR PURCHASE OF DRESS WHITE UNIFORM.

6. IF OFF UNABLE COMMENCE TRAVEL BY 16 OCTOBER ADVISE THIS OFFICE AND CINCPAC BY MOST EXPEDITIOUS MEANS, INCLUDING TELEPHONE.

> BY ORDER OF THE SECRETARY OF THE ARMY
> STEPHEN L. MORGAN
> BRIG GEN
> DEPUTY, THE ADJ GEN

"Jesus, he was mad, wasn't he?" Lowell said.

"I beg your pardon?" Major General Jiggs asked.

"I suppose, sir, that I may infer from your presence here that I cannot promise to sin no more, and ask you to get me out of this?"

"I don't have anything to do with it, Craig," Jiggs said. "I just came to ask you myself if there is any bona fide reason you can't go."

"No, sir," Lowell said. "I really can't think of one."

"When can you leave?"

"I'll need two hours to pack my bags," Lowell said. Then, bitterly, "That little sonofabitch! I never thought he'd do this to me."

"Felter, you mean?" Jiggs asked. "Is he behind this?"

The question made it clear that Jiggs didn't know.

"Yes, sir, I think he is."

"All Bellmon told me was that it came from high up," Jiggs said, and then he changed the subject. "Don't go overboard, Craig. You must be tired. Why don't you get a good night's sleep and leave in the morning?"

"I can sleep on the plane, sir," Lowell said. "As I recall, it's a rather long flight to Hawaii."

(Three)
Atlanta International Airport
1730 Hours, 14 October 1960

When the Aero Commander taxied up to Southern Airways gate number 7, the Atlanta station manager of Delta Airlines, accompanied by two baggage handlers, came through the glass door and stood waiting until the plane's door opened.

"Major Lowell?" he asked, smiling and offering his hand to the tall, mustachioed man in civilian clothing who came out of the airplane. He had been told an hour before by the executive vice president, finance, to "make every effort to smooth things" for Major Lowell.

"Right," Lowell said.

"My name is Dietrich, Major. I'm the Eastern station manager here."

"How do you do?"

"We have you on Flight 330, which will board in forty-five minutes, nonstop to San Francisco, and connecting with Northwest Orient Flight 203 to Honolulu. First class, of course."

"I thought maybe," Lowell said dryly, "that if you looked hard, you could find me a seat."

Dietrich handed over the tickets.

"We'll see your baggage is loaded, Major Lowell," Dietrich said. "And you can wait in the Club."

"Thank you very much," Lowell said.

Bill Franklin handed three pieces of luggage through the door. Two of them were brand new Mark Cross leather suitcases (bought by Major Lowell in anticipation of his honeymoon) and the third was an ancient and battered canvas Valv-pak on which was stenciled Lowell's name, rank, and serial number. He had had it since he was a lieutenant. LT and CAPT had been successively painted over, so MAJ was now two lines above the line with his name and serial number.

"Send a postcard," Bill Franklin said.

"You may use my car to dazzle the local ladies," Lowell said, shaking his hand, "providing you don't drive it over thirty-five or get heel prints on the headliner."

Franklin chuckled, and then he saluted.

"Take care, Major," he said.

"If you go south, watch your ass," Lowell said.

"I'm very good at that," Franklin said.

Lowell punched him affectionately on the arm, and then followed Mr. Dietrich into the terminal building. Franklin waited until Lowell was out of sight before he got back in the Commander and fired it up.

He felt sorry for Lowell—for being taken out of the action—and doubly sorry that his buddy Felter had done it to him. But still, the bottom line was that he shouldn't have flown to Nicaragua when he had been told not to.

In the Club, Mr. Dietrich installed Major Lowell in a leather armchair. A hostess appeared immediately with a tray holding nuts, cigarettes, and cigars and asked if she could bring him something to drink and/or something to read.

"Bring me two double scotches, please," Major Lowell said, "I always require a little liquid courage before getting on an airplane."

A second hostess appeared, bearing a telephone on a long cord and a pad of telegraph blanks.

Lowell took one of the cigars and accepted Mr. Dietrich's quickly offered match.

"It was important that I get to Honoluly as quickly as possible," Lowell said. "Someone used a little clout to get that done. But I'm not a VIP, Mr. Dietrich, and I'm sure you have more important things to do than sit here and hold my hand until the plane leaves."

Dietrich took the army officer at his word. They shook hands and Dietrich left.

Twenty minutes later he was back with a teletype message:

FROM STATION MANAGER NORTHWEST ORIENT HONOLULU

TO NWO STATION MANAGER SF
   EASTERN STATION MANAGER ATL
FOR C. W. LOWELL PASSENGER ENROUTE HON VIA EASTERN ATL-
SF, NWO   SF-HON

ROYAL HAWAIIAN HOTEL CONFIRMS PENTHOUSE SUITE B. ROYAL
HAWAIIAN REPRESENTATIVE WILL MEET YOUR FLIGHT WITH LIM-
OUSINE. AIRCREW AUTHORIZED INFLIGHT RELAY ANY FURTHER
REQUIREMENTS.

> CHARLES D. STEVENS
> STATION MANAGER
> NORTHWEST ORIENT AIRLINES
> HONOLULU

By that time, Lowell, who was obviously more of a VIP than he said he was, had downed the first two double scotches and was working on a third. Dietrich had no way of knowing, of course, that Lowell had flown from Nicaragua that day—on a diet of sandwiches and two hamburgers in Miami. All he could see was that Lowell was a little bit tipsy.

"I think I'll send a telegram of my own, if I may," Major Lowell said.

"Certainly," Mr. Dietrich said.

Lowell, grinning with pleasure, wrote out a brief message and handed it to Mr. Dietrich. For one thing, it proved that he was a VIP, and for another, that he was tipsy.

"Can you say *that?*" Mr. Dietrich asked.

"I don't think," Lowell said, smugly, "that many Western Union operators in Atlanta are going to speak Yiddish. If one says something, tell her it's code."

"I'll get it right off, Major," Mr. Dietrich said.

Fifty minutes later, as Major Lowell was wolfing down a filet mignon in the first-class cabin of Eastern Flight 330, ATL-SF, a somewhat strange telegram came off a Western Union printer on Pennsylvania Avenue in Washington, D.C.

ATLANTA OCT 14 555P
SANFORD T. FELTER
THE WHITE HOUSE
WASHINGTON DC

I AM GOING TO NAIL YOUR SCHWANZ TO THE WALL FOR DOING THIS TO ME. YOUR EX PAL DUKE.

After some discussion, it was decided between the Communications Center duty officer and his counterpart at the Defense Communications Agency that there was more than likely a hidden message within the clear text. It was therefore encrypted as Top Secret–Gardenia No. 60–56003 and relayed by radio to Nicaragua.

(Four)
Penthouse B
The Royal Hawaiian Hotel
Honolulu, Hawaii
0700 Hours, 15 October 1960

A long shower and two pots of coffee did nothing to shake loose what felt like a terrible hangover, but which was more fatigue and jet lag than the product of all the brandy he had consumed between Atlanta and Hawaii.

As he examined his image in the mirrored walls of the bathroom, he saw that his eyes were both sunken and bloodshot and that his face, looked white and drawn. He looked hung over, which would probably not at all surprise CSP-CINC-PAC—whoever the hell that was. CSP-CINCPAC, to whom he was ordered to report, had certainly been advised that he was getting a fuck-up to be kept on ice and would not be surprised when said fuck-up showed up looking as if he had just come off a two-week drunk.

He looked so bad that he seriously considered taking off his tropical worsted uniform and going back to bed for several hours. He would then seek out a Turkish bath, have a long steam and a massage, and spend the rest of the day on the beach trying to get a little color back in his face and some of the blood out of his eyes. When he reported the following morning, he would look less like death warmed over.

Which would, he decided, accomplish exactly nothing. A healthy looking fuck-up sent to Hawaii to be kept on ice would be treated the same as one that looked like he had just crawled out of a bottle.

He left the suite and went to the desk, where he was given the keys to a Hertz convertible Lincoln and a map marked with a Magic Marker giving the route to Headquarters, U.S. Army Pacific, where he would report to CSP-CINCPAC for duty.

CSP-CINCPAC turned out to be full bull artillery colonel, a tall, heavyset, deeply tanned middle-aged man with the look of someone who spent a lot of time keeping in shape.

"Sir," Lowell said, "Major Lowell reporting in compliance with orders."

"You can stand at ease, Major," CSP-CINCPAC said. "We didn't expect you until tomorrow or the next day."

"Would the colonel like to see my orders?"

"Give them to my sergeant on your way out," CSP-CINC-PAC said. He looked at Lowell appraisingly, and then dialed his telephone.

"Sir," he said a moment later, "Major Lowell just walked into my office." Whoever he was talking to said something, to which the colonel replied: "Right away, sir."

CSP/CINCPAC stood up and motioned for Lowell to follow him out of the office. He stopped before the master sergeant in the outer office.

"You know what to do for Major Lowell, Sergeant," he said.

"Yes, sir," the master sergeant said.

Lowell handed him his letter orders.

"Thank you, sir," the master sergeant said. "Welcome to Hawaii, Major."

"Thank you."

He followed CSP-CINCPAC out into the corridor. Toward the end of it, Lowell noticed a plastic sign on a door: 106 CINCPAC ENTER THROUGH 110.

CSP-CINCPAC pushed open the door to 110.

There was a familiar face in that office, a very large, very black master sergeant. Master Sergeant Wesley, General E. Z. Black's longtime orderly.

"Hello, Wesley," Lowell said.

"Hello, Major Lowell," Wesley said, offering his massive hand. To CSP-CINCPAC, Wesley said, "The boss expects you, go right on in, Colonel."

They walked into CINCPAC's office and CSP-CINCPAC said, "Good morning, General."

Major Lowell saluted.

General E. Z. Black returned the salute, looked at Lowell

thoughtfully, and said, "Lowell, you look like hell."

Lowell was not surprised at the comment. It was apparently Step One in the speech he was going to get. At first he had been surprised to be sent to face E. Z. Black himself. But now that he thought about it, it fit in with the pattern. He was going to be (a) told that he had failed the trust General Black had placed in him when he had not thrown him out of the army, (b) advised in some detail of his current status, and probably (c) advised of what would happen to him if he talked at all about what he had been doing before Felter had arranged for him to be sent halfway around the world to keep him out of the way.

There was a knock, a quick rap of knuckles, at another door to General E. Z. Black's office, and a major general came through it immediately without waiting for permission to enter.

"This is Major Lowell, Pete," General Black said. "Two days sooner than we expected."

The major general smiled, and said something astonishing as he offered his hand: "And not a second too early. How do you do, Major? I've heard a lot about you."

"Wes," General Black said, raising his voice. "Coffee, please, and then see we're not disturbed."

M/Sgt Wesley had anticipated the command. He came through the door almost immediately, pushing a cart on which sat a coffee thermos, cups, saucers, and a plate of doughnuts.

"The last I heard," General Black said to Lowell, "you were on a trip, and no one knew when you'd be back."

"I returned day before yesterday, sir," Lowell said.

"And came over here right away?" Black asked. "No wonder you look terrible. Well, this won't take long. I wanted General Day to meet you, and to give you a quick picture of what's going on. Then you can go to bed. Maybe a steam bath would help."

It didn't seem like the opening remark in an ass chewing.

"Your being here," CSP-CINCPAC said, "eliminates a lot of problems. I've been trying to arrange for you to catch up with us, and I've learned it's not easy to get from here to there. Now you can go with us."

"We're going to Saigon the day after tomorrow, Lowell," General Black said. "They did tell you to bring civvies?"

"Yes, sir."

"It looks," General Black said, "as if we're going to have

to greatly augment our force of advisors in Indochina—which, by the way, we now refer to as South Vietnam. I asked DCSOPS to send me an expert, somebody familiar with the aviation companies we've been forming, and someone who knew something about the airmobile division we're forming. Your name came up, of course, but you were otherwise occupied. But then Bellmon decided you were just about finished with what you were doing and could be spared."

"I thought," Lowell said, "that I was being sent into durance vile."

General Black was not amused.

"Why would you think that?"

"I made an error in judgment, sir," Lowell said.

"Another one? Who's annoyed with you this time?" Black asked.

"Felter, sir," Lowell said. "Or I thought he was."

"You'd better hope he was not," Black said. He did not ask for an amplification, and Lowell did not offer one.

"If we go into Vietnam in any strength, Lowell," General Black said, closing that subject, "and I'm afraid we will, we're going to have to go in with somewhat unconventional forces— unconventional in the sense that we haven't used them before. And I mean aviation heavy, not just Special Forces. Since the country is primitive, that means that there are insufficient aviation installations in place. We're going to have to build our own. What I want you to do is recommend what we should build, and where."

"Sir, isn't that an engineer function?"

"So the engineers have reminded me," Black said. He paused, as if debating whether Lowell should have an explanation, and then went on.

"There are two ways to go about this," he said. "According to the book, the engineers would prepare a report of existing facilities and of facilities they are prepared to build. They'd turn this over to aviation and tell them this is it: adjust your plans accordingly. If it looked as if we were going to send conventional forces, that's the way it would be."

"Yes, sir," Lowell said.

"The other way is the way I've decided to go. Have an aviator come up with what aviation would like to have, and then make the Engineers justify not giving it to them."

"I understand, sir," Lowell said.

"You hear a lot of smart-ass remarks about the 'Big Picture,'
Lowell," General Black said, "generally from officers who
have not yet learned that no matter how important what they're
doing is, the army is also doing something else which is of
equal or greater importance. I think you know that there *is* a
Big Picture, and that everything has to fit in it."

"I hope I do, sir," Lowell said, aware that he had been
complimented.

"I thought, Lowell," General Black said, "and so apparently
does General Bellmon, that you would be able to walk the edge
of the razor and come up with a list of facilities that was right
in the middle between an aviation "Wishful Thinking List" and
an engineer "We'd Really Rather Not Do That List.""

"I'll try, sir," Lowell said.

(Five)
Near Bahia de Cochinos
Republic of Cuba
25 March 1960

There was no reason for the supervisor of the midnight to
four shift in the radar-filled room at Jose Marti Airport in
Havana to suspect that Honduran Air Force Six Six Four was
anything but what he said he was: a Curtiss C-46 "Commando"
en route from Miami home.

He personally thought if Honduran Air Force Six Six Four
was in the employ of the Yankee imperialists and/or some
counterrevolutionary group, they would not have got on the
horn and requested permission to pass through the airspace of
the People's Democratic Republic of Cuba.

But orders were orders, and he picked up a red telephone.
Accordingly, five minutes later two P-51F piston-engine fighters of the Cuban Air Force rose from Jose Marti to have a look
at Honduran Air Force Six Six Four.

When they saw that Honduran Air Force Six Six Four was
a battered and ancient C-46 painted in the Honduran scheme,
which was able to exchange a few friendly words with them
in Spanish, the fighters returned to Jose Marti.

Honduran Air Force Six Six Four proceeded on course, at
13,000 feet, toward Honduras. Havana area control continued
to monitor the flight on radar, of course. And the radar, twenty
minutes after the fighters had completed their investigation,

showed little blips leaving the aircraft.

The radar operator didn't even report this to the supervisor. The radar had not been properly maintained since the fall of General Batista's regime. And since then, the servicing of radar had become something of a problem. No longer did the pleasant young men from Sperry catch a quick flight from Miami carrying attaché cases full of "short-life" parts.

They didn't come at all, and no parts were available. By Herculean effort, the radars were kept working with one make-do fix after another, but they weren't up to specs. They showed more and more glitches.

When the new and all-around superior radar came from East Germany, the problem would be solved of course. But there had been minor delays in getting the East German equipment at all, and then when it had arrived, certain parts had been missing. Havana area control was having to make do with what it had, and what it had often showed little blips that weren't really there.

Twenty-two minutes after passing over Havana, eight men in black coveralls stood up in the cargo compartment of the Curtiss Commando and, on signal, jumped out the door.

"A" Team No. 64, Third Special Forces Group, First Lieutenant Thomas J. Ellis commanding, landed within two hundred yards of one another about a mile from their intended landing zone; a field several miles above the village of Aguada de Pasajeros. No one was injured and there had been no indication that they had been seen.

There was a stand of trees three hundred yards away at the upper end of the field, and they made their way to it. There they buried their parachutes and jump equipment and unpacked the equipment bags.

SFC Eaglebury and Lieutenant Ellis made a quick reconnaissance of the immediate area, determining their exact location, and then led the team across country to their destination. When they arrived, they made camp, and settled down for the night.

In the morning, Lieutenant Ellis and SFC Eaglebury made another reconnaissance, from which SFC Eaglebury did not return.

"Hey, Lieutenant," SFC Juan Vincenzo Lopez asked, in English, "where the hell is Eaglebury?"

"Eh!" Lieutenant Ellis replied. *"Por favor. En Espagnol."*

It was understandable, Lieutenant Ellis thought, that Lopez would forget to speak Spanish. But correction was necessary.

SFC Lopez, of Los Angeles, California, was the second radio operator of the team. He had a very colorful vocabulary of profane and obscene words and phrases in the Spanish language, and now was the time he should use it.

"To tell you the truth, Lieutenant," Lopez now announced, in English, "I'm not what you could call fluent in Spanish."

Lieutenant Ellis now learned that SFC Lopez—despite his suggestions at Bragg that he was a "card-carrying wetback," and despite his fluent Spanish profanity—was in fact a third generation Mexican-American who was considerably less fluent in Spanish than the first radio operator of the team, M/Sgt Stefan Karr, who had gone through an intensive three-week course in that language at the U.S. Army Language School at the Presido in San Francisco. The only Spanish SFC Lopez knew was what he had picked up while visiting the Los Angeles *barrio* (his father, a successful Mercedes salesman in Brentwood, housed his family in Marina del Ray) in search of ethnic food and feminine companionship.

"Goddamnit, one of the reasons you were picked for this mission was because you spoke Spanish," Ellis exploded. "Why didn't you say something?"

"*I* never said I spoke Spanish," Lopez said. "And if I had said something, I'd be at Bragg, picking up cigarette butts . . . I really wanted to make this operation."

He could not, of course, Ellis realized, be sent home in disgrace.

"You dumb sonofabitch," Ellis said, in English.

"Where's Eaglebury?" Lopez pursued.

"You don't want to know," Ellis said.

"What's that supposed to mean?"

"Just what it sounds like. You don't want to know," Ellis said.

Lopez looked at him a moment, and then nodded his head.

In point of fact, all Lieutenant Ellis knew about SFC/Lt. Commander Eaglebury was that his bag had contained civilian clothing and that Eagelbury had put it on before walking down the mountain.

And while Ellis was curious what Eaglebury was up to, he really didn't want to know. Ellis and the others on the team had been kept in the dark against the possibility of their capture.

If they were captured, they would be interrogated. Their only defense against a determined, skilled interrogator equipped with the best mechanical and chemical tools of the trade was ignorance.

Lieutenant Ellis's "A" Team had a mission, of course, a mission which was both bona fide and a splendid cover for Eaglebury's more secret mission. Ellis's team was to install, at a precise location, a radio transmitter which—when the word was received—they would activate. This transmitter would allow the aircraft involved in the invasion to determine their precise location.

By noon of the first day, Ellis had learned that Lopez's nonfluency in Spanish was not the only shortage he was going to have to cope with. The communications portion of the radio which the team had been equipped with had somehow been rendered inoperable during the insertion. The receiving function worked, but it was impossible to transmit. Neither M/Sgt Karr nor SFC Lopez were able to repair it.

Even that contingency had been planned for. At prespecified times during the night, flares were to be ignited for precisely sixty seconds and then extinguished. They lit the flares that night, and radio confirmation came quickly that Base understood that the team was intact and operational and that only their radio acknowledgment of orders was impaired.

From that point until they got the word, the team would have little to do except avoid making waves. Other flares were ignited at predetermined times to confirm that the team remained operational, but that was it.

XX

(One)
Headquarters
U.S. Army, Pacific
Honolulu, Hawaii
2230 Hours, 12 April 1961

Major Craig W. Lowell had been assigned a room in the basement. It contained two desks, one of them with a shelf holding an IBM electric typewriter, two chairs, a standard issue table, and a telephone on a stand.

He had originally been assigned a clerk-typist, but the Adjutant General, on whom the levy for a typist with a Top Secret security clearance had been laid, had naturally not deprived his organization of his best typist.

The typist he got was a nice kid, and Lowell didn't want to send him back with the humiliation of being relieved for incomptence, so he told him to make himself scarce until he sent for him.

Then he did the typing himself, and there had been a good

deal of it. It had taken him six days.

He took the covering letter from the IBM and looked at it.

TOP SECRET

HEADQUARTERS

U.S. ARMY, PACIFIC

HONOLULU, HAWAII

14 April 1961

SUBJECT: Letter of Transmittal

TO: Commander in Chief
              U.S. Army, Pacific
              Honolulu, Hawaii

1. Transmitted herewith in triplicate is the report of the undersigned concerning aviation logistic requirements in the event the United States Army should be required to participate in operations in the Republic of South Vietnam.

2. The report consists of this letter and eighteen (18) separate documents, attached as Inclosures 1 through 18 hereto. The report is classified Top Secret. Copies 2 and 3 are in the custody of the Clasified Documents Officer, Hq, USARPAC, under control numbers TS-61 107 and TS-61 108. Copy 1 has been delivered personally by the undersigned to CINCPAC.

                                   Craig W. Lowell
                                   Major, Armor

Incl:
    1. General topographical observations (w/maps) as they apply to the operation of conventional U.S. Army forces within the Republic of South Vietnam.

    2. General topographical observations (w/maps) as they apply to the operation of airmobile U.S. Army forces (i.e., 11th Air Assault Division [Provisional] [Test]) within the Republic of South Vietnam.

    3. General topographic observations (w/maps) as they apply to the operation of unconventional forces under

U.S. Army control (i.e., native forces under the control of U.S. Army Special Forces).

4. Evaluation of existing air facilities at Saigon, together with an appraisal of their capability for expansion to meet U.S. Army needs under the following conditions:

    (a) U.S. Army strength level to 25,000 personnel
    (b) U.S. Army strength level to 50,000 personnel
    (c) U.S. Army strength level to 100,000 personnel
    (d) U.S. Army strength level to 200,000 personnel
    (e) through (h) Same as (a) through (d) but assuming forces include 11th Air Assault Division (or equivalent)

  5. Same as 4 above for Hue
  6. Same as 4 above for Tourane (Da Nang)
  7. Same as 4 above for Gia Lia (Pleiku)
  8. Same as 4 above for Ban Me Thuot
  9. Same as 4 above for Da Lat
 10. Same as 4 above for Nha Trang
 11. Same as 4 above for Vung Tau (Cap St. Jacques)
 12. Same as 4 above for Long Huyen
 13. Same as 4 above for Phu Quoc Island

14. Evaluation of existing aviation petroleum storage facilities at Saigon, together with an appraisal of their capability for expansion under the conditions specified in 4. above.

 15. Same as 14 above for Qaung Ng Ai
 16. Same as 14 above for Binh Dinh
 17. Same as 14 above for Vinh Cam Ranh (Cam Ranh Bay)

18. An appraisal of special aviation requirements in the event of deployment of U.S. Army Special Forces in the highlands (w/maps).

Craig W. Lowell
Major, Armor

TOP SECRET

He took a pen from his pocket and wrote his signature above his typed name.

Then he called the Classified Documents Officer and asked him to send somebody over to help him carry everything to the vault. There was no way he could carry it all by himself.

He thought that what would happen now was that he would present it to General Black in the morning. Black would tell him to amuse himself—while keeping himself available—until he had time to read it. That would be followed by two days of nit-picking and answering questions he hadn't answered in the report. Or maybe a week of that. It was an enormous report.

He misjudged again what General E. Z. Black would do.

"There's no point in you sticking around, Lowell," Black told him. "If I have any specific questions, I'll get them answered by someone with fresh eyes."

"Yes, sir."

"Thank you, Lowell," General Black said. "Jiggs was apparently right."

"Sir?"

"The problem dealing with you is keeping you busy; when you're busy, you're everything that can be expected of a good officer."

"Then I shall try to keep busy," Lowell said.

"Perhaps they'll have something for you to do when you get back," Black said, offering Lowell his hand.

There was more in that remark than the words, but of course Lowell could not ask him.

He went back to the Royal Hawaiian. He went to his suite and took a long shower, and then he made himself a drink.

He gave into the temptation, and reached for the telephone, as he knew he would. He had written Cynthia his own version of her "Get Thee Out of My Life, My Darling" letter, just before he'd gone to Vietnam.

He had told her that he simply couldn't settle for the odd weekend now and again. He told her he was being "sent away" and would use the time to think the whole thing through. And he wrote that it seemed only decent to say that he thought it would be better if he never tried to call her again—and that he probably wouldn't.

And now that he had changed his mind, the editorial offices of *Time-Life* in New York would not tell him where he could reach Miss Cynthia Thomas. But, they said, if he would leave his name and his number, they would try to get his message to her.

He controlled his temper and gave the name. Porter Craig or that press agent would have known someone at *Time-Life* who could get him through to Cynthia, but obviously—under the circumstances—he could not call Porter.

He looked out his window at the beach and the Pacific Ocean. It would be a shame to have been in Hawaii and not taken a swim, he decided. And it was not entirely beyond possibility that there would be a female on the beach who had come to Hawaii in search of romance. But just as he was about to leave his room, the telephone rang. He would have given odds that it was some sonofabitch at HQ USARPAC who had seen his report and wanted to talk to him about it.

"Lowell," he snarled into the telephone.

"You drop out of sight for six months, and you *snarl*?" Cynthia Thomas asked.

"Jesus!" he said.

"Where were you? Where are you? How come not a lousy postcard?"

"I'm in Honolulu."

"What are you doing there?"

"I'm about to leave."

"I have the feeling we've had this conversation before," she said.

"I hope it ends the way the other one did."

"Excuse me?" Cynthia said, not taking his meaning.

"With breakfast, so to speak," Lowell said.

"Oh, so that's why you called me?"

"It was in my mind."

"Tell me where you've been while I think about it," she said.

"I'm sorry, I can't do that."

"Oh, here we go again. C. Lowell, defender of the world!"

"I can't."

"I'm in Los Angeles," she said. "But I'm leaving."

"Oh?"

"For Mexico City."

"Mexico City is lovely this time of year," he said.

"It is. But I'll be working for a week."

"At night?"

"Night and day," she said. "How about a week from today?"

"All right. Where will you be?"

"You get a place," she said. "And then call me at the bureau, and I'll rush over with a rose between my teeth."

The phone went dead. He looked at it. Cynthia for a couple

of days was not as nice as Cynthia forever, but Cynthia for a couple of days was a lot better than no Cynthia at all.

He tapped the hook with his finger. He asked to be connected with the manager and told him he would be very grateful if a first-class seat could be found for him on the next plane to the States.

(Two)
Near Aguada de Pasajeros, Cuba
0650 Hours, 7 April 1961

Sergeant First Class Juan Vincenzo Lopez had philosophized with maddening frequency: "Operations aren't so bad. It's sitting around with your thumb up your ass that gets you down."

For Ellis, keeping the troops occupied had posed something of a problem. Troops with a lot of time to think can come up with very imaginative worst-possible scenarios for their future, and troops hiding out in the mountains of a hostile country can not play intramural softball or be assigned to whitewash rocks to keep them busy.

Then M/Sgt Karr and SFC Lopez presented Lieutenant Ellis with a proposal to go into Aguada de Pasajeros to steal a truck to provide an additional power supply; this would (a) obviate the necessity of turning the bicycle pedals at all, (b) save the batteries for an emergency, and (c) permit the team (when the word came) to get their asses down to the beach and away several hours earlier than the plan called for.

At first Lieutenant Ellis was opposed to the idea. He had been ordered to make every effort to avoid capture, so that the United States would not be embarrassed by the public display of captured American soldiers involved in what was a *native* Cuban effort to overthrow the communist regime of Fidel Castro. Any project like this was bound to involve some risk. But as he thought about it, he saw that the plan had two things going for it. The sooner he got the team to the beach after the invasion started, the less chance they would be captured. And putting Operation Hot Generator into effect would give his men something to think about.

He decided that what M/Sgt Karr and SFC Lopez proposed was worthy of execution. The only problem with their carefully thought-out plan was that neither of them spoke Spanish well. Consequently Lieutenant Ellis had accompanied SFC Lopez into Aguada de Pasajeros, leaving M/Sgt Karr behind and in command. The theft of a 1948 Ford pickup had gone smoothly. By noon the next day, the truck had been installed in a camouflaged position with its rear wheels off the ground, its hood removed against possible engine overheating, and its carburetor and gear box arranged so that—at just above normal idle—the rear wheel drove the bicycle pedal mechanism at precisely the right speed to power the aviation navigation aid.

SFC Lopez then devised and built a switch that would instantly switch the batteries on in the event the engine stopped. When the word came, all that would be necessary for them to do was start up the truck, wait until the engine appeared to operating normally, and then haul ass for the beach to be picked up.

Other missions had been launched, primarily to keep up troop morale. Their execution had seen the only shots fired—three rounds from Lieutenant Ellis's silenced .22 caliber pistol. Ellis had gone three times to the outskirts of Aguada de Pasajeros with various members of the team, where he had shot three pigs in the ear with the silenced pistol, gutted them, and then carried them back to the camp for an alfresco pig roast.

And then there was a message from Base that Ellis did not immediately recognize. He had to consult his code book (actually, two sheets of very thin paper designed to dissolve very quickly in water, or saliva) to decipher them.

"Augmentation Two Men Equipment Time M Site 8 Acknowledge"

The message required that Lieutenant Ellis make an important decision: The dropping of two men and equipment (unspecified, but he thought it was likely that it would be replacement transmitters) at Time M (first light) at Site 8 (a field three miles away) was the wrong time and the wrong place.

If he had a functioning transmitter, he could inform Base and recommend other sites and places. The area where Base intended to HALO the augmentation was one of the few places where the People's Revolutionary Militia, or whatever the fuck those clowns called themselves, operated patrols.

The fields in that area were being sown. Lieutenant Ellis didn't have the vaguest goddamn idea what they were planting. But whatever it was, it was stuck into the ground by three-person teams. One dug a hole, one stuck something in the hole, and the third covered the hole. The persons doing this were female, many of them young. Members of the team had spent many hours observing the native woman through binoculars. Only a few of the women, it had been determined, wore brassieres.

The area was thoroughly patrolled by two or three pickup trucks, each carrying two or more Cubans armed to the teeth. There was no evidence of counterrevolutionary activity in the area (except for one missing truck and three missing pigs), but vigilant patrol gave the revolutionary guards a splendid opportunity to swagger around the girls, manfully handling their weapons.

Lieutenant Ellis realized he had only two options. He could either use the flares to acknowledge receipt of the order and announce his preparedness to meet the augmentation team or to signal that the intended augmentation should be aborted.

He decided that he better go along with what the higher ups had in mind. Since he did not know the purpose of the augmentation team, he had to presume that inserting it had a higher priority than even the mission of "A" Team No. 6. There had probably been at least one more team like his inserted elsewhere. They would want insurance. That meant that it had been decided that inserting the augmentation team was worth the risk of losing "A" Team No. 6 and its capability.

Ellis ordered the flare signal which told Base to send the team.

That night, he divided his own team in two: M/Sgt Karr, and four others would remain at the nav-aid site. They would make every effort not to be discovered, they were authorized to eliminate the intruders or to take any other action they saw fit.

Ellis took the remaining three men with him through the woods to Site M. He sent one man who spoke passable Spanish to the high end of the field. If the augmentation team landed near him, he was to wave them into the woods, and, if necessary, provide covering fire from his machine gun.

Ellis positioned the other two men in the trees on either side of the road leading to the field. Each had a machine gun, a submachine gun, and fragmentation hand grenades. They would be in a position to delay—for a time—vehicles and personnel moving either from the town to the field or from the field to the town.

Lieutenant Ellis himself took up a position in a tree on the low end of the field. From there he could see the entire field. Everyone was in place an hour before the first faint rays of the sun were evident on the horizon.

The sun came up quickly. The sky was clear. Thre was no sign, no contrail of high altitude condensation. He was to wonder about that later. He thought there was always a contrail.

He saw the canopies, three of them, pop open. And as if the popping open of the canopies was a cue, he heard the faint sound of truck engines coming up the hill.

The two parachutists and the cargo bag landed almost in the center of the field. They did not run (as Ellis thought they would) for the tree line at either edge of the field. He saw SFC Haywood, whom he had sent to the far endge of the field, standing at the tree line frantically waving a handkerchief.

But the parachutists—looking down the hill—did not see him. And apparently they couldn't hear him. They stood where they were and divested themselves of the leather HALO gear. And left it where they were.

They were, Ellis saw, in civilian clothing: flower-printed shirts and cotton pants. They were not armed, either, he saw with surprise. What they took from the cargo container was suitcases. They were either Cubans or Americans intending to pass themselves off as Cubans.

Cursing his stupidity for not thinking of it before, he realized that the jumpers had seen the trucks coming up the mountain and had realized that it was more important to get off the field immediately, even though that meant the inevitable discovery of the chutes and other equipment later.

It was also entirely possible, Ellis realized, that even though they had popped their chutes no more than 800 feet off the ground, the chutes had been seen by the truckloads of farm girls and their escorts from the People's Revolutionary Militia.

Why they didn't run instantly for the woods became immediately evident. A pickup carrying a cabful of revolutionary guards appeared on the road. The jumpers apparently had decided that they would appear less suspicious walking down the road than running for the trees.

It took the revolutionary guards longer to spot the two men walking down the road than Ellis thought it would. But when they saw them, the driver immediately raced toward them, skidded the truck sideward on the road, and stopped.

The guards leaped from the truck brandishing their weapons. The two parachutists, who had made no attempt to run, put their hands in the air.

Ellis slid down the tree and ran back through the woods to the road. It was further than he thought it was and when he finally reached the road, he understood why. He had become disoriented in the woods, and was much further down the hill than he had planned to be. He didn't know exactly where he was, only that he was further down the hill than the two men he had left to guard it.

He ran up the road, once almost dropping his Thompson .45 ACP submachine gun. He had been given his choice of weapons, and he had elected to take a stockless Thompson with a 50-round drum magazine, for no better reason that he had once seen Alan Ladd use one against the Japanese on a late, late movie on television.

He heard the truck coming down the hill.

He kept running up the hill.

He saw a familiar stand of trees. He was almost to the men he had left by the side of the road. But there was no time to talk to them, to explain what had happened.

Now that he was faced with it, he knew there was no chance at all that he could stand in the road and mow the bad guys down with the tommy gun. For one thing, if he did manage to hit the pickup truck, he would more than likely kill the people he was trying to save.

He ran to the side of the road and dropped the Thompson in a ditch. Then he tore off his fatigue jacket and dropped it on the road as he ran.

When he saw the truck, he ran up the middle of the road toward it, frantically waving his arms.

The truck skidded to a halt. Two revolutionary heroes were in the back of the truck training their weapons, a Thompson and a Garand, on the two prisoners in the bed of the truck. One of them very nearly lost his seat as the truck skidded to a stop.

The driver opened the door and stepped onto the running board.

"Qué pasa?" he demanded.

"There's more of them," Ellis shouted in Spanish. "Fifty of them! Maybe a hundred!" He gestured excitedly behind him toward the woods.

The two men in the back of the truck stood up to get a better look. The driver of the truck ran toward Ellis, taking a Model 1911A1 Colt from a holster as he ran. He was in the process of chambering a round when the first machine gun burst came. It struck him four times in the chest and face. He stopped and dropped to his knees, a surprised look on his face, and then fell forward.

Before the driver had dropped to his knees, there was, a second and longer burst of machine-gun fire from the opposite side of the road. It knocked one of the revolutionary guards out of the truck and blew off the top of the head of the second one.

Ellis ran to the truck.

The prisoners jumped out of the bed. Ellis recognized one of them, a little Jew.

"God, Ellis," Lt. Colonel Sanford T. Felter said, "am I glad to see you!"

It was the little Jew who had been given a green beret the day Ellis had graduated from McCall. Ellis, with an OCS reflex, saluted.

Felter smiled, and returned it casually. Then he jumped into the cab of the pickup truck and raced the engine, furiously. He jumped out, raised the hood, and looked inside.

"Nothing wrong with this except old age," he announced.

Ellis saw that burst of machine-gun fire which had taken out the driver had stitched the pickup truck. But the damage was to the door, which had been open, and there was only one neat hole in the windshield.

Felter went to the bed of the truck and handed Ellis one of the suitcases.

"There's a transmitter in there for you," he said. "When you get it on the air, tell him we're on our way to Objective Delta. Your orders remain otherwise unchanged."

By then the man with him was in the driver's seat of the pickup truck. Felter ran around to the other side and jumped in. The truck spun its wheels and headed down the hill.

Ellis ran into the trees and lay down, his chest heaving, his eyes fuzzy.

A moment later, two more pickups came around the turn. There were two short bursts of machine-gun fire, and one more long one. And then, a moment after that, a two-or three-shot burst.

When got to his feet, he saw that the two trucks had gone off the road, one on each side. The five men they had held were all dead. He wondered if that had been the smart thing to do, or whether it would have been better to just let the trucks pass.

It didn't matter. He went onto the road where the machine gunners could see him. He made a gesture, "pack it up, get away," and then he ran down the road until he found his Alan Ladd tommy gun. He picked it up and ran into the woods.

It occurred to him that he had just been in his first combat, his first firefight, and he had not fired a round.

When they got back to the camp, Lieutenant Ellis found that the blisters he earned carrying the suitcase with the transmitter in it were in vain. There were two barely visible holes in the cheap artificial leather. Two .308 inch diameter bullets, had gone through the transmitter before passing out the other side.

There was nothing to do but sit tight, hoping that when they discovered the fight, Castro's soldiers would decide that whoever had been in the area had left in the missing pickup truck.

(Three)
227 Melody Lane
Ozark, Alabama
2030 Hours, 16 April 1961

"He's got a visitor," Jane Jiggs said to her husband as she turned off Melody Lane and into the driveway of 227 Melody Lane. There was a Cadillac already there.

"It doesn't have a post sticker," Paul Jiggs said. Then he saw the CD plate. "Diplomatic plates," he added. "It must be Jannier. I heard they were back."

Major General Paul Jiggs started to open his door.

"Let's get this over with," he said.

"I don't want to block that car," Jane Jiggs said.

She backed out the driveway and parked the car on the street. Her husband and the two men in the back seat, a colonel and a master sergeant, got out of the car and walked across the lawn toward the house.

They were, she knew, a notification team. An ad hoc, unofficial notification team, but nevertheless a notification team about to discharge an unpleasant duty.

They had left her behind. Not out of discourtesy, she thought, but because their minds were on something else.

She caught up with them at the door in time to hear Colonel Paul Hanrahan say to M/Sgt Wojinski, "Push the doorbell, Ski."

Wojinski pressed an illuminated button by the door. Chimes sounded.

Major Craig W. Lowell appeared at the door in a powder-blue polo shirt and pale yellow plants. When he saw them, he smiled broadly.

"My God!" he said. "This is wonderful! We'll really have to kill a fatted calf. Jean-Philippe and Melody just this moment got here!"

There was no reply.

"To judge by your faces," he said, "old Silver Cloud Lowell has jumped to the wrong conclusion again. Now I'm afraid to ask why you're here."

Colonel Hanrahan handed him the yellow teletype message:

SECRET

CIA MCLEAN VA VIA DEFENSE COMM AGENCY

FOR COMMANDING GENERAL FORT RUCKER ALA

FOLLOWING CLASSIFIED TOP SECRET EYES ONLY COMGEN FORT RUCKER QUOTE PLEASE PASS SOONEST FOR ACTION TO COL PAUL T. HANRAHAN BELIEVED TO BE AT YOUR STATION: THE DEPUTY DIRECTOR THE CIA REGRETS TO INFORM YOU THAT LT COL SANFORD T FELTER PRESENTLY SERVING WITH THIS AGENCY IS MISSING ON A FOREIGN ASSIGNMENT AND MAY BE PRESUMED DEAD. NO FURTHER INFORMATION IS AVAILABLE AT THIS TIME. THE DIRECTOR BELIEVES THE ARMY IS THE AGENCY WHICH SHOULD INFORM SURVIVORS. ANY FURTHER INFORMATION RECEIVED WILL BE RELAYED AS RECEIVED. ENDQUOTE END TOPSECRET PORTION. IF COL HANRAHAN NOT PRESENT YOUR STATION PLEASE ADVISE LOCATION MOST EXPEDITIOUS MEANS. FOR THE DIRECTOR. JAMES W. STEMME. DEPDIR FOR ADMINISTRATION.

"Oh, shit!" Lowell said.

He turned from the door and went into the house. The others trooped after him.

Madame Melody Dutton Greer Jannier, very pregnant, and her husband were in the living room.

Jane Jiggs went to her and kissed her.

"How are you, honey?" she asked.

Melody gave her an impatient smile.

"What's wrong, Craig?" Melody asked. He handed her the TWX. She read it, said "Damn!" and handed it to her husband.

Both Major General Jiggs and Colonel Paul T. Hanrahan were uncomfortable with Lowell's violation of security regulations. Neither Jean-Philippe nor Melody should have been shown a Top Secret TWX.

"Ah, mon Dieu," Jean-Philippe Jannier. *"C'est le petit Juif féroce, n'est pas?"*

"Right," Lowell said very bitterly. "The ferocious little Jew. I think he would like that for an epitaph."

"We thought," Jane Jiggs said, "that you might want to tell Sharon."

"I've got a 23 laid on to take you to Atlanta," Paul Jiggs said.

"No way," Lowell said, firmly, coldly. "I did that the last time the Mouse was playing hero and they thought he'd gotten himself blown away."

There was no reply.

Major Lowell said "Shit!" again, and there were tears in his eyes.

Then he asked: "How do we *know* he's dead?"

"They must have a pretty good idea, Craig," Hanrahan said, "or they wouldn't have sent the TWX."

"Well, I'm not going to put Sharon through that ordeal again on the strength of a CIA guess," Lowell said, flatly.

He went to the bar and set glasses neatly in a line, one for everyone present, and poured brandy in each glass.

He picked his up and sipped at it.

"There's soda and ice, if anybody wants it."

No one moved until Jane Jiggs picked up one of the glasses and drank it down neat. Then she poured more. After that Jiggs, Hanrahan, and Wojinski helped themselves.

"Sharon has a right to be told," Jane said.

"Let me tell you something about Sharon, Jane," Lowell said. "Every time the Mouse goes off on one of his little trips, Sharon is convinced she's seen him for the last time. I'm not going to be responsible for telling her he's dead for sure . . . until *I* know for sure. I repeat, 'How do we *know* he's dead?'"

"Because the CIA says so," Jiggs said.

"Screw the CIA," Lowell said. "What do we *know* for sure?"

Hanrahan started to speak, stopped, and looked at Paul Jiggs, who nodded his permission. The security dam had been breached; they might as well go all the way.

"We know Sandy jumped into Cuba on the morning of 7 April," Hanrahan said.

"He jumped into Cuba? In Christ's name, why?" Lowell exploded.

"Because Eaglebury was captured and executed," Hanrahan said.

"Did you get that from the CIA, too?" Lowell asked, bitterly. "Or is that a fact?"

"Unfortunately, it's a fact," Jiggs said. "The Mexican ambassador gave the State Department a photograph. Which came into their hands from unspecified Cuban sources. Apparently they wanted to inform us they know of certain plans."

"A photograph of what?"

"Of Commander Eaglebury after he had been tortured and shot through the back of his neck," Hanrahan said.

"Oh, my God!" Jane Jiggs said. She had not heard that before.

"He was the man you stole the radios with?" Melody Dutton Jannier asked.

Jiggs and Hanrahan looked at her in confusion.

"Yes, ma'am," M/Sgt Wojinski said.

"The CIA is apparently going on the assumption that during Eaglebury's interrogation, other things came out," Hanrahan said, carefully.

"That means the Mouse jumped right into the bastards' arms," Lowell said. "With all he knew, he shouldn't have gone anywhere near Cuba!"

"I can't comment on that, Craig," Hanrahan said. "Did you know he was relieved as Action Officer?"

"No, I didn't," Lowell said. "Why?"

"When Kennedy took office, they put the whole thing in the hands of the CIA."

"Those bastards play games," Lowell said. "Are you suggesting that he was set up?"

"I am not," Hanrahan said. "He must have been picked up in the execution of his mission."

"Which was?"

"Obviously what Eaglebury failed to do. I can't tell you

more than that, Craig," Hanrahan said. "I don't even know if what I was told was the truth."

"Jesus Christ!" Lowell said, angrily. He glowered for a moment at the TWX, and then went on. "But we *don't* know for sure that he's dead, right? For all we know, he could be sitting with Ellis and that goddamned nav-aid in the mountains."

"What makes you think he's with Ellis?" Hanrahan asked.

"I set up that nav-aid mission," Lowell said. "And I know Eaglebury jumped in with it."

There was no reply.

"Well, do we? What do they have to say?" Lowell snapped.

"Communication with Ellis is limited," Hanrahan said. "He doesn't have a transmitter. Felter took him one, but it hasn't been on the air."

Lowell screwed up his face thoughtfully, poured himself another drink, and then poured it back into the bottle.

"Someone's going to have to tell Sharon," Jane Jiggs said, softly.

"Not me," Lowell said. "And I don't think anybody else should, either, at least not until I get back."

"Back from where?" asked Jiggs.

Lowell looked at him and raised his eyebrows at what he obviously considered a dumb question.

"General, I respectfully request ten days' ordinary leave," Lowell said. "I have something like ninety days accumulated leave to my credit."

"Don't be an ass, Craig," Jiggs said. "What the hell could you do down there?"

"I won't know until I get there," Lowell said.

"That show is about to get going," Jiggs said.

"Within the next couple of days, I would guess," Lowell agreed, "if Ellis and his guys are still there . . . They can't stay forever."

"Next Monday," Hanrahan said. It was Thursday. Jiggs, startled, gave him a dirty look, started to say something, and then changed his mind.

"Then I'll have plenty of time to get down there," Lowell said.

"I officially forbid you to go anywhere near there, Craig," Paul Jiggs said. "I'm sorry, Craig."

"What the hell can you do to me?" Lowell asked.

"Court-martial you, if it comes to that."

"Let me tell you something, Paul," Lowell said. "Just before I left Hawaii, I had a couple of drinks and made a telephone call. I told my cousin to get our senator on the horn and discreetly inquire when I could expect to be promoted. Black's going to send an aviation battalion to Vietnam. In my innocence—and since Black had just expressed his deep appreciation for my splendid services—I thought, if I could get that little silver leaf, I could command it."

"You're getting the Legion of Merit for what you did for Black in Vietnam," Paul Jiggs said.

"You'll mail it to me, of course?" Lowell said, sarcastically. "Pray permit me to finish, General. What our senator found out, General . . . and I find it difficult to believe that you didn't know this . . . is that I have been passed over twice for promotion, and as soon as this Cuban thing is settled, I will be involuntarily separated. So let's stop the crap."

"They're throwing you out, Duke?" M/Sgt Wojinski asked.

"On my ass, Ski," Lowell confirmed.

"Sonsofbitches!" Wojinski said. "That ain't right!"

"But it is the fact. So what else can you threaten me with, Paul?"

"OK," Jiggs said. "Go ahead, make a goddamned fool of yourself. You won't get near Cuba. Or for that matter, Nicaragua. If the Cubans don't shoot you down, our people will. I told you, it goes on Monday."

"Don't be a fool, Craig," Jane Jiggs said.

Lowell picked up the telephone and dialed a number.

"You want to get your ass in a really big crack?" he said to whoever answered.

"Who is that?" Jiggs demanded.

"Bring the Commander and a change of underwear to the Ozark airport," Lowell said, not replying to the question. "Right now. I'll be there."

He hung up.

"Who was that?" Jiggs demanded.

"Franklin," Lowell said.

"You're willing to get him in trouble, too? In this childish gesture of yours?"

"*If* we get in trouble, I'll hire him a good lawyer," Lowell said. "Franklin is a freak like me, General. When his friends are in trouble, they worry about paper-pushers later."

"That was a cheap shot, Craig," Hanrahan snapped.

Lowell looked at him, and then at General Jiggs.

"Yes, it was, and I'm heartily sorry," he said.

"Forget it," Jiggs said. "I realize you're out of your mind."

"I'm going to pack," Lowell said. "Will you see yourselves out?"

"Colonel," M/Sgt Wojinski said, "I want to go."

Hanrahan looked at him.

"And I am going, too," Jannier announced.

"No, you're not," Lowell and Melody Jannier said in almost perfect unison.

"I have no intention," Jannier said, "aware that I am about to become a father, of doing anything that would in any way endanger me. But I do travel on a diplomatic passport, and diplomatic passports are often very convenient."

His reply shut both his wife and Lowell up. Lowell because he knew that a diplomatic passport was more valuable than money, Melody because she knew that she could not stop him from going anyway.

"Obviously, Sergeant," Colonel Hanrahan said, breaking the silence, "I cannot approve in any way your getting yourself involved in Major Lowell's insanity. You are officially forbidden to do so. On the other hand, if you have any leave coming, I see no reason why you can't take a few days off."

"You don't actually think," Jiggs said, "that this is going to be anything but a useless tragedy, do you?"

"I think the odds are against them," Hanrahan said.

"You got some kind of a weapon for me?" Wojinski said.

"Sure," Lowell said, "come along."

Wojinski followed him into the house.

Major General Jiggs poured himself another drink and then went into the bedroom after them. Lowell was wearing a German Luger in a shoulder holster, and Wojinski was closing the lid on a case which held two shotguns and a .45 Colt pistol.

"Jane will drive you to the airport," General Jiggs said. "For obvious reasons, I can't afford to be seen seeing you off on this escapade."

"Thank you," Lowell said.

"The last time I saw that GOTT MIT UNS holster," Jiggs said, making reference to the Wehrmacht belt buckle that Lowell had mounted to the custom-made holster, "was a long time ago."

"When I was a bright young major, with a very promising career, right?" Lowell replied, dryly.

"In those days, Craig, I thought you thought very clearly."

"You going to wish us luck, Paul?" Lowell said.

"Sure," Major General Jiggs said, and offered his hand.

Jane Jiggs was surprised that Melody didn't try to stop her husband. And then she understood that Melody knew that she could not have stopped her husband except at a price she was unwilling to pay. Melody was wiser than she should have been at her age. It might be because she had already lost one warrior husband. Or it might be that she, like Jane herself, was that rare woman who understood the price that had to be paid for being married to a warrior.

"Melody," Lowell said, "I need a favor."

"I regret," Melody mockingly quoted, "that I have but one husband to give to my country."

Lowell looked as if he was going to reply, and then changed his mind.

"Call Cynthia at the *Time-Life* bureau in Mexico City," Lowell said.

"Cynthia *Thomas?*" Melody interrupted.

"Yeah," Lowell said.

"Well! well!" Melody said.

"I was supposed to meet her down there," Lowell said.

"You don't say?" Melody asked, innocently.

"Call her and tell her I can't make it," Lowell said.

"Why don't you call her yourself?" Melody asked, pointing to a telephone.

"Because if I call her," Lowell said, "she'll want to know why I can't come, and I can't tell her. And that would make her mad."

"What I should do to you, Craig, is call her and tell her the reason you're standing her up is a peroxide blond with a forty-inch bust named Wanda."

"I thought we were pals," Lowell said.

"We were," Melody said, "until you blew the 'charge' on your trumpet. You should have known that would cause the goddamned Pavlovian response in the father of my unborn child."

"All he's going to do is go wave that diplomatic passport around," Lowell said. "Nothing more."

"Said the Tooth Fairy," Melody said.

"OK, don't call her," Lowell said.

"Melody," Jean-Philippe Jannier, now the French husband, said, "you will do what Craig asks."

Melody stuck out her tongue at him.

Then they went out and got in the car and drove off.

Major General Jiggs waited until it was clear that Lowell was not going to come back to the house for something he had forgotten before he got on the telephone.

Melody watched as he placed a person-to-person call to Mr. James W. Stemme at the Central Intelligence Agency in McLean, Virginia.

After some delay, General Jiggs reached Mr. Stemme at his home in Silver Spring, Maryland. When he'd explained what was up, Mr. Stemme assured Jiggs that there would be no problem. When Lowell arrived in Miami he would be met by agents of United States Customs. Acting on a tip, they would search his aircraft, find contraband, and arrest the airplane's occupants. After everything was over, they would be released with applogies.

Mr. Stemme thanked General Jiggs for bringing the matter to his attention.

Jiggs hung up.

"Why didn't you just have the MPs hold him here?" Colonel Paul Hanrahan asked. "Was all that necessary?"

"It's a long way to Miami," Jiggs said. "Craig's a smart fellow. He'll come to his senses long before he gets there."

Hanrahan nodded.

"And I didn't want to have him arrested for wanting to do something I wish I could do myself," General Jiggs added.

"You underestimate them, General," Melody Jannier said. "Good try, but it won't work."

General Jiggs and Colonel Hanrahan looked at Melody but they didn't respond. They thought that Melody simply didn't know what she was talking about.

(Four)
Montego Bay, Jamaica
0945 Hours, 17 April 1961

Lowell, dressed in khaki pants and a T-shirt, found Captain Archibald Needham in the bar of the Prince Charles' Arms' Hotel. Captain Archibald Needham, chief pilot for Air Hire

Jamaica (and its sole stockholder) was, despite the hour, visibly drunk.

"Needham, you sonofabitch!" Lowell said.

"Well, good morning, Mr. Lowell," Needham said.

"You gave me your word," Lowell said.

"Oh, don't be an ass," Needham said, so clearly and so angrily that Lowell suspected he wasn't quite as drunk as he wanted to appear. "Haven't you heard the radio? Radio Havana is already boasting that your invasion is a disaster."

"So what?"

"So I have no intention of flying you anywhere. This isn't the Battle of Britain, you know. Western civilization is not really hanging in the balance."

"How the hell are we supposed to get there?"

"Don't go," Captain Needham said. "Discretion, I've heard, is supposed to be the better part of valor."

"And I thought I could take an English gentleman's word," Lowell said.

"You must know how absurd you sound, Old Boy," Needham said. "And I don't think you're naive. So I must ask myself, why did he say that?"

"I'll fly it," Lowell said. "You just come along."

"But that's why I got drunk," Needham said. "So I would not be of any use to you in case you were either very persuasive or kidnapped me at the point of a gun."

"Just come along and show me how to fly it," Lowell asked, reasonably.

"I'll tell you what I will do," Needham said. "I will buy that Catalina of yours . . . for ten thousand American dollars less than you paid me for it."

"You are a miserable sonofabitch," Lowell said.

"And the day after tomorrow, I will be a live, if miserable, sonofabitch," Needham said.

"Fuck you," Lowell said, ineffectually. It was all he could think of to say. Hitting Needham would accomplish nothing.

He walked out of the bar.

He heard Needham chuckling behind him.

When he got to the airfield, Jannier, Franklin, and Wojinski were sitting in the shade of the wing of the airplane. The airplane was an amphibian, a Consolidated Vultee Catalina. This particular airplane was relatively new. It had been delivered to the U.S. Navy as a PBY-6A in 1944. Two 1,200-hp Pratt & Whitney "Twin Wasp" radial engines, sitting on the wing above and just behind the cockpit, drove it at a top speed of 179 miles an hour.

The airplane was designed for long-range reconnaissance before radar was more than an engineer's interesting idea. Two ovoid bubbles were on the sides of the fuselage. And there was another observation position in the nose in front of the cockpit windows.

When the airplane had been sold as surplus, the machine-gun ports in the observation windows had been filled with Plexiglas, and the cabin interior outfitted with sound-deadening insulation and seats. No other changes were required to modify the plane for commercial use. Indeed, the Catalina was ideally suited for service in the Caribbean and West Indies. If there was an airfield, it used the wheels. When there was no airfield, the wheels folded up against the fuselage, and the Catalina had the water to use for a landing field.

Flying south from Ozark, Lowell had known they would need an amphibian. And he knew that he was going to need a Catalina, because all the other amphibians (the Grumman Widgeon, for example) would not be able to carry Ellis's "A" Team.

He had also suspected that Paul Jiggs (with Hanrahan's unspoken agreement) had given in to his going to Cuba too easily. There would almost certainly be military police waiting for them at Miami. And so, twenty miles out of Tallahassee, he had gotten on the horn and told Valdosta area control to close out his Miami instrument flight plan. He had announced his intention of going back to Tallahassee for fuel.

He had then dropped down to the deck and flown right down the center of the Florida peninsula to Palm Beach.

The only thing that surprised the proprietors of the Palm Beach Flying Service was that the pilot of the Craig, Powell, Kenyon and Dawes Aero Commander was colored. It did not surprise them at all (for this was Palm Beach, where the rich were accustomed to getting what they wanted) that they wished to charter another aircraft with crew to continue their journey to Jamaica.

The American Express card offered in tender of payment identified the holder as Vice Chairman of the Board, Craig, Powell, Kenyon and Dawes. A quick telephone call to American Express had gotten a blanket OK for whatever Mr. Lowell wished to charge.

They weren't even surprised that the big, Polish-looking character with them had a Colt .45 pistol tucked in the waistband of his trousers. Bodyguards for the very rich were not at all uncommon in Palm Beach.

"Couldn't find Captain Needham?" Jannier asked Lowell.

"He chickened out when he was sober," Lowell said. "Now he's drunk again."

"You want me to go talk to him?" Wojinski asked. There was a good deal of menace in the innocent question.

"It wouldn't do any good, Ski," Lowell said.

"So what do we do now?" Franklin asked.

"If I can get this machine started," Lowell said, "I'm going to drive it into the water, see if I can find out how to make the wheels fold up, and then I'll shoot some landings. Then you can decide if you still want to go along."

"No," Franklin said.

"I understand, Bill," Lowell said. "You want to pick up the Commander at Palm Beach? Take Ski to Bragg and then wait for me at Rucker."

"I meant no touch and go's," Franklin said. "Since your experience with a seaplane is nil, the more landings and takeoffs you make, the greater the chance that you'll dump it."

"You mean just get in it, fire it up, and go?" Lowell replied.

"We've been listening to the radio," Wojinski said. "The fucking Cubans have announced that the invasion's failed."

"Then there's really no purpose in going, is there?" Lowell said.

"Why don't we just stop the bullshit, get in the fucking airplane, and go?" Wojinski said, flatly.

When Lowell looked at him, Wojinski crossed himself, folded his hands before him in an attitude of prayer, and raised his eyes toward heaven.

By that time, Franklin was already tugging at the fuselage door to open it.

Lowell put out his hand to Jannier.

"Merci, mon vieux," he said. "Thank you for coming. You'll be able to get back into the States all right?"

"I am going back to the States in that airplane," Jannier said, pointing to the Catalina.

"The deal was that all you were going to do was bring along the diplomatic passport, to be used if needed."

Jannier didn't reply.

"That's what you told Melody," Lowell said.

"But she knew I was lying," Jannier said, and crawled into the Catalina.

(Five)

An hour after British Jamaican Airways One Seventeen (which is how Lowell had decided to identify himself to the air traffic control people) departed Montego Bay for Grand Cayman Island, Georgetown tower came on the air and announced that due to "conditions," Georgetown Field was closing down. Jamaican Airways One Seventeen was directed to return to Montego Bay.

"British Jamaican diverting to Montego Bay at this time," Lowell said.

He pushed the stick forward.

"What are you doing?" Franklin asked, in alarm.

"I'm going down on the deck," Lowell said. "I don't believe that bastard for a minute. They know it's us. There's no reason Georgetown should be shut down. Jiggs almost certainly turned us in before we were off the ground at Ozark, and they've been looking all over for us. That radio call meant they just now found out we where we are."

"Why on the deck?" Franklin asked.

"Maybe they've got radar."

"I'll bet the Cubans do," Franklin said.

Lowell didn't reply.

He had the ADF tuned to Ellis's nav-aid, which was transmitting. That meant that Ellis was probably operational—unless he had been overrun, and the ADF permitted to operate because that would attract Cubano airplanes to Fidel Castro's antiaircraft batteries.

An hour later, three U.S. Navy fighters appeared on their wing. Their flight commander got on the horn and ordered them out of the area. Lowell pretended not to hear. When the navy pilot made violent "get out of this area" gestures, Lowell chose to interpret these as friendly waves. He waved back in a very friendly fashion.

When, five minutes later, they approached several tiny islands, the navy fighters turned back. Lowell and Franklin could now see a small fleet of ships. Beyond these was the land mass of Cuba.

He turned right until he was several miles from the Bay of Pigs itself, then crossed the coastline where he could see nothing but a road. He homed in on Ellis's nav-aid—and circled when the ADF needles reversed. He knew he was there, and he knew the area from maps, but he could see nothing.

He kept circling . . . until Wojinski leaned over his shoulder and matter-of-factly told him they were taking fire. There had been hits on the left wing.

Lowell looked back and up. He couldn't see anything.

"I think we're losing fuel," Wojinski said, coolly.

Lowell headed for the coastline.

"Do we go in now, or not?" Lowell asked.

"If you could put it down by them ships," Wojinski said, "I could go ashore and have a look. There's a life raft in the back. You pull a lever, and it falls out and blows up. Or that's what it says."

Lowell got the plane onto the water, which took longer than he expected. When he finally touched down, he touched down hard. Water splashed over the airplane. But he was down.

He taxied closer to the beach and turned at right angles to it, two hundred yards offshore.

"When you get close enough," Wojinski said. "Stop the sonofabitch, and I'll pop the raft."

He went into the cabin.

Lowell suddenly advanced the right engine throttle and pushed on the rudder pedal. The Catalina turned left again, directly toward the beach.

"Jesus H. Christ!" Franklin said.

Fifty yards offshore, Lowell turned at right angles to the beach again.

A dozen or more landing craft appeared to be moving around nearby—apparently without purpose. A flickering caught his eyes. He was being signaled by someone on the beach with a signal lamp. And then there was a man gesturing for him to come in.

"Wounded, I think," Wojinski said. "They want us to take them."

"I'll give them five minutes," Lowell said. "And then we'll pick up whoever we can."

He taxied slowly along the edge of the bay.

Suddenly, the water in front of them erupted in small splashes.

"Shit!" Wojinski said. "Fucking machine gun!"

At that instant Lowell experienced terror. His stomach turned into a small hard ball; bile came to his mouth. He was chilled, and the skin on the back of his skull moved with a life of its own.

They had missed with the first burst. There was no way they would miss with the second.

And then reason returned. They had missed with the first burst only because they had wanted to. They were sending a message: *Stop that airplane and pick us up, or nobody goes anywhere.*

He looked in the direction of the fire.

There were two men standing at the water's edge. They had M60 machine guns cradled in their arms. They had belts of .308 ammunition draped around their shoulders. One of them was a very large man with a green beret on his head.

The other one was small and bareheaded. He was bald. Lowell recognized him. His name was Sanford T. Felter.

(Six)
The Presidential Apartments
The White House
Washington, D.C.
1925 Hours, 23 April 1961

"You know the way, Colonel," the elevator operator said when he opened the door.

"Yes, I do," Lieutenant Colonel Sanford T. Felter said. He walked down the corridor. He thought if he got this far, the Secret Service agent would simply pass him through. But he didn't, and before the agent passed him into the presidential apartments Felter was required to show both his Adjutant General's Office identification card and the Temporary Visitor's Pass he had been given at the main gate.

The butler recognized him.

"It's real nice to see you here again, sir," he said. "And

don't you look *spiffy* in your uniform with all those medals?"

Then he rapped the door gently with his knuckles, and pushed it open.

"Mr. President," he announced. "Lieutenant Colonel Felter."

The President, who was sitting in a rocking chair, smiled, rose half out of the chair, and offered his hand.

"Can I offer you something, Colonel?"

"No, thank you, sir."

The President nodded.

"It should go without saying that I was happy to hear, as Mark Twain said, that the report of your death was considerably exaggerated."

"Thank you, sir."

The President wasted no time. "I would like to ask you a question, Colonel, and then I would like to hear why you think the Cuban operation turned into a disaster. When you've done that, I would like the hear the details of your evacuation. In that order, please."

"Yes, sir."

"First question, why did you jump into Cuba? Was that appropriate for someone of your position? With your knowledge?"

"I was the person best qualified, Mr. President, to replace Commander Eaglebury. So far as my position is concerned, I had been relieved as Action Officer some time previously. There was a certain element of risk that I would be captured between the time I went in and the time the invasion started. At that point, of course, my knowledge of invasion plans would have been of little use to them. I considered that risk justified."

"Why?"

"There were only two people who believed that the Russians intend to install offensive missiles in Cuba," Felter said. "Me and Commander Eaglebury. We were not believed. Commander Eaglebury felt that getting proof that the Russians have already sent in support equipment justified his going to Cuba. When his mission failed, I didn't have much choice but to try to finish it."

"Despite orders from the CIA Action Officer to the contrary? How do you justify that, in your mind?"

"I have two answers, Mr. President, both of which might strike you as flippant."

"Try them," the President said.

"There is an old army expression, Mr. President, that some people are so dumb they can't find their own rear end with both hands. That was my assessment of the Action Officer who replaced me. Further, I..."

The President interrupted him by holding up his hand.

"Why were you relieved as Action Officer?" he asked.

"I wasn't given any explanation, sir," Felter said. "My relief came shortly after you assumed office."

"You think your relief was a mistake, is that it?"

"Yes, sir, I do."

"You don't think the CIA should control an operation of this nature?"

"I believe it should, sir. When I was Action Officer, I was not functioning as an army officer."

"Why did you remain in Nicaragua after you were relieved?"

"I served as liaison officer between the man who replaced me as Action Officer and the Special Warfare School."

"You were about to give me your second reason for going into Cuba yourself," the President said.

"I took an oath, Mr. President, when I was commissioned, to defend the country and the Constituion against all enemies, foreign and domestic."

Their eyes met.

"What would you have done in the event of your capture?" the President asked, after a moment. "Taken a pill?"

"The pills are not always effective, Mr. President," Felter said.

The President's eyebrows went up.

"You are apparently as you have been represented to me, Colonel," he said. "I am now interested in your views concerning the disaster we've just gone through."

For a moment Felter remained silent, as if gathering his thoughts—or maybe deciding if he was going to reply at all.

"Go on, Colonel," the President said.

"The tactical reason it failed, Mr. President, was the absence of air cover."

The President thought that over for a moment.

"I made that decision," he said after a moment.

"I can only presume, Mr. President, that you were not aware of the situation," Felter said. "Or that there were other considerations. In other words, that you knew the invasion would fail without air cover and you had decided that loss must be accepted."

"I was advised by the CIA," the President said, not defensively.

Felter didn't reply.

"The use of naval aircraft would be an act of war," the President said.

"Mr. President," Felter said, "providing arms to one side in a civil war is an act of war."

"I don't need a lesson in international law from you, Colonel," the President said.

"I meant to suggest that the Soviet Union committed the first act of war in Cuba," Felter said.

"A nuclear war should be averted at all costs, Colonel."

"The Russians have begun installing missiles, Mr. President," Felter said. "By now, I presume, you have the proof of that? What I brought out?"

"In other words, Colonel, you're saying that what happened is my fault?" the President asked, smiling with his lips, but not his eyes. "And that I have the responsibility for whatever happens next?"

"In my opinion, sir, under the restrictions you judged necessary, the operation should not have been launched."

"I was led to believe there was a chance of success," the President said, "without U.S. Navy air cover."

"You were ill advised, Mr. President," Felter said.

"Is that hindsight, Colonel?" the President asked, coldly.

"I held that opinion before the operation was launched, and so advised my replacement as Action Officer."

"Apparently your views were not thought to be valid," the President said.

"I was led to believe you wished to see me regarding the missile installations, sir."

"You were then ill advised," the President said. "I didn't say *why* I wanted to see you, only that I did."

"Yes, sir," Felter said.

"But since that has come up, what do you think should be done about the missiles?"

"I would not presume to offer you an opinion beyond my level of expertise, Mr. President."

"Your modesty is commendable, Colonel," the President said, dryly.

Felter was aware that he had infuriated the President of the United States, the Commander in Chief. And he also realized that he didn't give a damn. He was sorry about only one thing, that he had naively thought he would be permitted to return to the Special Warfare School and complete his twenty years. His military career, obviously, was over. In this fiasco, they would be looking for people to blame. He was a certain target.

Sharon would be pleased that it was over for him.

"Is there something else, Mr. President?" Felter asked.

"The details of your withdrawal, if you please," the President asked.

"There is not much to tell, Mr. President. We made our way back from Havana to the Green Beret team, and from the transmitter site to the beach. We made our evacuation by air from the beach."

"That's not quite the story I get, Colonel," the President said. "I heard that it was necessary to fight your way to the beach, and that the aircraft waiting for you there was not—how shall I say this?—in the regular service of the United States."

Felter said nothing.

"I understand," the President said, "that it was an old Navy PBY Catalina."

"That is correct, sir."

"Flown by an army aviator."

"Yes, sir."

"Who had never before flown one?"

"I believe that is the case, sir."

"I further understand that the CIA was aware of his plans, and proved incapable of stopping him," the President said.

"I have no information about that, Mr. President," Felter said.

"Where the hell did he get a Catalina?"

"It was in previous service as an interisland passenger aircraft in the Bahamas, sir."

"He stole it?"

"I believe he bought it, sir."

"Money talks, doesn't it, Felter?" the President said, and laughed.

"Yes, sir."

"I have had three communications regarding Major Craig W. Lowell in the past several days. The CIA wants him court-martialed."

Felter did not reply.

"And I received a letter from the Commander in Chief, Pacific, who asks me to nominate Major Lowell for promotion, inasmuch as the army has not seen fit to do so."

"Major Lowell is a fine officer, sir," Felter said.

"So the senior senator from New York has informed me," the President said. "He also told me the major's father and my father-in-law played polo together."

Felter didn't reply.

"Perhaps, Felter, we left-wing geopolitical virgins aren't as blind to reality as some people feel," the President said. "Nor solely concerned with getting reelected from the moment we enter office . . . to the point where we cave in to every kiss-the-Russian-ass pressure group."

It had obviously reached the President's ears that he had been so described by Colonel Felter during a CIA debriefing. Colonel Felter did not reply.

"Do you plan to see Major Lowell anytime soon, Colonel?"

"Major Lowell is out of the country, sir," Felter said. "I believe he is in Mexico City.

"On personal business, I hope?"

"Yes, sir."

"Well, when you do get in touch with him, perhaps you will be good enough to inform him that bowing to pressure from the Harvard Alumni Association and the National Association for the Advancement of Colored People, I have judged it politically *in*expedient to court-martial both him and Warrant Officer Franklin—despite the CIA's strongly expressed views to the contrary."

"Yes, sir, I will be happy to tell him."

"I have also decided to nominate Major Lowell to be a lieutenant colonel, Mr. Franklin to be a first lieutenant, and with one eye on our Polish-American voters, Sergeant Wojinski to be a warrant officer."

"The promotions are merited, sir."

"One more thing, Felter," the President said.

"Yes, Mr. President?"

"I'm sorry if you've had your heart set on Fort Bragg, but I'll expect you to be available to me at 0800 as of Monday next week."

"I don't quite understand, sir."

"My predecessor, who telephoned three times to inquire about you, informed me of the valuable services you rendered him. I would like you to do the same for me."

Felter paused a moment.

"I'm at your service, of course, Mr. President," he said.

"Pity we can't publicize it," the President said dryly. He rose out of his rocking chair and put out his hand. "I'm up for reelection in only forty-two months, and there's a lot of Jewish voters out there."

When Felter didn't reply, the President said, "That will be all, Colonel Felter. Thank you for coming to see me. Thank you for everything."

"Thank you, Mr. President."

ABOUT THE AUTHOR

W.E.B. Griffin, who was once a soldier, belongs to the Armor Association; Paris Post #1, The American Legion; and is a life member of The National Rifle Association and Gaston-Lee Post #5660, Veterans of Foreign Wars.